THE PROMISE KEPT

Echo Springs Book Two

MAGGIE MAE GALLAGHER

Published by Blushing Books
An Imprint of
ABCD Graphics and Design, Inc.
A Virginia Corporation
977 Seminole Trail #233
Charlottesville, VA 22901

Maggie Mae Gallagher
The Promise Kept

EBook ISBN: 978-1-64563-428-7
Print ISBN: 978-1-64563-429-4
Audio ISBN: 978-1-64563-430-0
v1

Cover Art by ABCD Graphics & Design

This one is for my sisters:
Christal, Loren, Brianna & Jess

Chapter 1

From Old Man Turner's Journal:
Sometimes fate and life have other plans for you. The same can be said of dating and falling in love.

"Oh, yes. Right there," she murmured.

Cybil sighed at the strong hands kneading her tense shoulders. Golden sunshine warmed her skin. Azure waves lapped against the pristine, ivory sand not fifteen feet from where she lounged on a luxurious padded chaise. Her tanned skin glistened in the sun. The coconut scent from her suntan lotion wafted on the gentle breeze and mingled with the salt from the ocean waves. The simmering heat of the tropics caused perspiration to bead on her forehead and evaporate with the light wind. The sunglasses perched on her nose shaded her gray eyes from the radiant sunlight.

It was without a doubt a perfect day.

The light breeze played with the loose tendrils of her inky hair while the sexy-as-sin Pablo—he of the broad, tanned shoulders, gorgeously thick black hair, and soulful eyes—massaged her shoulders with his long, talented fingers. The man had the most wonderful, gifted hands and knew precisely where to exert the most pressure. And those thumbs of his were singularly skilled at ferreting out every ache and pain.

God, she had needed this getaway—away from the cold, the snow, the dreaded holidays, and nonstop work.

She muffled a moan.

Cybil couldn't remember the last time she'd felt this relaxed. She could still taste the lime and salt from her frozen margarita. And she was a breath away from suggesting to Pablo that they take the massage indoors to her beachside bungalow. The thought of those hands massaging other regions of her body left her achy and needy. It had been so long since she had been with a man. Since this was a vacation, she didn't have to worry about getting attached. Cybil moaned as he dug into a knot on her left shoulder.

Pablo lowered his face. Cybil shivered, heady anticipation humming along her skin. Was he going to nibble on her ear? Suggest naughty, decadent delights to be had if they retreated indoors? She was ready and willing for anything the guy had in mind.

"Purrr." A cold, wet nose pressed against the side of her cheek where it met her ear, amplifying the sound. The purr increased in tenor. Something tickled her nose.

Cybil cracked an eye open. A pair of golden eyes stared at her with expectation and determination, with a side of feline disdain that she had yet to acknowledge their owner. Midnight and ivory fur decorated her cat's face, with the ivory creating a point on his crown between his eyes, and his black pointed ears were twitching. He blinked slowly so he wouldn't miss the slightest movement from Cybil. Rather incessantly, his purr grew louder. His white whiskers blurred with their proximity, and teased the tip of her nose.

Shadows filled her bedroom in that hazy pre-dawn, moments before the sunrise, gray light. The dark mahogany panels of her sleigh bed were visible. Overnight, her rumpled linen bedding had tangled around her body in a cocoon fashion so that she resembled the stuffing inside a burrito.

"Meeeooow." Gus nudged his nose and face against Cybil's cheek in a soft headbutt. It was his way of telling her: *hey lady, get up and feed me.*

Cybil blew out a breath. The sweet furball had interrupted a rather magnificent, sexy dream right before the good part. Wasn't that what was wrong with her life—that she was always stopped before she could get to the good parts? Shoving her hair out of her face, she contemplated the ceiling. It was rather pitiful that the only male kissing her was a sixteen pound, three-year-old, portly tuxedo cat by the name of Gus instead of her fantasy beach cabana man, Pablo, with his dashing, dark good looks, and magic hands.

As the light increased, she noticed some spots on the ceiling where the paint was beginning to fade and get dirty. This summer, she would see about repainting the interior of their little abode. It had been a few years, and the wear was beginning to show.

At the next caterwaul meow and more forceful headbutt from Gus, which made her inhale fur, she sighed. Wiping hair from her lips, she said, "Oh all right, you big baby, I'll get your breakfast. It's almost time for me to get up anyway."

Gus purred even louder at her acknowledgement and rose into Bastet pose, his imitation of the cat goddess. The tomcat Cybil's sister, Tessa, had adopted three weeks ago had taken a peculiar liking to Cybil. Since joining their little family, Gus chose to wake her every morning in this fashion.

Given his girth, he definitely could go without a meal, but he wouldn't stop his crying until someone fed him. The sweet furball was a lovable lap cat who liked food and naps, in that order.

Cybil scratched him behind the ears before gently shoving him off.

Fluffy and chunky, he jumped down and waddle-strutted to the door, his thick black tail swishing in expectation as she shivered and slipped on her soft, pale blue robe. Not a lot had changed in the years since they'd moved in here. She still had the same dresser and nightstands of her youth. The king sleigh bed was the one big upgrade she had made furniture-wise this last year. But that purchase had been more out of self-preservation, since she had been waking up in pain each morning because the bed she was sleeping in had been around since they had moved to Echo Springs when she was a teenager.

Downstairs, once Gus was happily chowing down on his kibble, she texted Tessa a picture.

Cybil: See, he's fed and happy. Awaiting your return on Sunday.

Tessa: Oh, he's so cute. I just want to squish his face. They're trying to talk me into a panel for Sunday and changing my return flight to Monday. Will let you know. Only doing it if they pony up the money for the flight and hotel.

Cybil: Supposed to get snow next week. Might want to nix the extra panel, even though I know you live for that stuff.

Tessa: Will let you know. Give my Gus-Gus a cuddle for me.

Cybil: Will do later. Full day today. I let him sleep in my bed.

Tessa: Aw, I told you that you'd love him. LOL

Cybil: Tolerate him. Especially when he wakes me up from a sexy beach dream before Pablo can get to the good part.

Tessa texted a laughing smiley face. Cybil studied Gus, who was now lying on his back next to his bowl, cleaning his fur, those golden eyes full of blissful contentment. She snapped another picture and texted it to Tessa.

As much as she enjoyed the solitude while her sister was away on a work trip, signing her comics at an expo in Boston, Cybil missed having her around, even when they were competing for time in the one full bathroom they shared.

Over the last few years, the dynamic of her relationship with her sister had undergone a metamorphosis from being a mother figure to a deep friendship of equals. They depended on one another, always had each other's backs, and enjoyed hanging out together. There was no one else Cybil would want more on her Apocalypse Survival Team, especially with all her sister's geek knowledge.

Cybil dressed in layers, in deference to the biting cold and unpredictable Colorado weather. The layers were useful because, while the current temperature was in the low thirties, as the day progressed, it could warm up and reach the sixties by mid-afternoon—and then drop into the twenties overnight, with a sudden snowstorm. But even with Mother Nature's ever-present temperature roulette, she decided to walk to work today instead of drive. Snow was forecast the next couple of days, but today was supposed to be crystal clear and sunny. A perfect opportunity to soak up as much vitamin D as possible—the real kind, not the sexy beach dream kind.

Cybil strolled the eight blocks to her yoga studio while munching on a protein bar. There was a banana in her bag she would have once she made it to the studio. She yawned. As soon as she reached the studio, she'd brew a cup of coffee. Maybe this morning, she'd go with Kona coffee, continuing with her tropical island dream theme. If she couldn't get to Hawaii, at least she could bring the flavor of it directly to her door. If she made it to the studio fast enough, she should be able to inhale half a cup before her client arrived. Shoving her hands in the pockets of her puffy red coat, she quickened her speed to a brisk pace.

The sun crested the nearby mountain peaks, illuminating the town of Echo Springs in a golden glow. In the early morning light, the mountains were shaded a deep purple-gray, with bands of white crowning each peak, making them picture perfect. The crisp air carried an aromatic hint of snow and pine—or, as Cybil liked to call it, home. She loved this place, with all its eccentricities and delights.

The town was nestled in the heart of the Colorado Rockies, with the shadowy backdrop of the mountains. It was one of those postcard-worthy places that tourists oohed and aahed over. Echo Springs was located along Interstate 70, which bisected the Rocky Mountains. It stood as one of the main crossroads pitstops for travelers on their way to ski resort towns like Vale, Breckenridge, and many others. The bulk of the town was situated along the northern edge of the interstate, with the mountains beyond forming a natural crescent shape.

Echo Springs had grown a bit throughout the years Cybil had lived there. There were new fast food restaurants offering burgers and tacos, and new shops along Main Street with an eye toward luring tourists. New homes and subdivisions had been built as the township expanded, and another bank had opened off Main Street. But there was also a persistent resistance to change here in Echo Springs. It took time for anything new to take hold, if it took hold at all.

It was part of the town's charm that she had grown to love over the years.

Once upon a time, she'd hated how stagnant—and, at times, how archaic—this town could be, with its entrenched traditions and beliefs. Families had lived here for generations. The biggest source of revenue were the tourism dollars. Most of the businesses that had developed and thrived catered more to out of town guests just passing through than to yearlong residents—with exceptions of course, like Fitzgerald's Grocery Store and the post office. Many of the festivals and events had been designed with the intent of skimming some of the tourists' cash before they made it to their final vacation destinations at the ski resorts, or camping in one of the nearby national parks.

But Cybil no longer considered Echo Springs as a mere stopover in her life. It was home. She might want to visit all fifty states, tour Europe, stand on the Great Wall in China, and touch the sky at Machu Picchu, but this was the place where she would always return. Now, as she neared her thirty-first birthday, she saw her hometown as a steady comfort instead of a prison.

Wrapping her arms in front of her chest to ward off the cold, she trudged the short distance from her duplex to her yoga studio.

A bright yellow school bus rumbled down the street, making its rounds to pick up kids and ferry them to class. She loved the sounds of the world waking up: the birds chirping as they scouted their morning meals; a dog barking from behind a privacy fence she passed. Lights were on in the windows of the Victorian style homes as people started their day.

She yawned and muttered a curse under her breath. Today was going to be a long day. She had picked up an extra shift at Smitty's last night, and had worked until one. Smitty's Bar and Grill was one of the local hotspots for the over-twenty-one crowd. They had a thriving business, mainly because most people didn't like to drink alone. The job paid well in tips, even though the occasional dumbass tried to cop a feel on occasion. After being a waitress at Smitty's for almost a decade, Cybil knew how to handle men who figured it was their god given right to grab things that didn't belong to them. She had attended high school with the current owner, Burke Smitt, who'd inherited the bar and grill from his uncle Tim a few years back when he'd passed. Burke was a good boss. He and Cybil were friends and had even dated for a time, until they realized they were better friends than anything else.

If there was anything wrong with Echo Springs, it was the lack of available, eligible dating material. Hence her fantasy man, Pablo with the great hands. Rarely did anyone new move to Echo Springs. Not on purpose, at least—with the exception of her newest friend, Abby, who had recently moved here from New Jersey and wound up falling madly in love with the town's sexy sheriff, Nate Barnes. Pure circumstance had brought Abby to their town, as her great-aunt, Evie Callier, had willed her big old Victorian house to Abby. Falling for her neighbor, the town sheriff, had been a stroke of luck.

Cybil was thrilled for Abby, really, she was, but it had been longer than she cared to admit since she'd gotten horizontal—or anything else—with a guy. Her girly bits felt sorely neglected and downright testy lately. It was probably because Cybil knew Abby was getting all the sex—nightly, judging by the satisfied glimmer that seemed to glow from her friend, stating quite clearly for all and sundry to see that she was enjoying every blessed minute with Sheriff Stud Muffin.

Cybil wasn't jealous—at least, not very.

The tiny smattering of jealousy made her feel a wee bit bitchy, as well as a side heaping of self-pity that there was no one special in her life who looked at her the way the sheriff did Abby.

Cybil's pity party, table for one, could be the reason why she had lost her effing mind and signed herself up for the hottest new dating website, Matchmakers.com, a week ago. She was bound and determined to find someone to date. She missed male companionship, and sex. Maybe she wouldn't find the love of her life or a keeper, but it would be nice to get taken out to a meal she didn't have to buy herself. And perhaps, if she was really lucky, she might experience a few good orgasms that weren't of the solo-expedition variety.

She wasn't desperate, by any means, but there were times, like now, when she felt lonely. When she would love to have someone to lean on, and not have to worry about every blessed thing, all the damn time.

After week one, the dating app hadn't produced any winners—not that she'd expected a crown prince when she'd made the decision to join after a night of wine and a pint of her favorite ice cream, but she had hoped to find at least one guy with a little substance whose profile picture didn't resemble a mugshot. She might be crazy but she didn't think finding a halfway decent guy who was appealing to the eyes, gainfully employed, not an asshole, and didn't live with his mother should be on the same level as the quest for the Holy Grail.

Her breath puffed out in plumes of crystalized white. She shoved her gloved fingers deeper inside her coat pockets. Maybe she should have driven today, given the frigid temperatures. But her aging truck could be temperamental at best during the summer months. In the winter, the ancient beast tested her patience. She tried to save her gas and engine for things like working at Smitty's, or dates from hell in case she had to abruptly flee. A new vehicle wasn't in her financial plans or within her reach for a few years yet.

Her yoga studio was located at the corner of Continental Drive and Pine Street, on the second floor of a building owned and operated by Clark Biddle the Third. The man was old enough that he likely remembered the formation of the Rockies. Cybil liked the old guy. He was always wheeling and dealing and had a keen eye for profit. But he was fair too. He'd given her a fabulous rental rate, and allowed her to refurbish the space to the specifications she needed in order to make her business work.

Local contractor Aiden O'Toole had helped her realize her vision for her studio. It was too bad they didn't have any chemistry together, because Aiden was gorgeous, with his molten dark chocolate eyes and buns of steel. Who knew a tool belt on a pair of lean, masculine hips could be sexy? Unfortunately, there was no connection between them, no blip of something more. Otherwise, she would have already made a play for him. And he had been of the same opinion. They had been friends and known each other since high school. Although some days it felt like they had known each other since the Stone Age.

Cybil had sweated, literally, and saved every extra penny she had earned in tips that didn't go toward her bills for years to bring her vision, her dream, to fruition. She had taught classes at the local community center, building her following. And while her profession wasn't what she'd originally thought she wanted to do with her life, it suited, to the core of her foundation, the person she was today.

The building itself, with its forest green roof and exterior of sandstone-colored brick, had been built back in the fifties. The three-story structure held an eclectic mix of businesses and apartments. Two-thirds of the first floor were taken up by the offices of Clark Biddle, and the realtor firm Echo Springs Realtors took up the rest. Mr. Biddle was also the owner and landlord for the building. He had dabbled in real estate, in addition to being one of the few practicing attorneys in town.

On the second floor was Cybil's studio, Roe Yoga and Fitness. It was small, only twelve hundred square feet, but it was enough to fit twenty adults on mats comfortably on the golden wood floor. There was also a small workout room, with an elliptical and treadmill, along with a plethora of weight machines and free weights. Along the interior wall near the door was a row of metal coat hooks and built-in shelf cubbies for people to store their personal items. There was also a single bathroom the size of a broom closet that held a commode and sink for clients; a storage room for extra equipment like yoga mats, blocks and weights; and an office. The office was large enough to fit her desk, a chair, a dorm-sized refrigerator and a coffee maker, leaving barely enough room for her elbows, but she had her own private bathroom in exchange for giving up the elbow room. It was picky on her part, but this way she could store feminine items and not have to worry about sharing a bathroom with all her clients.

The space was perfect. Perfect for Cybil, at least.

Across the hall was an office that had been vacant since she had moved in two months ago. Three studio apartments, all currently occupied, were on the third floor. She'd made sure to introduce herself to those tenants, and gave them a discounted rate that she extended only to the building residents. Now Lily Daniels, Harper Emerson, and Eva Monroe each attended a few classes a week.

There were days when Cybil still couldn't believe that the studio was hers, that after all these years, she finally had achieved her goals, and she took pride in it. The path to achieve her dream had taken several years, during which she'd had to balance waiting tables to make an income while attending classes to become a certified yoga instructor. And, to fully make her dream work, she'd added many more types of fitness styles, like Pilates and Zumba, along with personal training certifications. With all those qualifications under her belt, the diverse number of classes she could offer provided her with a solid platform to launch her studio.

And so far, in the month she'd been open, she was seeing an inkling of success. It wasn't much. Yet. Funds would still be tight for a while longer. She had to continue waiting tables in addition to her workload at the studio. But it was a start. And a good one.

It gave her hope that she had a future that didn't simply include serving other people adult beverages, but making a difference in people's lives, in their health, and helping them reach their fitness goals.

In addition to her already loaded schedule, Cybil continued to teach a few classes at the community center for the elderly residents of Echo Springs. The location was easier for them so that they wouldn't have to navigate the stairs in this building. Most workdays were a race to the finish line. She constantly ran from one class and one job to the next.

She worked in her studio Wednesday through Monday, with Tuesday being her one day off a week—mainly for her sanity, and a chance to do things like grocery shopping and laundry, since house fairies didn't exist. Or, if they did, she'd not been able to coax them out of hiding to convince them to do the household chores.

At night on the weekends, she waited tables at Smitty's, and picked up extra shifts when she was able, like she had last night. For a Wednesday, Smitty's had been hopping. Her week had started off with a frenzied bang. And she had three more double-duty days between her studio and Smitty's until she had another day off.

And then she wondered why her most committed relationship was with streaming television while she dreamed of paradise and companionship.

Cybil entered the building with her key, locked the door behind her, and headed up the wooden flight of stairs to her place. The building itself didn't open until eight in the morning, in consideration of the tenants who lived there. She had a personal-training client scheduled at seven. Otherwise, she would still be in bed after her late night, since her first class wasn't until eight-thirty.

She didn't hate mornings. It was more like she was in a tacit agreement with them that if they weren't too awful to her, she wouldn't curse their very existence. The tentative arrangement worked for Cybil.

Her client would call when he arrived, so she could let him in. She wasn't necessarily fond of Alex Dotson, but he was a paying client. That was what mattered.

Besides, she had bigger problems to worry about than Alex. Mr. Biddle had informed her last week that he'd decided it was time for him to retire, and he was not only selling his law practice but had found a buyer for both his practice and the building. Cybil had mixed feelings about the situation. While Mr. Biddle had promised her that the terms of her lease would stand throughout the remaining ten months of it, the change-up was coming at a crappy time of year.

She loathed the holidays. Epically loathed them.

Between Thanksgiving next week and Christmas a few short weeks afterward, this was the time of year when Cybil tended to just survive. While everyone else was getting holly and jolly, she felt it was a monumental win if she didn't drown herself each evening in a pint of ice cream. It was hard to be sad when that first taste explosion of rocky road hit her beleaguered soul. But it was only a Band-Aid measure and wasn't kind to her waistline. Plus, she didn't want to make it through the holidays and then not be able to fit into her pants.

That was yet another reason why she was trying to date as much as possible. Perhaps if she could find a man to spend some time with, maybe of the dual-orgasm variety, she wouldn't focus so much on the holidays, or braving them solo, or the impending annual return of the anniversary of the day her life had changed forever.

Cybil entered her studio and flipped on the lights, admiring the way the soft golden glow illuminated the custom sandalwood flooring that helped cushion a body during strenuous poses. She'd had Aiden install flooring that catered to the fitness styles she offered. Once in her office, she started her coffeemaker, sighing at the potent scent of Kona roast filling the air as she organized the equipment and weights for the day.

Alex Dotson had said he'd hired her as his trainer because he wanted to build his resistance strength and increase his muscle density. In truth, Cybil figured he just wanted an excuse to show off. Lately, the man had been rather insistent on trying to get her to go out with him.

It didn't matter what floated his boat, because she wasn't interested. Not tempted in the slightest. Alex was a decent guy, for the most part, and was reasonably attractive. But she got nothing, not a tingle or zing in her girly bits, when she looked at him. And wasn't that part of her problem? When she examined the available eligible bachelor pool in Echo Springs, there were four distinct categories: the elderly grandpa crowd, the already dated and not going out with them again, the perfect-age bracket but so not interested, and then lastly, the hello Mrs. Robinson group.

Echo Springs was slim pickings when it came to men. At least for Cybil.

If she ventured farther afield, there were the park rangers at the nearby stations in Arapaho National Forest, or the next town over, Frisco. It was only twenty miles up the interstate, but it wasn't like Cybil had an inordinate amount of spare time. At the last town meeting, Mayor Fred Bailey had announced that the Colorado State Troopers had leased one of the historic buildings near Main Street, and were planning on opening a division in Echo Springs by this summer. Plus they had a new Search and Rescue Field Office with the Rocky Mountain Region Mountain Rescue Association opening up this spring as well, so there was that.

It was great news for Echo Springs residents—especially the single-female population, if the troopers and crew with the MRA stationed here ended up being single as well. It wasn't often that there was new man meat in town.

As great as that was, spring and summer were months away. And Cybil wanted co-ed orgasms now. It didn't make her feel any better that her inner monologue on the situation resembled Veruca singing, *Don't care how, I want it now*. And that was why both her id and ego on wine had convinced her to join Matchmakers.com.

She could face the dreaded holidays one heck of a lot better if she were being treated to nightly orgasms. Cybil disliked being in the same category as Scrooge, but the truth was, every year, a melancholy descended over her from Thanksgiving through the New Year. There was nothing for it, and no way to change it.

Boy, her thoughts were maudlin today.

Shaking herself out of her funk, Cybil got her studio prepped for the Hatha Yoga class at eight thirty. That way she could move seamlessly from her personal training session with Alex to her first class of the day.

At five to seven, Alex texted her that he was outside the building. Cybil headed down the wooden stairs that tended to creak in spots. At least the lighting in the stairwell was decent, glowing off the muted tan walls to create a warm atmosphere. When she strode across the small building lobby that was really nothing more than an oversized foyer, and opened the door, she noticed that the lights in Mr. Biddle's office were on already. The old codger did like to get an early start.

She pushed open the front glass and wood door to permit entry to her client. Admittedly, Alex was an attractive man in his black workout gear. His naturally wavy blond hair was meticulously trimmed, his angular jaw clean shaven, his cheekbones sharply pronounced, and he had a mocha gaze that always seemed set to smolder anytime he glanced in her direction. She just wished his smolder, along with his six-foot lean build, did something for her girly bits, but it didn't. Maybe it was because she knew him well and thought he had the personality of a turnip. Not to mention she sensed an undercurrent of menace that he tried to hide behind a polished sheen, which she didn't trust. She kept her grimace to herself and said, "Alex, come on in."

"Cybil. You look refreshed this morning," Alex said, telling her with his gaze that he appreciated her, the way a man did a woman he found attractive: his gaze roving over her body, warming over the sweet spots like he was a lion envisioning sinking his teeth into a gazelle.

A part of her wished she could feel something for him, anything really, other than mild annoyance.

Before she could reply, Clark Biddle shuffled out of his office, dressed in gray tweed slacks with a matching suit jacket, a bright canary yellow dress shirt and a multicolored plaid bow tie to complete his ensemble. For a man in his eighties, he was rather spry and moved with efficiency.

"Cybil, I'm glad I caught you. If I could have you come into my office for a few minutes so I can introduce you to your new landlord?" Clark's voice boomed and echoed in the stairwell.

"I have a personal training session. Can it wait?" she asked, indicating Alex with a slight nod as he crowded her. Really, the man needed to learn about personal space.

"It shouldn't take more than a minute," Clark said, his bushy, stark-white eyebrows raised. The tufts of his matching white hair were in wild disarray, looking windblown. Clark's hair, for all his styling clothing wise, always looked like he'd stuck his finger in an electrical socket and was just too busy to care about taming what was left on his balding dome.

With a sigh of defeat, because she knew Clark well enough that he wouldn't let up until she capitulated, Cybil turned to Alex. "Would you mind going on up and getting yourself warmed up on either the treadmill or elliptical? I'll be right up."

"Sure thing, as long as you don't forget about me," Alex teased in an attempt to flirt with her.

Her annoyance at his insistent innuendos climbed, but instead of showing it, she pasted a bland smile on her face and said, "I won't. I'll be up shortly."

Alex gave her what she was sure to his mind was a sexy half grin and a swaggering tilt of his head intended to make her swoon. Too bad it made her want to roll her eyes and ask if that move had worked for him in the past. As Alex ascended the stairs, Clark steered her into his office. The man without fail smelled of peppermint and Old Spice aftershave.

"Now, as I mentioned last week," Clark said, "the terms of your lease will stand for the full twelve months. Then you will have to negotiate a new lease with your new landlord."

Cybil replied, "Thank you, I appreciate that. I—"

Oh, sweet biscuits and gravy, no!

Not him. Anyone but him. She'd take the devil himself in exchange. Give her Beelzebub, give her Hades, give her the Hells Angels biker gang, all of them, over the man sitting so casually in Clark's office like he owned the place—which from all indications, he now did.

"Cybil. Good to see you. From what I understand from Clark, you're one of my new tenants," Miles Keaton said in his deep baritone voice as he rose from his seat when she entered the office.

"No," was all she could say. He couldn't be her new landlord. Surely she was still in bed and having a nightmare. That was all. She would wake the moment her alarm rang. Any minute now.

Miles raised a golden brow in her direction. His turquoise eyes, the ones that had haunted her dreams for thirteen years, regarded her coolly, with indifference.

It would have been far better if he had gotten fat or gone bald over the last thirteen years, losing some of the tousled golden hair that always looked like he'd run his long, sturdy fingers through it a hundred times. But if anything, he was like a fine wine or scotch, where he'd only gotten better, more potently gorgeous and alpha with age. The handsome, strong lines of his face had matured, and there were crinkled lines at the corners of his enigmatic eyes that glimmered with intelligence. He hadn't shaved today, and there was a hint of darker golden stubble gracing his square jaw, framing a pair of the most kissable lips she'd ever seen and tasted on a man. His six-foot-two, broad-shouldered frame, which had always been solid, had thickened and filled out with muscle. He wore a pair of tailored black slacks that rode low on his lean hips, and a crisp salmon dress shirt, unbuttoned at his neck, that should have looked girly, but which made Miles appear even more dominant and alpha, if that were possible.

The man had always been a walking wet dream. And dammit, but her girly bits awoke like a princess awakening from true love's kiss, and were throwing an excited rave at his presence. Although sadly, in her case, it was probably closer to a mummy emerging from his sarcophagus than a princess.

"I see you already know each other, Cybil, Miles. I just finished signing all the contracts for the transfer of my practice and the sale of the building. It will take another thirty days for the close of the sale, but for the sake of an expedient and painless transfer, as of today, Miles is your new landlord."

"I see. Well, thanks for the heads up. I have a client waiting." Cybil took a step back, ready to retreat to a place of strength and to figure out just what the heck she intended to do about Miles as her new landlord. She didn't know if there was anything she *could* do, with the exception of clearing the local supermarket out of their supply of rocky road ice cream.

"Cybil, I want to reaffirm with you, as I am doing with all the tenants in the building, that your lease will stand as is, and then we can discuss new terms once you are up for renewal," Miles stated. He studied her reaction intently. Too closely, to her mind. Uncomfortable with the scrutiny, she felt an all too familiar ache lance through her chest.

Her smile tight, she said, "Thank you for putting my mind at ease. I will sleep so much better now. If that's all you need, I have to go."

"Yes, yes, you young folk, always running from one place to the next," Clark said, shooing her out.

Miles didn't say anything, he just nodded, like a king granting a boon.

Miles had been visiting Echo Springs quite a lot recently. Coming into Smitty's frequently to hang out with his best friend, Nate. Escorting his mom to brunch or dinner at one of the local eateries. And now she knew why. Miles was back, back in Echo Springs. It took every ounce of her composure to maintain a straight face, when she wanted to act like a five-year-old and stick out her tongue at him, then go throw a temper tantrum that would make the Big Bang look like a bottle rocket explosion.

Agony, guilt, and regret infused her being any time they had the misfortune to meet. Guilt over the things she'd said to him and the way she'd treated him. Regret, large heaping piles of it, that she had ended their relationship and the real reasons behind the break, damn near choked her. It never helped that whenever he looked at her, it took her right back to that time, like the last thirteen years had never happened. She didn't know what was worse, his stony indifference or studious curiosity. They rarely said more than two words to each other; today's little conversion was an exception.

And she wished like hell it didn't hurt, that looking at him didn't feel like a thousand knives piercing her heart. But it did. Every. Time. It was the price of keeping the promise she had made long ago. Now, instead of just having to dodge him occasionally, it would become a daily occurrence.

Cybil feared what being around him all the time would do to her. And with a simple roll of the dice, her day had turned into pure, undiluted crud. Rather different than the first time they had met.

When he looked at her with that cold indifference, she wondered if he ever thought of that time. But then she tried to think of it no more as she escaped into her studio and used the buffer of work to shove it all out of her head.

The thing was, when it came to Miles, there was never a time when he wasn't there in some form in the back of her mind.

Chapter 2

13 years ago

Things could be worse.

Yeah, right!

Moving to a new town right before her senior year bit the proverbial big one. She had one year in which to pay penance in this Podunk spit of land along Interstate 70. Cybil grimaced from her perch, angry at the world in general for her predicament.

Not that she was from a large town to begin with, but at least her hometown of Salina, Kansas, had a few shopping malls and things to do. Here, all she had to do was look at the mountains.

She'd never seen anything like them. The way they speared the heavens in shades of slate and gruff gray, dotted with patches of glimmering ivory crests from year-round glaciers. A pair of bald eagles danced on wind currents above, and she marveled at their wingspans, the graceful arcs and dips as they soared through the clear blue sky. She had to admit, if only to herself, that the land captured her in a way the rolling fields back home never had.

They had moved to Echo Springs because Mom and Dad had wanted a fresh start. Really, it was more her mom's doing. When Dad had received the job offer as sheriff's deputy, they'd jumped at the opportunity. Mom couldn't handle all the close calls her dad had in Salina anymore.

Cybil didn't blame them. She wanted her dad alive too. And if this Podunk town helped keep him alive on the job, well then, she was all for it.

But it sucked balls that she didn't know a single person in this town on what should be her best year of school. While her friends in Salina had said they would keep in touch, Cybil was a bit more realistic about the situation. She was a good ten-hour drive away from them. And in truth, Echo Springs really couldn't be considered a town. It was more like a pit stop on the way to bigger and better things.

That was what Cybil planned to do: make this place a pit stop on the journey of her life. She had the world to conquer. She didn't know precisely how, but adventure was out there. She was so ready to grab life by the proverbial horns and go for a ride.

A person couldn't do that stuck in the middle of nowhere.

At least she'd gotten out of the house for a bit today. Since arriving, they'd barely left their new house two short blocks over off Main Street, mainly because Dad wanted everything unboxed and set up before his job started next week. Their house was near the heart of Echo Springs, straddling the good side of town compared to the area where the homes were rundown, and shabbier. Not that there was much town to begin with. She thought she'd read on their insufferably long drive that Echo Springs was two and a half square miles. Granted, from what she'd seen, there were outlying roads with additional homes beyond the tiny center.

Plus, there was the added bonus of the nearby ski resorts. She wanted to try skiing at least once. Discover precisely what it felt like to strap your feet onto two wooden slats and hurtle down the side of a mountain covered in fresh powder. She bet it would be exhilarating.

Cybil sat on a stone bench and gazed out over the shimmering silver-blue body of water the town had dubbed Echo Lake. They were very original around here with naming things. Currents rippled and swirled in the water in tune with the breeze whipping across the surface. Her perch was a stunning spot, filled with majesty, and made her feel small in this great big world. The air was crisp and clear, with a hint of a brisk chill. Cybil had not realized how cool it could get at the higher elevations. The next time she came up here she'd have to remember to bring a jacket, because she was freezing in her cargo capri pants and sky-blue cotton tank top.

The lake crested the lip of a mountain on its northern shore with a sheer two-hundred-foot drop-off. According to travel brochures, if you stood on the ledge and spoke, your voice would echo in the valley below, and you would see a series of springs flowing from one lake to the next along the side of the mountain. That was how the lake and town got their name.

As much as Cybil wanted to see the great big world out there, in this instance, sitting near it on a bench was close enough. She didn't mind heights or have a fear of them, but there was that whole *one teensy slip and you're a goner* thing she didn't care for much.

The stone bench was pleasant. It gave her a spot to people-watch as tourists—mainly families and couples—hiked the area trails. She wanted to try her hand at hiking; take one of the dirt pathways and experience nature with all that it entailed. Her only problem with the great outdoors was the lack of indoor plumbing.

She'd have to see if she could get her parents to buy her a pair of hiking boots. Money was tight because of the move, but she hoped she could persuade them. Then again, maybe the pizza place over on Main Street, Papa Beau's Pizza, would hire her part-time this summer, because then she could buy her own boots. She'd put in her application a few days ago. Fingers crossed that she would get a call. She should be a shoo-in, since she had worked at a pizza place in Salina.

"Mind if I join you?" a deep, gruff voice said behind her on the left.

Startled, Cybil shifted in her seat and glanced up. She gasped involuntarily.

He looks like an avenging archangel, was her first thought. His golden hair was illuminated by the high-noon sun, and a pair of aviator sunglasses, glinting silver, covered his eyes. His lips were firm, but full—kissably full—and softened the lines of his square jaw.

He was tall and rangy, with broad shoulders, but it was what he was wearing which caught her attention the most. A suit. Like this was his Sunday-best, going-to-church suit, in so dark a gray that it cast her initial theory of avenging archangel into new light. The crisp, ivory dress shirt and black tie he wore were loosened at the firm column of his neck. The guy was drop dead gorgeous; he looked like a model stepping off the pages of Cosmo. And Cybil's body reacted to him in a purely feminine manner, with a deep flutter in her belly.

"Um, sure," she replied, her voice breathy, her insecurity coming through loud and clear.

So much so that one of his golden brows quirked up from behind his sunglasses and her mystery guest asked, "You sure you don't mind? I only have a few minutes before I need to head back, and this bench is my favorite spot."

"No, not at all," Cybil murmured, feeling like a ninny, and shifted over to give his broad frame more room on the stone bench.

His shoulders were tense, his movements precise. Like it took all his energy to maintain an unaffected front of nonchalance.

"Thank you." He folded himself onto the bench, and Cybil felt a tremor of female recognition deep inside her as she caught a whiff of his masculine scent. It was raw, earthy, and unapologetically male. It made her want to turn in to him, this man, this stranger, and nuzzle his chest to inhale his enticing scent more fully.

"So, I have to ask, *Men in Black* audition? Is some alien dude coming to destroy Echo Springs and you're here to whisk everyone to safety?" Cybil asked, and slanted a sidelong glance at him.

Her question drew a surprised chuckle from her unexpected guest. The deep, masculine rumble curled deep inside her. Warmth unfurled within her breast.

Shaking his head, he murmured, studying her, "No. Nothing like that. I've not seen you around Echo Springs before."

She squinted as she tilted her head to look at him, and her lips curved up. "Perceptive. My family moved here two weeks ago, after school let out."

"Oh, yeah? Where from?" he asked. The tension that rippled off him in invisible waves unclenched little by little as they talked.

"Salina, Kansas. Human population forty-five thousand. Cow population nearly double that."

Her response coaxed a small grin from him. She couldn't help but glance at his lips, watch how they moved and formed words. She wondered how they would feel against her own. "So, from one interesting small town to the next, huh?"

"Pretty much. Granted, I like the view here. We definitely didn't have anything like it in Kansas," she admitted.

"Yeah, you picked a choice spot here too."

"Your spot apparently," she murmured in a teasing fashion.

"One of them. You gotta name, Kansas?"

She slid him a glance. "Perhaps, as long as you're not from a secret government agency, here to conduct experiments."

He grinned and shook his head. "I'm not, no."

"Well, then. I guess I can tell you. Cybil Roe. Nice to meet you…" She cocked her head and held out her hand for him to shake.

His much larger hand closed around hers, accepting it in congenial greeting. Where their palms touched, her skin burned, and a livewire of energy zapped through her. But it was over in a blink when he released her.

"Miles Keaton. Thanks for the conversation and for sharing the bench. I have to get back. Maybe I'll see you around," he said, his gaze on her as he stood. She wished she could see his eyes behind his sunglasses, get a better read on his expression. Had the momentary touch rattled him the way it had her?

Miles. It was a good name. It suited him.

Before he turned away and left, she blurted out, "I need to know, what's with the suit?" She gestured with a wave to his clothing.

Miles inhaled a deep, shuddering breath, squaring his shoulders before he replied, "My dad's funeral."

"That sucks balls," she exclaimed. Then heat infused her cheeks.

She wanted to smack herself upside the head. *Way to go, moron. Get the hot guy to talk to you, and completely screw up any chances of seeing him again because of your curiosity about his choice of fashion in the great outdoors.*

But he didn't appear offended. Her response drew a lopsided, half grin out of Miles, and he said, "That it does. See you around, Cybil."

Then he departed with a nod in her direction. As he strode away, she watched his retreating form, somehow aching for him. And, if truth be told, wanting to know more about Miles Keaton with the great laugh and kissable lips, who'd just lost his dad.

She stared after him long after he had vanished from her sight, replaying their conversation over and over in her mind. On what had to be one of the worst days of his life, he'd been kind and funny. Added to that, he was stunningly gorgeous. Miles was quite intriguing.

And he lived in Echo Springs. Cybil smiled. Her move to Podunk USA had suddenly become far more interesting, and much less of a travesty. She wondered when she would see him again. In a town this small, they were bound to run into each other.

Chapter 3

From Old Man Turner's Journal:
Change happens. It's how you deal with it that matters.

Fate was quite the bitch. Miles grimaced as Cybil hightailed it out of the office with a swish of her shapely, slender hips.

His office now. For better or worse.

Perhaps he should have inquired more deeply into who all his tenants would be before signing on the dotted line. While he and Clark had hammered out terms, he had been informed of the yoga fitness studio in the building, and Miles liked the idea. Granted, he'd not realized Cybil was the owner until he signed the papers and noted the name of the studio. Learning he and Cybil would be in close contact often was sort of like looking both ways before crossing the street and getting hit by an airplane.

Clark Biddle had explained that there was a realtor's office, a yoga fitness studio, and three tenants renting the apartments on the top floor. The monthly rents from his five tenants more than covered the cost of the mortgage and any upkeep this place might need. Clark kept Aiden O'Toole on retainer for any maintenance needs. It was a relationship Miles planned on keeping. Aiden was a good guy, and a hell of a contractor.

Cybil had been none too happy to spy his sorry ass in the office. Not that he could blame her, not with their sordid history. And she'd taken his breath away, even though he had known it was coming that he would see her at some point today. Cybil packed a one-two punch, with a slender, toned body in her athletic wear—and then there was her face. She had smooth, unblemished, cream-colored skin he knew pinkened under the sun and felt like silk beneath his fingertips, and high cheekbones gave her an exotic, seductive look, with a slim, pert nose, the tip slightly upturned, pale pink lips that were almost too wide and generous, and delicate arched black brows. But her eyes were the feature that had always sucked him in. They were sultry, goddess eyes that had the ability to offer a man heaven or cut him to the bone with a mere glance, surrounded by a wealth of inky lashes.

The expression on her beautiful face had registered abject horror instead of a warm welcome. At one time—in another life, it seemed most days—a smile would have lit up her face and turned her gray eyes molten silver with the entirety of her heart beaming for all the world to see. But he didn't get that from Cybil, hadn't for a long time; nor would he get warmth from her. Not after the way she had so brutally dumped him after her parents died all those years ago. Frankly, he did not expect anything less than a sneer and cold shoulder from Cybil. They had both made mistakes in the years since, in their treatment of each other. Their relationship, what there was of it, tended to skew toward tension, clipped words, and retreating to a minimum safe distance. At one time, she'd looked at him with something bordering on hero worship. He shook his head at the memory, at the visceral ache it ignited when he thought of what they had lost.

Still, he planned to change that reaction. What would she say if he told her she was part of the reason he'd decided to move back here? That after all this time, seeing her again these last few months had resurrected feelings he'd thought had died long ago.

Miles knew it was a long shot, but he knew Cybil and figured with time, with patience, he would win her back. Because this time, he was no longer a boy playing at being a man. He knew what he wanted for his life, for his future, and was playing for keeps.

Christ, she looked good. Better, even. Then again, Cybil had always been a sensuous little minx with the ability to rouse him to extremes, either anger or passion. And there was a fine line between the two.

Remorse weighed heavy on his soul, because now there was only awkwardness, bitterness, and an aching longing in him for what might have been had he been stronger, had he not caved and chosen the easy road, but fought for them instead. When she had pushed him away after everything they had been through, Miles had let her. It had been easier. He'd been arrogant enough that he had figured it was for the best, and like a fool, he had even been relieved. It had been the coward's way out. Deep down, he understood that, and had never forgiven himself for not standing his ground.

Time supposedly healed all wounds. Miles called bullshit. Not a day had passed that he hadn't thought of Cybil and the promise of what they had lost. He'd always wondered about her, wherever he had gone. She had always been in the back of his mind, even when he'd been mired in other relationships and dating other women. He'd enjoyed himself in college, and as a hotshot attorney in Denver. The world had been his proverbial oyster where women were concerned. Not a single one of them had ever held a candle to Cybil.

The opportunity to buy Clark Biddle's practice had been the chance he'd been looking for to move back to Echo Springs. It was rather ironic that all he'd thought about in high school was leaving Echo Springs for greener pastures. And now, at thirty-three, he had transferred back to his hometown because he wanted to be here.

"Cybil is a good tenant. Hard worker, that one," Clark Biddle said. The old geezer stared at Miles with his wizened green gaze, as if he remembered that Miles and Cybil had once been an item. While they'd not hidden their relationship, they hadn't necessarily taken out an ad about it either. That was because most of the people in this town didn't know how deep they'd gone, how inseparable they had been all summer. They didn't know that the couple had experienced the heights of ecstasy, and had been flattened by the double-edged sword of reality.

"I know Cybil." Or he had, and planned to once more. "It should be fine. Who else do we need to meet with today?" Miles deflected with a canny grace that had served him well in the courtroom, redirecting the meeting back to the business at hand—shifting ownership of Clark's business and the building into his hands.

"The realtors should be in later this morning, but I think, ah, there's the next one," Clark said with a grin.

Miles spent the morning meeting his new tenants, and reading over and signing the final documents with Clark. The older gentleman was a pistol with his contracts. It was one of the things Miles enjoyed about the law and legal system—how a single word or phrase could change an entire clause and contract, if you weren't careful. He'd won a lot of cases on technicalities because people didn't necessarily read a contract thoroughly before they signed. Case in point: all those online user agreements for every computer program and website. But the law worked for him; the ins and outs, the puzzle presented with every case, suited his personality. And a side benefit was he'd made a ton of money and had the wherewithal to invest wisely. It was one of the reasons he could move back to Echo Springs to work a smaller practice.

By noon, they had completed all the transfers and had everything signed, and even though the closing on the building was in thirty days, it all technically now belonged to Miles. Ready for some fresh air, he left the office, just as the movers Clark had hired to relocate his furniture had arrived.

Miles already had an office suite of furniture he would move in. That furniture currently occupied a storage locker on the outskirts of town, along with most of his worldly possessions, while he decided on a more permanent place to live. As it was, he was renting Abby Callier's house. She was shacking up with his best friend, which left the house she'd inherited from her great-aunt unoccupied. He liked the old Victorian. It was solid, had good bones, and could be updated if Abby ever decided to sell.

Truthfully, Abby's house was not the right space for him for anything other than a temporary stay, even if that stay was six months or longer. That was how he viewed his time at the Callier place: as temporary, though Miles did need a more permanent place to lay his head at night, one that was not his mother's house. There wasn't anything wrong with his mom's home. It was the home he had grown up in. There was a lifetime of memories, both the good and the bad, in that place. But if he lived with his mom, she would constantly try to set him up with one of her friend of a friend's daughters even more than she already was—and that was with him at Abby's. It wasn't that he didn't want to date. He did. Once he was settled both in his new business and home, Miles would implement his plans to win Cybil back.

Just not at or from his mom's house, no matter how much he loved her.

Miles had a plot of land, Prospect Point, that he had inherited from his father when he passed away. Prospect Point was up off Miner's Way Road, on the very outskirts of town, about a mile from the McKinley Place. It was a remote, isolated few acres, but one of the prettiest spots in the world, to his mind. Growing up, it had been his spot. First, with his dad when he was a kid, they would go camping there. Then, when he was a teenager, it had been a spot where he and Nate and some of their high school buddies would go to drink beer and talk about women. Until that one summer when it had become their spot: his and Cybil's.

That was a carrot he would dangle—the house he wanted to build there, and he didn't plan to live there alone.

Since he made the decision to move back to Echo Springs, Miles had started moving forward with building his own home on that stretch of land. He had contacted Aiden O'Toole about it and had a meeting scheduled with him next week. He knew Aiden was a damn fine contractor with a background in architecture. Aiden had been two years behind Miles at Echo Springs High, and they had regularly run into each other over the years.

If he was being fanciful, the idea of constructing a home—his home—at Prospect Point, filled Miles with a sense of destiny, as if it was the place he had been heading toward his entire life and was only just now realizing it. Building a home made his return to Echo Springs permanent and real. Miles did not regret his decision to move here. And it wasn't purely for his mom that he'd moved back to his hometown, even though that was his story, and he was sticking to it for the time being. In truth, he needed the change. His entire routine, his daily life, had become nothing but work. For years he had thrived on it, working on cases, scoring big hauls for the practice, putting in ninety hours a week without fail.

But now, he was burned out and hollowed out. The truth was, he had begun to feel like the job had leached out his soul, and all he was doing was going through the motions.

When he had come back here for his mom's retirement party

months ago and run up against Cybil at Smitty's with the gang, it was the most alive he had felt in years. Electrified over a haughty glare, Miles started planning, searching for the perfect opening and opportunity to move back here.

Cybil wouldn't do long distance a second time. And that was part of his bargaining chip: that he was here, and here to stay.

For now, renting Abby's place gave him time as it was open-ended, which suited him and his purposes.

When he left the office, he did so with one thought in mind: food. Miles wasn't losing himself in willing female flesh and, in his book, food was the next best thing. Which was one of the reasons he ran six miles a day every morning—not because he wanted to wake before the sun rose to get a run in, but because he loved to eat.

Miles walked the block from his building over to the Emporium Diner. The eatery had been around since the late 1930s and was famous for its burgers and milkshakes. As tastes had changed over the years, items had been added and removed from the menu, but it was still one of the best places—not just in town, but in Colorado—to get a burger and their famous green chili, a tradition in the state.

Inside, the diner looked like a time warp back to the 1950s. What with the Formica countertop and red booths with the sheen of wear at the edges, one might expect to see women in poodle skirts and guys in jeans folded at the cuffs, sporting black leather jackets.

It was a favorite spot for both the locals, and tourists passing through. It was open twenty-four hours and always had a gaggle of patrons lining the counter and stuffed in the booths.

Miles met his best friend, Nate, at the diner. He and Nate had met in kindergarten at Echo Springs Elementary. They were family, considered each other brothers, and were about as opposite as they came, at least in appearance. Nate's work attire consisted of jeans, flannel shirts, a gun belt and today, with the chilly weather, a black coat with the town's emblem and *Sheriff* embroidered underneath.

The pair had added Jacob and Sam to their circle in college. The four of them were as thick as thieves. Sam was off in Hollywood, dating actresses and being a stunt double for some of the biggest action stars gracing movie screens. Jacob ran his own tech company and, word had it, was poised to move back to Echo Springs himself. That would put three of the Four Musketeers back together again.

Their waitress, Genevieve, a petite, girl-next-door strawberry-blonde who had been behind Miles in school by about five years, gave them a warm smile as she dropped off their orders. They were never ones to break tradition when they stopped in at the diner. Their meals consisted of a couple of loaded double bacon cheeseburgers and extra-large baskets of fries. Miles skipped the soda and the milkshake.

"How's the new office?" Nate asked, then took a bite of his burger.

"It's a good space. Little odd being back," Miles said, which was the understatement of the century considering his little run-in with Cybil this morning. That was all they seemed to have anymore: tense, anxiety-filled interactions where Miles got to relive the mountains of regret he still harbored over their ending.

One step at a time. It would take time and the patience of the Dalai Lama to win her back. To change them into what they were once, and could be again.

"I experienced the same when I returned. I, for one, am glad you're back. We could use your skills on our flag football team this winter. And I'm sure your mom is thrilled."

"I'm down with the football. Just let me know when. I'll build it into my schedule. Mom's happy I'm here, of course. If only all the women in this town were," Miles bit out, annoyed that Cybil had riled him and cast a shadow of doubt over his agenda. No one else could get under his skin like she could. His body electrified in her presence, and tended to short-circuit his brain.

Nate quirked a dark brow. His lips twitched at the corners, and he said, "You mean Cybil?"

Shit.

Miles sighed in defeat. Nate knew him too damn well. It was a hazard of a lifelong friendship. There were very few secrets that they had kept from one another.

He had only one, and it was a doozy.

Although, due to the fact that any time Miles and Cybil were in proximity to one another, they tended to resemble two feral cats barricaded in a room together, it wasn't a shocker that Nate, with his detective skills, surmised Cybil was the woman in town who wasn't thrilled at his return. Interactions between them had been difficult to avoid because Nate's fiancée and Cybil were bosom buddies. And they were about to level up, now that Miles was her landlord, and had ulterior motives to woo her back into his life on a permanent basis.

"What she'd do this time? Snip your balls off?" Nate asked good-naturedly, then stuffed a French fry in his mouth.

"Not this time, no." Although Miles wouldn't put it past her. That woman was downright scary when she was pissed. "She's one of my new tenants."

Nate's brows rose in stunned surprise before he howled with laughter, a wide grin splitting his face. "Seriously? Cybil's your new tenant? But I thought she lived with her sister over in the duplex."

Miles could only wish that were the case. "She does live with her sister, as far as I know. It's her fitness studio that she opened a month ago. She's only been a tenant there for two months."

"Okay, let me get this straight. You and Cybil will be working in close quarters on almost a daily basis? Is your life insurance policy paid up? There are no firearms on the premises, right? I should ask Abby to see if she knows whether Cybil has a firearm."

"No, there aren't. Cybil wouldn't do that." At least, Miles didn't think she would.

"What's the deal with you two, anyway? You've never said. There's enough chemistry between you to power the town's generator," Nate said, dredging a handful of fries in ketchup.

"Leave it. It's nothing. I don't want to talk about it."

Nate cocked his head at Miles's tone. "I'm not the enemy here. But my cop Spidey-senses are on alert, and what's more, I know you. We have been friends our whole lives, so what gives? You've never told me why you and Cybil can't stand one another."

There were very few things Miles had kept from Nate over the years. However, his relationship with Cybil had been a life-altering whirlwind, and at the time, he had kept it to himself because she had mattered more than any woman ever had before—and, he had to admit now, ever since. His life was divided into two distinct epochs—Before Cybil and After Cybil. Glancing around the diner to ensure no one was eavesdropping on their conversation, he leaned forward and said in a low voice, "Remember the year my dad died?"

Nate's blue gaze turned sympathetic. "How could I forget? We'd just finished freshman year at CU in Boulder."

"Yeah, well, I stuck around Echo Springs while you went back to Boulder for summer classes and football." The memories of that time in his life always brought with them a twinge of profound sorrow. He'd willingly drowned himself in Cybil. After he'd lost his dad so suddenly, she had been his salvation, had kept him treading water when the rest of his life had so drastically changed.

"And?" Nate asked, breaking him out of his reverie.

"Cybil and I were a thing that summer. She'd just moved to

town, and we dated. I had told you I was dating someone, if I remember correctly. I just never said who," Miles admitted.

"I knew there was something there. How could I have missed this? I'm guessing by the way Cybil's claws come out whenever you're in the vicinity that it didn't end well between you two."

That was the understatement of the century. It had ended with her parents dying, then Cybil shutting Miles out with him not fighting for her—for them. And there was a part that they had lost that he had never really come to terms with, not in all the years since. She had broken things off with him, and he'd let her. He'd loved her with everything he was, and had let her down spectacularly by allowing her to push him away.

Miles snorted. "What do you think? Of course it didn't end well."

And much of the blame could be laid at his feet. Looking back, it had only been a little over six months after his dad died, and his head space had made him want the path of least resistance. That was still not a valid excuse for letting her go without a fight, though, and a complete dick move on his part.

Nate scraped a hand over his face. "Well, your secret's safe with me. I need to head back to the station. If you're not doing anything for dinner, you're welcome to join Abby and me."

"I'm meeting movers at my storage unit in fifteen minutes to have them move my office furniture into my new headquarters. If we get everything transferred and I don't finish up that late, I will definitely take you up on that offer. I haven't had a chance to get more than the basic supplies. As long as you're certain that Abby won't mind," Miles replied after they'd settled the check and headed out of the diner. The last thing he needed was another woman in this town being pissed off at him. One was bad enough.

"She won't. Let me know if you need any help getting settled," Nate said, climbing into his Explorer.

"Will do." Miles trod the block over to the office building, where his Escalade was parked, to head off to meet the movers.

Miles spent the better part of the afternoon with the moving company, getting his office furniture carted from the storage unit into his office. There was the mahogany desk he had found at an estate sale in Denver a few years ago that had come with matching bookshelves. He had not been able to pass the set up. Desk chairs, chairs for the waiting room, a leather loveseat for his office, a second desk for the waiting room, and what he hoped would be his assistant's desk, as soon as he hired one. He had that task on his agenda to get squared away in the next week or so. There was also a larger leather couch for clients while they waited outside his office, with a few comfortable padded chairs if they were needed. While the movers transferred everything into his new suite of offices, Miles carted boxes of supplies from his Escalade inside: computers, printers, boxes of printer paper, boxes of file folders and legal pads, along with all the stationery items one could need. There were also all his law books on statutes, both federal and state, that would go on his shelves, as well as artwork and accent pieces to add to the walls.

His new office had four rooms—six, if you counted the two restrooms. There was the main waiting room with the desk for a future assistant, along with what he considered the public restroom. There was an employee breakroom with a refrigerator, toaster oven, microwave, and sink. Clark had left the breakroom furniture: a round wooden table and chairs, and an ancient, albeit still nice, couch in a seventies brown plaid. The room beyond the breakroom would serve as his storage room.

Then there was his office, where he would spend the bulk of his time when he wasn't in court. The hardwood floors were something that had sold him right off the bat. Miles spent time unboxing things, beginning with his office. He'd have to remember to bring his tools with him tomorrow to get the pictures hung.

The sheer volume of items needed to run an office was unreal. He schlepped boxes into the storage room, figuring this was the room he would tackle tomorrow. Which reminded him that he needed an office manager, like yesterday. Once he had his computer set up in his office, and had the internet transferred and arranged in his name, he would submit an ad to the local newspaper, seeking an office manager. Hopefully, he could get someone in here at least part time to start. But for now, without any support staff, he'd be running the show on his own. It was too bad he'd not been able to entice his secretary at the firm in Denver to move here. Marcia had kept him organized and on point, an invaluable asset that he hated to lose.

It was pretty sad that the person he missed most from Denver was his former secretary.

Miles made lists of things he needed to do this week. He worked better with lists and tasks that he could cross off as they were finished. Deep down, he had always been an organized soul, even as a kid. He emailed the cleaning company Clark had suggested to set up a meeting. Also on his agenda for this week was getting new business cards and a letterhead designed, as well as mailing out a welcome letter to all the clients transferred into his business with the buyout. He'd need to look at online office supplies stores and establish an account with one of them. There was no way he could get into Denver once a month to buy supplies. It would be much easier if he had it all delivered. Although, he was considering running into Denver and finding some area rugs, one for his office and another for the waiting room. He added that to the list. As soon as this place was in working order, he needed to familiarize himself with the previous cases, the ones in progress, and work forward from there.

This office—his office—was going to run at a much different

pace than what Miles was used to after serving as a corporate attorney defending companies for one of the top firms in Denver. He was looking forward to the most exciting thing on his docket being a will or land dispute, perhaps a few speeding tickets or driving under the influence citations.

Not for a minute did he regret living in Denver, or the experiences he'd had over the years. Still, he wouldn't miss the ninety-hour work weeks that had made it so the only person he truly missed was his secretary. That was something he wanted in moving back to his hometown—he wanted a life again.

Miles glanced up and caught sight of Cybil rushing out the front door of the building like her feet had hyper jets attached to them. Her body was sleek and toned, but all woman. Her yoga pants sported a snakeskin pattern, and hugged her curves like a second skin. She was bundled up in a fire-engine red parka, and knee-high black boots. A thick, raven-hued braid streamed down her back. He remembered what her hair looked like unbound and spread out beneath her, and rubbed at the spot in his chest. Even covered like she was against the colder temperatures that had swooped in from the north this week, she was more lusciously feminine than most women.

He wondered where she was running off to with such enthusiasm. At one time, she'd been that way with him. Christ, being back in this town, seeing her again all the time, made the past thirteen years dissolve. He could still remember the day they'd met, the day of his dad's funeral. She'd been a refreshing breeze amidst the sudden tragedy of his father's passing, the first person inside of a week who hadn't glanced at him with pity or sorrow. And when it had come to light that he'd just left his dad's funeral, she hadn't offered a canned condolence but had been blunt and outspoken instead.

He shook his head at the memory. There was always an ache whenever he thought of his dad and that day. That was yet another reason why he'd moved home. As he was an only child, and with his dad gone, there was no one else here to take care of his mom. At fifty-nine, she was still spry and wildly independent, but he knew better than most that that could change from one heartbeat to the next. He was a big fan of being prepared and playing the long game.

That way, when the next big life surprise came, he would be ready for it.

Miles shut down his equipment for the night, turned off the lights, and locked up before heading out. On his way home, he stopped at the grocery store and picked up a few things for the house, remembering to grab a bottle of wine and yellow roses for Abby as a thank-you for feeding him dinner this evening.

Chapter 4

From Old Man Turner's Journal:
When it comes to love, time has no meaning.

Cybil pulled her aging brick-red truck into Nate and Abby's driveway, and parked behind Abby's Land Rover. This way, she wouldn't block Nate in. It would save her a trip outside if Nate was called into the station. As the town's sheriff, he was pretty much always on call.

Until recently, Nate had lived in the slate blue and ivory two-story Victorian all by his lonesome and had been considered one of the town's most eligible bachelors. But that had all changed when Abby, grand-niece of the recently deceased Evie Callier, moved into the house Evie had left her next door.

Abby had officially moved into Nate's house a month ago. Those two were so in love with each other, anyone could see it. It was a palpable, tangible thing. Cybil was over the moon for Abby, while at the same time it shone a light on her singleness. Cybil particularly felt like an absolute heel anytime she grimaced over the two lovebirds.

Everyone else seemed to be falling in love, getting married, having babies, and had their lives on track, while Cybil could only say things like: *Look, a bill was paid on time*, or *I got out of bed on time and didn't kill anyone*, or her favorite: *Everyone else's life is moving forward and progressing, while I feel like I'm just standing still.* Cybil, as much as she blustered and pretended that she had her act together, was just getting by most days. Just finally beginning to shape her life into what she wanted, instead of the life that had been thrust upon her.

And any time petty jealousy crept in at her new friend being in love, she was swamped with guilt to the point where she wanted to thunk her head against her steering wheel and repeat the mantra: *I am a good person*, until she believed it.

Maybe she should have canceled the invite for the meal with her friends. She was in a rotten mood because her first love—in truth, the only man she had ever loved—was her new landlord and back in town after thirteen years. Cybil had no clue how to feel or how to deal with the new circumstances. The situation made it seem like she had a cosmic bull's-eye positioned above her head whose only job was to continually disrupt her life and plans. Would it be so much to ask to have one thing go right? She would dearly love to know what deity she had angered; that way, she could atone and make amends.

Running into Miles all the time, she could say goodbye to any Zen in her life.

With a deep sigh at the state of her world, Cybil emerged from her truck, the old door creaking at the forced movement. She straightened, pasting a smile on her face that she didn't feel, and headed up the stone path toward the front door. It opened before she arrived at the porch. In a blur of dark fur, Rufus, Nate's hundred-and-fifty-pound Great Dane, bounded toward her, every inch of the big lug vibrating with excitement. The way his mouth hung open, tongue dangling out, looked like a smile. If there was anything that her many years of waiting tables and hefting platters had done for her, it had given her fast reflexes for dodging unwanted hands and huge dogs that had no idea how big they were. She shifted her body just before Rufus could pounce, and he skidded past.

"Oomph! Jesus, Rufus," a male voice said behind her. A voice she knew all too well. One that made her heart trip over in her chest. "This dog is a menace."

"He's harmless, just gets excited over company. Rufus, get back in here, you moron," Nate shouted, shaking his head while he waited on the porch. Did Rufus listen? Nope. He waded into the yard to smell every bush and shrub, happy as a clam to be in the great outdoors.

"Sheriff," Cybil acknowledged, climbing the stairs, charmed by Rufus's antics but refusing to turn around and greet the man striding up the walkway behind her. She could feel him. His potent, dominant energy was powerful enough to blot out the sun. It was bad enough that she'd thought about little but Miles all day long. Now she was going to have to deal with him all through dinner.

Lovely.

It made her wish she'd gone home and responded to one of the interested men on Matchmakers.com instead.

"Cybil, glad you could make it. Abby's back in the kitchen if you want to go on in," Nate said with a friendly smile. The man had certainly earned the nickname *Sheriff Stud Muffin*. He was tall, with a full head of dark hair and blue eyes that were shades darker than Miles but no less handsome. Nate seemed to have a permanent shadow of dark stubble lining his jaw. He'd removed his gun belt and was minus his badge, but his air of authority lingered, as if his rangy frame was always ready for action.

But Cybil didn't stop her forward progression, not with the icy breath of her past panting down her neck. She sailed past

Nate and into the house. Her heart stuttered as she inhaled deep, calming breaths on her way back to the kitchen.

Cybil liked the house. Nate had fully remodeled the interior little by little, creating a beautiful home full of warmth, with gleaming hardwood floors. Cybil thought it was sweet how he and Abby had finished this place together. It was homey, with Abby adding some decorative touches that were feminine and added cheer and comfort to the place, like the vase of fresh flowers on the table in the foyer, and some of the artwork that graced the hall.

"There you are. I was starting to think you weren't coming tonight." Abby shot Cybil a welcoming grin from her stance at the stove. Her brunette hair fell in soft waves around her shoulders. The ivory cashmere sweater she wore clung to her curves and fell past her waist, almost to mid-thigh. Completing the look with dark brown leggings and riding boots in a matching brown, Abby looked chic and urbanite, but then again, she always did. One of the things Cybil loved about her was her sense of fashion.

Abby wiped her hands on a towel before giving her a quick hug of greeting. Abby had become one of her best friends in the relatively short time she had lived in Echo Springs. She and Tessa both considered Abby their triumvirate addition.

"I got caught up at the community center. I still have one class there, and it went extra-long tonight." Cybil shrugged, leaving out that it was because Alex Dotson was becoming a thorn in her side. In addition to their personal training session that morning, he had attended her power yoga class this afternoon, and then waited until the rest of the class had ushered out of the room before asking her to dinner. What was the man thinking? She had never given him any reason to think she was the slightest bit interested. At least she had already had plans tonight, so she hadn't needed to lie and make excuses. But she and Alex were going to have a little chat soon if he didn't back off. Yes, she wanted to date, but not him.

"It's too bad Tessa's out of town. It would have been nice if we could have all gotten together," Abby said, moving around the kitchen with the ease and confidence that spoke of her comfort in the room. She did a fabulous imitation of Julia Child with her cooking, too. Cybil was an okay cook—okay in that she preferred picking up one of those precooked rotisserie chickens, adding a salad to it, and calling dinner done.

"Yeah, she's at a comic book expo back East. She'll be sad she missed this little gathering." If Cybil's sister had been here, there would have at least been more of a buffer between her and Miles. As it was, she needed to steel herself to handle him without Tessa there to run interference.

"It's not the same without her around. Miles, you made it." Abby moved forward and gave him a hug even though his hands were full. Abby had no qualms or hang ups when it came to Miles, welcoming Nate's friend with the same effusive joy that she had Cybil. And Miles's smile for Abby was chock full of affection and friendship; a far cry from the mysterious glint in his eyes when he looked at Cybil over Abby's shoulder as they embraced.

The strange look vanished as he withdrew from Abby's arms, replaced by congeniality and a familiar rapport toward Abby and Nate. Miles still wore his dress slacks and shirt from earlier that day, meaning he had not stopped working in enough time to stop and change. There was a twinge in Cybil's chest when he offered Abby a bottle of wine and a bouquet of flowers he was carrying like some gallant gentleman. It was totally in keeping with his personality. When they had been dating, he had always brought Cybil little trinkets.

"As a thank you for feeding me tonight," Miles explained with a dashing smile at Abby.

"You didn't have to do this, but I must admit I love flowers. Here, Nate, why don't you open this up while I put these in some water?" Abby said, distributing tasks like a seasoned veteran. Carting the flowers over to the sink, she retrieved a vase from a cabinet and arranged the flowers in it.

"Slick moves. Get your own woman," Nate added good-naturedly with a teasing glance at Miles. He moved around the kitchen confidently, opened the wine, and then pegged her with a glance, his brow cocked in question. "Cybil?"

Slipping her hands in her pockets, she nodded, keeping a smile on her face when she felt anything but happy. "Sure, I'll have a glass."

"Miles? This, or would you like a beer?" Nate asked, retrieving wine glasses from an overhead cabinet.

"Beer would be great. I have to say, Abby, whatever you made smells fantastic. I might have to steal you away from Nate so I can have you cook for me all the time." Miles winked at Abby.

"Is that all men think about?" Cybil said, her voice dripping sarcasm as a punch of anger powered through her. Instantly, guilt accompanied her words. Why did it always have to be hard words and angry looks? Why couldn't she move past it, him, after all this time? Why was there a part of her that was jealous that he could be so easy with her best friend, while with her it was angry barbs?

Miles's gaze slid over her. At first it was filled with reprimand but then shifted—as he took in her manner of dress, noting that all she had done was toss a sweater on over her workout gear—to male appreciation, with the corners of his mouth curling up. An emotion Cybil had not felt in years stirred to life. Heat at levels that could spark nuclear fission flushed her limbs. She hated that Miles could rev her internal combustion when he was near. A simple searing glance from him was more potent than any wine.

"Not all. But it's definitely a nice bonus," Miles murmured and shrugged nonchalantly, his baritone husky and laced with condescension, berating her for bad manners. His voice curled inside her chest and wound its way down into her belly, leaving a scorched trail in its wake.

"I'd like to see you try," Nate said, and pulled Abby in for a quick kiss. And there it was: the ease, the beauty of the two of them together, just how well they fit. The aura and bubble of love surrounding them. It reminded her of when she and Miles had been together. Cybil was not prepared for the lightning strike ache inside her chest.

She slanted a glance at Miles only to find understanding mirroring her feelings, and internally cursed the promise she had made all those years ago. If things were different… She looked away and took a long sip of wine. They weren't different. They were never going to be.

But then Abby shoved Nate away, blushing profusely. "Why don't you guys have a seat? Dinner's ready. And you, mister, keep your hands to yourself so we don't embarrass our guests."

"I solemnly swear to be on my best behavior." Nate winked at Abby.

Abby shook her head and gestured for them to take their seats. Abby and Nate sat at either end, leaving Cybil and Miles to each pick one side. It was going to make it that much harder to avoid looking at him. Dinner was a succulent pot roast, with carrots and red potatoes, warm, crusty French rolls with fresh butter, and a garden salad tossed with a balsamic vinaigrette Cybil was sure Abby had made herself.

"Miles, Nate was telling me that you bought Clark Biddle's practice." Abby slipped into the role of hostess, ensuring everyone had what they needed.

"Yeah, I did. We finished signing all the paperwork transferring the practice to me this morning," Miles replied, taking a swig of his beer.

"Oh congratulations! That's got to feel wonderful, knowing you'll be your own boss," Abby murmured.

"Why did you decide to buy his practice? I thought you were

living the life in Denver as a hot shot attorney," Cybil said politely—as politely as she could, anyway—more curious than she wanted to admit.

Miles zeroed his full attention her way, assessing her before he answered. "I decided I wanted to move home. Now that my mom has retired, I prefer to be close by if she needs me. And Denver was great, but I was ready for a change."

Figures. Life and its opportunities had always come easier to Miles. He had visited places, experienced life, and moved on from Echo Springs. Moved on from Cybil without any trouble.

She toasted him with a smile she didn't feel. "Well, welcome back."

Abby, sensing that Cybil was close to losing her cool, deftly switched the subject. "By the way, Thanksgiving is next week. We wanted to invite you guys to celebrate the holiday with us. Cybil, if you and Tessa want to join us, we would love that. Miles, I'm not sure what you and your mom are doing, but you're both welcome. I will be cooking the turkey and all the trimmings, so you don't have to worry about a thing, just show up and eat."

"Maybe," Cybil said. "I'll talk to Tessa when she returns from her comic expo. And it depends on the time. I'm working at Smitty's that night as part of the annual charity auction."

"The last few Thanksgivings Mom's spent in Denver at my place; we would definitely love the hospitality, and will join you. I'm sure my mom will want to talk to you, Abby, about bringing a dish or two. I'll give her your number so she can coordinate with you. And Smitty's has a charity auction? Since when?" Miles reached for another roll in the basket by his elbow.

Cybil tried for an olive branch, considering she had been rather bitchy. "When Burke took over Smitty's from his uncle, he started the charity auction to benefit the neediest families in Echo Springs. It helps provide Christmas presents and meals for Christmas Day. It's a really good cause, and all the proceeds stay in our town. Burke's way of giving back to the community."

"That sounds like a great cause. What do they auction off?" Miles asked.

"Dates," Nate commented with a shake of his head and an eye roll.

Yeah, it was a little ridiculous to offer dates to make money. But Cybil also knew that it tended to haul a huge crowd to Smitty's, and accrue quite a bit in cash donations. It was one of the reasons why she worked the auction. She was only on stage for a few minutes at most, and tended to score primo tips due to the festive nature of the event. The local VA even provided free shuttle rides home at the end, for the inebriated patrons.

"Come again?" A smile tugged at the corner of Miles's lips. Cybil had always been fascinated with the firm fullness of his mouth. And damn it all but that charm hadn't diminished one bit.

"They auction off the single people in town for a date. Both Tessa and I are participating. Even Burke offers himself up as a prize. Burke roped you in again, Nate, even though you're taken?" Cybil asked, rather surprised Abby was going to allow it.

"He did. I couldn't get out of it," Nate replied with a deep sigh.

"And I will be bidding on him. No way am I letting someone else get their hands on him," Abby said defiantly.

Nate threaded his fingers with Abby's and gave her a sly grin. "Fighting over me. I like it."

"You won't be liking it when I relegate you to the couch if someone else should win. And I'll let Rufus sleep in bed with me," Abby murmured. At his name, Rufus, who'd been silently watching them at the table, clearly hopeful that someone would drop some food, pranced a bit and nudged his head onto Abby's lap.

"And you're part of the auction, Cybil?" Miles pinned her with a glance.

"I am. Have been every year since it started. It's harmless, really. Granted, there was that one year when Martin won me. But there are parameters for the date," Cybil replied, and shuddered at the memory of the date with Martin. That guy had had more hands than she'd been able to keep up with, until she had finally left in the middle of the so-called date.

"That wouldn't be Martin Long, would it?" Miles's expression shuttered, his eyes became as hard as diamonds.

"One and the same." Cybil sighed and took a swig of her wine.

"What happened with Martin?" Miles inquired with a steely gaze, his voice low.

The absolute worst date of Cybil's life, but he did not need to know the nuts and bolts of it. "Nothing I couldn't handle. Burke banned him from bidding the following year, after his shenanigans. But I think he's been reinstated for this year." Cybil prayed that Martin would not bid on her if that was the case. She would have it out with Burke if he allowed that. Not after last time.

"Martin's always been an ass, even in high school," Nate said with disgust. "Some things don't ever change."

"You've got that right. Abby, Nate's going to need to buy bigger belts with your cooking. This was the best pot roast I've had in years," Miles complimented as he laid his napkin next to his empty plate.

Abby beamed. "Thanks. You're welcome to come for dinner any time, Miles."

"I appreciate the open invite and dinner tonight. I wish I could stay to socialize, but I still have more unpacking to get squared away, and an early start tomorrow." Miles carried his plate over to the sink before he returned to the table and gave Abby a brief hug. He glanced at Cybil over Abby's shoulder as they embraced, and Cybil wished she could tell what he was thinking when he looked at her, but he kept his thoughts from her. Although the frost that had been present the last thirteen years was conspicuously absent.

Did that mean that perhaps after all this time, they could be friends and not enemies? It would be so nice to not be on the defensive around him all the time.

"I'll walk you out." Nate shoved his chair back. At the movement, Rufus leapt to his paws and shadowed Nate and Miles. The pup probably needed another trip outside. Then again, most dogs loved going in and out a hundred times a day. It was one of the reasons Cybil had not objected to her sister adopting Gus. A cat didn't need to be let outside, and with the number of predators in the mountains, was best kept indoors anyway. Besides, their little butterball was perfectly content to watch the world from the window nearest his food bowl.

Once the guys had left the kitchen, Cybil helped Abby clear the table and whispered so that her voice wouldn't carry, "You could have warned me that Miles would be here."

Abby glanced her way, interest filling her warm gaze. "What do you have against Miles? Has he done something to you?"

What was done was all in the past. And her attitude toward him was a mixture of guilt, grief, and regret, piled on top of memories that ached and were even more prominent at this time of year.

With a heartfelt sigh, she replied, "Nothing much. We've known each other a long time, is all. I'm working on accepting the fact that he's back in town for good."

"And?" Abby asked with a slanted look as she piled dishes into the dishwasher.

Cybil stared at her new bestie. Very few people knew about her and Miles. It wasn't that they'd hidden the fact that they'd dated that summer. But neither of them had shared how deeply they had fallen for each other, or the other facts and sordid events of their relationship. Only her parents and Miles had known the depths of it, where they planned to take it, and how it had all fallen apart.

"What do you mean, *and*?" Cybil deflected. Her relationship with Miles was a topic she hated discussing, laden as it was with emotional land mines at every turn.

"Honey, Miles looks at you like he wants to eat you up with a spoon—after shaking some sense into you."

The kindness in Abby's expression almost made Cybil spill the whole enchilada. Maybe that was how Miles had looked at her at one time, but he didn't anymore; hadn't for thirteen years. And the divide those years had created was wider than the Grand Canyon and, to her mind, insurmountable because of a vow she had made. The damage done if he discovered the bargain she'd struck would be on a cataclysmic level, and it wasn't just her life it would upend. If she didn't honor her word and stay away from him, then what kind of person did that make her, besides weak and selfish? "Look, Miles and I dated when my family first moved here, okay? We were teenagers. It was a long time ago. We're different people now. And ever since it ended, there's always been this underlying tension between us. I don't know that it can be helped or healed, it's just the way it is, unfortunately."

She didn't want to talk about the rest. She couldn't. It hurt too much to even think about it. Not the soul crushing loss, or the bitter ending.

Abby's jaw dropped open, her eyes widened, and she sputtered, "What? You and Miles were a couple? I can't believe you never told me. How did your sister not spill the beans?"

"Because I asked her not to, not just to you, but to anybody." Tessa, for all her quirks, was one of the most loyal people Cybil knew. When Tessa was asked to keep a secret, she was like Fort Knox. "It's not that I was trying to keep you out of the loop. But things ended painfully, as painfully as these things can, and I know it's been a long time since we were together, yet some of the pain still lingers. He was and always will be, my first love."

She left out that he was her only. The only man who had ever made it inside her heart.

Abby stared, her expression infused with compassion and understanding. "Well, I'm glad you told me. Now the way he looks at you and you at him makes sense. I'm guessing there's more, but I won't push. When you're ready, you know I'm here and have an ear if you need it."

Cybil's heart warmed. Abby had been in town for only a few months, but she'd become the third pea in her and Tessa's pod. Cybil didn't necessarily have a ton of girlfriends to talk to, other than her sister—at least none she felt comfortable enough with to delve deeper, rather than have a surface-value friendship. But Abby had clicked with her and Tessa right from the start, with her wicked sense of humor, stalwart loyalty, and the warm affection that radiated from her being. Nodding, Cybil replied, "I do know. Thanks for dinner, it was wonderful. Even with Miles here. I wish we could sit and chat more tonight, but I have an early client."

"No explanations needed. You know mornings and I don't get along well. But we really need another girls' night soon. Once your sister comes back, I'll send Nate to spend the night next door and we can have the place to ourselves."

Cybil grinned and slid her coat on. "You're on. And you know Tessa's always up for it."

"Leaving?" Nate asked as he entered the kitchen and assessed her.

"Yes, thanks for letting me invade," Cybil said, giving both him and Abby quick hugs. Then she side-stepped a prancing Rufus with a quick pat on his head, and made her exit. Outside, there was a hint of frost mingled with a rich pine tree scent in the air as she inhaled a steadying breath.

Miles was back in her life.

It was something she needed to buck up and get used to, because this town was small. They had friends in common and were bound to run into each other socially. As for running into him in the building where her studio was… she grimaced, striding to her truck and climbing inside. That was going to be a trial on her sanity, and even more so on her heart.

Before she backed out, she happened to glance up at the second-floor light which was on in Abby's old house. Framed in the window was Miles, his stance pensive, staring out at her. Even from this distance, she could sense the tension in him. After all this time, it still hurt to see him, like a fist punching a hole through her chest. She'd loved him with her whole heart. It was the curse and the beauty of youth, she supposed. She'd held nothing back from him but had jumped in feet first and not looked back—at least, until reality had burst their bubble.

Miles was silhouetted in the illuminated window, the angle of the light casting his big frame in shadow so that she couldn't see his eyes. Cybil had wondered about him over the years, usually on the anniversary of the day they'd lost it all. Or when she'd caught glimpses of him in town while he was visiting his mom.

She turned away when a crack slivered open in her chest. She couldn't allow herself softer emotions where Miles was concerned. It was self-preservation when it came to him. He'd always seen her so clearly. Cybil reversed out of the driveway and didn't look back. There was no point in reopening old wounds, regardless that they'd never fully healed to begin with.

Chapter 5

From Old Man Turner's Journal:
Women are always right. Even when they are wrong, they are right.
The sooner you make peace with that fact, the better your life will be.

Miles yawned as he infused himself with another cup of black coffee. He'd slept like crap, tossing and turning all night.

And why had sleep eluded him?

Mainly because of a certain recently acquired tenant. Being near Cybil again, interacting with her last night at dinner, had dredged up memories and cast doubt upon his aims. All it had taken was a day in her presence to resurrect them in full-color, the-hills-are-alive surround sound.

He remembered it all. That first meeting up at Echo Lake. How she'd coaxed him out of his misery that day, and had made him smile when he'd worried that nothing ever would again. He remembered the powder-blue tank top she'd worn, how it had clung to her supple form, and how she'd obviously been a little cold, because her nipples had been beaded into hard points beneath it. He had never told her that, but it had been a damn fine view and one heck of a distraction for his nineteen-year-old self. Hell, if he saw her that way now, it would be a fantastic view. And that in a nutshell was the crux of the problem that had kept him awake last night, staring at the ceiling.

When she'd ended their relationship thirteen years ago, he'd walked away without putting up a fight. Were his actions—or rather, the lack of them—something she would forgive?

Miles had no clue. As confident as he was that moving back to Echo Springs was the right course of action, the conundrum Cybil presented made his path forward to win her affections difficult at best. Especially when he felt like his future happiness hung in the balance.

Today, he hit the ground running, literally, first with a six-mile run outdoors. With his workout done, he didn't squander the morning away, but made it to the office before nine. There was still plenty of organizing to be done with the files, and he remembered to bring his tools for the artwork. Throughout the day, in between fielding calls and arranging his workspace, he had a few walk-in hires from some of Clark Biddle's current clients. One was a divorce, with a nasty custody battle brewing. Another was a land dispute over a tree and a hedge, and which neighbor said tree and hedge belonged to. Those first two credit card charges with signed contracts were a thing of beauty. Miles booked two appointments for the following week for clients needing wills drawn up. Plus, he had a smattering of clients coming in with traffic tickets today, letting him know that Nate was keeping the speeders in check.

In the afternoon, Miles combed through each of the leases for the tenants in the building, checking to see if there were any maintenance requests or other problems. The tenant in 3C, Harper Emerson, was having issues with her stove. Miles contacted Aiden and scheduled an appointment to have it looked at the following day, then emailed the tenant that he was having it checked out and that any repairs would be handled.

Miles had never intended to be a landlord. But with the mortgage on the building, he understood why Clark Biddle had lumped it in with the practice. What the tenants paid in rent more than covered the cost of the mortgage each month. It ended up being a win-win on his part. Which was good, considering what buying the practice had cost him.

Not that he couldn't afford it. He'd made plenty during his tenure with Farland Law Firm and Associates.

Miles left his office and headed to Cybil's studio. There were additions he wanted to make to the building, like installing security cameras in the common areas, and offering tenants the opportunity to have a security alarm and panic button installed in their rental space. Not that Echo Springs was a hotbed of illicit activity, he just recognized that all his tenants were women, and wanted to ensure their safety. But he trudged up the stairs because he and Cybil needed to have a conversation, one where others were not listening. He didn't want open warfare between them, quite the opposite. He wanted her, and not merely for the night.

Miles understood Cybil's defensive, back-the-hell-off stance. He'd fucked up epically when she'd needed him the most. He didn't blame her for her hostility but hoped that today's conversation would begin to bridge the space between them. And he figured that with the two of them being this close to one another, asking for a truce was a good place to begin.

He'd never wanted anything but the best for her, even if at times when he'd seen her, he'd given her the cold shoulder, especially in those first few years while he was away at college and would come home and see her around town. They had burned so bright and hot that one summer that it had taken him a long time to come to terms with how it all ended—in flames and death.

The door to Roe Yoga and Fitness was made of frosted privacy glass framed by golden wood, and bore the studio logo—a rose in full bloom—above the name of the business. Pushing open the door, he entered and was surrounded by the tune of gentle instrumental music that would put him to sleep if he had to listen to it for long. There were a mix of aromas infusing the air, lavender and cedar, with the underlying hint of sweat.

There was glossy golden wood flooring, soft calming blue walls, and a studio packed with bodies on mats.

But his gaze zeroed in on Cybil, her body contorted like a pretzel in a yoga pose. He had no idea how she maneuvered her lithe form into such a position. Lust, pure and undiluted, lasered through him.

"That's it. Now, on the next exhale, I want you to straighten your legs out behind you. And once you do, I want you to curl your toes underneath, and draw your pelvis up into downward-facing dog." Cybil's voice seemed to float over the room in a gentle, soothing rhythm.

She was hypnotic, her movements graceful. Seeing her like this, all soft and open, tugged at a very male part of Miles. She'd always drawn him in, with her body, her voice, her intelligence, her warmth. Attraction had never been the problem. It was a rather inconvenient truth that in all these years, his attraction for her hadn't diminished one bit—if anything, it had grown. The enigmatic pull Cybil had on his senses clobbered him any time she was near.

Cybil in her element, with a confidence that shone through her movements, in the way she worked with people, stirred him, made him ache. His mouth went dry. The class was crowded, with barely any empty floor space.

Unexpected pride swelled within his chest. She'd always impressed him. But she'd really built something for herself, in the town she'd had every intention of leaving the moment she had the chance. Then everything had changed. Sorrow gripped him with a vengeance. By now he should be familiar with the ache in his chest, but it never lessened. Perhaps it was more pronounced since they were back in each other's lives, and he knew that part of what he wanted from her wasn't merely to have her back in his life, but for her to forgive him for how badly he had fumbled things.

After all this time, she still called to him on an elemental, nearly primal level, making him want to beat his fists against his chest and go all caveman on her sweet ass.

"Namaste. My spirit honors your spirit," Cybil intoned. "Good class, everyone. I'll see you all next week. Remember, we will be closed on Thanksgiving, but we'll be back open on Black Friday, so you can come work off that extra helping of pumpkin pie."

The crowd laughed as they began moving, feet shuffling, rolling up yoga mats.

And then, finally, Cybil's gaze landed on Miles. Fury turned her gray gaze into thunderous storm clouds. She had known the moment he had entered the studio.

The class began filing out, and he was shocked to recognize one of the students.

"Mom?" he said, surprise filling his voice as he approached her.

His mom looked up from rolling the mat and smiled. "Miles. I didn't expect to see you today, and didn't want to bother you in your office. Are you thinking about taking one of Cybil's classes?" Rising, she gave him a big hug.

"No. I own the building now, remember? Just need to talk to Cybil once she's done with the class," he said, looking into eyes that were so like his own. She was nearly as tall as Miles, her trim build willowy. There were more lines around her eyes these days, but she was still beautiful. At the mention of Cybil, he spied a flicker of something in his mom's face. If he would have blinked, he would have missed it before it passed.

What was that all about?

"I know. But it wouldn't hurt you to do something that would help you relax. And Cybil's classes are wonderful for that." She patted his cheek affectionately, much like she had when he was a kid.

The only thing that would truly help him relax was a nice sweaty bout of spine-tingling, mind-numbing sex with the woman in question. And he sincerely doubted he could entice Cybil back into his bed just yet.

"I'm not that bad," he said to his mom, but caught Cybil watching them with a hooded expression.

"Well, as long as you're sure. Dinner on Sunday?" she asked, zipping up her coat and shouldering her purse strap.

"I wouldn't miss it," he said, gave her another quick hug.

While he and his mom talked, the rest of the class had filed out. When his mom walked out the door, Miles was alone with Cybil. The music, some flute and piano number, had been shut off. He would prefer hard rock or heavy metal any day. But the silence was deafening as he approached Cybil.

She stood, her body tense, like a mythic Valkyrie goddess about to do battle. "What do you want, Miles?" she asked, her annoyance evident.

"Just to talk."

"I can't. I have another class in a bit that I have to prepare for," Cybil said with a shake of her head and turned, giving him her backside as she went about her business. The quite delectable ass had been honed from years of yoga. And he found himself lusting for her, to feel her slender curves, and lose himself in her flesh. Cybil had always tempted him. She could wear a trash bag over her body instead of the spandex that molded to every blessed curve, and he would still find her the most desirable woman of his acquaintance. She rolled out a weight rack and then carried a new set of mats.

Shoving his hands in his pockets when he realized she

planned to continue to ignore him, Miles said, "Look, I realize this situation is not how either of us would like it."

Her head whipped around, and she shot him a steely glare. She snapped, "Are you kidding me? Not how I would like it? Well, no one asked me what I would like—not you, nor Clark Biddle. So, you'll have to forgive me if I'm less than welcoming."

"Jesus, Cyb, I realize the situation is difficult with our history. I didn't know who any of my tenants were until I'd signed the papers. Clark had only indicated that he had a tenant already in place for one of the second-floor spaces, and wanted to make sure that I would accept the lease he had in place. He explained the terms of your lease, and I agreed, not knowing it was you. I didn't do this, move back here, buy the practice and the building, to harm you. I needed a change in my life and wanted to move back to my hometown, both for myself and my mom. When Clark approached me and told me a few months ago that he was selling his practice, the timing was right. That's all."

He decided to leave the part about him wooing her back into his life for another time.

"Is your mom okay? She seemed fine in class. If there's something wrong, maybe I can help," Cybil offered. And she was earnest with that offer. It was part of what had drawn him in and had him wound around her little finger thirteen years ago. When Cybil cared about someone, she was always there to offer help whenever it was needed.

"I appreciate your concern, but she's fine. I just wanted to be around more, now that she's retired, to help her out. It's harder to do from Denver and when I'm working ninety hours a week. My move here was not about you or meant to upset your life," he said, feeling his own antagonism rise—especially since he'd arrived feeling guilty before the conversation even began. He was irked because she had her nose bent out of shape and was treating him like an irritating fly she kept swatting at.

"Miles, as long as you stay in your space, I will stay in mine, and we should get along fabulously. If we cross paths, I promise to be civil."

"If that's how you want it." He clenched his hands, seething. She was the most maddening woman. He wanted to shake some sense into her. He wanted… her. Christ, this was not going the way he wanted it to. He'd figured he could charm her back into his life, but that was going to be difficult if she wanted nothing to do with him.

She swiveled his way with consternation on her face. "What? Did you think that we could be BFFs? Hang out, laugh about old times?"

"Well, yeah, in time. Get to know each other again. Jesus, it's been thirteen years, Cyb. I know I failed you."

"I'm sorry, Miles, but that's not possible, at least not for me. I'm sorry if that hurts you or pisses you off. But I can't go there." She pressed a hand to her chest. "It's too hard, and there's too much between us. Deep down, you know what I'm saying is true. Now if you don't mind, I have a class shortly that I really need to focus on prepping for," she said with a slight nod toward her door, dismissing him. Then her back was to him, shutting him out entirely.

He wiped a hand over his face. She eviscerated him with her words and deeds. How could his heart still ache after so many years? Regret and shame kept him from pursuing the matter further—for today, at least. Perhaps he needed to devise another plan of attack, because this wasn't going the way he had hoped it would.

Miles spun on his heel, disappointment shrouding his steps as he strode out the door of her studio. Their conversation had not gone in the direction he had hoped. Quite the opposite; it had been more like a train derailment that he couldn't stop watching until it was finished. He had thought, given everything, that the first step—declaring a ceasefire—would be something she would agree to easily. And damned if he didn't want to be ornery and do the exact opposite of what she'd asked. He wanted to push her to accept him, accept that he was there to stay, and that they would be in each other's business and, he hoped, their lives.

But he didn't. He let her be, as she requested, in part as his penance and his surrender.

Because at the end of the day, he still cared about her and wanted her back in his life. Although after that unpleasant interlude, he had to accept it might not be the way he wanted. This time, he was putting her needs first.

But that didn't mean he wasn't going to fight like hell to change her mind.

Chapter 6

13 years ago

It turned out that Cybil ran into Miles much sooner than she would have imagined. Three days after their first meeting, to be precise, on her first night as hostess at Papa Beau's Pizza. The pizza joint was located in one of the historic storefront buildings along Main Street that had been built at the turn of the nineteenth century. The walls were old-fashioned red brick that had paled slightly with age. The dark hickory wood floors were scarred smooth. There were ceiling fans with lights, whirring away at a brisk pace, helping to keep the building cool, since the summer sun tended to turn the inside of the building into a brick oven—and that was with the air conditioning that had been added to the building when they'd modernized it.

At this time of night during the dinner rush, the cinnamon-colored wooden tables were crowded with families, groups of teenagers, couples, and friends. There was a small line at the salad buffet. Heady aromas of fresh-baked pizza dough, tomato, garlic and basil, and the hint of melted cheese hung in the air.

Cybil liked the restaurant. And as long as she primarily stuck to the salad bar and didn't inhale pizza every time she worked, she'd be fine, especially considering there was the side benefit of a free meal every night she worked. They made the pizza crust thick at the edge so you could pour fresh honey over it once you'd finished the other part of the slice, turning it into dessert. It was apparently a unique Colorado delicacy, and super yummy.

Cybil was thrilled that she had scored the job at Papa Beau's. Getting a job meant adding funds to her blowing-Podunk savings—something she planned to do the moment she graduated high school next spring.

She studied the plastic-coated layout of the dining room with Shirley Preston at her side. Shirley was the owner's wife, she managed the place with her husband, and was closer to Cybil's parents' age than hers. But she was nice enough, in her black jeans and red polo with the store logo written on the chest. Shirley's light brunette hair had a few strands of silver at the temples and was pulled back into a tame ponytail. The woman's appearance was practical, the only jewelry she wore was her wedding bands and small gold hoops in her ears. Shirley seemed to have a knack for putting people at ease with her smiling chocolate eyes and calm manner, and she always had a kind word for everyone who came in.

On Cybil's first shift, Shirley was training her in the method they used to seat customers. They had a laminated seating chart with all the tables numbered, and they used erasable markers. It was a fairly easy system, one Cybil figured she would have down pat relatively quickly.

A large, tall presence stepped up to the hostess stand. Lifting her gaze, Cybil nearly bit her tongue off to hold back her excited gasp.

It was him. Her avenging archangel, Miles.

Gone was the dark suit, replaced by a black T-shirt bearing the name of some heavy rock band; the material stretched over his muscular chest and hung loose over his belly. A pair of blue jeans rode low on his lean hips. As spectacular as he had looked in the suit, he had seemed untouchable, out of her league even. In well-worn jeans that were distressed at the knees and a pair of battered black Converse, he was infinitely more accessible.

He was stupendously gorgeous. She had fantasized about seeing him again. Wondered about what it would be like, and whether she had bungled things with her comment about his dad's death.

Her pulse fluttered at his nearness, and she had the sudden urge to fan herself. Her tongue stuck to the roof of her mouth.

If anything, he had grown more handsome since that first meeting. And she finally knew the color of his eyes—a stunning turquoise blue, making her think of the ocean surrounding Tahiti she had admired in pictures. They seemed to glow in his tanned face. Upon spying her, he cast her a smile chock full of pure masculine satisfaction and interest.

His presence commanded her attention, blotting out the rest of the restaurant. Her insides trembled at being near him once more. She ached for him, instinctively knowing it was desire and need on a scale she'd had yet to experience until his advent into her life.

Oh, she'd had boy crushes before. But they had been paltry by comparison. This was much more than a crush. It wasn't only a crush, it also had a mile-high serving of lust. Miles's golden hair was untamed and windblown, and she itched to run her fingers through it.

"You? I was wondering if I'd run into you again," Miles said, and those killer eyes of his caressed her body from head to toe. Heat flushed her cheeks, and the bass resonance of his words vibrated within her chest. He was looking at her like he wanted *her* on the menu.

"Yep, it's me. Kind of hard not to run into one another in a town this size. Did you need a table?" Cybil asked, her voice throaty and infused with a hint of sarcasm as she tried to play it cool with the hottie. Her girlfriends in Kansas would be so jealous. He had admitted, with witnesses present, that he had thought about her since they'd first met. On the inside, Cybil was jumping up and down and screaming at the top of her lungs in excitement. On the outside, she remained cooler than a cucumber.

"You're supposed to welcome guests, Cybil. Remember the spiel I mentioned earlier?" Shirley explained with a patient expression on her kind face. She was a bit like a mother hen with the employees.

"Me and Cybil go way back. We're old friends now, so it's no big deal." Miles stepped in and saved her. His flirtatious words and come-hither stare made the breath hitch in her throat.

Warmth spread through her chest. "Way back, huh? So, do you want a table or not?"

"Cybil, you can't talk to customers that way," Shirley admonished, with raised brows and annoyance on her pretty face.

But both Cybil and Miles ignored her.

His turquoise gaze roamed over her, from her Papa Beau's tee shirt with the name written across her chest, to her short jean shorts that left her legs bare. When their gazes clashed, the air sizzled. "There are a lot of things I want. Starting with your phone number and what time you get off tonight."

"I work through the dinner rush until eight but am free after that," Cybil replied. No way would she turn him down. She'd thought of little but him since their accidental meeting up at Echo Lake. Her curfew was eleven, which would give her three solid hours with Miles. She would call her mom on her break and let her know she was going out with some new friends.

"I'm picking up dinner for my mom but will swing back by and pick you up at eight, then," Miles responded with a sexy grin.

Cybil's cheeks heated as she blushed, and she prayed it wasn't too noticeable. "Sounds good. I'll go grab your order from the back," she replied, the corners of her mouth turning up. She headed into the kitchen, aware of Miles's gaze on her backside as she strode through the double swinging doors.

In the kitchen, she fanned her face, not because of the heat belching out of the pizza ovens, but because of Miles and his potent magnetism. Working quickly, she collected his order: a fully loaded pizza, and chef's salad. She added some extra salad dressing, packets of honey, and Parmesan cheese, along with plastic utensils and napkins to the bag holding the chef's salad. With as much grace as she could muster, she sauntered back out to the counter with her hands full, praying that she didn't do something that made her look foolish, like trip and send the food flying.

"I already took care of his bill, Cybil," Shirley said when she reached the hostess stand.

"Okay, great. Hope your mom enjoys her dinner." Cybil handed the to-go order to him and their fingers brushed. Electric currents shot through her system.

"See you at eight," Miles said with a wicked wink.

He left, but not before she noticed the long lean lines of his back, or the way his jeans perfectly cupped the sexiest set of buns she'd ever seen on a man. There she went again, needing to fan herself as if she were having hot flashes.

"What was that all about, Cybil? You really can't talk to customers that way," Shirley scolded, looking down her nose with a pinched scowl.

"Look, I know the drill with what you want me to say, and I will work very hard for you. But I know Miles." Or at least, she wanted to know him with every fiber of her being, and was already counting down the hours—two, to be exact—until she would see him again.

Shirley huffed and shook her head, her exasperation crystal clear. "We'll see. Now, I want you to greet guests and seat them, going through what we discussed. I will be here shadowing you, helping with anything you don't understand, and then when it gets close to the end of your shift, I will run you through the end-of-night prep work that you will be required to do."

"I'm ready," Cybil said. And she was, for that great big slice of life that she knew was out there waiting for her. Perhaps, if she was really lucky, Miles might be part of that slice.

Chapter 7

From Old Man Turner's Journal:
Reality and the truth are most often two separate beasts; the sooner one understands this fact, the better your life will be.

Present Day

On Monday night, after a blisteringly long weekend, Cybil was ready to drop where she stood. But instead, she rushed into her house for a wardrobe change. She had a date, of all things. It had been so much longer than she wanted to admit—a full twelve months, if a person was counting—since she had been on a date.

Her sister, Tessa, stood at the stove in an oversized tee, flannel plaid bottoms, and fluffy slippers, with her black hair streaked with cobalt blue and piled on top of her head.

"You just getting up today?" Cybil asked.

Tessa yawned. "Nope, been up for hours. I just haven't changed out of my pajamas yet. You know how much those expos and traveling wipe me out."

"Yeah, I do. But I'm glad you're back." Gus rubbed up against Tessa's legs. "And so is your newest love."

"I know, Gus is my cuddle monkey, and agrees it's perfectly acceptable to snuggle on the couch all day in my pjs with no judgement."

"I wasn't judging." Cybil hung her coat and purse on the hook just inside the door. Sniffing the air like a bloodhound, she asked, "That's not mac and cheese is it?"

"Yep, with bacon and peas. The perfect comfort food, with like a bazillion empty calories, but considering how busy I am at the expos and how little I eat while I'm there, my body could use some comfort food. Want some?"

Cybil sighed. She would love some. She could use some old-fashioned comfort food to bury her sorrows in. And there was no greater comfort food on the planet than mac and cheese with all the trimmings. "I wish I had time."

"You working at Smitty's again tonight?"

"No. I have a date."

"Say what? You? A date? With whom? Spill the beans, missy!" Tessa waved her big wooden spoon at her sister.

"No one you know. Don't have time for beans or anything else. I have twenty-five minutes to get ready or I will be late."

"Do I know him, at least?"

They had very few, if any, secrets between the two of them. Cybil grimaced. "Doubtful. I don't really know him that much either."

"Then who is he and where did you meet him?" Tessa asked, stirring the noodles and adding ingredients to the pot.

"This is the first time we're meeting in person. I met him online on that new dating website."

"You signed up for Matchmakers? You? Okay, who are you and what have you done with my sister? Do we have an invasion of the body snatchers deal going on?"

"Yep, I joined. And I'm going to be late." Cybil hurried up the stairs with her sister calling after her.

Tessa's shout carried up the stairs. "I want to see your profile when you get home. And where are you headed?"

At the top of the stairs, she turned and glanced down at Tessa, who stood holding Gus. "The Aztec Mexican Restaurant. I figure I can't go wrong with margaritas and queso."

"Good choice. What's his name? I need details."

"Later. Right now, I need to make myself presentable and be out of the door in, eek, twenty minutes."

"Fine but expect the Spanish Inquisition when you get back, missy."

Cybil chuckled and waved her off. There wasn't time to wash her hair, but she took the time to shower with her hair up so at least she wouldn't reek of old sweat. She reapplied makeup, freshened her hair with some dry shampoo, and restyled it with a few big curls so that it fell in loose waves over her shoulders. It wasn't often that she went on dates, or even casual meet ups for drinks and maybe dinner if everything went well enough. So she put some effort into what she wore, selecting a blouse in fire engine red that displayed her wares. To her mind, every woman worth her salt should have a few tops that really showed off the girls, no matter how much or how little they might have. In her experience, men loved boobs, and thankfully she had been blessed with a decent rack. She picked a black skirt that fell to just above her knees, hugged her curves, and looked spectacular with her black leather knee-high boots.

After she'd added some dangly silver hoops to her ears, Cybil raced downstairs. "See you later? Save me some of that, will you, in case the date is a bust. I could use the comfort food. Especially with Miles back in town."

"Miles is back too? What do you mean he's back? Why am I just hearing about this now? You've got some explaining to do."

"I know. Sorry. I didn't want to text it to you while you were out of town." Cybil waved Tessa off as she grabbed her purse and keys. "He's not just living in Echo Springs, he's my new landlord. God help us all. I'll explain later."

"Wait a sec, he's your landlord? Oh, sweet Jesus! Well, don't forget to text me an hour into the date or I will call the cops. And we aren't done talking about Miles."

Cybil dashed out the door to her truck, leaving Tessa sputtering. She was meeting Ed for dinner and drinks. From his picture, she had to admit he was pretty cute. His profile said he was a thirty-five-year-old divorcé, had served eight years in the military, and now led tourists on hikes into the mountains. Cybil liked hiking. She and Miles had spent plenty of time in that long ago summer hiking the trails surrounding Echo Lake.

Damn. She swore to herself she wasn't going to think about Miles for the rest of the night. Tonight was about getting to know Ed, not traveling down memory lane.

From her few online chats with Ed over the weekend, she figured he sounded nice, normal, and average. One of the things she liked about the site was that it left their interactions to the chatroom and messaging until they were ready to move to exchanging phone numbers.

They had messaged each other through the dating app all weekend, and she had to admit she liked what he had to say so far. Granted, it was easy to sound suave and marginally intelligent over an internet connection. Cybil's expectations for the evening weren't high. She had the appointed check-in time with her sister, which gave Ed sixty minutes to wow her, although she would settle for an awkward, reasonably well-mannered conversationalist who might take more than one or two dates before she decided if he was a keeper, or should be tossed back into the dating pool.

In fact, so far, the dating app seemed to be working like a charm. Cybil had a couple dates lined up this week, which for her was an epic feat given the dry desert of her dating life.

Tomorrow night she was meeting Jeremy, and on Wednesday she had a date with Chris. Not a bad haul for a newbie to the world of online dating.

Cybil shivered as her truck's aging heater sputtered out stringy puffs of lukewarm air, and drove the short distance to the Mexican restaurant. She loved this place. They had epic, fish-bowl-sized margaritas in a wide array of flavors, and a mural on the exterior of the building, in bold, vibrant colors, that depicted a man being led to an altar to be sacrificed to an Aztec goddess. Her kind of place. It was all female empowerment. She and Tessa had spent many nights here with their margaritas and queso dip.

She hurried inside against the frigid wind and searched for the cute guy carting a white rose. Scanning the brightly colored restaurant, she made a few passes with no luck. She did spy a few people with fishbowl margaritas at the center bar though.

"Would you like a table?" the hostess asked. Cybil eyed the blonde teenager with the high ponytail and couldn't help but think she looked incredibly young to be working. But she probably wasn't much older than Cybil had been when she'd worked the same job at Papa Beau's Pizza. She might be thirty-one, but the fact that the hostess looked thirteen at most made Cybil feel incredibly old.

Cybil sighed, tamping down her anxiety. "I'm meeting someone here. His name is Ed. I can't see if he's here yet or not. Did he already check in with you? A reasonably attractive guy with a white rose?"

"Oh, yes, your party is already here. Won't you follow me?" The hostess' golden eyebrows rose briefly before she arranged her face in a benign smile once more.

Unease rippled through Cybil. What the hell was that look about?

Please don't tell me that my date was a jerk to the hostess. If there was one thing she detested, it was people acting entitled and treating wait staff like scum. The hostess led her down through the red tables to a booth near the back. Cybil spied the guy at the table and did a double take. He had a white rose, but that was the only thing that looked correct. Where was the good-looking guy? This wasn't what Ed looked like in his profile pictures at all. Instead of a full head of black hair, what hair was left on his head was no longer black but steel gray. Gone was the smooth angular jaw, replaced by one covered by a papa bear beard that trailed to his mid-chest in a matching gray.

His shoulders, while they at one time might have been broad and still held traces of strength, were hunched and more slender with age. Dread pooled in her chest as he stood and grinned. Cybil almost turned on her heel and ran when she spotted the gap where he was missing one of his front teeth. This was her nightmare date scenario—on steroids. What the hell?

"Cybil," he said, his voice crusty, and he opened his arms for a hug.

Cybil held out her hands in a back off gesture to keep him away. No way in hell was the man touching her. "Ed?"

She hoped with every fiber of her being that this was a practical joke and that the real Ed would poke his head around the corner and say, *Gotcha*, and they would all laugh. As it was, Cybil was ready for a shot of tequila.

"Yep. It's me, darlin'. I'm so glad you made it. Won't you have a seat?" He gestured to the side of the booth he'd been sitting on.

She selected the opposite side and slid in, thoroughly unamused. Although, that didn't seem to faze her date as he slid into his side with a leering grin. She had given up her sister's killer mac and cheese for an evening with Grandpappy Ed with the toothless smile. *Kill me now*.

As soon as she was seated, a perky waiter, Evan, appeared, his smile flashing overly bright. His vest displayed several lit-up pins—his vest flare, if you will—and made her wonder if he was auditioning to join the circus after his shift ended that evening. If she were one of the judges, he'd be a shoo-in thanks to all the swag glaring at her.

"What can I get you folks to start?" Evan asked. He had this peppy energy which, if she had to endure it for longer than the sixty minutes she had set aside for this *date*, Cybil was certain would make her want to hurt him.

"A margarita, please," she beseeched him. Between her ready-for-circus-tryouts waiter and Papa Grizzly date, she was going to need every drop of alcohol she could find.

"Absolutely," he said with a clap that made Cybil wonder if he would break out into choreography if they ordered dinner. *If* being the optimal word here, because she was giving Papa Grizzly just the time it took her to finish her margarita to explain why his picture looked nothing like him.

Ed chimed in, "I'll have a margarita as well. Now, I have a coupon for a senior citizens discount. Do you still accept them this late in the evening?"

Oh, sweet gravy! Her date wanted a senior citizen discount. This was beyond bad. This date was turning out to be epically horrific. Cybil weighed whether to stay or to just get up and walk out.

Evan replied, "Yes, we do. I can take that now, if you have it."

"Evan?" she said before he could walk away, lifting her hand to stop him from leaving.

"Yes, miss?" Evan asked with an over bright grin.

"Make mine the fish-bowl size." It was a forty-four-ounce margarita. And looking across the table at Papa Grizzly, she figured she was going to need it.

"Absolutely, I'll be right back with your drinks." Evan left the two of them alone.

"I've got to say, you are every bit as gorgeous as your picture." Ed gave Cybil what she was sure to his mind was a smolder, but it came across as more of a creepy leer that made her skin crawl.

"While you look nothing like yours. And why is that, exactly?" Cybil pinned him with a glare, folding her arms across her chest, and leaning as far away from him as possible.

"I may have exaggerated the truth a bit. But there's no harm done. You're here, I'm here, we might as well enjoy ourselves." He wasn't bashful or remorseful in the slightest over lying about his age.

"Be that as it may, you said that you were thirty-five. With a picture that made it look like you were."

"I was thirty-five, once; it was 1988, but that's not a big deal."

Ed had been thirty-five… in 1988, the year after Cybil had been born. Why was it so hard for people to be honest? Cybil was a straight shooter. Always had been. She didn't understand people who lied about who they were to try to make themselves look better. Not that she gave the farm away on personal matters, but things like a person's real age shouldn't be subjective. Cybil had always figured honesty was the best policy when it came to dating.

"Cybil."

No!

Not here. Not right now.

Cybil froze. Panic blared code red. She wanted to hide under the table. She wanted to melt into a puddle of mortified embarrassment. She wanted to kick herself for not running out the door the moment she spied her date.

Of all the nights and places to casually run into him. This had to be a nightmare. She was at home, in bed, *alone*, and having a horrifically vivid nightmare. That was all.

Surely Miles wasn't here. She glanced up in dawning horror, taking in the expensive cut of his black slacks, and buttoned up dark pewter pea coat that emphasized his powerful build. Their gazes clashed. Electricity sizzled. And tingles erupted low in her belly. Oh, she should have ordered two margaritas. What was he doing here? Pasting a smile on her face, with as much dignity as she could muster, she said, "Miles. Didn't expect to see you here."

Why her? Why did these things happen to her? Was she cursed when it came to men, was that it?

Miles shrugged, glancing between her and Papa Grizzly with amusement dancing in those blue depths. "Just picking up a to-go order. Long day at the office and all that. I'm being rude. Miles Keaton, and you are?" Miles held his hand out toward Ed in a smooth move Cybil was certain he had executed more than once. That was something that had changed about Miles—he had a level of suave sophistication that he hadn't had at nineteen.

And damn him, but it was sexy as hell. The sheen, the layers he had added to himself so that they were as much a part of him as breathing, were a total turn-on.

"Cybil's date. I'm Ed." Ed shook Miles's hand and sent Cybil a wink. Cybil wondered if the restaurant had ever had a woman run screaming from a date before or if she might wind up being the first. The only thing that kept her stuck to the seat with a forced smile glued to her features was the thought of Miles seeing her run. He'd laugh his ass off over her cowardice. Damn him. Not that she would blame him for it. If their positions were reversed, she would do the same.

"Is that right?" The corners of Miles's mouth twitched. Cybil curled her hands into fists beneath the table. She wanted to wipe the smirk off his handsome face. Miles was doing his best not to laugh outright at the scene she and her senior citizen date presented.

"That's right. Problem?" she asked with waspish undertones. Where the hell was that margarita when she needed it most? That twinkle of glee in Miles's eyes infuriated her. The jerk. She knew how the situation looked. He didn't need to rub it in with such unrepentant delight. Or maybe he did, since she was the one who had called it quits on their relationship.

"Well, I will leave you to your *date*. Have fun. Ed, pleasure." Miles nodded and sauntered off, holding the to-go bag bearing the restaurant logo clutched in one hand.

Cybil glanced over her shoulder. The man damn near strutted to the doors. Cybil hated that he still looked like an avenging archangel who left her wanting to fan herself due to the combustible heat between them. At the exit, Miles turned back and flashed her a knowing smirk before he headed out into the night.

Her brain clicked off for a moment. It was the same grin he had used on her countless times. The same one that made her bones melt and left her wanting, on the edge of her seat, waiting for the next time she would see him.

Sweet Mother of God!

She couldn't lust after Miles while on a date with another man. Even when that man had lied and there wasn't going to be a second date. Miles was her past—a past she had fought to, if not forget, at least move on from with as much dignity and grace as she could muster. Besides, she couldn't want him, not after the promise she had made at the hospital all those years ago, the one where she had vowed to stay away from him.

Evan delivered their margaritas. Finally. Cybil's was in a glass large enough that she thought she might be able to fit her head inside it. The waiter plunked a basket of chips and dish of salsa down as well. "Would you folks like to order dinner?"

"I think that would be—"

Cybil cut Ed off. "Dinner won't be necessary tonight. Thanks. Just the drinks for now."

Evan, obviously sensing the tension at the table, said, "Okay, great. Just flag me down if you folks decide you want to order something."

"Thanks so much, Evan," Cybil murmured with a strained

smile. She ignored Ed for a moment and tried to find a measure of calm as she slurped at the margarita as if she had been wandering the desert for forty days without water.

"Now, I can tell you're a little miffed that I stretched the truth a bit."

Cybil slanted him a look and stopped sucking on the straw in her margarita long enough to reply. "No, you think? You really can't understand why I might be a little angry that you blatantly lied on your profile and then conveniently forgot to mention any of this when we were messaging one another?"

"I think we should just move past it and make the best of what we have."

The best of what they had. The only good thing about the night was the margarita she was mainlining. "That may be good for you, Ed. But then again, you aren't the one who was lied to."

"Well, you know…" His voice droned on as he made excuses and attempted to smooth over what he considered her ruffled feathers.

Cybil just worked on her fabulous margarita, figuring she could still make it home and heat up some of her sister's mac and cheese. When she'd finished half the cocktail, she realized that if she had to stay and listen to him a moment longer, the drink would end up over his head. She was done with his sly innuendos and out and out lies. She plunked some cash for her margarita on the table with enough of a tip for the server. "Here you go, Ed. It was nice to meet you, but I have to get home."

"You don't want to come back to my place? I thought we had a connection." Papa Grizzly leered, giving her probably what he thought was a sexy smile, but it just made her skin crawl.

Um, ew. "No, I'm sorry, it's not going to happen. And can I make a suggestion? Stop lying on your profile about your age. It's really not a nice thing to do to someone."

"But it's the only way I can score with you sweet young things," Ed explained with a harmless, *aw shucks* attitude.

Again, ew. "Yeah, well, don't take this the wrong way, but first of all, women don't like to be lied to. And second of all, how many women my age have actually fallen for that line and still slept with you?"

"Four so far." He grinned.

Not even if she was desperate and he was the last man on the planet. She didn't care if humanity died out. Never in a million years. But hearing that really shone a light on what slim pickings there were out there and how many women would toss away their good common sense. Her gorge rose. "Okay, then. Well, it's not going to happen tonight or ever with me. So yeah, I'll just go."

Cybil slid out of the booth and left without a backward glance. Date number one on the dating app could be marked as a complete catastrophe. And she wasn't going to think about the fact that she still lusted after Miles.

Nope. Not going to think about that at all.

Chapter 8

From Old Man Turner's Journal:
Dating and romance don't come without a few lumps. Be brave enough to risk getting flattened.

The next morning, Cybil crawled out of bed a little after nine. Days off where she didn't have to wake before dawn were her favorite sort of days. She loved indulging by sleeping in. And since Tessa had returned Sunday night, Gus had been sleeping with her. Was it odd that Cybil missed the furball waking her up and snuggling against her through the night?

Maybe they should have gotten a cat years ago. At the time, she just hadn't wanted the responsibility of an extra mouth to feed and care for, not when it had been hard enough keeping a roof over their heads.

Now they were past that tenuous hand to mouth existence they'd gone through the first few years after Mom and Dad died, thank goodness. Over the years, Cybil had worked hard to ensure she had a rainy day fund, and had instilled that same practice in her sister. No one could make a penny stretch like Cybil could. Despite her investment in the studio, she had a nest egg of savings. It had dwindled and was smaller than she would like because of the funds she plunked into the studio, but it was there, nevertheless. And she had every intention of adding funds back into her savings each month as the studio turned a profit.

Today she had the whole day to herself, if she wanted it. Although she figured she should spend an hour or so rectifying her business accounts, pay some bills, and brave the grocery store two days before the holiday. She probably needed to do a load or two of laundry, too, and ensure she had clean underwear for the coming workweek. Was it any wonder she dreamt of relaxing on a white sandy beach with nothing to do? With a deep sigh, because the work was never, ever truly done, Cybil grabbed her robe and slid it on before she headed downstairs.

"Me-e-e-ow."

"Who's the best kitty in the whole world?" Tessa said in a manner one normally reserved for babies.

"You know those things are like giving him a Snickers bar, right?" Cybil indicated the handful of treats Tessa was feeding the butterball on his perch from one of the chairs at the kitchen table.

After Gus sniffed Tessa's empty hand, she picked him up and cuddled him like a baby, with Gus purring up a storm in adoration, his gold eyes slitted in ecstasy. "I know, he's just so fluffy and cuddly. I love seeing him so happy. How was your date? I heard you come back early but was too tired to want to get out of bed. I love those expos, but man do they flatten me for a day or two after the fact."

"Let's just say my date had a teeny tiny problem with lying about his age." Cybil made a beeline for the coffeepot and the elixir of her life. It might technically be a day off, but that didn't mean she would go a day without the stuff.

"What, was he too young for you?" Tessa teased as she cuddled Gus in her lap and went back to her laptop.

"God, no. Too young, I could have handled better. He was far too old. Much older than his picture and profile suggested. As in: Grandpappy, eligible to collect social security and retire old. Not to mention, he was doing an imitation of Grizzly Adams with his appearance. And then Miles turned up at the restaurant to catch the unfortunate show. All in all, a total bust."

"Ugh, I hate when they lie like that. It's too bad it was a bust. And hey, does Miles have a tracker on you or something?"

"God, I hope not, although it sure seems like it. He was picking up dinner and stopped by the table to say hi." Cybil shook her head at the memory. At least the margarita, what she'd had of it, had taken some of the sting away.

"No! He stopped at the table? That bites. Okay, well it's time for the inquisition. Sit yourself down and we can begin."

"I need coffee first before I get into it all." Cybil poured herself a cup of coffee in a big twenty-ounce mug, adding a dollop of cream and sugar, since her sister tended to brew java extra strong. She winced at the boldness of the drink. "Good God, Tessa, this stuff could power a generator."

"I know. I woke up early this morning and couldn't get back to sleep. I needed the kick in the pants to get motivated. It's a holiday week and I want to be lazy with no classes to teach, but I also have a deadline on my next comic."

"I'm right there with you. Maybe we should look at taking a vacation next year, on a beach somewhere with free flowing margaritas. And speaking of the holidays, Abby and Nate invited us to spend Thanksgiving with them. Abby's planning on cooking. You up for it? I know we've got the auction later that night, but Abby's willing to work with our schedule and have dinner at an early time."

"I would be down for a gathering with them, as long as you promise to make your pies. It won't be Thanksgiving without your pies. It's tradition. We've got to have the pies," Tessa said staunchly. "And I could dig a beach vacay. We should start looking at dates, maybe see if Abby and Nate have set the date for their wedding yet and work around that. Maybe we could even invite Abby to go with us, make it a pre-wedding, bachelorette deal to somewhere like the Bahamas."

"I like the idea of a bachelorette weekend in the Bahamas. We should start looking soon," Cybil murmured, sipping her coffee. Apple pies were one of the few things she knew how to bake, and bake well. She would easily pit her apple pie recipe against anyone else's, including any of the celebrity chefs on television. It was their mom's recipe, handed down from their grandma. Since their parents had died, the sisters had turned those pies into a Thanksgiving tradition. They might not make a big meal with it being just the two of them, but they always had apple pie. "I guess I could make a couple of apple pies, especially since I ate the rest of your mac and cheese last night. Some for Abby's, and then one specially for us that we leave here. I've got most everything already. Although, I need to make a run to the grocery store today to get the rest of the supplies. If there's anything that you know we are running low on that you want, put it on the list, will you?"

Tessa did a little dance in her seat that had Gus scrambling up off her lap. "Oh, poor Gus-Gus. I didn't mean to make you move. Just wait until you taste Cybil's pie."

"I don't think pie is an acceptable food for a cat, Tessa."

"Well, perhaps Abby will send us home with some turkey. Gosh, it's been so many years since we've had an actual turkey on Thanksgiving. Not since…" Tessa trailed off and paled in horror.

The loss of their parents… the pang was always there, always present in some form. And during the holidays, the grief always seemed sharper and much swifter in the way it could eviscerate them at the recollection. She didn't think it was something that would ever go away, even if the pain had become easier to carry.

Cybil had tried so hard in those first few years, almost driving herself insane to keep their parents' memories alive, to keep their lives as normal and the same as possible. And she had kept it up that first year—until she finally realized her sanity and peace of mind mattered more than keeping traditions going. "Not since Mom and Dad died. Sorry I didn't keep that tradition."

"Well, after that first year when you tried to make a turkey and nearly set the place on fire, I figured it wasn't worth it. Besides, we have our own food traditions for the holidays."

"Yeah, there is that. Remember how the fire department showed up that year, with all the smoke billowing out of that oven? We lost the security deposit on that place and had to move in here."

"If I remember correctly, a few of the firefighters gave you their phone numbers that night, too."

"Yeah, they did. I even went on a date with one of them." Cybil laughed at the bittersweet memory of their first Thanksgiving on their own.

"I still miss them. It's hard to believe they've been gone almost thirteen years," Tessa said, her eyes brimming with moisture.

"Me too. You want any eggs? I can at least make those without needing to call the fire department," Cybil said, pulling ingredients out of the fridge and blinking the tears from her eyes at the unexpected trip down memory lane.

"Nah, I had the last of the cereal, but thanks though. Although, it might be a good way to score some dates other than Matchmakers."

"I'm not that desperate." At least, she didn't think she was, and convinced herself that having the fire department called to get a date was the wrong way to go about it.

Cybil scrambled up some eggs, tossed some red peppers, goat cheese, and avocado in with it, and sliced up the last pear.

"So Miles is back, huh?" Tessa asked when she joined her at the kitchen table.

Landmines. This time of year, her life was laden with them. Now more so than ever, given Miles's return. It didn't matter how much she tried to avoid stepping on one, they were everywhere. She cleared her throat at the sudden lump lodged there. "Yep. For good, it seems. He bought out Clark, with Clark's blessing."

"I just cannot believe Clark sold his practice to Miles. I didn't think that man would ever retire," Tessa exclaimed.

"I know. I mean, he'd told me he was selling it and had a buyer lined up. But I never for a minute thought it could be Miles." For a small town like Echo Springs, Miles moving back and buying Clark's practice was newsworthy. The local gossip mill would already be discussing it, considering it was the hottest news since Janice Murphy plowed her Buick into her neighbor's hedges and Nate Barnes was moved off the eligible bachelors list.

"Did Miles know you were one of the tenants?"

"No. Which means I can't be mad at him for wanting to move back to Echo Springs." Cybil sighed and reached down to pet Gus, who seemed to sense her disquiet and was rubbing his face against her calf. Either that, or the furball wanted her eggs and figured he could appeal to her with some cuddling. She didn't mind, and was grateful for it no matter the cause.

"God, that has to be… how are you so calm? Really, after everything?"

Cybil snorted. "I'm not calm. Granted, I'm calmer than I was, but it's definitely been a shock to the system having him back in town and in my building. I haven't handled it well at all, really. I've snapped at him a few times. He probably thinks I'm a complete bitch at this point. It's not fair, and he's no happier about it than I am. But there's nothing I can really *do* about it." She jabbed her fork into her eggs, her appetite fleeing at the thought of Miles. She couldn't explain his attitude last night—

beyond the amusement; the simmering undercurrent she'd picked up from him.

"What are you going to do about it? Do you need me to help you kick his ass? I have a shovel handy if we need to bury the body."

Cybil laughed. Her sister was a nut. A lovable, loyal nut. She sighed. "I don't need to kick his ass. He hasn't done anything that would warrant an ass-kicking. It's a small town, we're bound to run into one another, and it's just something I have to adjust to. As for him being my new landlord, there's not much I can do about it. I invested heavily in the renovation of that space, and haven't made that money back yet. The terms of my original lease stand as is through the end of its term for the next ten months. Which is good. Only now, I will be paying Miles each month instead of Clark."

"Oh Jesus, that's got to sting, paying your ex. Although, maybe it won't be so bad. I mean, really, how often did you see Clark?" Tessa tried to cheer her up about the dreadful situation.

"Not very much, other than to drop off my monthly check, or in passing. But it's more than the running into him at work. He was at Abby and Nate's when I went to dinner at their house the other night. He's going to be there at Thanksgiving." She sighed. "For better or worse, we're back in each other's lives. I don't think there's a way around it unless I move out of Echo Springs or stop seeing Abby, and I don't want to do either of those things."

"It's a tough break all around. It sucks and I'm sorry, I wish I could make it go away for you. But that's why we are going to use that new dating app of yours to find you a new man. That way, running into Miles all the time won't matter one bit." Tessa's fingers flew over her keyboard as she brought the site up on her laptop and turned it Cybil's way. "Here, enter your password."

The bright pink Matchmakers logo glared brightly on the screen. After last night, the last thing Cybil wanted to do was go on another date. She protested, "Tessa, I'm not so sure. It might have been a mistake signing up for that thing."

"Oh, come on. It will be fun." Tessa gestured with an enthusiasm that had her sighing.

"I already have another date scheduled for tonight and one with another guy tomorrow. That's enough for now, don't you think?"

"Oh pish posh, we will get your calendar so booked up that you won't think about he who will not be named, and find you a new hunk of burning love who will keep you too busy between the sheets to even think about your past. Heck, we might find a man for me too. One never knows with these things. And I've certainly been on the lookout for a new beau."

"I thought you were interested in Jacob. And word on the street is he bought the McKinley place and is moving to Echo Springs."

A shadow passed over her sister's face and she pouted. "Jacob's not interested in me. I don't think he's interested in anyone, to be honest. The guy appears to be a monk." She shrugged and, with a defiant jut of her chin said, "It's his loss. I would have rocked his damn world."

"That's too bad. I know you've had a crush on him. All right, fine. Let's find some male companionship for the both of us." Cybil typed in her password and had no sooner clicked the login button than her sister confiscated the computer.

"You, eat." Tessa flexed her fingers with a wicked gleam of excitement in her gaze. "I've got this. Let me see who we can find for you."

Cybil ate her eggs, not really out of hunger, but knowing that if she didn't, she would get hangry later—that combination of hunger mixed with anger—because she was starving. It wouldn't go over well at Fitzgerald's if she walked into the grocery store without eating beforehand. In her current mood, she would walk out owning both the ice cream and wine aisles.

"This one isn't too bad. I'm going to mark that you viewed *BigCountry*," Tessa murmured thoughtfully. "Oh, yeah, we need to take a look at this one. Username: *HoohahWhisperer*. If he doesn't work for you, maybe he would do it for me… oh god, my eyes, my eyes! Nope. Nope. Definitely not." Tessa waved her hands in front of the screen with her face turned to the side in abject horror.

"What? Let me see."

"Don't say I didn't warn you." Tessa turned the computer around.

Cybil recoiled. In his profile picture, the man lounged on his side wearing nothing except a leopard print bikini and a leer. No man should ever wear bikini underwear, as it was really nothing more than a banana hammock. But this guy? Hell to the no. "Oh my god. You weren't kidding. He makes Papa Grizzly last night almost marginally appealing."

"I told you. It's like if the Clampetts and Uncle Fester made a baby. Not even with a bag over his head, the poor guy," Tessa said, laughing so hard she wiped at tears.

"If you feel that sorry for him, Tess, maybe you should see if he really knows how to whisper to your hoohah," Cybil teased and snorted a laugh at her own brilliance. How anyone would think it was acceptable to dress like that for a profile picture was beyond her.

"Sis, my hoohah took one look at him and put the *closed for business* sign in the window. No way in hell. I'd join a convent before I went out with him. I'd rather go online and look at the latest offerings from the adult goody store for battery operated options."

"It's so wrong, but you are so right. Good lord, I can't believe anyone would make that their profile image."

"Well, I learned from the best. It's always the ones who shouldn't put it all out there that do. Let's keep looking. There have to be a few winners. We're in the land of rugged mountain men. Oh, there's this one. He's cute and, bonus, he has all his teeth," Tessa continued with a chuckle.

They spent the remainder of the morning laughing as they combed through the dating website. And at Tessa's insistence, Cybil messaged two new guys: *Cuddleguy* and *NormalDude*. As for the rest, they would see.

Chapter 9

From Old Man Turner's Journal:
Dating is a bit like standing naked in the middle of town square. It's awkward, scary, and everyone is laughing at you.

On Tuesday, Miles began his day with a six-mile run outdoors. The morning was crystal-clear with a cloudless blue sky. The air was pure and crisp, with a tinge of frost-coated pine, and didn't carry even a hint of smog like it did in Denver. Miles wanted to take advantage of the weather. Before too long, when winter set in, he would be forced to relegate his morning run indoors. He mentally added looking into buying a treadmill to his agenda.

He settled into a rhythm with his stride. It had been a while since he had run up Echo Lake Drive. Living at Abby's house, all he had to do was exit his front door and turn left onto the road. As he ran, Miles kept an eye out for bears, elk, and cougars beginning their morning search for food as his feet flew over the pavement. Instead of what normally would have been an easy run, he had to push his lungs, paying attention to his oxygen intake.

Living in Denver had thinned his blood some. By this time next year, he would be back in form and wouldn't notice the lack. He had forgotten how peaceful it could be up in the mountains, how much it could remove the mental load he carried even if only for a time. And how much he had missed taking time out to brood over his problems until he figured out a solution.

Take running into Cybil on a date last night as an example. To say that Miles had been shocked that Cybil had gone out with the man was the understatement of the century. But the pained expression she had been wearing told him that one, she hadn't been happy to see Miles, and two, she wasn't happy with her date either.

But what last night had done was make it abundantly clear that she was single and searching. Which meant he could toss his hat back into the ring. And that perhaps he needed to shift his approach, from patiently chipping away at her walls into a full-on siege to break them down. Miles was betting on the possibility that Cybil still had feelings for him. If she didn't, she wouldn't be so bothered by him being her landlord.

By the time he reached the lake, he was gasping for breath. His lungs burned from the exertion, but the physical movement, the endorphin rush, had been exactly what he needed. Even panting and gulping oxygen into his lungs like a trout tossed onto dry land felt terrific. His bench was still there, on the banks of Echo Lake. The gray weathered stone was just waiting for a body to come sit and contemplate their life.

It was the same bench where he had met Cybil.

Their meet cute seemed like it had happened yesterday, the memory clear and distinct as any one of his life epochs. Yet in reality, years had passed, and he was no longer that angry, broken college kid on the cusp of true adulthood. Miles had been drowning in stunned grief, his world ripped to shreds. While he and his dad might not have always seen eye to eye, Miles had loved his father. He had never had to wonder whether his dad loved him like his buddy Nate had with his absentee father. Miles's dad had coached his Little League, had been there when Miles had run All-State track in high school, and had cheered him on when he had received his acceptance letter to Colorado University in Boulder.

Miles remembered the staggering regret that he had not made it home more often during his freshman year. That he hadn't called his dad more. They'd both been so busy—his dad with his hardware store, he with his classes and fraternity. So he'd driven up to the lake, needing a moment to clear his head after his dad's funeral. The heart attack had happened so suddenly. One minute his dad was there, robust and alive, the next, they were lowering his body into the ground.

After the burial, he'd asked his aunt to take his mom back to their house for the bereavement meal. He'd needed a few moments to catch his breath, a little peace amidst the chaos.

He could still remember the way she looked that day. Her profile had been stunning. And when he had asked to sit beside her, the full brunt of her beauty had sucker-punched him. But it had been her eyes, the color of storm clouds and bursting with vivacious life, framed by thick, inky lashes, that had sucked him into her sultry, enchanting vortex.

Meeting Cybil on the day of his dad's funeral had been a surprising, refreshing interaction that had made Miles momentarily forget that his heart was bleeding. And when she had smiled at him, he had felt like the sun had finally emerged back into his life.

Before Cybil's advent into his life, Miles had dated a few girls in high school and during his freshman year in college. But Cybil had been different from the moment they met. She had been daring and smart, independent with an adventurous streak that had called to him on every level of his being. She had become his solace, the place he ran to when he needed a measure of peace as much as his spot at Echo Lake had been.

Miles raced back down Echo Lake Drive toward Abby's house, inundated by memories of that summer with Cybil. Like the first time he had kissed her on the night of their first date; she had tasted like sunshine and sweetness. And Miles had not been able to get enough of her after that initial taste.

He had craved her like his body needed air. And Cybil had been right there with him, along for the heady, wild ride as they tumbled headlong into lust and love. They had been inseparable. All summer long, whenever they weren't working—he at his parents' hardware store and she at the pizza joint—they'd been together. Just the two of them against the world.

It was the most authentic and carefree time of his life. Miles had loved Cybil with everything he had inside him, and been blinded to all but her.

Miles shook his head at the deluge of memories while he finished getting ready for his day. It wouldn't do any good to dwell and linger over days gone by. Not that he didn't wonder whether, if he had been strong enough, if he had fought for them, they would have made it and gone the distance.

During the drive into town, he stopped at the Emporium Diner for coffee and a breakfast sandwich on his way to the office. Really, some things never changed, and if it weren't for the Emporium and Abby's cooking, he'd likely starve. He really needed to make a grocery store run at some point, and stock more than beer and leftover takeout cartons in the fridge. When he parked at the office, he noticed the lights in Cybil's studio were off.

He wondered what time she would be in that day. From what little he had witnessed, he could not fault her work ethic. The woman worked hard every day. Then again, she always had been a hard worker. Miles wanted to start chipping away at the ice around her heart.

By ten that morning, Miles had met with a handful of clients, and read through a few resumes for the office manager position when JoAnn Fincher strolled in.

"Howdy, neighbor," she said, her tone dripping honey. Her voice had always made Miles think of a cat in heat, even when they were in high school. JoAnn wore a man-eater of a suit, with a red skirt that ended at mid-thigh. He couldn't fault her figure, she had one heck of a body, but she always made him think of a praying mantis that tended to castrate any man she wrapped within her clutches. Her ex-husband, Joel Fincher, worked over at the local inn, and was a shell of his former self. JoAnn owned the realty company across the hall, and she liked to poke her refurbished, plastic surgeon special nose into everybody's business.

"What can I do for you, JoAnn? Is there a problem?" Miles asked, instantly on guard. As much as he would like to get laid, there was no way in hell he would touch JoAnn. He wasn't that desperate. Besides, word on the street was that JoAnn had slept her way through the entire eligible male population and was always on the lookout for husband number two—the wealthier, the better.

"Oh, there's no problem at all. I just wanted to bring this by for you, to welcome you back home and to our little building. It's my prize ham and potato casserole. It won the blue ribbon three times at the Fourth of July Town Fair. I put the heating instructions in the envelope here on top," she said with a bat of her fake lashes, her smile predatory.

"Ah, thanks. That wasn't necessary. I appreciate it, though." Miles sensed a trap as he took the dish from her. It would be rude to refuse. But he wasn't exactly sure how to handle the situation without pissing off a paying tenant. Thankfully, his phone rang. "I'm sorry, but I have to take this."

"It's no bother. If you need anything, and I do mean anything, you let me know, all right?" JoAnn said and strutted out the door, leaving him with the casserole. Miles wondered if she had roofied the casserole with something other than ham and potatoes.

"Keaton Law," he murmured as he picked up. The caller was a job applicant he'd contacted that morning. Eva Monroe was also, as it happened, one of the tenants who lived in a third-floor apartment in his building, and she was returning the message he'd left her that morning. They made an appointment for an interview the following day.

By noon, his eyes were crossing after he'd begun to wade through Clark Biddle's files. The man was a brilliant attorney but had organized his files by just shoving documents into folders and then putting them in a filing cabinet. There was no order or methodology to it. The mess drove Miles's obsessive-compulsive need for organization crazy. Clark was lucky no one had ever sued or audited him, given the sad state of his files.

Before Miles left to grab a bite to eat at Papa Beau's with Nate, Sally Little strolled in. The voluptuous redhead was the town clerk, and had been a year behind him at Echo Springs High. She had always been sweet and perky, on student council and yearbook and just about everything else a person could participate and volunteer in.

"Sally, to what do I owe the pleasure?" Miles said from his desk. He rose and approached her, surprised by the visit.

A rosy blush spread over her ivory cheeks. Sally held up a foil-covered ceramic dish. "I know you just moved back to town. I wanted to bring this by to help you while you're getting settled and all, as a welcome back."

"Ah, thanks. What is it exactly?" Miles asked, a mite suspicious at the unexpected gift.

"Oh, you'll love it. It's my chicken enchilada casserole, made special with green chili," Sally replied with a sweet, expectant grin. Sally had always been nice. He doubted there was a mean bone in the woman's body. Miles had enjoyed interactions with her throughout the years. But what the hell was going on? Two casseroles in one day?

"Um, you really didn't have to do this."

"Oh I know, but a runner like you needs to keep his strength up. And this dish is so hearty." Sally extended her hands with said dish for him to take.

"Thanks. I'll just set it in the fridge." He put it next to the one from JoAnn, sensing a theme. Was there a bulletin at the supermarket? Had his mom mentioned he had a fondness for casseroles at the last townhall?

"Oh, did someone else beat me to the punch?" Sally asked, peering over his shoulder.

He hadn't heard her creep up behind him. He sidestepped away, rather uncomfortable at the rapacious gleam on her face. If he didn't know better, he would say that Sally Little was sizing him up for a tux.

"I appreciate the casserole, Sally, I'm sure it will be delicious. I hate to do this, but I have a lunch meeting and need to run out," he explained as a way to escape the situation that was making him sweat. The woman was undressing him with her eyes. Normally, he wouldn't mind, but he'd known Sally practically his entire life. He had never been interested in her, not even in high school. What the hell was going on with the women in this town?

"No problem at all. I'm at lunch myself," she said, with hope swimming in her eyes that he might invite her to eat with him.

"Sorry, but it's a business meeting. Attorney-client privilege and all," Miles explained, and realized he was going to hell. Sally was a nice, mild mannered woman. Surely he was the one over-reacting to her nice gift.

"It's no problem. We can do it another time, like when you return the casserole dish." She flashed him a seductive, come-hither smile, and exited the office.

Jesus H. Christ, if the woman had stared at his crotch any

longer, Miles wasn't sure he could have kept himself from putting his hands in front of his junk. What in the everlasting hell was going on? First JoAnn and now Sally.

Maybe he and Nate should meet at Smitty's so he could grab a beer. He scooped up his phone and was just about to text him and suggest that when he received an incoming text from Nate.

Nate: Stuck at the station, can't get away. Reschedule?

Miles: Sure. But you're buying for standing me up.

Nate: Sorry. Bad accident on the interstate with a DOA and have a shit ton of paperwork.

Miles: That's a lot to deal with. Fuck, I'm sorry. I'll buy you a beer at Smitty's next chance we get.

Nate: Thanks. It's a deal.

Instead of leaving the office, Miles ordered a pizza for delivery from Papa Beau's and shut himself away in his office, then proceeded to work through the afternoon. He wondered about the accident on the interstate and hoped like crazy the DOA wasn't someone from Echo Springs. By mid-afternoon, he was in the midst of brewing another pot of coffee when Katie Conroy, a kindergarten teacher at the local elementary school, waltzed into his office. He'd been friends with her brother Matt in high school. His brows rose when he spied the blue flowered dish in her hands. Katie was a sweet blonde, with a girl-next-door air, and had been two years behind him in school.

"Katie, what can I do for you? How's Matt?" he asked with a smile hovering over his lips.

"Off saving the world as usual, working on creating environmentally friendly energy for a tech company in Silicon Valley," Katie explained with a sweet smile that displayed her dimples.

"He always was sharp. And you, how have you been?" Miles poured coffee into his mug, his thoughts on the stack of files he had yet to get through today.

"Ready for the Thanksgiving holiday break from school. I love my kids, but they can be a handful this time of year."

"I bet. So what's up?" Miles asked, eyeing the dish in her hands as if it was a rabid dog about to attack.

"Oh, I just wanted to welcome you back to town and make sure you were eating well enough. This here is my French toast casserole. It's awesome for breakfast, or anytime, really," she explained, holding the oven dish out toward him.

He eyed the damn thing like it was a bomb with a timer ticking down to zero. He didn't want to take it. But as he stared, he realized he had been backed into a corner and had to accept it whether he wanted it or not. He was back in his hometown after more than thirteen years away. He'd just purchased a law practice that he wanted—dammit, *needed*—to do well. That wouldn't happen if he pissed everyone in town off within the first week.

But another casserole? Miles scraped a hand over his face, trying to hide his unease. What in the hell was going on? He couldn't remember there being a casserole brigade in this town. Then again, who was he to say? Maybe they were all being nice and welcoming, and he was being an asshole for reading too much into it.

"Um, thanks. You really didn't have to do that. I assure you I'm not starving," he replied, pasting a smile on his face.

"Oh, I just wanted to welcome you back. It's no big deal." She set the dish on what would hopefully soon be his office manager's desk.

"No, I appreciate it. I've barely had time to make it to the grocery store." That was something he damn well planned to rectify at the soonest. Had a memo gone out to the town that he had returned, and some ladies' club decided he needed to be fattened up like a Thanksgiving turkey? If so, he wanted a follow-up memo to clarify that he was just fine, thank you very much. And that while he might enjoy a casserole now and again, he did not need or want the kind hospitality.

"Great. Well, enjoy. And if you don't have any plans tonight,

I'm meeting some friends at Smitty's. You're welcome to join us," she offered with an interested, hopeful gleam in her baby blue gaze.

"Ah, thanks. I can't tonight." He made a mental note to avoid Smitty's, and to stop at the grocery store on the way home. That way, his eating habits, or lack thereof, wouldn't be fodder for the local women's league. Hell, he didn't even know if there was one. Maybe he should ask his mom if they had started something like that in Echo Springs. It would make him feel better if he didn't think he needed to be on the defensive. As it was, Miles felt like he was the newest selection on the town menu and every single eligible woman wanted a bite. Well, not all of them, but enough for him to stop and take notice.

Although, hell, he now had three casseroles that he could eat for dinner if he wanted to avoid the grocery store two days before a holiday.

He and Katie chitchatted for a few more minutes before Katie finally left the office. Miles thought seriously about locking his office door and pretending he wasn't in for the rest of the day. His phone rang, and he sighed.

He picked it up just as one of his tenants raced down the stairs and out the front door. He wasn't prepared for his disappointment that it wasn't Cybil he had spied on her way out, or at all today. After all, not one of the women who had visited his office had stirred his interest, or his body, the way the flash of Cybil's midnight hair and her supple form—dwarfed in her big red parka—did.

With a grimace at the weird twist of events, Miles plowed through the rest of his workload for the day, all the while wondering what to do about the casserole brigade and Cybil. He was worried that the one woman he wanted, whom he planned to fight for this time around, wanted nothing to do with him.

Chapter 10

From Old Man Turner's Journal:
Trust your gut and your heart. There's no time for anything else.

That evening, pleased that she had accomplished the grocery shopping, done a few loads of laundry, and gotten some bookkeeping out of the way, Cybil headed to Hiker's Oasis for date number two she had arranged through Matchmakers. The restaurant and bar was situated on the outskirts of town, nestled at an overlook plateau on the way up to the Eagle's Nest Ski Resort. The place was a smidge out of the way. It was more of a tourist stop which most of the locals in Echo Springs tended to avoid, preferring Smitty's Bar and Grill instead for their nighttime get togethers. However, when you were trying to date in a small town and didn't want *everyone* talking about it over the produce section in Fitzgerald's, or preferred not to run into your ex while out on a date, having an out-of-the-way destination was a good place to start.

Hiker's Oasis looked as if it had been carved out of the

mountain. Constructed of slate gray stone and dark walnut-colored wood, the two-story building boasted a full tourist shop, with tee shirts and all manner of trinkets with the restaurant's logo for people to buy on the first floor. Up on the second floor was the full restaurant with a circular wooden bar in the center. There was a grand fireplace constructed of cobbled gray stone, with a plethora of wooden tables and seats in front of it for guests to warm themselves by the roaring fire. In the summer, they opened the patio and doors to allow in the breeze. Across the road from the restaurant was a prime overlook of the valley below where tourists stopped, sometimes in droves, for a chance to snap a selfie or group photo with the landscape in the background.

Hiker's Oasis prices were on the higher end of the scale, but it was the upcharge for tourism dollars. People were willing to pay twenty bucks for a hamburger when it came with the stunning view out the bank of windows of the western valley and surrounding snowcapped mountains.

Cybil bypassed the store in favor of the bar. They were doing decent business tonight. But she knew with it being this close to the holiday, people tended to meet friends and family and eat out a lot. Smitty's would be packed tomorrow night, and she almost wished she was working for the load of tips she could get. Granted, she would make it up Thanksgiving night during the auction, so she didn't feel too bad about missing out. She headed toward the walnut bar, where the counters gleamed with a reddish undertone. Cybil knew the bartender working tonight, Paige, who had been a year behind her at Echo Springs High and a huge fan of grunge. From all indications, she still tended to walk on the wild side, given that her blonde ponytail sported teal highlights, and her eye makeup was on the heavier, spackled on side of things with thick lines of coal black liner. Still, she was far more sedate than she'd been in school. At least, Cybil thought she was.

"Cybil, good to see you." Paige flashed her a grin and wiped a rag over the bar top in front of the leather stool she chose. "What can I get you?"

"Hey Paige, haven't seen you in a while. How about a Guinness?" Cybil was looking for comfort, and nothing said comfort in a cup like a Guinness.

"Good choice." Paige pulled out a clear stout glass and began working the tap. "Been working some crazy hours around here. How's the yoga studio? I've been meaning to come take a class."

"Things are good." Except that her ex was back in town and she had no idea how to handle it, or him. "And you know, the first class you take at the studio is free. The schedule is up on my website. You should come; I have plenty of classes that I think you would like. For you, I would suggest the power yoga or the hot yoga, I think those would suit you well."

"I'll check it out. What brings you up here? I didn't think you normally left Echo Springs for much of anything," Paige replied, setting down a disposable coaster with the bar's logo on it before placing the nicely stacked Guinness on top.

It was ironic how much of a homebody Cybil had become since high school. The comment reminded her that she had never gotten away from the tiny town and sought all the adventure that was out there, like she had planned. It made her sad. If she could change how everything had turned out, she would. Then her parents would still be alive, she and Miles might have worked out, and she would have traveled the world. But she couldn't change the past, not without a time machine. And the thing was, even contemplating a different life for herself dismissed everything she had accomplished and become, which in her mind, was pretty damn great. She shook off her malaise.

"You definitely should come. I'm here because I'm meeting a date."

Paige's eyes widened and her eyebrows rose in surprise. The woman had one of the most expressive faces. "Really? Good for you. Who are you meeting? Is it someone from Echo Springs that we went to high school with?" she asked, leaning forward, not hiding her curiosity.

"No. He lives in one of the neighboring towns and works at Eagle's Nest. His name is Jeremy." Or, as his profile name read, *Skier4Ever*. Really, some of these guys need to come up with a better uscrnamc. But at least his profile image didn't look like a mugshot, so there was that.

Paige snickered and slapped a hand on the bar. "Well, you tell me how that works out for you."

"You know him?" Dread settled in the pit of Cybil's belly. What was Paige not telling her? That look made it seem like she pitied Cybil.

"He comes in here quite a bit. You tell me what you think after your, um, date. In fact," Paige wiggled her eyebrows and nodded to a point behind Cybil, "he's coming up on your six now."

Cybil inhaled a deep breath, then swiveled on her bar stool and stood. *Here goes nothing.* She spied her *date* and mentally applauded herself for keeping her smile firmly in place. Jeremy's profile proclaimed he was six feet tall. Cybil snorted. Actually, he was pushing maybe five-foot-six, if that, and that was only because his sun-kissed brown hair was arranged in a windblown fashion, spiking up an inch from the crown of his head. In her four-inch-heeled black boots, she towered over him.

"Cybil. Nice," he said with a smug grin, undressing her with narrow eyes the color of burnt toast. "I see you've already started. Hey, Paige, why don't we start with a round of shots?"

"Oh, I don't need a shot. I'm set with my Guinness," Cybil murmured, sliding back onto her stool, noting the baggy jeans, tee shirt, and dress shirt buttoned only halfway. No way in hell was she doing shots and then driving on the windy mountain roads at night. If she drank too much at Smitty's, she walked home. But this far up was way the hell too far and out of the way for that; she would end up a meal for a mountain lion. Not to mention, she wasn't getting hammered with Mister Liar-Liar-Pants-on-Fire. Really, was it that hard not to lie on the dating websites? Did everyone on those things lie about who they were and what they actually looked like?

Six feet? Yeah, in his dreams.

"I can dig it, sweetheart." He slid onto the barstool beside her, and she forced herself not to grimace. She'd give him one drink. If things didn't improve, she was out of there.

Leaning against the bar, Paige asked, "You still want a shot, Jeremy, or do you want something else?"

"Why don't you bring me the round of shots? Make 'em Cuervo. I'll drink hers and then will chase it with a mojito."

"Suit yourself," Paige said with a grim smile and shake of her head, like she had seen this act from Jeremy one too many times. Cybil understood that. After waiting tables at Smitty's, she knew the regulars who came to drink their cares away. Cybil was all for a good time, but for her it wasn't at the bottom of a bottle. Never had been, nor would it ever be.

"So, sweetheart, tell me about yourself." Jeremy scooted close and laid his hand on her knee.

Cybil glanced at the hand and beat back her anger. They were not yet familiar enough or friendly enough for him to take that sort of liberty. She wasn't a prude by any means, but that didn't mean she didn't have boundaries. And this jerk seemed not to care, judging by his blatant move. Paige returned with his drinks as Cybil delicately shoved his hand off her leg.

"There's not much to tell. Like I mentioned in our conversation online, I run a yoga studio." Cybil blew out a breath, hoping for some of that inner peace she always impressed upon her students.

"And I can't wait for you to give me a private lesson and show me some poses." He gave her a sly wink and then knocked back a shot of tequila without batting an eye. The man drank Cuervo as if it were water.

Cybil enjoyed a good drink now and again, and she had to give the guy props for his drinking ability. However, there was no way in hell she was giving him a private lesson, now or ever. In fact, she already knew from this minor exchange that he would be lucky to make it to date two.

"What do you like to do when you aren't teaching tourists how to ski?" She tried to get a conversation started.

"Oh, I'm not an instructor or anything. I work in the ski rental booth for the owners. In exchange, I get to ski as much powder as I can handle, and a place to lay my noggin. It's a cool gig. Some buddies of mine are renting a place in Breckenridge, and I plan to head there for the holidays. They have some awesome skiing in Breckenridge. Ever been?"

"Sadly, no." Cybil played with a drop of condensation on her glass. *Come on inner peace, I don't have all night.*

"Well, if you want to come crash with me, I'm sure I could make some room for you. It will change your life."

"I bet." And not for the better. Cybil might still hold the dream of seeing the world, but she wanted to see it under her own steam. Not as some dude's bed bunny addition.

Jeremy's hand found its way onto her thigh. Again. She was surprised steam wasn't emitting from her ears. In a more forceful manner where she hoped he would get a clue, she pushed his hand off.

He shot her a lopsided smirk. "Problem, sweetheart?"

Of all the insufferable, odious, ham-handed men to be stuck with! That did it. Rage bubbled and boiled over inside to a point where she could no longer ignore it. Cybil understood that meeting new people and trying to date was difficult, but this guy's boorish, overblown ego and sense of entitlement that he could put his hands on her without her permission was unreal. And that was on top of being a liar. If the man told her to just relax, she might do him bodily harm. Nate wouldn't arrest her, he'd give her a high five for smacking the leering smirk off the jerk's face. She couldn't make the hour or the full drink. "Yep. First, if I want your hands on me, I will tell you. Until then, keep them to yourself if you don't want to start losing body parts. Second, I'm not now, nor will I ever be, your sweetheart. Third, if you're six feet tall, I'm the damn Queen of England. Paige, what do I owe you?"

"It's on the house," Paige said, smothering her grin, her brown eyes dancing with merriment.

"You get a week's worth of free classes on me, Paige. Good night, Jeremy. Have a nice life."

He gave her a disgruntled shake of his head. "Not cool. Chill out… sweetheart," he sneered with a chin jut.

Cybil clenched her hands to restrain herself from strangling the little shit. Nate might look the other way if she smacked him. She doubted he would be able to do the same with murder.

"Grow up," she snapped and marched out of Hiker's Oasis without a backward glance. So far with her Matchmakers pickings, she was batting zero. Was she going about this all wrong? It made her wonder if she should keep the date scheduled for tomorrow night, or not. If she wasn't so bound and determined to find a decent guy to date, some of which was fueled by Miles's return to Echo Springs, she would cancel it.

Instead of an interesting night that she had hoped would lead to more, Cybil headed home and drowned her sorrows in a pint of rocky road. She didn't indulge often, but the chocolate and marshmallows hit the proverbial spot. While it wasn't the exciting date that could potentially one day lead to some orgasmic bliss between the sheets, the ice cream came in a close second.

The day before Thanksgiving rolled around way too early, and Cybil's belly was none too happy with her ice cream indulgence last night. At least Gus had resumed his morning ritual of waking her before her alarm with his cold, wet nose pressed by her ear, purring and nudging her so she would feed him.

This morning, she had another training session with Alex Dotson. Also on their agenda was a long overdue chat. Theirs was a professional relationship only. If he couldn't stay within those parameters, she would have to stop training him. Cybil noticed the lights on in Miles's office when she went to the front door to let Alex in.

"Cybil, you look refreshed this morning." Alex crowded her as they ascended the stairs to her studio.

The man invaded her space, he was practically breathing down her neck, and it took everything inside her not to snip at him to back off. A part of her knew she should be flattered that he found her attractive and appeared interested in taking their relationship past the tentative friendship level, but she wasn't in the slightest. And the other part of her said to hell with that, the guy was acting like a creep and needed to be put in his place—preferably beneath her heel.

She waited until they were inside, with the door to her studio shut behind them for privacy, before bringing it up. "Alex, we need to talk." She clasped her hands together and nibbled on her bottom lip.

His eyes lit up with an interested male gleam. A satisfied smirk tilted the corners of his mouth. "I've wanted to talk to you, too. We should have dinner sometime soon, just the two of us, and see where the night takes us." He approached her with a cocky swagger. It took all her willpower not to roll her eyes. She realized he was misinterpreting the situation. It was up to her to set the record straight. Cybil lifted a hand to stop his forward progression.

But did Alex read her back off signal? Not a chance. He had

her backing up when he tried to grab her around the waist and bring her up against him. "Alex, stop."

"Don't be a tease, Cybil. We're both feeling it. We should lock the door and make sure we aren't disturbed." Alex kept pursuing her, boxing her in against the wall.

"Alex, you're misunderstanding the situation. Back off."

"Oh, don't be like that. Especially when we both know you want it." He seemed to grow additional hands. When he grabbed her ass as she dodged his mouth, Cybil saw red.

She did the one thing she knew for sure would get his attention and make him back the hell off: she brought her knee up between his legs and slammed it into the family jewels. Pain mottled his features and he stumbled away with a roar.

Cybil moved then, holding her hands up defensively. "Just stop, Alex. That wasn't a come on."

"You bitch! What the hell did you do that for?" Alex shouted, cupping himself, red faced, his features contorted with rage.

Cybil couldn't believe he'd truly thought she was interested and would be okay with him copping a feel in her studio. The jerk. It was nice to know she hadn't been reading him wrong. "Let's get one thing straight. You seem to be under the impression that our relationship is something it's not. I like you, Alex, as a *friend*, but it doesn't go beyond that, nor will it *e-ver*. I would appreciate it if you would stop with the innuendos and flirting. It makes me uncomfortable. I cannot do my job properly if I'm worried I will have to field advances from you. And whatever that just was, try to touch me again without my permission, and you will know the meaning of true pain."

"You've been coming on to me this whole time, sending me all these flirty signals. I don't see why you're getting bent out of shape over it," Alex replied with a sneer. There was a meanness, a cold, calculating anger in his eyes that she'd always suspected lingered below the surface, and she shivered at seeing it on display.

"I have not, and you know that. While I appreciate the offer, my answer is no. And there's nothing you can do to change my mind. I think that you might need to find another trainer."

Alex exploded, still cupping his junk with one hand, and sniped, "Don't be like that. And so yeah, I thought we could have some fun. Nothing serious. No reason for you to get so bent out of shape and kick my balls through my stomach."

"Well, you can stop thinking that because it's never going to happen. Now—"

"Is there a problem?" Miles said from the door of her studio. Tension oozed from his form in the clean lines of his mint green, linen dress shirt and tailored dark gray slacks. He looked like he had stepped off Fifth Avenue with his gray silk tie and the Cartier watch on his wrist. His demeanor screamed that he was seconds from ripping Alex's head clean off his shoulders.

Alex's expression turned mutinous. But Cybil had this. She didn't give the man a chance to reply to Miles's question. "No, no problem at all. Alex was just leaving."

"Are you serious?" Alex snapped. His fists were clenched, his lips drawn back in a sneer. A violent, unholy rage vibrated from every fiber of his being. The man was dangerous, and Cybil decided to bar him from attending any classes at the studio.

"I think it's for the best." While she would hate to lose the money, there was a reason Miles and his buddies called Alex Dipshit Dotson. In this instance, Cybil had a feeling she would have had to continue to dodge his advances.

"You're a lousy trainer," Alex snarled and stomped away. He and Miles met at the door. Miles pinned Alex with a glare and a small smile, making Alex understand that his pissy attitude didn't scare him, but in fact amused him, until finally Alex growled, "Out of my way, Keaton."

"Stop being such a prick, Dotson," Miles said, with enough insinuation and meaning laced into his words that it was clear if Alex didn't, Miles would do something about it. And then Miles stepped to the side, giving Alex room to storm out the door. He slammed it behind him, the glass inside vibrating at the force.

Cybil winced at the sound of the door to the building thunking shut. That was one way to kick off a morning. She sighed. "Well, that went swimmingly."

"Are you all right?" Miles asked as he approached, his gaze roving over her form, searching for any harm done.

Did he have to look like a walking wet dream? Especially after walking in acting like a knight in shining armor, ready to defend her honor from Alex.

"I'm fine," she assured him with more confidence than she felt. "I don't need you rescuing me. Do you think he's the first guy I've had to say no to?"

"No, I don't. I think you should call Nate, let him know about this incident. Did he touch you?"

"He did," she held her hands up at the murderous look that entered in his eyes, "but not for long. I dislocated the family jewels with a knee to his groin and took care of it."

"Still think you need to call Nate and report it. Dotson won't let this slide. He's been known to retaliate."

"I know, and I will take care of it. I've been handling guys like him on my own for a long time." She blew out a frustrated breath.

Miles slid his hands into his pockets and glanced down pensively, like he had been about to mention something but thought better of it. He shook his head and headed for the door.

Cybil couldn't let him leave and think what he'd done had not mattered, because it had. And she did appreciate it. "Miles, thank you for coming to my rescue. I didn't need the help but thank you just the same. And I'm sorry about the other day. I know this situation isn't what either of us wanted or planned for, but I'm willing to declare a ceasefire if you are."

It was the best she could do for now.

With his hand on the door handle, he cocked his head,

studying her. A small smile tugged at his lips. "I'm waving my white flag, and agree to a ceasefire."

"I never wanted hostility between us. It doesn't mean I think we can be friends, though."

Consternation filled his eyes. "Then what do you want?"

It was that look, the one that called her a fool, that could see through all her defenses to the very heart of her, that rattled Cybil more than Alex Dotson grabbing her butt. Defeated, she sighed. "I don't know. I just know that I don't want to fight anymore. That I'm tired of the song and dance that seems to be a constant repeat when it comes to us. I snipe at you, then you snap back, and on and on."

"Cybil, I don't want to fight with you either. I haven't for a long time. I'm sorry for the part I've played though, over the years."

"Are we actually having a conversation without one of us getting bent out of shape? We should mark it on a calendar."

"Yeah, look at that, the two of us acting like adults." He grinned. Sexily.

She couldn't stop the smile, or the warm flutters in her chest. "Imagine that. It was bound to happen one of these days."

Miles laughed. Crinkle lines appeared at the corners of his eyes. "Well, I'll let you get your day started. Sorry that you lost a client."

She shrugged and shook her head. "You were right in that he's always been a dipshit. It's not a big loss, and I'm not worried about it."

"That's good then. See you at Abby and Nate's tomorrow."

"Yep. Thanks again." She watched his retreat as he exited her studio, noticing he still had a mighty fine posterior. Then Cybil walked to the door and flipped the lock. She needed a few minutes without any interruptions to find her Zen before her slate of classes today.

How was it that two dates couldn't get a rise out of her?

Then a perfectly acceptable man for her to date did the opposite and pissed her off so much, she kneed him in the balls when he made an advance. But five minutes in Miles's company, five measly minutes alone with him, and her entire being lit up like Main Street decorated for Christmas.

How was that right? Why did fate seem to want to throw them back in each other's lives? Yes, she'd softened toward Miles and declared a ceasefire. She hadn't been lying when she said she was tired of fighting with him. Besides, what woman in her right mind could remain angry at a man when that man was willing to defend them from danger?

But it also confirmed an idea, a theory, she'd had for years: that no matter where she went, what she did, and with whom, they would never measure up to Miles. That she would never have it in her to love another man the way she had Miles.

Instead of prepping her studio for the day, she curled up in her office chair with a mug of coffee and pondered the implications of a ceasefire. Could they be friends? Or at least, friendlier toward one another than they had over the last thirteen years?

And was that opening herself up to more heartache where Miles was concerned?

Cybil had no idea. But she hadn't lied to him. She *was* tired of the constant suspicion and animosity, especially because she'd started it. It was the only way she had been able to keep her promise.

When Burke Smitt called and begged her to fill in that night at Smitty's, she said yes unequivocally and canceled her date with *Softheart282* aka Chris—she had no idea what his last name was and at this point, didn't care one bit. Cybil would rather go run her legs off than go on another failed date, especially since the night before Thanksgiving traditionally was one of the busiest bar nights of the year.

It had nothing to do with Miles and the smoldering intensity in his eyes. Heat and passion had never been the problem between them. In the end, she was the one who messed up when she made that stupid promise. Because there hadn't been a day that had passed since then where she hadn't missed him. They had not just dated and been lovers that long-ago summer. They had been best friends.

And she didn't know if she could maintain that line of demarcation if she allowed herself to be friends with him again. Because the thing was, she had given Miles her whole heart, and she never really got it back.

Chapter 11

From Old Man Turner's Journal:
In life as well as in dating, there are the plans we make, and then the plans that life has for us. And most of the time, fate knows better than we do.

Temperatures had dipped into frigid territory while Cybil worked the night shift at Smitty's. Exiting out the front door, she shivered in her red parka while she waited for Burke to lock up. They were the last two to leave. This late at night, they always made sure to leave in pairs as a safety precaution. Not that they had to worry about crime as much as they did in the city, but there was always a chance of running into a mountain lion or two.

The parking lot was deserted except for his truck and hers at the edge of the lot nearest McKinley Drive.

"Thanks for coming in tonight. I really appreciate you helping me out of a bind and filling in for Shelly," Burke said with a nod when he reached his black truck. The Army ballcap hid his full head of chestnut hair. His six-foot lanky frame always carried a hint that he was ready for action and wouldn't back away from a fight if needed. Cybil had watched him evict more than one drunken lout from the premises.

"No problem, Burke. I made quite a nice haul in tips tonight. I might even treat myself to a pedicure next week." She shot him a grin and unlocked her truck.

Burke chuckled. "I'm sure they'll look pretty too."

"Oh honey, you know me. They're awesome."

"Ha. Well, thanks again. Get some rest and I will see you at the auction in about sixteen hours," Burke replied with a salute, and climbed in the cab of his truck. The big black beast of a vehicle roared to life.

Burke waited until she'd slid behind the wheel of her truck before rumbling off in the direction of home, leaving her alone in the parking lot. There was an owl nearby hooting up a storm.

Cybil slid her key in the ignition and turned it. The engine turned over like it wanted to start but had no juice. She tried again. "Come on, baby, don't let me down."

She pumped the gas and turned the key again. The engine sputtered and coughed but didn't start.

Shit.

Cybil lowered her head to the steering wheel. This was what she got for putting off taking the damn thing into the garage. She knew it was up for service, but with all her expenses lately with the studio, she'd hoped she could put it off a little longer. Make it a task she crossed off her to-do list next month.

Dammit, the last thing she wanted to do tonight was walk home. She'd done it many times before, but she was exhausted. At this point, she had been up for twenty-one hours, had run her damn legs off, her feet ached, and all she wanted was her nice, warm bed and a few uninterrupted hours of sleep.

She could call a tow truck or even the police station, to see if someone could help. But Cybil hated depending on someone else or asking for favors or help. It was stubborn and stupid of her, she knew that. That didn't mean it made asking for assistance any easier.

She waited a minute, thankful that at least being inside the truck protected her from the arctic wind—even if it was still cold enough her breath fogged out in front of her. She tried turning the key one more time, mumbling a prayer that it would start and get her home. She could deal with repairs and maintenance needed once she got there. But the engine sputtered and clicked, it didn't give the tiny bit of juice she had gotten before. It had to be the battery. Maybe one of the cables had come loose. She would check it and call the station. Surely one of the cops on duty could come give her a jump. With a sigh, she popped the hood latch beneath the dashboard, and climbed out with her keys. She had a small flashlight keychain that would help her see this late at night.

Cybil propped the hood up and shone the light on the engine. The battery cables looked fine. As for the rest of the engine, she had no clue. The parts under the hood were one of life's little mysteries to her, like the possible existence of extraterrestrials, or why some people couldn't stand cilantro, or what people who didn't drink coffee actually did to wake themselves up each morning.

Headlights flashed nearby. Cybil glanced over and recognized the Escalade pulling into the lot and parking a few feet away from her truck.

Just to cap off her long, arduous day, she would get another interaction with her ex. *Oh joy*. That was what she wanted at three in the morning—another sad trip down memory lane. Was she on some god's hit list? She couldn't explain her bad luck any other way. At least she wouldn't have to walk home, she thought with relief.

Miles emerged from his vehicle and joined her at the front of hers. "Problem? Truck not starting?"

"Nope. I think it's the battery. What are you still doing up? It's three in the morning."

He shrugged, still looking rather dapper in jeans and his dark gray coat. "Just had burgers with Nate and Jacob at Emporium. It's a tradition when we all get together after we finish up a night at Smitty's."

"Figured you would have gone home with one of the members of your fan club."

He chuckled. "What can I say, the single female population is happy I'm home."

"That's only because it's slim pickings around here."

"Well, you should know. When a woman has to resort to the senior citizen population for a date, one has to wonder."

"Ha! I can't help it when someone lies. Did you stop just to rib me over Monday night, or were you going to help? Cause if you hadn't noticed, it's freezing out and I've been on my feet for hours."

"You can warm up in my car if you need to, and I'll get this taken care of."

"No, it's fine. The sooner we get it done, the sooner I can go to bed." She shivered, wrapping her arms around her chest. "So why didn't you go home with one of your fan club members?"

He shot her a pondering look. "They're nice, but I'm not interested in them. Shine your flashlight on the engine again for me."

Miles leaned beneath her hood and checked a few things. "Probably just needs a jump. Although, when was the last time you had this thing serviced? Your cables are corroded and need to be replaced. Some of your belts look worn. Probably why you are having a hard time with the battery."

"Yeah, I know. I've been meaning to get it into Mike O'Toole's garage. Aiden's brother doesn't overcharge me for parts and labor just because I'm a female. I don't have any jumper cables." She held up her hands. "I know with a vehicle this old, I should. So sue me."

"Not sure you could afford me, babe. And you're in luck, because I do. It will just take me a few minutes." He headed over and popped the hood on his vehicle, connected cables to his battery, and then brought them over to her truck. "Jesus, how old is this battery? There's quite a bit of rust when you remove the cables," he said, connecting the jumper cables.

"I'm not sure. At least five years, perhaps more."

"Well, that's part of your problem. I think at the very least, you need a new battery. Go try to start it." He jerked his head toward the cab of her truck.

Cybil did as he asked, leaned inside the cab, and turned the key in the ignition. The truck sputtered to life. It didn't roar. But at least it started. Hallelujah! No walking home for this girl. She could already envision just how heavenly her bed would feel.

"Okay, good. Now leave it running. Given the state of that battery, we should let it run about five or so minutes and let it charge up," Miles said, still looking beneath her hood.

With a sigh, she shut the door to allow the interior cab to heat up as the battery charged. Cybil leaned back against the side of the car with her arms crossed, and lowered her head.

"You look tired."

She lifted her gaze. Miles was standing before her. He didn't look tired. In fact, he looked even better than in her memories—gorgeous, with that same razor sharp intensity that could cut through all her defenses with a mere glance. "Good to know I look that bad."

"That's not what I meant, Cyb," he admonished her.

She winced. She was always doing that: snapping at his outstretched hand of friendship. "Sorry. It's just been a really long day. And, well, you know it didn't start on the right foot."

"Did you report the incident to Nate?"

She shook her head. "There wasn't time."

"Dammit, you need to make time. Dotson was watching you tonight. What if it had been him that showed up and not me?"

She felt a prickle of fear at the thought of being alone with Alex in the dead of night in a parking lot versus in a building that had other people in it. "I know. I will. Sorry, I meant to, I'm just so tired."

"You promise?"

She watched his mouth form the words. God, there was no one who could kiss the way Miles did.

His stance was anything but casual, and he was no more than a foot away. It would be so easy to lean into him. There was a part of her that wanted to say to hell with it, erase the distance and years between them, and that wanted it fiercely. Her gaze dropped to his lips as an acute yearning filled her chest. She curled her fingers into her palms to keep herself from reaching for him. She squeezed her eyes shut. She couldn't go there with Miles and not get burned.

"Cybil, look at me, babe."

She opened her eyes and lifted her gaze until it connected with his. A sizzle of kinetic energy whipped through her being. Awareness entered his eyes, and the concern on his face transmuted into carnal hunger.

"Do I make you nervous?"

"No. Don't be silly," she denied with a shake of her head. She was denying what she felt, even as there was a flutter and pulse deep in her center that she recognized—anticipation and arousal.

"You sure about that?" he said with a husky bass in his tone that shivered through her.

"Yep."

"Uh huh, and that pulse in your neck is racing, just like it used to when you wanted to kiss me back in the day." He lightly traced his finger along said vein in her neck, and she felt that simple, gentle touch from the point of contact all the way down to her toes.

She quivered like a damn schoolgirl. Trying to save face, she countered, "Why are you always around? Since you've been back, I can't seem to go anywhere without you showing up."

He flashed a grin. Sexily. "Huh. Would you look at that? I am making you nervous. I've never known you to be nervous, about anyone or anything."

"Times change. And no, you don't make me nervous."

"Liar. You want me." His throaty chuckle made her girly bits quiver. Miles stepped forward and pressed his entire hard length against her. Unlike when Alex had tried the same move that morning, Cybil didn't experience revulsion at his touch. Quite the opposite. It lit her body up, awakening a clawing need to feel his rock-hard flesh, and surrender to the wild, carnal madness that it seemed only he could provoke.

She sputtered, "I do not."

Oh, sweet biscuits!

How could she have forgotten how decadent the man's body felt against hers? His move brought that sinful mouth of his within striking distance. And yes, the man could still turn her inside out with need.

"Yeah, you do. I know you too well, Cyb. And the thing is," he boxed her in against the truck. One hand toyed with her braid, "I want you too. I don't think I ever stopped wanting you."

What? "No, you don't. You can't." She shook her head in denial and put her hands against his chest to push him away, fighting back the whimper. She was touching him again, after all this time. Even with the barrier his clothes and coat made, it didn't matter, because she was touching him again.

"You do. I see it in your eyes. You forget, I know you. I remember with perfect clarity the way the pulse right here," he stroked it again, "tends to race when you want me to kiss you, or you're thinking about kissing me. Wanna neck in the parking lot of Smitty's like old times, Cyb?"

Her body shouted an unequivocal yes.

Bad body.

The thing was, when it came to Miles, it wouldn't only be a kiss. She would end up in bed with him. And while her body might rocket up onto cloud nine, she couldn't keep her emotions out of it. Not when it came to him. There was too much history between them for her to maintain that line.

"I can't, Miles," she whispered with regret.

"You sure?"

Cybil fought her emotions back and nodded. "Yes. Thanks for helping me. I think it's best if I go home. It's late."

He studied her reaction, and then said, "Here's the thing, Cybil. I want us to try again."

"What? Why?" Why was he doing this to her? Was this some joke? Her heart squeezed. "Try again? You can't be serious."

"I've never been more serious in my life. With the amount of chemistry between us, we owe it to ourselves to try. Besides, I have all my teeth and no AARP card. Given that, I'm a catch."

She wanted to laugh. She wanted to cry. She wanted… him. But she couldn't travel down that road again. "No."

"Why not?"

"Miles," she fought against the need, the desire to surrender, "I don't know that I can. I barely survived the first time. And I don't think it would be a good idea no matter how much chemistry there is, because that was never the issue."

His gaze shuttered, closing her out. "Well, I'm not going anywhere. Think about it. You're almost frozen. Let's get you inside. I'm going to follow you home, make sure your truck doesn't break down on the way."

He'd backed off, and Cybil didn't know what to feel. A part of her wanted to take back her words, pull him back against her, and capitulate to the ever-present need clawing at her to be set free. But the other part told her to run as far and as fast as she could, away from the danger he presented to her heart.

Miles disconnected their vehicles and shut both of their hoods. In that time, she wrangled her emotions back into control. Before she climbed in, she said, "Thanks again for the save."

"Anytime. Think about what I said. I'm not lying or playing games, Cyb. I want you. In fact, you're the only woman in this town I want."

She just nodded because the words were sticking in her throat, and shut her door. Miles did as promised and followed her all the way home to ensure her truck made it. She waved him off after she parked on the street in front of her place, and sat for a moment, watching his taillights disappear down the street.

Miles wanted her. Cybil had no idea how to even begin processing that tidbit. It wasn't a question of wanting him. She had always—and feared she would always—crave him. But how was she supposed to respond? Every part of her body was on board with him, but it was her heart that trembled, that questioned whether she could let him touch her body and not let him affect her emotions.

Cybil feared the answer was no. And the thought of opening herself up to that kind of pain again, even just the mere potential of pain, left her quaking in her boots. She rubbed a tired, chilled hand over her face. With no idea what to do about him, she headed inside. The man had lost his mind. Exhausted, physically, and emotionally, she did a nosedive into her bed. A few hours of shut eye were all she needed, and then she could think with a clear head to determine the correct path.

She couldn't be with Miles again, not without devastating consequences, could she? That thought followed her into her dreams—dreams of the past, the present, and of what they might be again.

Chapter 12

From Old Man Turner's Journal:
Don't sweat the small stuff. In the end, you realize it's all small stuff.

Thanksgiving arrived bright and sunny—far too damn bright and sunny in Cybil's book. The holiday brought with it frigid temperatures, the promise of snow forecasted for the weekend, and gnawing indecision over what to do about Miles.

No clearer in the light of day about the choice before her, Cybil spent the morning inhaling coffee, getting herself ready for the afternoon at Abby and Nate's, and working on her pies. At least while making the pies, she concentrated on her task, instead of the nagging uncertainty plaguing her. Or rather, she tried to.

Miles… What in the world was the man thinking? Did he not remember how their relationship had ended? She still bore the scorch marks on her heart from the disastrous flames.

She burned her finger on a pie pan because she wasn't

paying attention. No more thinking of Miles, and how he felt like sin pressed up against her.

Work was what mattered. If it snowed Friday night, she had a fifty-fifty shot of people not showing up for classes at the studio Saturday morning, which would put a dent in her earnings for this month. She did have quite a few people who had signed up for her monthly, all-access class pass. However, she also had enough drop-ins—on the weekends in particular—to warrant worry if she had to cancel classes due to Mother Nature's finicky temperament.

Cybil moved around the kitchen, cleaning up spilled flour and spices, while her three apple pies bubbled and baked in the oven. She loved the homey smell of apple pies baking. She made a killer apple pie, with a buttery, flaky crust that people tended to lose their minds over. Her mom had taught her the recipe. Anytime she made it, she felt close to her mother, like she was still there with her. She remembered the soft smile her mom had worn when she cooked, typically humming a tune, off-key, but blissfully happy. Her parents' marriage had never been perfect, but Cybil had never doubted for a second that they were madly in love with each other, even after twenty years of marriage. They'd been high school sweethearts and were married right after graduation. Her mom had Cybil when she was twenty, then died at thirty-eight.

No matter how much time passed, not a day went by where she didn't miss them terribly. It was worse during the holidays. Her mom had taken such joy in cooking Thanksgiving dinner for the family. Many times, her dad had been on call or had to work the holiday. One time, when Cybil was twelve, her mother made the entire Thanksgiving meal, boxed it up, and they'd taken it to the station so they could eat the feast together as a family. Some of the other officers on duty had joined in, with grand appreciation of the meal her mom had created.

Their parents had given her and Tessa such a firm foundation, showing them not just with words but also their deeds what a healthy, stable, loving relationship should look like. Cybil supposed that was why, when it came to dating, she didn't want booty calls, or for-a-good-time hookups. She wanted the all-in-forever type of affair. It was part of what made her first two dates with the Matchmakers app so disappointing.

And her reaction to Miles even more alarming.

At one time, she had believed with her whole heart that they were forever. That he was the man she would be with her whole life. And the thing was, she wanted him still. There was no question in her mind on that point. No, her bone of contention, what made her hesitate, was whether she could be with him and not allow it to touch her heart.

There was this little voice inside her whispering: *but what if it could be even better than before*? Yet she was too afraid to hope for that, although she realized it made her a coward.

The thing was, the implosion of their relationship and the mitigating factors that led to it had defined her existence. It had turned her into the person she was today. But the pain of that time, her broken heart, had never truly mended or ceased to ache.

Cybil glanced at the timer on her pies and sat at the kitchen table with her laptop.

She could use a drink—or twenty, considering the week she'd had—and it was only Thursday. For now, she needed to ignore Miles, even though she feared the magnetic pull would only get worse the longer he was in town.

On the bright side, she had received a notice on her phone app from Matchmakers that she had a perfect match. Apparently, this *Runner4Life* prospect was ninety-nine-point-seven percent compatible with her. The two guys she had met this week had barely been eighty percent. So she was infinitely curious as to whom it might be. The guy she'd canceled on last night had messaged her back and told her that if she wasn't willing to keep their date then she shouldn't bother contacting him again. Which meant suitor number three was a dud as well.

Fingers crossed on prospect number four. She logged in to the site and clicked on the profile.

Sweet Jesus on a biscuit!

No. It wasn't possible. This couldn't be happening.

Miles? Again? She was trying to avoid him, not date him. Miles was *Runner4Life*? As in: the only man she'd ever loved, Miles Keaton? Matchmakers rated him as her perfect match. What was the weird algorithm that had decided her fate?

It boggled her mind. Cybil never would have thought Miles would sign up for online dating. She hadn't been lying when he'd come to her rescue last night—the single female population at Smitty's had thrown themselves at him, standing in line or in groups to talk to him.

And yet, he claimed that she was the only one he wanted. She hated what hearing those words had done to her, the tiny thrill that had shot through her and melted her insides to the consistency of a campfire marshmallow. Miles was a lot of things, but he wasn't a liar, nor did he say things he didn't mean. Those words had wedged a crack in the foundation of the wall around her heart.

However, the proof was in the pudding. He was on Matchmakers, and looking for that special someone. He smiled back at her from his profile picture. Her belly flipped over and exposed its soft underside. This was the face that had haunted her dreams for the last thirteen years. He made her heart ache. They'd been so young—far too young to be prepared for the consequences of their actions.

In the years since their relationship had ended in flames, she had dated and slept with other men. But none of them had stuck. None had made her feel even half of what she'd felt for Miles.

It hurt to be near him. He was a reminder of everything

she'd lost. There were parts of her soul that had died in the fallout.

"Oh my god, those pies smell amazing. Are you ready yet? Oh, you've got another match. Let's see who it is, it's… oh my god!" Tessa exclaimed, her mouth dropping open as she stared at the computer screen.

"I know. What the hell is wrong with this site? And that's not even the worst part."

"Miles is your perfect match? What do you mean, that's not the worst part? Your ex is a perfect match for you."

"My truck wouldn't start after my shift. Miles was driving by and came to my rescue. Once he got my truck running, he told me that he wants me. That he wants to give *us* another shot. And now this." Cybil gestured at his smiling face on her computer screen.

"Holy smokes! He said all that? Well, if he wants you, why is he on the dating site?"

"I don't know. Miles never lied, at least, not when I knew him. Who's to say that hasn't changed in thirteen years?" It all left her more confused than ever. If he wanted her and only her, why would he be on a dating website?

"Cybil, are you sure things are done between you two? Besides," Tessa gestured at the computer, "the algorithms on those sites are pretty damn accurate. I don't ever think I've seen a match rated that high before."

"I don't know. We called a ceasefire yesterday morning. And then there was his rescue last night. I won't deny that he makes me feel so damn much, it scares the hell out of me. I don't know that I can go there again with him. Tessa, he makes me ache, and not all of it's good. I don't know if I have it in me to separate the past from the present." Not to mention there was that damn promise that was mocking her at this point. A promise neither her sister nor Miles knew anything about.

"Okay, hear me out. Before you say no, I think you should really consider giving him another shot."

"But—"

"Just think about it. Don't shoot him down just yet. It's okay not to know the answer. But I remember when you were with him, and how happy you were. I know I've never been in love like that. All I'm saying is think about it, and him. Take whatever time you need, but make sure if you say no that it's not out of fear. And I've got your back, whatever you decide."

"I don't know. Can we drop the topic for today and come back to it? I just, god, I need time to think, because I don't know." The truth was, Cybil was terrified.

"Sure, but don't take too long or someone else will snap him up. Miles is pretty hot. I'm sure all the single ladies in Echo Springs will line up for the fresh man meat in town."

They already were, and Cybil hadn't cared for the vicious jealousy she had experienced seeing it.

"Man meat? Sounds like he's food for a zombie. I know you're right, and I'll think about it. Don't say anything though, even to Abby. Until I know what I want to do, I would rather he not catch wind of it." Cybil exited out of the website and shut her computer. A part of her wanted to run off to Bali and teach beachside yoga so that she could avoid her past.

"I won't, pinky swear." Tessa held up her pinky in their age-old tradition. Cybil hooked her little finger around her sister's just as the kitchen timer dinged to say that the pies were done.

Leaving her sister at the table, Cybil went to the stove and removed her steaming, bubbling apple pies. From the delicious scent, she knew they had come out perfect.

Gus waddled into the kitchen, his tail twitching and his nose up in the air, sniffing. Cybil pointed at the big ball of black and white fur. "This isn't for you, buddy, no matter how much you beg. Tessa, why don't you feed him before we leave? That way, he won't be tempted to get into our pie while we're gone."

"Not a bad idea. Come here, Gus-Gus. You want your Thanksgiving dinner, sweetie pie?" Tessa took care of a meowing Gus. "And you need to be good while we're gone, and maybe I can bring some turkey back for you."

Cybil covered the pie she had made for the two of them with a large casserole dish on the stove that should, hopefully, keep Gus away from it. They didn't allow him on the counters. That didn't mean she hadn't caught the furball up there, nosing through stuff. He was a cat; what could she do?

The other two pies, she nestled on a large cookie sheet and wrapped with aluminum foil.

"I need to change into something that doesn't have flour on it, and then we can head over to Nate and Abby's place." Cybil glanced at her stained shirt. It was why she'd waited until the baking was finished to put on her holiday wear.

"I like the look you're sporting now. Sort of a distressed, fashionably-dusted-with-cooking-splatters type of style," Tessa teased, lightening the mood.

Cybil raised a brow at that. "And you look ready for a turn on the catwalk instead of dinner at Abby and Nate's."

"Well, it is a holiday," Tessa replied. She was wearing a skintight—as in, the material was practically a second skin—black and burgundy horizontal striped dress that ended mid-thigh, and was paired with knee-high black leather boots.

"Uh huh."

"What does that mean?" Tessa blustered. Her spine straightened up a bit. Even in her heels, Tessa was still shorter than Cybil by about two inches. Her diminutive frame didn't diminish her larger-than-life personality.

"Only that I know you well. And you don't get this dressed up unless there's a man involved. That's an *I'm going to knock their damn socks off* kind of dress. You sure you don't have a thing for Jacob, still? Because from the way you're dressed, it looks like you're going fishing to catch a man. Spill the beans." Cybil gave her an arched glare, turning the tables on her sister for once.

Tessa returned her glance with a blasé, unfazed stare. "I don't know what you're talking about. There's nothing there with Jacob. Besides, I'm part of the auction tonight and want to look my best. Since your truck is on the fritz, we should take my car. Don't you think?"

"Nice deflection. Yeah, we should. I doubt lightning will strike twice, and I would rather not get stuck in Smitty's parking lot. Let me get dressed, and we can leave. Do you want to drive, or do you want me to?"

"Nope, you be the driver tonight. I would rather be able to drink."

So would Cybil. Then again, knowing that Miles would be at Nate and Abby's, she figured it was better if she maintained a cool head, clear of any substances. She was already having a difficult enough time around him sober.

"Give me ten minutes and I will be ready." Cybil headed up to her room. She already had her outfit picked out for tonight. But now that she had seen what her sister had on, she looked at the jeans and top with a critical eye. Damn. She couldn't be outdone at the auction by her little sis. She thumbed through her closet and settled on a bronze metallic sheath dress that fit like a dream, ended just above her knees, and still looked amazing with her black, heeled boots. Her boots did not kill her feet too terribly much waiting tables, and the vee neckline displayed her cleavage nicely.

She touched up her makeup, slicking on a merlot lipstick that really popped, and headed back down. "I'm ready. Let's get going."

"Where did you get that dress? If you're looking to impress a certain someone who shall remain nameless, you will."

"That last time I headed into Denver, I picked it up." Cybil shrugged her coat on, and grabbed her keys, purse, and the pies before heading out the door.

They left their house, leaving a single light on since it would likely be past midnight when they returned, judging by past auctions. Their place wasn't a house really, but one side of a two-story house that had been split into a duplex. It wasn't in the best part of town, but it wasn't in the worst part either. They'd moved in there not long after their parents had passed, when it became evident that Cybil wasn't going to be able to afford the house her parents had rented on her own. Even with everything the town had done for them, Cybil had had enough foresight to understand that, if they were going to survive on their own, she'd have to get smart about money. Moving into the duplex had cut their rent payment by a third, which Cybil had been able to squirrel away for other things. Like paying for her sister's braces, and helping Tessa attend college. Hell, just getting her through high school had been challenging enough.

There had been a stretch while Tessa was in high school that she'd resented Cybil acting like she was her parent. They'd butted heads all throughout Tessa's junior year, and Cybil had wondered if she was going to get her sister to graduate at all.

But then Tessa had pushed through her rebellion and settled down in her senior year. Their relationship was solid, even if at times Tessa did roll her eyes and reply with a yes-mom, exasperated mentality.

Cybil drove through town and grimaced, muttering under her breath. Every stationary object along Main Street had been decorated for the holidays. The town looked like Santa's Workshop on steroids. She breathed deeply. All she had to do was survive the holidays, and then she could go back to being… well, she didn't really know anymore. It wasn't like she was miserable, because she wasn't.

She had created a decent life for herself despite immense tragedy. A life she was proud of, and the fact that Tessa was a fully functioning, responsible adult meant she had managed the whole life-tossing-her-lemons bit well enough.

But that didn't mean she didn't feel a lack, because it was there, filling her with a rather glum outlook. She'd begun to wonder if this was all there would be for her. She was achieving her dream, and yet, she wasn't satisfied. And, she had to admit to herself, she was lonely. She had her sister and Abby, friends like Nate, and a town that had become hers, but she'd begun to feel like an island.

And suddenly, she had someone standing on her shore who had always understood her, telling her she didn't have to be alone anymore.

Chapter 13

From Old Man Turner's Journal:
Sometimes, you have to stop worrying about what you can't fix, and concentrate on the joy of the moment instead.

When Cybil pulled into Nate and Abby's driveway, she expelled a pent-up breath. Knowing she was going to face Miles again across the dinner table after the revelations of the last twenty-four revealing hours was going to be interesting, especially given the fact that she had no idea what to think or feel or do. One, because of what he'd said to her in Smitty's parking lot when he came to her rescue. And two, because he was on Matchmakers. Had he seen that they were each other's perfect match? If she knew Miles, he would use it as fuel to add to his argument.

His SUV wasn't in Abby's driveway. Maybe she had been granted a reprieve and he had been too busy to see that they had been matched. Could she delete herself from the app before he saw it? And did she really want to do that? The whole purpose of joining the dating website was to find someone other than Miles. Not that the stupid thing helped when they matched her to the one person she was trying to avoid.

Cybil had no idea what she was going to say to him if he brought it up. She couldn't date Miles again. Could she? Did she want to date him? It was a conundrum, since her heart and her head weren't in agreement.

"You okay?" Tessa asked, holding the cookie sheet with the pies in one hand with the other on the door handle.

"Not really. What do I say if Miles brings up the dating app?" Cybil refrained from nibbling on her bottom lip and ruining her lipstick, but just barely.

"Oh god, I hadn't thought of that. Uh, well, that's what I'm here for, right? Ride or die. If he mentions something, signal me, and I'll help change the subject or think up a distraction."

She nodded. "Okay, that's a good plan. And what if the change of subject doesn't work?"

"Well, I could always plant one on Jacob. That would take the focus off the two of you really quick."

"Would you do that, really?"

"Sure, why not? Who knows, maybe the guy will go all caveman on me." Tessa sighed dejectedly.

"You do still have a thing!" Cybil gasped.

"I don't know what you're talking about. Don't worry about today. I've got your back. Now, let's go break some hearts." Tessa winked with a gamine grin.

Cybil laughed. She couldn't help it. Her sister was crazy with her willingness to engage in over the top shenanigans merely as a distraction to help her out. And she would deal with Miles being on Matchmakers the best way she knew how today: by avoiding the topic if possible. If not, she had back up. "Thanks, Tessa."

"Hey, it's what I'm here for: to help you hide the body when you need it. Let's get inside, because I'm starving, and you know Abby will have a ton of food."

Cybil smirked. "I do. Come on. Let's go in before we freeze our asses off. Want me to carry the pies?"

"I've got them. No worries."

Cybil admired the decorations already displayed on the front porch. Christmas lights lit the concrete path, lined the roof ledge, and were wrapped around the porch balustrades. The front door sported a wreath with bright silver and blue ornaments. She had to admit, as much she as didn't like the time of year, the decorations were pretty. Ready to take the deep plunge, she knocked on the front door.

Nate greeted them with a warm smile on his handsome face as he swung the door open wide. "Tessa, Cybil, glad you two could make it. Happy Thanksgiving. Come on in out of the cold."

Even though it was a holiday, he was dressed in his usual jeans and a flannel shirt, this one a dark forest green with the sleeves rolled up to his elbows, displaying his muscular forearms. Cybil wondered if the man owned a shirt that wasn't flannel, and whether he would appear at his own wedding dressed in a flannel and jeans.

"Where's the horse imitating a dog?" Tessa asked, glancing around the foyer in a search for Rufus, the Great Dane who fancied himself a lap dog and was harmless, for the most part. The big guy had no concept of how large he really was, and tended to be the proverbial bull in a china shop.

"He's currently grounded and spending some quality time next door. He ate one of Abby's pies when neither of us were looking," Nate said, with an undercurrent of exasperation laced with love in his tone.

"Well, then I'm glad I made a few pies to bring along." Cybil nodded to the cookie sheet in Tessa's hands.

"Oh, that's great. Here let me take those for you, Tessa." Nate hoisted the sheet from Tessa as they entered. The house smelled divine, with mouth-watering scents emanating from the kitchen.

"Thanks for bringing these. You both remember Jacob? He'll take your coats for you," Nate said, indicating the Goliath lookalike in the living room. Jacob was a good six-foot-six and built like a linebacker, with a close-cropped black beard and full head of thick, black hair that fell in rich waves to his square jawline. He was dressed semi-casually in jeans that displayed thickly hewn thighs, and a deep cobalt dress shirt that was open at the neck. But it was the man's eyes that she'd always thought were beautiful—a pure, pale jade green that always seemed to carry a hint of sadness.

"It's nice to see you again," Cybil said with a smile, removing her coat, and handing it over.

"You too, Cybil. Happy Thanksgiving," Jacob replied, taking her coat, and then he glanced at Tessa. "Tessa, let me take that for you."

"Thanks, big guy. Happy Thanksgiving." Tessa dropped her coat into his large hands and sailed past them down the hall to the kitchen with an, "I'll just see if Abby needs any help."

Jacob's gaze followed her sister and was trained on her form with such blatant hunger and longing, Cybil almost took a step back. *Well, well, well, what do we have here?* She would have to tell Tessa about the overt display of desire later. Because the guy wasn't cold and uninterested in her—far from it. After Jacob hung their coats up on the rack in the foyer, he trod toward the kitchen, likely in search of Tessa.

"I'm going to put these pies where Abby wants them. Can I get you anything to drink while I'm at it?" Nate asked, holding the pies.

"I'm good for now, thanks."

Cybil followed Nate toward the back of the house. When they were halfway between the kitchen and foyer, there was a loud knock at the front door. Nate shot her a look over his shoulder. "Do you mind getting that for me?"

"Sure." Cybil headed back toward the door. Fingers of dread curled inside her chest. She knew that it had to be Miles, since everyone else who'd been invited was already in attendance. She steeled herself, straightening her backbone, and promised herself she would indulge in a bottle of wine when she got home tonight. She drew the door open with a prayer that the evening would go smoothly without any hiccups.

"Cybil, I didn't expect to see you here tonight. Miles never tells me anything. Don't you look stunning," Ella Keaton exclaimed, a smile transforming the older woman's elegant face. Her tall, willowy form crossed the threshold, and she pulled Cybil in for a tight hug. Her penchant for enthusiastic hugging was something Cybil had always adored about Ella. As she returned the embrace, Cybil spied Miles over his mother's shoulder.

Instead of the pain that normally accompanied their interactions, she experienced a feminine flutter, a recognition of the magnetic pull he exuded.

He was dressed casually—for Miles anyway, these days—in a pair of jeans that rode low on his lean, muscular hips, a turquoise button-down dress shirt, and a charcoal dress coat. The rich color of his shirt made the hint of a tan on his golden skin glow. The man simply took her breath away. After all this time, a single glance from him turned her insides molten and her body came alive.

Damn him. It wasn't fair that he could turn her inside out with his presence. He'd stirred her up last night with his whole spiel about wanting her.

His gaze traveled over Cybil's form, from the top of her head to the soles of her boots, and back up again. When his eyes met hers, she sucked in a breath at the lust darkening his gaze. And then he smiled that same *devil may care* grin he'd used on her in days gone by.

Awareness whipped through her.

A single, sexy, sardonic curve of his full lips smashed through her impenetrable walls as if they were tissue paper. Her body warmed beneath his hot gaze.

Stupid body for not listening to her tell it no, that he was off limits. She tore her gaze from his knowing one—she had to, or she would do something that she couldn't take back, like melt into a puddle of need at his large feet.

"Ella, it's good to see you," Cybil murmured as she withdrew from the embrace and smiled. Ella's golden hair was so like her son's, but with a smattering of silver highlights.

"Cybil, Happy Thanksgiving," Miles stated with a nod as he entered and closed the door.

"Ah thanks. You too."

Nate joined them in the foyer. *Thank god!* "I'll be back." And like a coward, Cybil escaped into the kitchen. If she was going to survive this dinner intact, she needed a breather and reinforcements. "Abby, your cooking never fails to impress me," she said, eyeing the pots and pans Abby had arranged on the professional grade, stainless steel stovetop. The granite counters were covered with dishes. And somehow, Abby made the canary yellow room the focus of the house.

"Cybil, I'm thrilled you and Tessa came today. I love your dress. Makes me think we need another shopping excursion before winter sets in. Maybe we could do a girls trip to one of the ski towns and check out their offerings." Abby happily moved around the kitchen with ease, not even consulting a recipe book. It spoke of her comfort in the kitchen; a skill Cybil had yet to master.

"I'm always up for shopping. It would be fun to do some holiday shopping in Vale or Breckenridge. We could make a day of it. What can I do to help?" Cybil asked, evaluating the organized chaos and wondering what she could handle without messing up.

Tessa's hands were full as she carted a dish into the adjoining dining room. Jacob stood at the kitchen table with an electric carver, carving a massive turkey.

"Here, why don't you help your sister take those dishes," Abby nodded at the ones she had just pulled from the oven, "into the dining room. There are extra potholders on the counter beside them. And there are food warmers set up in the dining room to put the dishes on," she added as she whipped the potatoes with an electric beater.

Cybil and Tessa worked alongside Abby, getting dishes arranged on the sideboard in the dining room, along with serving utensils. The dining table was already decorated with china, silverware, and crystal glasses. Cybil filled water goblets and wine glasses, admiring the simple pattern on the china. Nate and Abby's home looked like something out of a magazine. And she loved the hardwood floors complemented by taupe walls, with an ivory trim at the base and crown.

"Everyone, dinner is served," Nate's voice boomed.

The group adjourned into the dining room. Abby had decorated the table with her great-aunt's china. The ivory plates, bowls, and serving platters were rimmed with gold and had delicate yellow and blue flower patterns. Fresh-baked rolls and dishes with fresh butter were placed on the dining table within easy reach. There was a centerpiece of holly, and ivory taper candles in a sterling silver candelabra, the flames glowing softly golden. The air was festive as peopled filled their plates with turkey, stuffing, fluffy mashed potatoes, and all the delicious fixings Abby had created for their holiday feast.

With their plates full, they gathered around the table, with

Nate and Abby sitting at each end. Miles and his mom took one side, leaving Cybil and Tessa on the opposite side. Jacob, interestingly enough, sat beside Tessa—to her sister's dismay or delight, Cybil wasn't sure. But from the proprietary gleam on Jacob's face, Tessa's dress had done the job she had wanted it to do.

Once they were all seated, their plates overflowing with the delicious-smelling meal, Nate lifted his wine glass and said, "Thank you all for coming today. I'm thankful to share this day with each of you. And to Abby, for slaving away for all of us in creating this magnificent feast. Happy Thanksgiving!"

"Happy Thanksgiving!" everyone said, with glasses raised.

"Now let's eat," Nate exclaimed after he took a sip of his wine.

"I'm way ahead of you. Abby, you've outdone yourself. I'm already scouting for seconds," Jacob proclaimed. "You should toss this one over and run away with me."

At that, everyone laughed. The mood was congenial and friendly, the holiday spirit infusing everything. The food was spectacular, and Cybil enjoyed herself more than she thought she would. Yet it was taking every ounce of her energy to ignore Miles. She would glance up innocuously, and find him watching her with his intense gaze. More than once, her breath hitched in her throat and her pulse fluttered at the unexpected flares of heat in his eyes. Then he would shift his attention and smile at something his mom said, or join in the ongoing conversation flowing with ease around the table.

Cybil's teeth were on edge at the yo-yo-ing emotions tumbling through her at such a rapid pace that her entire being felt like it was on a tilt-a-whirl, and she couldn't seem to find decent footing.

"How's your sister doing, Nate?" Ella asked. "I'm surprised she's not here today."

Nate swallowed a bite then replied, "Well, she's not here because she's in the process of moving back to Echo Springs."

"Is she really? That's wonderful news," Ella exclaimed.

Nate nodded. "She's just waiting for her house to sell. She has a few offers. But she wants to get rid of the house first and is busy getting everything ready, or she would be here."

"Do you need me out of the house for your sister?" Miles asked, buttering another roll.

Natc shook his head. "No, if anything, we'll have her stay here if she needs it."

"Do you not like the house?" Abby asked, lowering her fork, her head tilted to the side with a worried expression.

"Well, since you moved the dolls up into the attic, it's much better." Miles quirked a grin. "But I'm actually going to be building my own place."

"Really?" Jacob said, rising to get another helping. "You didn't tell me that."

Miles nodded. "I have a parcel of land that I inherited from my dad. Prospect Point. I'm having Aiden O'Toole draw up plans for it now. We'll break ground this spring."

"That's right. I'd forgotten about that. It's up near the McKinley place," Nate said, rubbing a hand over his chin.

Cybil's heart dropped into her toes at the mention of Prospect Point. It was their spot—or it had been, once upon a time. They'd gone there so many times that summer. With perfect clarity, she could remember the way the earth smelled, how the starry sky looked from that vantage point, and the sounds of nature all around.

She had loved their spot. It had been their private Eden. Cybil had lost her virginity there on a hot Fourth of July night, when the stars had been out in full force.

"It's not the McKinley place anymore. It's officially mine. Now it's the Donovan place, and that means we'll be neighbors." Jacob toasted Miles with his glass.

Miles grinned and toasted him back. "Yeah, who would have thought we'd both end up here?"

Jacob nodded. "Yep. The bones of the house are good, but the interior of it needs a major overhaul. I've got Aiden working on it. The wiring is crap, and for what I do, I need it to be as high tech as possible."

"We should talk. I want to install solar panels and have a generator that's off the grid."

Jacob smiled then. "Yes, we should. Wait until you see all the gadgets I'm having installed."

"Great, we'll end up being ground zero when robots take over the globe," Tessa said with a roll of her eyes.

Jacob's massive shoulders shrugged in a totally male move. "Perhaps. But at least I'll be useful to the robots."

"For a while," Tessa murmured.

Abby said, "We heard from Sam this morning. He said to pass along his love to everyone, and Happy Thanksgiving."

"What movie is he working on now?" Ella asked.

Nate replied, "Some big blockbuster with that action star, Dirk Johnson."

"I just love watching him," Ella said with a sigh.

"We do too," Abby said with a wink.

Miles looked decidedly uncomfortable with his mom beside him. Then Ella glanced at him. "What? Just because I'm old that doesn't mean I'm dead. And that actor would make any woman's pulse race."

Cybil held up her wine glass and said, "Hear, hear. I agree."

"Us too," Tessa and Abby said, raising their glasses.

"And here I thought I was the one who made your heart race," Nate teased Abby with a sly grin.

Abby cast Nate a cheeky grin. "You do, but I've gotta say that if Dirk came calling, as much as I love you…"

"I bet I could convince you otherwise," Nate said, his voice husky.

Abby blushed. The heat between them could break a thermometer.

Miles interjected, "By the way, the last few days at the office have been a little strange. Is there a new ladies club that I've not heard about that brings people casseroles? I've been inundated."

Jacob barked with rich laughter, and Nate chuckled. Cybil sucked in a breath. Oh no. Code red. This wasn't good. She glanced at Tessa with wide, panicked eyes. Tessa gave her a thumbs up to let her know that she was ready to intercede.

"You did this to me?" Miles accused Jacob, his brows raised in shock.

"Nate and I did, yeah. We signed you up for that new dating website, Matchmakers. And one of the things you love most is a good casserole. Ha ha!" Jacob guffawed, his voice booming with glee.

"Take it back. Undo it," Miles demanded.

Jacob shook his head. "Nah, we think it's funny as hell." He whipped out his phone. "Oh, would you look at that? It's already found you the perfect match: *YogaRose*."

No!

Cybil blanched and almost inhaled her sip of wine. She choked. She had to make them stop.

"Well, I'll be damned," Jacob said, eyeballing Cybil, and then looking at the rest of the group. "Seems like the person who's your perfect match is sitting at the table."

Her palms went clammy and her stomach dropped into her toes.

Cybil shot Jacob a pleading glance, but he didn't see her. Instead, he shot a surprised glance, eyebrow quirked, at Tessa.

Cybil wanted to crawl beneath the table and start digging a hole to hide in. Everyone sat in a frozen tableau, forks and glasses in mid-air. She wondered if she would asphyxiate from the sheer lack of oxygen. Where was Tessa with the big save?

She couldn't look at Miles and stared down at her plate.

Abby must have sensed Cybil's mounting horror and blurted,

"It's me, I'll admit it. Miles and I are predestined to have a torrid love affair."

Abby's response drew a round of laughter from everyone at the table—except from Cybil—diffusing the sudden tension. Cybil kept her gaze off Miles, too uncomfortable to be able to look at him. At least now she knew he had not lied to her last night.

Then Abby asked, "Who's ready for pie?"

After the group's assent, they cleared the table of dinner dishes and helped Abby cart leftovers into the kitchen, with Miles getting Jacob to hand over the login for the account he had created for Miles.

Everyone already knew Cybil was the one on the dating profile. It wasn't like it was hard to deduce, or a state secret. But what did Miles think about her being on the dating app? And why did it matter?

While Abby was getting leftovers put away in the kitchen, Cybil dished up pie for everyone. She handed Tessa a slice. "Where was the save when I needed it?" she whispered furiously, glancing around to make sure no one overheard.

"Sorry, I didn't think he would be that blatant about it. I did kick his shin, for all the good it did," Tessa replied in a whisper.

So that's what that exchange had been about. "Don't worry about it." She waved Tessa off and handed out slices.

"Cybil, this apple pie is divine," Ella murmured.

"Thank you, it was our mom's recipe. It's a tradition we make every year," Cybil explained as she resumed her seat with her own slice.

"Oh, then that makes this even more special," Ella commented and glanced away, but not before Cybil spied the guilt in her eyes. Did she know what it cost Cybil every day to keep the promise she had made her all that time ago?

"The pumpkin pie is great too, Abby," Miles commented.

"I'm so sorry that there isn't more pumpkin available. But

Rufus, being the lovable knucklehead that he is, decided he wanted a snack when I turned away for a few minutes," Abby said with a sigh, and glanced at Nate. "Too bad I happen to love the big lug to distraction."

Nate gazed across the table at Abby, the love between them almost a living, breathing entity.

Cybil looked at her watch. She had time before she needed to get to Smitty's, but she wanted a chance to collect herself.

"Always in a hurry," Miles murmured, studying her with an unreadable expression.

"Just checking the time. Everyone participating in the auction has to be there by seven. Festivities kick off at seven-thirty. I don't want to be late and let Burke down."

"Burke knows everyone has family stuff to do with the holiday. I don't think he will hold being a little late against you. But we'll all leave here in a bit. I can even provide you with a police escort if need be." Nate winked.

"Yes, but I work for him, too, beyond the auction. The man can complain like a little girl when it's warranted," Cybil said with a shake of her head, drawing a few male laughs.

She shrugged. It was true. She liked Burke. He was a really decent guy. But when it came to running the bar and grill, he used the skills he'd learned in the army, and acted like a drill sergeant most days. When that didn't work, he complained. There had been more than one night when she had wanted to bash the man's head with her tray.

"Miles, I don't want you all to be late for the event, so we should get going. Abby and Nate, thank you so much for inviting us to share the holiday with you. It was one of the best meals I've ever had." Ella rose and did a turn around the room, giving everyone a hug and effectively ending the meal.

Cybil and Tessa weren't far behind, with Abby sending them off with leftovers they needed to drop off at home before they headed to the bar. It wasn't until they were back in Tessa's car that Cybil breathed a small sigh of relief. She had made it through, even with the hiccup of the dating app being mentioned.

But the question still plagued her: did she want to try again with Miles?

Chapter 14

From Old Man Turner's Journal:
It's better to take a roll of the dice than to sit on the sidelines and miss your shot.

"Dinner was lovely. It was wonderful getting to spend the holiday this year with your friends and then come home to my bed," his mom said with a pleasant smile when he pulled into her driveway.

"Yeah, it was nice. You sure you don't want to come to the auction? I'm positive people would love to see you there." Miles escorted her up the walkway to her front door, his mind on the auction and one woman in particular.

At the door, Ella waved him off. "Oh no, honey. After that feast, I'm ready to curl up in my pajamas with that romance Abby recommended. Unless you really want me to go."

He shook his head. "It makes no difference to me. I just didn't want you to think I was leaving you alone on a holiday."

"Is it because Cybil will be there?"

"No. Not at all," he deflected, when it was exactly the reason he'd asked.

His mom tilted her head. "Honey, you and Cybil have always been drawn to one another like magnets. It worried me how intense your relationship with her was back then. I know things didn't end well between the two of you when you were in college, but you're both adults now. It's perfectly okay if you're interested in dating her again."

"I love you, Mom." She had always had the unerring ability to see what was in his mind and heart with perfect clarity, often better than he could.

"I love you too. Have fun tonight and live a little. It's not going to hurt you." She kissed his cheek and hugged him.

"I'm going to bring in some more firewood for you and check the generator quickly before I go. If we get snow this weekend, I'll come by as soon as it's safe to clear your drive."

"What would I do without you?" Ella beamed.

"You'll never have to find out." Miles ushered her inside the large, two-story rustic chalet that resembled a modified log cabin. It was the house he had grown up in. Over the years, she had made changes to the place, although most of the exterior stone and wood remained the same. Much of the furniture had been updated, and now there was a flat-screen television he'd installed for her in the living room a year or so ago.

Miles double-checked that the generator battery was fully charged and brought in more firewood from the stack out back to ensure she had enough in case the snowstorm forecasted for tomorrow night hit.

He drove from his mom's house in the Echo Heights subdivision, with its manicured lawns and tasteful two-story homes, to Smitty's Bar and Grill. He liked Burke, the owner of the bar. Miles had been ahead of him by two years at Echo Springs High. They'd hung out a few times after Burke returned from his stint in the military. Smitty's Bar and Grill was pretty much the place to be in town if you wanted a drink, dinner, and some company. It was really the only venue to visit without teenagers hanging around, like they did at the pizza place, cineplex or bowling alley.

Miles couldn't believe the chuckleheads he called friends had signed him up for an online dating service without telling him. That did explain the myriad number of casseroles he'd received this week, though. At least he had gotten the login and password from Jacob so he could shut it down.

There was only one woman he was interested in.

Cybil.

And it explained why she had been out on a date Monday night with that old geezer. She was *YogaRose* on the dating app—she had to be—and she was his perfect match, apparently. Miles hated to admit it but he agreed with the website.

When she'd opened the door at Nate's earlier, he had been struck dumb at the sight of her in that dress that displayed her knockout form. It had taken him a few moments to find his voice. Need, hot and heavy, had blasted through him. If they had been alone, he would have charmed her into illicit activities over at his place.

The woman drove him insane. He'd not been lying when he'd told her that he wanted another chance, last night in this very parking lot. And she'd evaded him all throughout dinner this evening. Not once had he been able to get her alone, either, to ask if she had reported the incident with Dotson to Nate.

It made him wonder if the dating website was why Dotson had thought he could put his hands on her the other day. Miles had figured it was merely the guy being a prick as usual. But had she been dating him, hooking up through the website? What did he really know about her life now? He hadn't even known she had her own studio, or that it was in the building he was buying. For all he knew, she could be seeing Dotson.

The thought of Cybil with anyone made his gut clench. The thought of Cybil with his arch nemesis caused his blood to boil.

Miles fought back the urge to locate Dotson and beat the truth out of him. The only thing that stopped him was that he was a respected attorney, not some hotshot who felt he needed to defend his territory. Lord knew if he took a swipe at Dotson, it would put Nate in a pickle. Hell, Nate might join in, and then they would both be up a creek.

And Cybil being a member of the dating site—discovering that little nugget of information at dinner tonight—made Miles reconsider his approach to get her back into his life. He, rather egotistically, had thought he could make the first move, charm her, and that she would fall willingly back into his arms and, eventually, his bed. Instead, the confounded woman was avoiding him throughout the Thanksgiving festivities. Perhaps a bolder approach was warranted on his part.

That was why he was going to bid on the date with her tonight, and he would win. Cybil couldn't turn him down for the date then. It would chafe too much at her sense of honor and integrity to back out.

Tonight, the parking lot of Smitty's was overflowing with cars. Miles claimed one of the last remaining spaces, and wondered how Cybil would react to him bidding on her. Any time he got her alone, her defenses went sky high. Although last night, for just a moment, she had softened—her body pressed against his had lost its rigid stance, and seemed to melt against him.

Those few moments of surrender gave him hope that with enough patience and perseverance, he would win.

Determination filled Miles as he strode inside. The dark wooden tables had been rearranged near the stage for the auction. Holiday decorations abounded, with miles of garland wrapped around every stationary object. A few Christmas trees were spread throughout the bar, and lots of mistletoe hung from beams in varying intervals, giving the packed venue a jovial atmosphere. It appeared as if at least half the town was in attendance. He spotted Abby and Jacob in a row near the front. Nate must already be back behind the stage area, getting ready for his turn to be offered up as one of the dates. The two waved him over.

"We saved you a seat," Abby said with a friendly smile. Miles liked his best friend's fiancée. She was perfect for him. Her eyes had been haunted when they'd first met, but since she and Nate had fallen for each other, those shadows had vanished. And he'd never seen his buddy so happy.

Jacob grinned at him over the top of her head. "Get your mom home all right?"

"Yeah. I'm still pissed at you over the Matchmakers deal. Don't think you're off the hook for that stunt yet."

"Get your panties out of a twist. He never could take a joke." Jacob leaned closer to Abby with a conspiratorial smirk.

"Ass," Miles replied with half-hearted annoyance. Only Jacob would sign a friend up for a dating website as a joke. The man had a warped sense of humor.

"I like your mom," Abby said, and smiled at Miles. She wasn't gorgeous in the sense of Cybil's one-two punch to the gut, but Abby was the girl-next-door mothers around the globe wished their sons would fall for.

"Yeah, I do too," Miles replied. "You sure I can't convince you to throw over Nate and head to the Bahamas with me?" He playfully nudged her shoulder with his.

Abby smiled. "You're pretty, but—"

The lights went down.

"—I do love that man," she finished as Burke appeared on stage with Nate at his side.

Miles chuckled at Nate's tortured expression. His buddy really didn't want to participate, mainly because of Abby. Not that Miles blamed him. Nate's smile was forced, though the women of Echo Springs didn't seem to mind. They were losing their minds at the sight of Nate and Burke on stage.

Burke was grinning. The way the spotlight hit his chestnut hair, longer now since he was out of the military, made it look like he had an angelic halo. Miles snorted. Burke was anything but angelic. With a microphone in his hand, Burke said, "Thank you all for coming tonight to Smitty's Bar and Grill Annual Thanksgiving Charity Auction! All the proceeds tonight go to help our community's neediest families for the holidays. I would like to hear a big round of applause for all the volunteers tonight, who have graciously donated their time for this cause." He laughed as the crowd went wild. "And this year, we have added some fantastic packages we will be auctioning off, including dinner for two to some of the restaurants in town, great to take that special someone. Tonight is all about having fun and giving to a spectacular cause, so be prepared to open your wallets."

Hoots and hollers abounded.

"First up on our menu tonight is our very own Sheriff Nate Barnes. Our local sheriff grew up here, and this hometown boy works hard to keep the streets of Echo Springs safe for our community."

Another round of applause erupted from the women in the audience. Abby's eyes narrowed slightly as she stared down a few of the more overzealous women in the crowd.

Jacob murmured loudly enough that Miles heard it, "If you need any extra cash in case the bidding gets out of control, I'll cover it. Just bid on him."

"Oh, but I don't—"

"Consider it my wedding present," Jacob stated.

"Deal," Abby replied, and seemed to breathe a sigh of relief.

Burke opened the bidding at a hundred dollars. Abby bid first, but there was some fierce competition. Miles stood as a buffer to keep Abby from marching over to the group of ladies bidding against her and clocking them. One of them was none other than JoAnn Fincher. But finally, with Jacob's urging, Abby outbid them all.

"And the first winning bid of the night, for a date with Sheriff Barnes, goes to Abby Callier!" Burke exclaimed. Abby jumped up and down, then cast JoAnn a haughty glare. JoAnn lifted her nose and turned away with a shrug, ready to swim to less-infested waters, perhaps.

"Next up is Noah Jackson. Noah is a firefighter with our very own Echo Springs Fire Department. Let's start the bidding at one hundred. Do I have one hundred dollars?" Burke said.

The crowd really got into the auction from there. The alcohol was free flowing, and Miles could tell Nate was monitoring the crowd now that his turn on the stage was finished. He'd make sure no one over imbibed, and that those who did had a safe, sober ride home.

Harper Emerson was the next date on the auction block. She was a nurse at Echo Springs Hospital, with red hair and a sultry vixen smile over which the men in the audience got into bidding wars. Miles wondered when Cybil would be up on the auction block. But then he spied her next up, waiting in the wings.

Why was it he could be in a room surrounded by gorgeous women, and the only one who stuck out for him was Cybil, with her storm cloud eyes, raven's wing black hair tumbling over her slim shoulders, and a haughty expression whenever she glanced in his direction?

When it was finally her turn on stage, he leaned forward in his seat, prepared to start bidding. There might be a few men he would have to outbid—he spied interest in the audience.

"Up next is my lovely waitress and yoga guru, Cybil Roe. Can I get a hundred dollars for the chance to take Cybil on a date?" Burke asked.

Miles started to raise his hand.

"A hundred dollars," a voice Miles knew well shouted. He turned his head and saw Dipshit Dotson. Dotson's smarmy grin burned his ass and stoked his fury.

Without thinking about it, Miles shouted, "Five hundred dollars."

"Whoa! I've got five hundred. Can I get five hundred fifty?" Burke asked the crowd.

"Six hundred," the fucking prick yelled.

Miles clenched his hands into fists. "A thousand dollars."

"Holy cow! I've got a thousand big ones. Can I—"

"Twelve hundred," Dotson called out.

"Fifteen hundred!" Miles hollered.

"Sixteen hundred."

Fuck it. The prick was going down. "Two thousand."

Burke laughed. "I've got two thousand dollars for a date with Cybil. Can I get twenty-one hundred?"

Miles glanced at Dotson, who gave him a superior sneer, then Dotson shouted, "Three thousand."

Did the moron really think Miles was going to back down? Apparently so, given the smug satisfaction on the dipshit's face.

"Holy smokes, folks! I've got three thousand. Can I get thirty-one hundred? Anyone?" Burke searched the room and cast Miles a questioning glance. But it was the worry Cybil was trying to hide that pushed his overprotective buttons.

Miles smiled slyly. That fucker wouldn't poach on his territory, and he was putting an end to that bastard's smugness. With utter surety that he would win, Miles announced in a loud, crystal clear voice, "Ten thousand dollars."

The crowd gasped. Jacob sounded like he was choking. Abby cheered. Behind him, Nate laughed with appreciation because he knew what Miles was doing—that the idiot was going down, and doing so publicly. It made Miles feel all warm and fuzzy inside.

"Holy shit, folks! Pardon my language. I've got ten thousand dollars for the date with Cybil. Do I have ten thousand and one?" Burke peered at Dotson. The whole crowd looked at Dotson, all on the edges of their seats.

Dotson, well, he was mighty pissed off. The man appeared

like he had steam coming out his ears. With a scowl marring his face, he shook his head in the negative.

Then Burke said, "I have ten thousand dollars for the date with the lovely Cybil. Going once... going twice... *sold* to Miles Keaton."

The crowd went wild.

Nate clapped him on the back. Jacob applauded with a shit-eating grin. Abby gave him a side hug.

Jesus H. Christ, I've just spent ten grand on a date with Cybil. Well, she was worth every penny. Miles glanced her way and winced. He was going to let her cool off before he approached her to discuss the date and time of their date. The woman had murder in her eyes. Never mind that he had rescued her from Dotson yet again.

While Cybil appeared calm and smiling to most of the audience, Miles knew her well enough to see beyond that. She plastered a brittle smile on her face and strode off the stage, her gait dialed to pissed-off woman. Oh yeah, he was going to give her some time to cool down first.

He headed over to the cashier and was just paying when he felt Cybil's approach. The place was crowded but he could still feel her. After all this time, it was like they were two dowsing rods that seemed calibrated to each other whenever the other was in proximity.

After the cashier handed him back his credit card, he turned to Cybil. He was surprised steam wasn't coming out of her ears.

"Miles, ten thousand? Are you kidding me? He would have stopped before long. And if not, I could handle him. Why did you do that?" Cybil said with exasperation.

"Babe, there was no way I was letting Dotson get near you again."

"But ten thousand? Miles, it's too much."

"So are you upset that I spend my money how I see fit, or that you're not going out with Dotson?"

The rigidity deflated out of her shoulders. "No, I don't want anything to do with him. I just don't understand why you would spend that much on me."

"Because you're worth it. I wasn't lying last night. Besides, it's a tax write-off as a charitable donation." He shrugged and watched the interplay of emotions race over her expressive face.

No one was more surprised than he when she stepped in to him, wrapped her arms around his shoulders, and hugged him. It took him a moment to get over the shock of her touching him of her own free will, but then he pulled her close and held her.

She fit. Perfectly.

Always had.

There had never been any other woman who made him feel the way Cybil always did, like he was the closest to heaven that he would ever be. Every part of his being electrified.

He wanted her. Yesterday, today, and always.

"Thank you. I didn't need saving but thank you just the same," she whispered so that only he could hear, and started to withdraw.

But Miles held tight, not ready to let her go just yet, not when he'd finally got her back where he wanted her. "What night are you free? I'll make all the arrangements."

Cybil shifted in his arms and looked up at him. "Why are you doing this, really? And don't lie."

He noted the way her pulse was at a jackrabbit's pace. She was affected by his nearness, but she wasn't ready to admit it to herself, and least of all him. "I meant what I said last night. I want to be in your life. I want you to give me another shot. And now, you kind of have to go out with me. I mean, I did just spend ten thousand dollars for a night with you," he teased sardonically, taking that opportunity to play with a strand of her hair. It was as soft as he remembered.

The corners of her delectable mouth twitched. "Fine. But you keep your hands to yourself."

Miles smiled; he couldn't help himself. "You want me."

"No, I don't." She shook her head in denial as he backed her against the bar. Her pulse hammered at the base of her neck. Going out on a limb, he cupped her jaw with one hand, and watched her pupils dilate. The rest of the bar seemed to dim when her tongue darted out and moistened her lower lip.

Christ, he wanted her. He had since the moment he met her up at Echo Lake, and his desire hadn't diminished any. If anything, it had grown.

"Yeah, you do. You want me bad," he said, his voice husky and laden with need.

Her hands moved to his chest, pushing him back for some space, and he bit back a moan. How, after thirteen years, could her touch, even one meant to shove him away, still feel so damn good? He let her shove him back but kept boxing her in against the bar. He wasn't letting her out of his sight until he had confirmation of a date and time.

"Miles, I have to work. I need you to let me go."

"I will in a minute. When are we doing this… our date?" he murmured. "And remember, I just spent ten grand for the pleasure of your company. The least you can do is be gracious and give me a night of your precious time."

Cybil sighed. "You did this on purpose, didn't you?"

"And if I did?"

"You never could take no for an answer. Okay, fine, since you went to the trouble of paying way too much—and I will remind you that it was your doing and not mine—I am free Monday night."

He leaned in close. "You never could resist my charm. And remember it's easier just to agree when you know I'm right."

She laughed. "We'll see about that. I'll be done with classes by six on Monday."

"Great. I will pick you up at seven. Should be enough time

for you to get ready. I like this dress, by the way. If you have another like it, wear it for me."

Cybil rolled her eyes but there was a small grin tugging at the corners of her lush mouth. "I'll see what I can do. But I'm not making any promises. Now, will you let me get back to work, or is that against the rules?"

Miles stepped back to give her some space—not much, but enough that she could get by him. "Go ahead. I'll see you Monday."

She wasn't shy as she pushed him back further and slithered past him. He enjoyed seeing her all flustered, like she had no idea what to do with him. When she'd made it a few feet away without looking back, he called out, "Cybil."

She swiveled back around, consternation stamped on her brow. "What now?"

"Just so you know: for you, I would have paid double."

He was rewarded with wide-eyed shock, her mouth forming a perfect O. Emotion flickered in her eyes, and it was fascinating to watch the transformation.

Son of a gun. All her prickliness over the years had merely been her attempt to deny she still had feelings for him. Would wonders never cease? With his heart lighter than it had been for an age, Miles left her gaping, and headed back to his friends. He figured it was better to leave her with those words. Give her something to chew over the next few days. Because he hadn't been lying; he wanted her back. And he was willing to use every trick in the book to get her there.

They would have time to explore this development on Monday night. In the meantime, over the loudspeaker, Burke was announcing that Jacob had won the date with Cybil's sister, Tessa.

Huh, Jacob and Tessa? Go figure. Miles had to admit, this was the best Thanksgiving he'd experienced in quite some time.

Chapter 15

From Old Man Turner's Journal:
If you leave your past unresolved, be prepared to have it wallop you when you least expect it.

A few days later, Cybil stood in the bathroom, applying makeup with a careful hand as her curling iron heated on the granite bathroom counter. Tonight was it, the night for her date with Miles. The thought of being in such close proximity, just the two of them without any buffers, caused her skin to flush and her pulse to thrum with excitement and, heaven help her, anticipation like she was seventeen all over again.

Stupid body.

Miles had lost none of his potency over the years. If anything, it had increased tenfold. And Cybil found she was having a hard time resisting him, resisting the way her body had molded to his and she'd yearned to be skin to skin with him when he boxed her in at Smitty's the night of the auction. Not to mention his parting shot that he had been willing to pay double what he had for a night out with her. He'd said it to get under her skin, to make her wonder whether she should cave.

It had worked, damn him. She had thought of little but him or them all weekend long. It hadn't mattered whether she was serving shots at Smitty's or helping people find their Zen during crow pose, moments between her and Miles kept flashing through her brain, making her wonder what would have happened if she had said yes the night he rescued her. Either night, actually.

"Are you sure about tonight?" Tessa asked from the open doorway, cuddling Gus in her arms like a big baby. The feline's eyes were slitted in ecstasy, his purrs so loud they echoed in the bathroom.

"Honestly? No." Cybil glanced at her sister in the mirror and then went back to applying her makeup.

"You have to admit, he spent a ton of money just for a single date. It's more money than I make in advances on my comics."

Cybil realized that. And that there was multilayered reasoning behind the high amount. "He did. But he has ulterior motives. He wanted to beat Alex, because of that stuff that I told you about that Alex pulled in my studio. Miles walked in at the tail end—and they've never liked each other. And the other reason, that he wants us to try again, leaves me floundering, unsure how I feel about it, or him, or the situation."

Tessa set Gus down on the floor. The furball waddled over and rubbed his face against Cybil's bare legs. "I get that. I do. And thank goodness he did, or you would have to go out with Alex. But hear me out. I know it might sound crazy, but I think you owe it to yourself to give Miles a real shot. I mean, look at the dates you've been on lately, they were absolute disasters. And I don't know, but if a guy paid ten grand to go out with me, I would do it with an open mind."

"You mean whereas Jacob only paid four thousand for you—again, to beat Alex."

"We aren't talking about me here. Jacob and I don't have the history the two of you have."

Cybil finished applying her mascara with a sigh, her heart squeezing, and glanced at her sister. "I'll think about it. I will. It's just that I'm breaking a promise in seeing him tonight, and it only adds to the long string of promises made back then that were broken."

"What promise are you talking about? Like that you would love him forever? Cybil, you were seventeen. No one could hold you to a promise like that."

Cybil shook her head and cursed herself. Miles obviously had her emotions in turmoil, or she never would have said anything about that confounded promise. "No, not like that."

"Then what? You know you can tell me anything and it stays between us."

Cybil lowered her head and stared into the sink for a minute, trying to gather her courage. When it came to Tessa, Cybil knew she would peck away at her until she fessed up. Instead of looking at her sister, she began applying mascara to her other eye while she explained. "When I was in the hospital after everything, Miles's mom came to see me. And she asked me…" she trailed off at the wave of emotion, blinking back the sudden moisture.

"She asked you what?" Tessa asked, putting an arm around her shoulders.

Cybil looked at her sister, unable to hide it from her any longer. "To let him go. Let him get on with his life so that he could have a future."

Eyes wide with astonishment, Tessa's jaw dropped open. "No, she didn't. Ella is the reason you broke it off with him?"

"Yeah. And I've kept that promise to stay away for all these years." Cybil didn't think she could keep it anymore—or didn't know if she could.

"Does Miles know?"

"No, and you can't say anything. It would hurt him too much."

"I can't believe Ella would ask something like that," Tessa exclaimed.

"I can. She'd just lost her husband. With everything Miles and I had gone through, it was understandable. And as much as I hate to admit it, she was right. At the time, it was the right thing to do. But I don't think I've ever really recovered."

"Cybil, I'm going to say this: to hell with a promise you made a million years ago when you were still a kid. If you want Miles, then be with him. No one, including his mom, would think badly of you."

Cybil sighed and powdered her nose. "I know. It's just there's so much there, and not all was good."

"I realize that, but if you let your fears have power over you then you will never be happy, Cybil."

"You mean like when it comes to Jacob bidding on you," Cybil teased, needing to deflect the topic or she would lose her nerve in going out with Miles tonight.

"Jacob didn't bid on me because he's interested. He just did it because Alex moved on to me. I mean, he didn't even ask for my number so we could set up the date." Tessa sighed. "If only men were as good as the ones I create in my comics."

"I can agree to that. I will think about what you said."

"It's what sisters do. And your secret's safe with me. If you haven't picked out an outfit yet, go with the red dress and knock him dead," Tessa teased.

"That one won't keep me warm though," Cybil complained, thinking that she couldn't wear that one tonight.

"Honey, that dress is an *eat your heart out* one. And if you're going to do it and jump in, you might as well do it with a splash."

"I'll think about it. Now go on, and take the furball with you so I can finish getting ready."

"I'm heading out anyway to meet some friends for dinner at Emporium."

"Well, have fun."

"You too, and ah, don't forget to bring protection with you." Tessa wiggled her eyebrows and grinned.

"I'm not going to have sex with him." Cybil rolled her eyes. She wasn't going to jump into bed with Miles, no matter how much money he'd spent on their date.

"I'm just saying. I stocked up the drawer last week, so put one or two in your purse." Tessa gestured to the bathroom drawer that they used to store condoms and tampons—two of life's great necessities. "Better to have it and not need it than to need it and not have it."

"Go on, get out here," Cybil said with a laugh, and ushered out both her sister and a grumpy Gus, who was unhappy that she wasn't giving him love, and he let her know it with an annoyed swish of his black tail as he strutted out of the door.

The frigid arctic air had been so cold on Cybil's drive home that it had hurt her face. She wasn't going to wear the red dress. She'd be a popsicle by the end of the night. And she definitely wasn't going to wear it just because Miles had asked her to wear a dress. In these temperatures, she would be crazy to. She'd checked the weather before taking her shower, and Juno, Alaska, was currently warmer than Echo Springs, Colorado.

White covered the lawns and lined the streets. The forecasted snow had blown in Friday night and dropped eight inches, bringing with it plummeting temperatures that would make penguins feel right at home.

The memories of their first date all those years ago assailed Cybil while she added loose curls into her hair so it would lie in rich waves over her shoulders. Was Tessa right? Should she give it another go with Miles?

Then again, perhaps she was getting ahead of herself. It was one date.

She chewed on her bottom lip on her trek into her bedroom. She'd not meant to tell Tessa about that promise. Perhaps she needed to, though, to get it off her chest. It was a secret she had borne for thirteen years. She didn't hate Ella for it, either, because it had been the right thing to do back then.

In her room, Cybil thumbed through her closest, avoiding the red dress. After a few minutes of searching, however, she returned to the red one. Dammit, but Tessa was right. The three-quarter sleeve, vee neck, ruched at the waist dress was bright, scarlet red, with a pencil skirt that fell to an inch above her knees. It was the perfect dress to wow him in.

And strangely enough, she wanted to do that. But she didn't know what that meant. Uncertainty and yes, fear, were at the forefront of her feelings, and with good reason. Besides, Miles had paid ten thousand for the date tonight, the least she could do was wear a dress, she thought as she slithered into the thing.

Cybil had just finished applying her lipstick, in a color matching her dress, when there was a knock on the front door. Butterflies erupted in her stomach. She checked herself in the mirror one last time, liking the way her upscale black leather boots with three-inch heels complemented the dress. She prayed that there weren't any patches of ice she might embarrass herself on.

At the next knock, this one more insistent than the last, she huffed out a breath and turned from the mirror in her bedroom.

It was one night. A few hours, at most. She could make it through one evening with Miles. Nothing needed to be decided tonight. As she descended the stairs, he knocked insistently once again.

"I'm coming," she stated. The heels of her boots clicked on the wood floor of the foyer as she tried to step around Gus weaving his fat little body through her legs. "Not now, you big baby." Cybil pushed Gus back and yanked the door open. She nearly choked on her tongue as he entered.

Miles was wearing tailored black slacks, a blue button-down shirt that reminded her of shimmering sapphires, open at the collar to display the taut column of his muscular neck, and a black leather jacket that gave him an air of badassery.

He'd shaved, his square jawline smooth. His lips spread into an arrogant, decidedly satisfied smirk as he assessed her in the same head to toe fashion.

"I like the dress," he said with a husky murmur.

"Meow," Gus caterwauled.

"And who's this?" He bent down, letting Gus sniff his hand and, after deciding he wasn't a threat, rub his head against his fingers.

"That's Gus. Let me feed him real quick and we can leave. Tessa probably forgot, which is why he wants attention so badly. I didn't know you liked cats."

Miles shrugged. "I'm more of a dog person, but I don't mind cats. They're easier than dogs. Although this guy's a bit of a butterball, isn't he?"

"He is. My sister fell in love with him at the shelter and brought him home a few weeks ago. He's a sweetheart, if a bit insistent about getting fed." Cybil scooped out the diet high protein food she'd convinced her sister the cat needed. It gave her a minute to gather herself.

When Gus was happily munching away at his kibble, Miles asked, "Ready, Kansas?"

She shivered at the old nickname and nodded. "Yeah, I am."

She joined him at the door and grabbed her black pea coat off the coatrack. Miles gazed at her and said, "Here, let me."

When his hands closed around the fabric of her coat, the tips of his fingers grazed hers. Lightning energy arced between them. She dropped her hands like his touch had burned her. She let him assist her into her coat, acutely aware of him in the small foyer, of how his energy dominated the space. His hands inadvertently brushed along her collarbone as he settled her coat over her shoulders.

She bit her lower lip as heat coursed through her system. Cybil had forgotten that he gave such good woo. Grabbing her clutch purse from the small wooden table by the door, she noticed his gaze taking in the furniture with a light of recognition in his eyes because it was the same furniture that they'd had in high school.

"Ready?" He held his hand out to her.

Cybil expelled her pent-up breath and placed her hand in his. "Lead the way."

She couldn't help but think, as she slid into the passenger's seat and watched Miles walk around the front hood, how different this was from their first date so long ago. Gone was the euphoria and excitement of youth, replaced by wisdom and a healthy dollop of fear—along with a shocking amount of chemistry.

Chapter 16

From Old Man Turner's Journal:
You will need both patience and skill to win back the love of your life.

Miles didn't know what to think about his silent passenger as he drove out of Echo Springs, on the way up to the nearby ski lodge. Eagle's Nest Ski Lodge had a five-star restaurant offering some of the best steaks in the region. The other place in town with great steaks, Porto's Steakhouse, was being renovated because of a grease fire that had happened in the kitchen earlier this fall.

When he'd first arrived at Cybil's house, he'd worried how he was going to be received. He'd used the auction to get her to go out with him. He figured he'd start the night out with an apology first, and would then begin laying on the charm. But then she'd answered the door in that hot red number that hugged every blessed curve of her killer body, and he'd nearly swallowed his tongue. The voracity of need blasting through his system had nearly brought him to his knees. And it had taken every ounce of his willpower to push past the punch of lust to concentrate on his long-term objective.

Sweet mercy, no other woman had quite the same effect on him as Cybil.

"Where are we going?"

"She speaks," Miles murmured, navigating the winding road as it climbed up the mountain. In the glare of the headlights, the road was framed by snow that had fallen over the weekend. It was too cold for it to melt, and it created a glistening haze.

Cybil snorted. "Hardee har har. It's a two-way street, you know."

"It is. So how was your day, dear?" He shot a glance across the dimly lit confines of his vehicle.

Cybil chuckled. "It was fine; rather uneventful. Although, I did score two new signups for my monthly class membership, so yay. And you, what about your day? I don't figure you would have that many cases in a town like Echo Springs."

"You'd be surprised. Nate and his officers are good at their jobs, and I've gotten lots of speeding tickets just in the last week. My new assistant started today. I think it's going to work well, thank god. She's been keeping the casserole brigade at bay. And I've been looking forward to tonight all weekend."

"Smooth moves, but I'm not sleeping with you."

He barked out a laugh. Only Cybil would be so blunt. The woman didn't have a coy bone in her delectable body. "I bet I could convince you. Besides, sex between us was never the issue. In fact, I remember quite a few times in my truck—"

"All right, can we not talk about your truck or what we used to do in it?" she asked him.

"Why not? Those are some of my fondest memories." That wasn't a lie.

"Miles, please. Could we agree not to bring up the past, at least not tonight?" she pleaded, studying him in the darkened cab as he pulled into the lodge parking lot and into a parking space.

"So you want a new slate? For us to start over from the beginning?"

She nodded. "Perhaps that's the better place to start. Look, I'm not trying to erase what happened or forget it, but we aren't the same people we were back then. I've thought about what you said in Smitty's parking lot and the thing is, we don't really know one another anymore."

"But we can't ignore the past. We were more than lovers that summer, Cybil. We were friends, the very best of friends. I've missed that, and you. And I think you're wrong. We do know each other, which is why we know how to push each other's hot buttons." He felt her hesitation.

"Miles, I'm sorry. I know I didn't handle things between us very well there at the end all those years ago, and I've been kind of a bitch ever since. You were my only friend at the time. And it's not that I want to ignore the past or pretend like it never happened, because it did. I'm just asking: for tonight, can we try to get to know who the other is now, and not constantly put our past out on parade? It's still hard for me to think about. I'm sorry if that bothers you, but I don't want a trip down memory lane tonight." Regret laced her voice.

Sorrow punched through his chest. Like a coward, he'd left her alone to deal with it all. He itched to pull her close and comfort her. But he knew her well enough. If he tried in this moment, she would push him away.

"I'm sorry too. I'm sorry for leaving the way I did, but mostly I'm sorry that I didn't fight for us. Tonight, I promise to do my best not to rehash the past. Let's go eat some steak." Miles climbed out and walked around to her door, steadying himself on the way. He wanted to laugh at himself for being such a bonehead.

Had he actually believed winning her back would be easy?

Maybe she was right, and he was judging how their relationship had developed all those years ago and expecting it to follow the same pattern when in reality, they both bore scars, not merely from the fallout of their relationship, but the lives they had led apart.

When he opened her door, she looked at him, the overhead light in the interior of the Escalade framing her, and said, "Thanks, Miles. I appreciate it."

"For you, Cyb, anything." He quirked his lips and held out a hand for her to take. It was a start, maybe a start toward something new. He helped her down, and her boots started to slip on the slick ground. He caught her in his arms. "Whoa, steady there." He dropped his gaze to her lips. It would be so easy to close the gap. He ached to taste her again. But then she shivered against him. "Let's get you inside before you freeze."

Miles threaded her arm through his and guided her into Eagle's Nest Tavern.

Snow lined the sidewalk, but the ski lodge staff were meticulous about keeping the walkways cleared. Although that didn't mean he didn't use the slick path to his advantage, and as an excuse to touch Cybil.

Eagle's Nest Tavern had been constructed to serve as a bastion against the harsh, brutal environment of the mountain. It was constructed of stone and made to look like an inviting mountainside stone cabin, with two entrances—one from the parking lot, as well as access from inside the ski lodge attached at the rear of the building. Lights from the lodge glowed from where it spread out over the ridge.

Once inside the heavy espresso-colored oak front doors that barred the cold from entering, there was a fire roaring in the stone hearth. The tables were covered with crisp, ivory linen tablecloths. The lighting was soft and inviting against the bitter cold wind blowing outside. Miles knew that during the day, patrons could sit along the bank of windows along one wall and watch skiers fly down the slopes.

Miles gave his name to the concierge, who led them to a

table. Once there, Miles helped Cybil remove her coat, noticing the tiny quiver she tried to hide. Taking the seat across from her, he couldn't help but think she looked luminous, her ivory skin radiant in the low lighting. But then again, that was just Cybil. She never failed to capture him.

She perused the wine menu, her plump lips pursed in concentration.

"Do you trust me?" Miles asked her.

She lifted her gaze and considered him for a minute, long enough that Miles started to sweat. If she didn't trust him, it did not bode well for starting their relationship on new footing. Not that they couldn't build trust back up over time, but it would take immense patience on his part. And that was on top of needing to chip away at the walls she had constructed around her heart.

"Yes. Especially when it comes to food," she replied with wry humor.

He flashed her a grin. Relief flooded him. Even though they had agreed not to bring up the past, her response acknowledged that it was always present beneath the surface and that gave him a surfeit of hope. "Good. That should just about do it."

When their server arrived in his formal pants, crisp white dress shirt, and black tie, Miles ordered them both the filet mignon, medium rare, with mushroom truffle roulade, scalloped potatoes, Caesar salads, and a bottle of pinot noir.

"Well, you've certainly moved up in the world," Cybil said, studying Miles after their waiter left with their order, promising to return shortly with the bottle of wine.

He shrugged. "I'm still me, Cybil. I was fortunate enough to work with a high-caliber firm in Denver after I got my law degree. It was tough, grueling work. I routinely worked myself into the ground, billing ninety hours a week. While I didn't have much of a life outside of my career, I did make a good living."

"I'm proud of you. You knew what you wanted, even back then, and you got it. And then you decided to move here. I never thought you would. I figured if you moved anywhere, it would be to another metropolitan area."

Pleasure speared him at her unexpected praise. It mattered what she thought of him and the life he had made. "Don't get me wrong, I'm going to miss some of the conveniences of living in a large city. But truth be told, the last few years, I've been suffering from some pretty major burnout. I want the work I do to make a difference, and it got to the point where I didn't think that serving the interests of major corporations over people was the right thing to do."

"I had no idea. I'm glad you're back, and hope that living here gives you what you want."

"You mean that?"

Cybil waited until after their waiter had poured them each a glass of wine, placed their salads down, and left before answering him. With a considering glance, she replied, "Yes, I do."

A slow grin spread over his face. She was softening toward him, little by little. And mayhap he wouldn't be able to charm her into his bed tonight, but it would happen.

She pointed her knife at him across the table. "That doesn't mean I want you to get any ideas. It's just if you were that unhappy, then moving back to Echo Springs was the right thing for you, and I'm glad you were able to do it."

"Uh huh. Keep telling yourself that, babe."

"Please. I didn't say that to stroke your ego any. It's large enough on its own."

He chuckled darkly and let her see all the lust, the need in him. In a deep, low voice, he murmured, "I've got something large you can stroke."

She almost choked on her wine, then patted her chest and glared at him. But her form softened, and the air was suffused with kinetic energy. She glanced away and cleared her throat.

"Was it something I said?"

"Cool it with the innuendos."

Miles laughed. "Hey, you brought it up first."

"That I did. Now, if the peanut gallery is done, why don't you tell me about your plans for your house up at Prospect Point?"

"I'm not making any promises on that end. The plans Aiden has drawn up are great. Two-stories, four bedrooms with a full master bedroom and bath. A home office for days when I can't get to the office due to the weather. A full basement where I plan to install a home gym. Jacob's going to help make sure I have all the latest tech installed. And I'm making it as environmentally friendly as possible. There's a ton of work ahead there but I think once it's done, it will be worth the effort."

"It sounds wonderful. I'm happy for you. I always loved that spot." The wistful yearning in her eyes filled him with pleasure. This was all part of the plan. He knew she loved Prospect Point.

"You and me both. You should come by Abby's place sometime, look over the plans Aiden has already drawn up." Miles polished off his salad and took a sip of wine.

"What's it like living in Evie Callier's house?" she asked him.

"Odd. It's a beautiful home, no doubt. And the fact that Nate and Abby were willing to rent it to me, open ended, until my house is constructed is great. But it's still a little bizarre."

"I bet. Especially with all those dolls Evie Callier collected." She shivered.

"True. But Abby, Nate and I hauled those things up into the attic, while Tessa and Abby are working to get them all sold. That way, I don't have to look at them every day."

"They're still in the house. Those things creep me out."

Miles grinned. "Really? Nothing ever scared you that I recall. Although, maybe bears…"

"Ha ha! Seriously, you've got to admit, those dolls are creepy," she said with a wry grin.

"Okay, in all fairness, they are, but given the great rate Abby and Nate gave me, I'm not going to complain over a bunch of dolls, creepy or not. And it's great being near Nate again. Getting to see my mom on a regular basis doesn't hurt either, although I am looking forward to having my own house," Miles admitted. It was probably why he'd never bought a house in Denver—because over the years, the only place he ever saw himself in a house was up at Prospect Point.

Their steaks were delivered with an elegant flair. Cybil took a bite of the steak and moaned. Miles was instantly hard at the sound. Some of the girl he used to know shone through her enjoyment of the meal, that zest for life that had first attracted him.

And it was in that moment that he realized he'd never stopped loving her. All he had done was set that love aside.

"It's good, isn't it?"

"Oh my god, yes. I hate to admit that you were right about the food, but you were. And I'm sure the house will be stunning, Miles. You know, in all the years I've lived in Echo Springs, I've never been up here for skiing or a meal."

"Why not?"

"No time, mainly. I've been saying for years that I wanted to come have dinner up here. I just never found the time." Cybil studied her wine glass.

"You've never had a date bring you up here?" Miles asked her, finding that hard to believe. This was one of *the* places in the area to take a date—typically, a third date, in the hopes of getting lucky.

She shook her head. The waterfall of her raven hair shifted. The loose curls beckoned his fingers, and he had to occupy his hands with his wine glass to keep himself from reaching for her and toying with a strand.

"There haven't been that many dates," she admitted with a slight shrug.

"Why not? Cybil, you're a beautiful woman. I find it hard to believe men weren't beating down your door."

"For a lot of years, I had the responsibility of raising my sister. Then I was working and going to school to get all my certifications. The reality is there hasn't been a whole lot of extra time in my life to date. I have, but there's not been anyone noteworthy, not since…" She trailed off and glanced away.

"Not since me." He took one of her hands in his, rubbing the back of it. To know that life had been wretched for her after he'd bailed cut him to the core. "Cybil, look at me. Please." When she finally lifted her gaze and her eyes met his, he continued, "I know you wanted to avoid the past but when it comes to us, I'm not sure it's possible. And to be frank, there's not been anyone really important in my life since you, either. I was discreet, and tended to avoid women who wanted deep commitments."

"Really?"

He nodded. "Yeah, really."

A blush spread over her cheeks and she withdrew her hand, but there was a small smile playing about her lips.

"You should be proud of who you've become. I know I am. You've done well for yourself, Cybil."

Her eyes widened at his praise and she dropped her gaze, but not before he spied a sheen of moisture lining her lower lashes. Had no one in the last dozen years told her that, complimented her for the incredible job she'd done in the face of such daunting odds? In his mind, she was amazing.

As the meal and night progressed, they seemed to fall into the rhythm that was uniquely theirs. It made the time fly by so that before he realized it, dinner was finished. The waiter brought the check when Miles signaled him, and he settled the bill.

When Cybil started yawning, shielding the movement with her hand, he said, "Come on, let's get you home. You look dead on your feet."

"Sorry. Dinner was great. Mondays are the end of my workweek, and after all the shifts I worked at Smitty's this weekend, I intend to go to bed early. Although, I will probably spend an hour or so at the studio at some point tomorrow to get some paperwork done."

"No explanation needed. I know you work hard." Miles escorted her out to his vehicle.

He drove them back down the mountain and into town, then pulled up to her place and parked. Before she could escape, he strode around and escorted her to the red front door of her house.

"I enjoyed myself tonight. Thank you for the pleasure of your company. Maybe next time, I won't have to bid on you at an auction to get it," he teased.

"Maybe. Thank you for dinner," Cybil murmured, eyeing him. Her breath plumed in the air. Then she surprised the hell out of Miles by placing her hands on his shoulders, leaning up on her toes, and brushing a light kiss over his cheek. Before she could retreat, he nipped her around the waist, cupped her cheek, and claimed her lips.

Finally! was all he could think.

Electricity zapped through him at the first heady, seductive taste of her. Cybil had always tasted so fucking sweet, like the finest Bordeaux. He kept the kiss light, waiting for her surrender. Tracing his tongue along the seam of her lips, he nipped her bottom lip. With a shuddering moan, she parted her lips, her hands curled into the lapels of his coat, and yanked him closer.

The victory sent his head spinning, and Miles did what he had been longing to do for months now: he plundered. He ravaged her mouth, taking their kiss infinitely deeper as his passion boiled over. Slanting his lips over hers, he drank in her mewls. In her heels, she was almost as tall as he was, and in the heat of the moment, their bodies were aligned, hips to sternum.

Christ, she felt good, better even than his memories of her. He wanted to drown in her; lose himself in her flesh and not come up for air until they were both sated.

He kissed her and was home, after feeling like he had been

out in the desert without sustenance. His world was no longer askew as it clicked back into place because he was holding her: the only woman he had ever loved.

He wanted everything with her—everything he'd wanted to give her all those years ago but had been too wrapped up in his own world, and grief, to fight for them. Waves of desire rose, consuming him, and Miles wanted to suggest they take it inside. But he didn't want to stop kissing her long enough to say the words.

Cybil clung to him, kissing him back, and matching his passion with her own. Her hands fisted in his hair, trapping his mouth against hers.

"Um, yeah, hi. If I could just get past you two," a female voice said with amusement.

At the sound, Cybil sprang away from him as if she had been burned. Her fingers touched her kiss-swollen lips.

Miles rocked back on his heels, stunned by the intensity of his desire as he watched Cybil withdraw and toss up walls. He glanced in the direction of the voice and spied Cybil's sister, Tessa, bundled up like an Eskimo. "Tessa, good to see you, ah, sorry, we were just—"

"Checking each other's tonsils," Tessa said with a laugh.

Amused by the situation, he said, "That about sums it up. Cybil, thank you for a great evening. We'll talk more later. You ladies have a good rest of your night."

"Yep, thanks, Miles. Tessa, didn't realize you weren't already home. Why don't we go inside? It's too cold out here." Cybil smiled at Tessa and shot Miles a glance laden with meaning.

Miles nodded and headed to his Escalade. His body rode a sharp edge of unquenched lust, but what he felt for Cybil was so much deeper than physical. And after the way she'd kissed him back, he knew without a doubt that she felt something for him too.

From his vehicle, he watched the sisters head in, and Cybil

close the door with a last glance his way. She still wanted him. And with that knowledge, he considered the night a rousing success as he drove back to Abby's.

He and Cybil weren't done with each other, not by a long shot.

Chapter 17

13 years ago

By the time Miles reappeared at the Papa Beau's hostess stand that night, Cybil had run her darn legs off, seating folks at tables, carting out to-go orders, rolling silverware, wiping down menus, and restocking the table condiments. She'd been feeling like she was close to dropping from exhaustion but one glance at Miles flashing a sexy, devil may care smirk in her direction caused that feeling to evaporate. In his presence, energy crackled as if she'd stuck her finger in an electric socket or had had one too many double-shot espressos.

"Ready?" he murmured in a husky baritone that skittered tingles down her spine only to pool in her belly.

"Yep. I just need to clock out and grab my purse from the locker," she replied, her voice a breathy whisper as she tried to contain her excitement.

"Take your time. We've got all evening."

Shirley rolled her eyes when Cybil turned her way. With a nod toward the back and an amused expression, Shirley said,

"Go on ahead. Good first night. On Monday, we'll do some more training before feeding you to the grizzlies next week."

"Thanks, Shirley." Cybil gave her a dazzling smile. Hyper-aware of Miles's attention on her, she did not want it to seem like she was in too big of a hurry or overeager to hang out with him. From everything she had learned in magazines, a girl should make a guy work for it a little. Not that she was an expert, but she figured it wouldn't hurt to try. She clocked out and grabbed her purse from one of the employee lockers in the small break-room that held a bank of lockers along one wall. On her way back to the front, Cybil detoured into the ladies' restroom to freshen up a bit. She was in and out in five minutes, after applying a new coat of lip gloss and running a brush through her high ponytail.

Cybil walked toward the hostess stand with a sultry strut and locked gazes with Miles. The dining room in Papa Beau's seemed to dim until it was only the two of them. She was a bit surprised that a cherubic angel didn't hover above them with his bow and arrow.

Miles wore a sensual, enigmatic smirk on his face, like he knew the effect his presence was having on her, and his stare was suffused with a carnal hunger that called to her on every level of her being.

And she'd thought moving to this little town was going to be a nightmare.

"All good?" he asked, his gaze dipping to her lips, making her infinitely glad she had touched up her lip gloss.

"Yeah."

Miles clasped her hand in his, and his long, lean fingers and broad palm enveloped her smaller one. The warmth of his firm touch sent heat tunneling through her body. Then he whisked her out into the clear night. Temperatures had dipped from the mid-nineties down into the sixties. She'd didn't feel the chill being this near to him. He was like her own personal sun, and she basked in his presence.

"So where are we going?" Cybil asked curiously as they strolled hand in hand past storefronts. Main Street of Echo Springs was a thriving tourist attraction, especially during the summer. Stores were illuminated, casting a superficial glow of lights in the darkening twilight. People meandered along the drive, and they threaded their way through the throngs. A few blocks up, she spotted the lights of a police vehicle and an officer directing traffic. It wasn't her dad, but he was out on patrol tonight, keeping the streets of their new hometown safe.

"Hungry?" Miles slanted a glance at her with a grin teasing the corners of his full, firm lips.

"Starving, but didn't you eat already?" During her break instead of eating the free meal she received while working, Cybil had called her mom to explain that she was going out after work and would be home by curfew. Her mom didn't ask too many questions. Then again, her mother was all *see, little miss, I told you that you would make new friends*. She hated to admit her mom had been right.

Miles shrugged his large shoulders in a totally nonchalant, masculine gesture. "I can always eat. Have you been to the Emporium Diner and had their burgers yet?"

"No, they any good?" she asked as he led her across the street. The Emporium Diner sat on the corner of Pine Street and Continental Drive, a block away from Main Street. The exterior of the building was like a time capsule and paid homage to the post-World War II era. A neon sign in blazing red and vibrant yellow above the entrance to the squat, one-story ivory building displayed the name of the place. The windows were trimmed with a silver chrome that reflected the neon lights. Inside, the floor was checkered white and black tile, and had a long ivory Formica countertop with a row of round chrome seats topped with red leather padding. In addition to the counter, there was a mixture of high-backed red leather booths and wooden tables with red leather chairs.

The place was charming and smelled divine, with the aroma of fried food and grease scenting the air. In the corner by the restrooms stood an old-school jukebox that pumped out tunes that made Cybil think of poodle skirts and sock hops.

"They're the best. I still haven't found a place in Boulder that's as good."

Her heart sank. He wasn't local. Boulder was a world away from the little town of Echo Springs when you didn't have your own car. Without transportation, it might as well be on the other side of the world.

"So you live in Boulder and not Echo Springs?" she asked as they walked to an available table in the back.

"I go to school there. Just finished my first year at CU Boulder, but I was born and bred in Echo Springs." He pulled her into one of the nearby empty booths.

That made him a sophomore in college. That was what set him apart from the guys at her high school in Kansas—the fact that he wasn't in high school. It made him that much more intriguing, even as disappointment raced through her that he wouldn't be matriculating with her at Echo Springs High in the fall. "What are you studying?"

"I'm dual majoring in pre-law and criminal justice."

"You're not," she exclaimed in disbelief. Didn't that just figure? Assessing him, she felt it didn't fit with the wicked vibe radiating that declared he was always up for a good time. But what did she really know about him? Enough to fill a shot glass. And she wanted to know more, even despite the pre-law and Boulder deal.

Miles's long legs brushed hers underneath the table, and she shivered at the innocent touch. He handed her a plastic menu.

"You should try the bacon cheeseburger and the cheese fries. If that's your thing," he said, almost as a dare.

She glanced over the menu and noticed a few things that caught her interest. Their server, Dolly, whose age could be anywhere from fifty to eighty, given the lines and wrinkles on her face, not to mention the hefty coat of red lipstick slicked over her lips, and the way her hair had been teased to within an inch of its life, stopped by their booth. Her voice, sounding like it belonged to someone who smoked a pack a day, rasped out, "What can I get you kids?"

Miles gestured at Cybil to order.

With a cool glance at him over the menu, Cybil replied, "I'll have the bacon cheeseburger, side of cheese fries, and a chocolate milkshake, please."

"Same," Miles said with a devastating grin, his gaze glimmering with amusement.

When their waitress left to put their order in, he leaned forward and asked, "So why don't you believe I'm pre-law?"

The man was like the proverbial dog with a bone. But she was nothing if not honest. "It's nothing. It's just that my dad is the new sheriff's deputy in town."

"Is that right?" He chuckled, and gave her a cocky grin. "So, you like law and order."

She huffed, a little exasperated that of course he was studying pre-law. "That's because I live it. But why the dual major?"

"I'm not sure which area of law I want to practice yet, and in case I do decide on criminal law, it wouldn't hurt to have the extra knowledge. I take an extra class each semester and it will take me four and a half years to finish, which will leave me with some gap time in between graduating and law school."

"It seems you have your life all planned out. Pretty ambitious too." To her, that was a real plus in his favor. It seemed he had his act and life together when most guys were just looking for the next score, be it parties or women, or both.

"Some days. Others, not so much. And you're what, in high school? Senior year perhaps? Any idea where you want to go to college?" he asked as their food was delivered.

"Yeah, which was why I wasn't thrilled at the move. Leaving between junior and senior year just makes it less fun, I guess. As for college, I'm still trying to figure out what I want to do. Like, how do you know that law will be right for you? Besides, much of it depends on whether I can score any scholarships or not to help financially so I'm not burdened with a ton of school debt. It's not that I don't want to go to college, I do, but really it's there to get me to what I really want," Cybil admitted. She didn't mind school, she'd just always considered it a steppingstone to bigger and better things.

"And what's that? What do you want?" Miles asked, popping a French fry covered in melted cheese into his mouth.

"To see the world. To explore." She swiped a finger through the fluffy mound of whipped cream on top of her shake and licked it off her finger.

Miles arched a golden brow, his heated gaze trained on her mouth. "Really?" he asked, his voice husky.

She knew she was teasing him, flirting with him, but it was only because he fascinated her. "Yep. I want to backpack through Europe, visit all fifty states, and maybe not climb Everest, but at least see it up close. I want to stand on the Great Wall of China, see the pyramids at Giza, ride on a gondola through the canals of Venice, visit Stonehenge, visit pubs in the Temple Bar District of Dublin, and so much more."

"All that, huh? Eat. Trust me. Burgers here are like a religion."

She poured ketchup onto her plate and put some on her burger, then took her first bite. She moaned at the flavor. "It's so good. How did I not know about this place?"

"Told ya. You can't go wrong with a burger from Emporium," he responded before taking another bite.

They stuffed themselves to the brim with greasy, yummy goodness. Miles stole a few fries off her plate after he'd devoured every crumb from his. They discussed their favorite movies, favorite bands, things they had in common. It was easy. He was easy to talk to, even as her heart trembled in excitement in her chest.

"You surprise me," Miles said, leaning back in his seat. His gaze held approval and something more. It was the more that left Cybil breathless, riding an edge of thrilling excitement, as if she were on a roller coaster, experiencing the twists, turns, and high speed.

"How?" she asked, curious, resting her face against her palm.

"Most girls would want the burger and fries but order a salad and then steal my fries, but not you," he said with a shrug.

"Yeah, well, I love food. I think it's stupid to get something that I'm not in the mood for," Cybil admitted. Even though she did try to eat healthy most of the time, she didn't turn down the opportunity to have something she really craved.

"Noted. If you're finished," he indicated her nearly empty plate that she shoved away from herself, "let's get out of here."

If she tried to fit one more cheese fry in her mouth, she would likely burst.

"Where are we going?" she asked, worried that their night was already ending. Maybe she should have been more like other girls and gotten a salad. Maybe he didn't like her after spending some time with her.

"We… are going bowling," he said with a waggle of his eyebrows that made her laugh.

"Bowling? Really?" she said, taking his hand. Euphoria suffused her. He wasn't ending their date. Carefree and blissfully happy that he wanted more time with her, she checked her watch, pleased that there was still plenty of time before her curfew.

When she pulled out her wallet to pay her half of the check, he gave her a bemused glance and took care of the bill. Then he asked sardonically, "Why not? It'll be fun."

That's what they did. He drove them to the bowling alley. It wasn't far from the diner. They could have walked, but with her curfew, they decided not to waste time getting there, so that they could be having fun instead. They were able to score one of the last open lanes. On a Saturday night, the bowling alley was packed. Some of the people there, she recognized. They had been in Papa Beau's earlier for dinner. Cybil figured by this time next year, she would be able to distinguish the locals from the tourists.

Miles was amazing. He'd just lost his dad, and yet here he was, laughing and joking with her, ensuring that she had a good time. They didn't talk about their families. It was a topic she figured they could discuss another time. If there was another time. Their bowling games were competitive, and the excitement left her flushed with energy. During the first match, he beat her by quite a bit—210 to her paltry 136. By the second game, she'd warmed up enough to toss a couple strikes, and eked past him in the final frame to win, 198 to 190.

She whooped with her fist in the air at her victory, but he snagged her around the waist and leaned his mouth down by her ear. "Tied so far this evening, huh? Next game, winner gets a prize. Loser has to give the winner whatever they want."

Feeling cocky over her recent win, she challenged, "You're on."

The third game was animated, a distinct battle to the end, with each of them attempting to distract the other. But Miles snuck past her with a strike to claim the win.

He swaggered over and took the seat beside her, removing his rental shoes. "Good game, Cyb."

"You have to give me a chance to redeem myself. You were

distracting me," she admitted. Miles was potent. The last few times, having him near had scattered her concentration and made her clumsy.

"I like distracting you, how you get all flushed. I think it's cute. But we'll have to have a rematch another time. Let's get you home. Last thing I want to do is break your curfew and have your father arrest me," he teased with a lopsided grin.

Her breath hitched. Another time?

"Okay," she replied, disappointed that the night was over when she never wanted it to end, but thrilled at the same time that he planned to see her again. "It was a good game. But what do you want for your prize?"

He shot her a wicked grin filled with intent. "Not here. I'll tell you in the car."

They returned their rental shoes, and Miles escorted her out to his truck with an arm about her waist. After he opened her door, he helped her climb inside his truck. She watched him walk around the front hood, all lanky, lean muscle. She saw sorrow in his step and in his eyes when she looked past her own rose-colored sheen. He was hurting, even though he was trying to hide it. It was probably a macho guy thing. He didn't want to appear weak, but she saw through the act, and her heart hurt for him.

When he slid into the driver's seat and started the engine, she threaded her fingers through his. Miles glanced at her in the darkened cab, a brow raised in question.

"Thanks for tonight and making me feel welcome here when I don't really know anyone. I know you're going through a lot, and I'm here if you need someone to talk to about it. Or to just go sit with up at Echo Lake." Cybil bit her lower lip as she looked at him. The shadows of full night around them made it hard to read what was in his gaze as he studied her.

Then he leaned over and cupped her chin with his free hand. His thumb rasped across her lower lip as he stared.

"Cybil," he murmured, his voice a husky whisper.

Then he dipped his head and brushed his lips over hers. It was soft at first—so incredibly soft that she sighed. His stubble grazed her skin, and his lips commanded all her attention as he deepened the kiss, dragging her into a passionate abyss where they were the only two people in the world. She parted her lips with a moan, and clung to his chest. Miles drew her close. His strong arms surrounded her. Cybil's head spun and her heart tumbled as her hands slid up his firm chest, reveling in the way he felt beneath her palms, before sliding into his hair, thrilled that she finally got to touch him, and held him in place against her mouth.

Cybil had kissed a guy before—twice, if one was counting. There had been Joe Demarco her freshman year, when she'd played the game Seven Minutes in Heaven with a group of friends. He'd slobbered all over her face like a Saint Bernard lapping at his water bowl. The second time had been homecoming her junior year, with Lloyd Moore, the junior captain of the football team, and it had been awkward and wholly unappealing. Cybil had wondered after her first two experiences what the whole kissing thing was about.

But Miles kissed her, and her brain clicked off. Pleasure unlike anything she had experienced before swamped her body. Desire moved her as she kissed him back with passion and need overriding her system.

She moaned in the back of her throat as his tongue invaded her mouth, sliding against hers as he dominated the kiss, directing her, showing her with his touch how to kiss him back. Cybil had always been a fast learner. She clung to him, racing toward a precipice and need she didn't fully understand. She wanted his hands on her, a liberty she had not granted any other guy. But she wanted them on her with an urgency that defied all logic and reason until, finally, he lifted his head and broke their kiss.

They were both breathing heavily as they stared at one another.

"Let's get you home," Miles said, tracing his knuckles tenderly over her cheek.

Cybil could only nod in agreement, quite shaken from their kiss. She didn't want to stop touching him. Ever. He seemed to understand, and placed a light kiss on her forehead before releasing her.

As he pulled the truck out of the parking lot, his hand found hers and twined their fingers together, his thumb rubbing over the back of her hand. They rode in silence, but it was a comfortable quiet—soothing, even.

Miles parked on the street beside her house, then leaned over and kissed her again. It was the best kiss. Her unschooled heart trembled, and she let him lead. She curled her hands around his neck, loving the feel of his skin beneath her fingers. He lifted his head and gave her a warm smile.

"What are you doing tomorrow?" he asked, stroking a hand down her back.

"We have errands in the morning. I can't get out of that. And then we have family time since it's my dad's day off from work." She grimaced. Normally she hadn't minded the forced family time. She'd been glad for it after the move. But now she just wanted to see Miles again. Her heart thumped in her chest.

"Sometime this week, then. What I want from the bet I won is another night out with you." He tugged gently on her ponytail.

She tilted her head and said, "I'm booked this weekend with family stuff, and work most of next week, but I'm free on Wednesday."

"Good. Come out with me then," he said, then released her and surprised her further when he got out and walked around to her door. He escorted her up to her front porch. Giving her hand a slight squeeze before he left, he murmured, "Night, Cyb. I'll catch you later."

"Night," she replied, chewing on her bottom lip, and walked inside her house. She glanced at his retreating form as she shut the door, and her heart sighed as it did a big swan dive into the glorious abyss.

Chapter 18

From Old Man Turner's Journal:
Life can rip holes in your heart, but don't let that be a reason not to love.

The next day, Miles was in his office going over a stack of old case files, and freezing. He refused to put his coat on as a matter of principle.

"Eva?"

"Yes, sir?" She poked her blonde head in his office. Eva Monroe, one of his third-floor tenants, was a twenty-six-year-old single woman with the face of an angel and a mind like a whip. She was a paralegal, and had worked for a firm in Oregon before she'd left to take care of her aging grandfather, Carl, here in town. With Echo Springs being as small as it was, she'd had a hard time finding a suitable position.

"Call Aiden O'Toole, tell him we need the heater in the building looked at today. Or if he can't get to it, to recommend someone who would be available today."

"Oh thank god! I don't see how you're sitting there without a coat on. I've thought about running up to my place and putting on my long underwear with some jeans over them instead of this skirt."

"After you make the call, you can run up, no problem. I don't want you catching pneumonia. If it gets much colder in here, I will be wearing my coat, don't you worry about me. Make sure you explain I've already checked the pilot light and it's on."

"Will do, boss." Eva headed back to her desk in her navy-blue parka.

He hoped the damn heater wasn't on the fritz and was something that Aiden could get fixed today. The frigid temperatures that had roared in over the Thanksgiving holiday weekend had stayed, and hovered like a blanket of ice over the town.

Miles went back over the page he had been attempting to read for the better part of thirty minutes, all because he had seen Cybil enter the building and head up to her studio. After last night, he had thought about her non-stop. Thought about that kiss non-stop.

It didn't help that he was also feeling edgy because he'd missed his morning run. The ground had been too treacherous to risk it. He didn't mind wet pavement, but ice was another matter altogether.

"Aiden will be here in two hours, and if you truly don't mind, I'm going to run up to my place and change into much warmer clothes," Eva said from his doorway.

"Not at all, go ahead. I'll hold down the fort until you get back."

"Shouldn't take me more than ten minutes," Eva replied, and rushed out the door.

Miles had been churning over an idea all morning long that involved Cybil and her gym. While he preferred getting outdoors for his daily run, he knew that for as long as he lived in Echo Springs, he would need to get a treadmill. When he'd lived in Denver, whenever he was unable to run outside due to inclement weather, he'd had access to a company gym with state-of-the-art treadmills. It was one of the few things he would actually miss about that place—not the people, not the job, not his apartment or the clubs he'd attended. The gym. He shook his head. It was why, when the opportunity to purchase Clark Biddle's practice had come up, he had jumped at the prospect.

Miles figured it would be better to wait six months until his house was built to buy a treadmill. In the meantime, he planned on convincing Cybil to let him use her gym equipment until then. He'd have to change his schedule up a bit and run in the evening, since he didn't have a shower at the office. But it would be manageable. He would offer her a discount on her rent; make it profitable for both parties. And it would have the added effect of placing them in each other's pathway.

And her mouth, Christ. He scraped a hand over his face.

Kissing Cybil had rendered him deaf, dumb, and blind to anything else. There could have been a massive meteor on a path to strike Earth with Echo Springs as its ground zero trajectory, and he wouldn't have known—or cared, for that matter. He loved the way her lithe body pressed against his and created a kinetic energy that whirled between them, blotting out everything and everyone else until the only thing that mattered was having Cybil in his arms. A simple brush of his lips over hers, and he'd been sucked into a vortex of heat and need so profound it had shattered him, altered his state of being until all he could see was her.

It had always been this way with her. She eclipsed every other relationship he'd experienced. Cybil's passion and zeal for life moved him. And last night, he'd felt his heart roll over and expose its soft underbelly.

He loved her. There was no question in his mind that she was the woman for him. And not just for a few quick tumbles in his bed either. He wanted permanence with Cybil—one that stretched from here into eternity.

"I'm back, boss," Eva said, and that was his cue that he could run upstairs and continue to put his strategy into action.

"I'll be back in a bit. I need to go talk to the tenant up on two. I've got my cell with me, call if you need me."

"Roger that," Eva replied.

Miles headed up the single flight of stairs and entered Cybil's studio just as she was shrugging into her fire engine red parka. She was stunning, with her toned, mile-long legs sheathed in black yoga pants. Her ivory top clung to her supple form and lovingly cupped her breasts. In the soft light, she looked ethereal with her dark raven hair drawn away from her beautiful face into a single, thick braid that disappeared over her shoulder. Her gray eyes spied him, and a blush spread up her neck and into her cheeks.

Interesting. Very interesting.

"Hi, um. Thanks again for last night. Is there something you need?"

When her gaze dipped to his lips and sparks of hunger flashed like lightning bolts in her eyes, his reason for coming up here shifted. Desire hummed in his veins as he stalked toward her, erasing the distance between them. Cybil retreated as he prowled forward, until she ran out of room and he crowded her against the nearby wall. He placed his palms against the smooth surface, boxing her body in.

"Yeah. You," he murmured, his voice low and husky, chock full of a desire only she seemed to evoke in him. Cybil placed her hands against his chest, and they scorched him like firebrands. Miles lowered his face until they were at eye level, and then lightly brushed his lips against the soft silk of hers. She gave a soft moan and her hands curled into his chest, tugging him close. With a muttered groan, he slanted his mouth firmly over hers and unleashed his pent-up need.

Her lips were soft, heated silk moving against his mouth. When she opened her lips on a sigh, he took the opportunity to plunge inside. She tasted sweet, with a hint of cinnamon. He'd forgotten how much she loved cinnamon mints.

The exchange was carnal. It was elemental. Kissing Cybil was akin to ascending into the very fabric of heaven.

He reveled in the feel of her. How she fit him. His hands trailed down along her sides, past the swell of her chest to her narrow waist and hips. He ate her startled moans. As he pressed his body against hers, his eyes nearly crossed at the feel of her soft lines smooshed again the firm planes of his chest. Cybil's hand slid up into his hair and gripped him—hard—holding him steady and keeping him a prisoner against her mouth. Miles was on board. His entire system had activated the launch-code sequence.

Christ, he wanted her, had never truly stopped wanting her.

Desire and need drove him. He slipped his hands beneath the open edges of her parka to palm the globes of her ass. Cybil had a fucking spectacular ass, supple and perfectly formed, taut from years of yoga. His fingers sought her flesh, sliding beneath her layered tops to the silken skin of her lower back.

He groaned at the feel of her, the taste of her. She spun his senses like a shot of hundred-proof whiskey. He wanted her—right here, right now, until they were too weak to move.

He nipped at her lush lower lip before trailing his mouth down over her smooth jaw to the hollow at the base of her neck. His hands caressed the lines of her back, and he was about to suggest they lock her studio door.

"Stop." Cybil shoved at his chest with a shuddered gasp that went straight to his groin.

Miles regretfully lifted his head and stared. Her lips were swollen and puffy from his kiss. Her pupils were dilated with lust. The pulse at the base of her neck hammered wildly.

When he would have reclaimed her lips for another taste, she stopped him. "Miles, let me go. This can't happen again."

"Cyb, there's still something here between us. I don't think it's ever gone away. And I want to explore it." It was as much of an admission as he was willing to give. He would scare her off if her told her everything just now.

"I can't go there with you again. I'm sorry, but I can't." She grimaced, and visibly withdrew. Her gaze shuttered, dampening the passion she'd expressed a moment prior. Miles spied the distinct glimmer of moisture lining her inky lashes.

"Why not? I know you feel the connection," he said, stymied over her refusal to see how good they were together—when she allowed herself to be in the moment, in the present, rather than dredge up the sorry past.

"You really want to know why?"

"Yes, I really do." He was done playing games. He wanted Cybil. He had always wanted Cybil. He loved her. Time hadn't diminished his desire or love for her.

"Fine. Follow me," she said, finally pushing her way around him. With her purse and keys in hand, she led him out of the studio, locking the door behind them.

Miles grabbed his coat on the way out, telling Eva he would be back in a bit, and followed Cybil to her aging truck.

"We should take mine. This bucket of bolts could break down on us. What is it that you want to show me?" Miles huffed against the cold.

"Just get in the truck, Miles," Cybil ordered, bossy and determined as usual.

Miles climbed into the passenger side. In unerring silence, she drove them down Main Street, past Papa Beau's Pizza and Smitty's, past the reception hall where he'd hosted his mother's retirement party. About a mile past the edge of town, she pulled her vehicle to a stop and climbed out.

Why the hell were they at Echo Springs Cemetery? The oldest headstone in the manicured lot dated back to the 1880s. Intrigued at what she had to show him here, and how it could possibly relate to why she wouldn't give their relationship another go-round, Miles trailed behind Cybil, watching her long legs in heeled boots navigate the terrain. Even with snow covering the ground, she was nimble on her feet.

About a quarter of a mile into the cemetery, Cybil came to a halt near a set of smaller headstones. These weren't fancy monoliths, but smaller, more refined grave sites. Miles noticed the names on the two small slabs of marble, and his heart squeezed.

David Evan Roe, Beloved Husband and Father

Then the one beside it.

Mary Elizabeth Roe, Beloved Wife and Mother

"Why are we at your parents' graves, Cyb? What do you want me to understand?" They had tragically died in a head-on collision on Interstate 70 on their way to see Cybil in the hospital. Miles ached for Cybil over the loss. She'd had far too much grief shoved onto her plate at such a young age. And what had he done at the time, when she'd told him they were through? He hadn't put up a fight—in fact, he'd barely lifted a finger, more relieved than anything that he didn't have to figure out a way to help her. He had walked away. His actions back then were something he would regret for the rest of his life. He had failed her in an epic, almost unforgivable fashion. He'd not fought for them, for her, and instead had chosen the easy route. Perhaps he was asking too much of her.

Cybil's normally expressive face was shuttered, her arms wrapped around herself in a defensive, hands-off move. The lines of her body vibrated with tension.

"We aren't here for them, but for this one." Cybil trudged a few steps past her parents' headstones and gestured to one beside them. Miles's heart tripped over in his chest and stopped.

"That's… that's—"

"Our daughter's grave," Cybil said solemnly, pain flashing in her quicksilver gaze.

The light gray marble headstone was engraved with a name. It read: *Amber Rose Keaton-Roe.*

He hadn't known she was buried here—or at all, for that matter. It was the reason why Cybil had been in the hospital all those years ago. She'd miscarried their child when she was six months along, just days after Christmas.

"You never told me that you had her buried. Why? Why didn't you tell me about this?" Miles couldn't keep the accusation out of his tone. This grave represented everything they might have been, all the hopes and dreams they had built that long-ago summer, buried beneath six feet of earth.

"If you'll remember, we weren't speaking with each other at the time. And my world had come to a shuddering halt, what with the miscarriage and then dealing with my parents' deaths."

"Still. It would have been nice to know," Miles said angrily, his heart aching.

"And I'm sorry for that. I know I made mistakes, but we were so damn young. I told them I wanted to bury her when they were working on me. I saw her before the drugs fully kicked in, you know. She was so tiny, Miles. And I felt so damn guilty." Cybil's hands were clutched at her chest, her body rigid, while her lips quivered.

"Why?" he asked, wanting to go to her, to hold her, but he knew she'd fight him if he tried.

Tears spilled over her inky lashes. "Because a part of me was relieved. If she had lived, I would have loved her with everything I am and would have devoted myself to raising her, but life chose differently. And in those days, after everything with the miscarriage and then my parents' accident on the way to the hospital, their dual funerals in the days that followed, I was just trying to make it from one minute to the next. I used some of the life insurance money Tessa and I got to put her next to her grandparents. I owed her that."

"Cybil. Jesus. I'm so sorry I wasn't there. I should have been. When you told me it was over, I should have fought for us. I'm sorry I didn't." Crushing regret weighed heavily upon his heart and soul. He couldn't be angry with her over this. He'd played just as much a part in their demise and how things had turned out. She was right. They'd been so damn young. Neither of them had been prepared for the strength and intensity of their feelings, nor for the consequences of their actions.

He'd already been back in Boulder after the holiday, interning at a local law firm, when she had contacted him and told him that she'd lost the baby. To be fair, he had been relieved too. They hadn't been ready to be parents. Miles had left Boulder and come home, wanting to support her, be there for her. And it was that very day, when he was on his way to the hospital to see her, that her parents were killed in a head-on collision on their way back to the hospital.

When she'd turned him away and told him to leave her be, he hadn't put up much of a fight. He'd buckled, unable to deal with the turmoil, still so raw over his own father's death.

"We both made mistakes and choices back then that we can't change. But now you know why I can't go back there, to that place with you. As much as I want you, Miles, how do we know that we wouldn't make things worse?" Cybil murmured, pain etched over her features.

Miles didn't buy that. "That's a cop-out and you know it. Have you ever considered it could be better? I love you, Cybil. I always have, and always will. I know you have feelings for me."

She shook her head in denial. "I'm sorry, but I'm not going there. I do want you, Miles. But I can't. It's a self-preservation thing, and I know that's not the answer you want to hear. I'll give you a few minutes alone with her and wait for you back at the truck."

Then she walked away. Cybil always seemed to be walking away from him. Miles watched her leave for a moment, her shoulders hunched forward, her feet treading the same path they'd taken to get here. Then he redirected his gaze to the small headstone and inhaled a deep breath. He knelt in the snow. It soaked the knees of his slacks, but he didn't care. He placed a hand on the cold marble bearing his daughter's name. His fingers traced the lettering.

"I'm sorry that we never got a chance to meet, Amber. I would have tried to be as good a father to you as my dad was to me. I—shit, I'll come back and visit again. Bring you flowers next time."

Miles stood, feeling old and tired, his heart sore. Icy wind whipped against his face, drying the wetness trailing down his cheeks. He wiped the remaining traces away before stuffing his hands into his pockets. He inhaled the pristine, frigid mountain air, feeling lost as to the direction in which to proceed. Cybil pushed him away and ran anytime things started to get complicated between them.

He loved her, and would always love her. It was time he stepped up and proved that he would be there for her no matter what.

They weren't who they had been thirteen years ago. Both of them had been tempered by life, forged by grief and world-altering experiences.

But that didn't mean they shouldn't head down this path again. Cybil was the only woman he'd ever loved. He'd had girlfriends, women he dated in college and law school, and beyond. But not a single one had ever touched him the way Cybil did. She was it for him. He knew that fact to the far-reaching corners of his soul.

That had to count for something. Miles wasn't entirely certain how to prove to her that he was all in, for good this time. All he knew deep down in his gut was that he was meant to love Cybil for the rest of their lives.

Now he just had to convince her of that fact.

Chapter 19

From Old Man Turner's Journal:
If dating wasn't hard, everyone would do it.

Later that night, Miles got home from work frustrated and emotionally depleted. The revelation of their daughter's grave had hollowed him out. It brought with it all the heartache and memories of that time. How useless he had felt, not knowing what he could do to help Cybil. But hearing that a part of her had been relieved took away some of the shame he had carried with him all these years.

If Cybil hadn't miscarried, he would have done right by her and their daughter. But Christ, he remembered the deep-seated fear he'd hidden from her the day she told him up at Echo Lake that she was pregnant. And then when they had stood as a united front to tell her parents, with him wondering in the back of his mind if her dad would use his police-issued service revolver on him for knocking up his daughter. Miles's mom had been supportive, even though he had seen the disappointment in her eyes.

After hanging his coat, he headed straight into the kitchen and to the fridge, unable to get the image of his daughter's grave out of his mind. He pulled a beer out, and stood with the door open as he took a long drink.

With his beer in hand, he turned and startled, sloshing some beer over the lip of the bottle.

"Jesus Christ, dude. Warn a guy next time," Miles exclaimed, rather perturbed at the interruption.

Nate was leaning against the frame of the back door, a rather bemused expression on his face. "You're just a bit of a pansy." He nodded at the beer. "Bad day?"

"Something like that. Want one?" Miles asked, and withdrew another longneck bottle of Corona.

"Shit, yes." Nate walked in and took the beer, sliding into one of the kitchen chairs.

"What's your excuse?"

"Other than the criminal case against Denny Filbert heating up? I pulled over Martin Long for speeding today, had him threatening once again to go to the town council about me—when he was the one doing fifty in a school zone during school hours. The state boys are putting in a station here and have already started working on the building. It will be nice to have the extra support, but this is Echo Springs. I'm hoping it doesn't become a bureaucratic nightmare."

"Shit. Do you really think Echo Springs needs a state patrol division?"

"Yes and no. With all the tourists passing through on the highway, it will be nice to have extra support for traffic violations. You will likely be busier on that account when there are more patrols in the area. And it will be nice to have extra backup if needed, but it depends on the troopers who are assigned to this division. They could end up being real assholes. What's your excuse?"

Miles contemplated his beer for a moment before he replied. "You remember how I told you about me and Cybil dating back in the day?"

Nate chuckled. "Yeah. What she'd do? Or did you do something to her?"

"It's not what she did today, but what I did back then. I didn't tell you the full story, I omitted some details. The short version is, I got her pregnant."

Nate choked on his beer. "Excuse me? Pregnant?"

Miles nodded and took a swig before replying. "She miscarried the child. The day after that, her parents died in the car wreck on the way to see her in the hospital. Our relationship imploded in the fallout."

"Are you serious? No wonder she hates you. I'm sorry, dude, that's a raw deal. For both of you."

Miles contemplated a bead of moisture on the beer bottle. "The thing is, I don't think she hates me. I know I don't hate her. In fact, I've been trying to convince her to give me another shot since I happen to love the woman to distraction."

"Seriously? You sure about that?"

"Yep. She's one of the reasons I moved back here. And I don't know how to break through her walls. She took me to our daughter's grave today to drive home why she didn't want to start anything with me again. I didn't even know she'd been buried. Amber Rose Keaton-Roe; doesn't that beat all?"

"I need to get you Old Man Turner's Journal. He's the reason I was able to figure things out when I fucked up with Abby. There might be a kernel of wisdom that could help you."

"What the hell, at this point I'll try anything."

"Then you just might be able to win her back. To Amber." Nate hoisted his beer bottle in a toast.

"To Amber." Miles clinked his beer against Nate's.

"And I'm sorry about the baby. I wish you would have told me about it back then."

"It was just too much to deal with, and it was only six months after my dad died. I handled things poorly with Cybil, which is the understatement of the century."

"Tough break all around," Nate said.

"Speaking of Cybil, did she ever mention anything to you about Dotson trying to grope her in her studio last week?" Miles asked.

Nate's gaze flipped to cop eyes. "No. This is the first I'm hearing about it. What the hell happened?"

It figured that Cybil hadn't said anything. If she wasn't going to do anything about it then Miles would. "He put the moves on her, she kneed him in the family jewels, and I walked in at the tail end when she was telling him to leave. Dotson isn't one to let things like that go."

"Nope, he's not. Thanks for telling me. I'll keep an eye on him, and tell my deputies to do the same. He's always been an asshole."

"No kidding." Miles tipped his beer up. "Where's Abby? Please tell me you didn't piss her off and she tossed you over. It would be a sad state of affairs if we were both in the doghouse."

Nate snorted with a shake of his head. "She's with Tessa and Cybil tonight for an emergency girls' night, which I'm now assuming is on account of you."

"Most likely. Well, we can drink beer and order a pizza. If Jacob's around, we should invite him over and we can all get piss drunk."

"Jacob left this morning for a week of meetings up in Boulder. He likely won't be back until Christmas. I'm up for pizza and beer tonight. Probably won't get piss drunk, but I won't let you drink alone. Let me go get that journal and rescue Rufus."

"You want to bring the mutt over?"

"For a guys' night, absolutely. He'll give me grief otherwise.

Why don't you put that order in for the pizza—extra-large, loaded—and I'll be right back."

It was as good a plan as any. "All right, bring the furball. And the journal. What the hell." Miles pulled out his phone. At least Nate knew about Dotson now, so there was that. As for the rest, he was more resolved than ever to win Cybil's heart back. Even if he had to use tricks from a dead guy.

Chapter 20

From Old Man Turner's Journal:
Fear makes fools of us all.

Across town, Cybil, Tessa, and Abby shared the remaining apple pie and a bottle of chardonnay. Curled up in the living room on the plaid couch, Cybil figured nothing else had worked at soothing her battered heart, so she might as well try baked goods and wine.

"God, this pie is so good. I need the recipe. It's seriously amazing. Although, perhaps not, I want to look good in my wedding dress," Abby said, glancing at her near empty plate.

"Have you guys set a date?" Tessa asked.

"Yep. It's in May. We have save the date cards going out next week. And while we're on the subject, before we get to the emergency behind our impromptu girls' night, I wanted to ask if you guys would be my bridesmaids. My sister's going to be my maid of honor. But I really would love it if you both said yes. And I solemnly swear not to put you in ugly-as-sin bridesmaid dresses. I have a few styles in mind that we can look over at the next girls' night. What do you think? Are you in?"

"Yes. Count me in!" Tessa exclaimed and toasted Abby with her half empty wine glass.

Moved, Cybil said, "Hell yeah, I'm in. I'm touched that you want us in your wedding."

"Well, you two have become my ride or die. I've never had girlfriends like you before. If it weren't for you, I'm not sure I would have had the courage to go after what I really wanted."

"Oh, you're going to make me cry," Tessa said with Gus on her lap.

"Me too, truly. And thanks for coming tonight on such short notice. I've been a wreck all day." Cybil figured putting the problem out there would help her make up her mind. Because her head was saying one thing, while her heart was saying another entirely.

"Well, why don't you start with what happened and go from there," Abby said.

"Okay, so you know how I told you about Miles and I dating when we were teens."

"Yeah, and that there was more to the story." Abby laid her empty plate on the coffee table.

"Well, here's what has happened over the last two weeks." Cybil rehashed her run-ins with Miles, ending with her date with him the previous night. It was the tip of the iceberg of their sordid tale, but it would lay the foundation for what had transpired today.

"Wait, I figured you were the *YogaRose* that Jacob mentioned, but I didn't realize you've been on a few dates. Why didn't you tell me?" Abby exclaimed with hurt in her eyes.

"I didn't want to say anything to anyone. Tessa knows because we live together. And I would have said something the other night when you invited me to dinner, but Miles was there and I didn't want him to know," Cybil admitted, staring into her wine glass.

"It's nothing to be embarrassed about. I've done online dating before," Tessa said with a shrug.

"Me too," Abby replied. "Although not with any great success."

"No, you just had to move to a new town to find love," Tessa teased good-naturedly.

Abby sighed with a small smile. "Yeah, I did. But I want to hear about these other dates."

"And most especially why you were kissing Miles on our front porch last night," Tessa stated, quirking a questioning brow.

"She what? You and Miles? You were kissing him? What?" Abby asked with surprise written all over her face.

"I'm not ashamed of doing online dating. The two dates I went on last week from Matchmakers were total and complete duds, so there was nothing to talk about. Other than the horror of running into Miles while on the first." Cybil shuddered in horror. "But forget about those, because they meant nothing. And yes, I kissed Miles at the end of our date last night."

Abby clapped excitedly. "I knew that there was something more there. You guys have so much chemistry together, it simply sparks like bolts of lightning."

"It was totally hot. You really missed a show, Abby. We're talking full-on tonsil hockey Olympics with Miles." Tessa toasted Cybil before taking a sip of wine.

"It was really hot, although not as hot as the kiss today in my studio.," Cybil admitted.

They gasped.

"Are you getting back together with Miles?" Abby asked her.

"What happened in the studio today? Because any hotter than what I saw last night, I'm surprised you didn't melt all the snow in town. Unless you… oh, did you *do it* in your studio?"

Cybil laughed. "No. We didn't do it, in my studio or

anywhere else. And I don't know what I should do about Miles. After what occurred after our kiss today…"

"Spill the beans," Abby demanded.

Cybil studied her sister and friend. There was no judgement here, and that stoked up her courage. "I stopped the kiss from progressing and showed Miles something today. The thing is, Abby, you were right, there were things about my relationship with him that I didn't tell you. You see, when we were dating, I got pregnant. Miles was so great when I told him, making plans for me and the baby to come live with him in Boulder while he was going to college. But when I was six months along, I miscarried."

"Oh Cybil, I'm so sorry." Abby gripped her hand and squeezed it in a show of support.

"That's not all. I hemorrhaged pretty badly. And it was before we had a full hospital here, so I had to be transferred from the clinic to a hospital on the outskirts of Denver. The day after I miscarried, our parents died in a car crash on the way to see me in the hospital. Tessa was in school, thank god, or she would have been with them."

Abby hugged her then. "I'm so sorry. God, I can't even imagine how hard that must have been for you. And for Miles too."

Cybil blinked at the tears filling her eyes after Abby released her. "And I'm the one who ended our relationship, for a number of reasons. But today, because he brings it all back up for me, I did something I should have done years ago; something I never told him about. I had our daughter's remains buried next to our parents, and took him to her grave today."

Abby put her hands over her mouth with a shimmer of tears in her eyes. She glanced at Tessa, who had silent tears sliding down her cheeks.

"There's more. When I told him that was why I couldn't be

with him, Miles told me he loves me." That had been weighing on her ever since they'd returned from the cemetery.

"Cybil, are you sure you're not letting fear of being hurt guide you?" Abby asked her.

"It was my fault. Our parents' deaths," Cybil held up a hand to stall any words to the contrary, "because if I hadn't gotten pregnant and then miscarried, they wouldn't have been on the highway and in that accident."

"Sis, it's not your fault. Our parents dying in that accident was not because of you. I've never blamed you for their deaths and you shouldn't blame yourself. It was tragic, and I miss them too, but you cannot blame yourself."

"Too late."

"Cybil, I need you to listen to me carefully," Abby said, looking her in the eyes. "I cannot imagine the pain you've been through. But here's the thing: you are letting your fear of getting hurt again keep you from a man who loves you. Can you honestly tell me that you do not have feelings for him?"

Cybil sighed. "No. I can't."

"A few months back, you gave me some really great advice, and now I'm going to return the favor. You already know what your life without him is like, bad dates and all. Don't you owe it to yourself to give you guys a second chance and see what it could be like with him back in it? I know that if it was Nate, I would do it in a heartbeat."

"Sis, Mom and Dad, if they were here today, would tell you that you are being silly. And in my opinion, you've been using their deaths as a reason to shield your heart. In doing so, you dishonor their memory. Mom and Dad always said when it comes to the people we love, we always give them another chance. Stop sitting on the sidelines, letting life pass you by. Because I think if you let this chance go, you will regret it for the rest of your life," Tessa said.

Cybil closed her eyes and lowered her head. They were both right. A set of paws walked over her thighs and a wet nose touched her cheek. She opened her eyes and found Gus in her lap, rubbing his face against her. Abby and Tessa flanked her, each putting an arm around her.

"We're here, whatever you decide to do," Tessa murmured.

Cybil laid her head on her sister's shoulder as Gus made himself at home on her lap. "I know. I will think about all you both said. I've carried this for so long."

"I have a question for you," Abby said.

"Shoot."

"How was it with Miles before all those things happened?" Abby asked her.

And wasn't that the crux of her issue? "Wonderful. He's the only guy I've ever loved."

"I think you have your answer. But I support you whatever decision you make," Abby replied.

"Me too," Tessa said, squeezing Cybil's shoulders.

"Thank you, guys. I need to think about what I want to do, but I will take your advice to heart. In the meantime, I think I'm ready for some more wine. And enough about me, let's talk bridesmaid dresses." Cybil shifted the conversation away from her problems. It was either that or she would be a basket case, sobbing into her wine for the rest of the night.

Because her friends weren't wrong. Her reaction to Miles this afternoon—telling him to leave her be after he'd said he loved her—had been a knee-jerk response. Had she been wrong in blaming herself over her parents' deaths? Maybe. And just that shift in her perception lifted some of the weight she had been carrying all these years.

A simple kiss had left her tossing and turning all night long, burning, aching… for Miles.

Getting involved with him was a slippery slope. She feared

she would only end up crashing and burning, only this time around, there wouldn't be any pieces left to pick up afterwards.

But the truth was that she was tired of standing on the sidelines because what if, like he said, it could be better than before? Wasn't that something worth fighting for? Wasn't he then someone worth fighting for?

Chapter 21

From Old Man Turner's Journal:
It's the unexpected side trips that make life worthwhile.

A few days later, Cybil grimaced as she trudged to her truck at the end of a long workday. Blinding torrents of snow fell around her, coating her head, her shoulders, and the rest of her body. Icy wind slashed against her like knives. She shivered as she climbed into the driver's seat and slammed the door. At least Burke had already called and let her know he was closing the bar due to the storm walloping the town. She slid her key into the ignition and turned it. Nothing happened. No sputter, no grunting chug of belts turning.

She tried a second and third time. Dammit. The battery was officially dead. The one she had been meaning to take into the garage and get replaced for the last two weeks.

Her breath plumed white in the truck cab. She couldn't stay in her frigid vehicle. Cybil mentally calculated the odds of walking home in the blizzard versus sleeping in her studio tonight. At the next gust of wind that rattled her truck like it was a toy, she thought: *to hell with that.* She wasn't walking in this crud. She would never make it home.

Her stomach grumbled.

She glanced at the passenger seat, and the bottles of wine she'd picked up at the store today. Well, on the menu for tonight was wine, and some protein bars she had stashed in her office. It was as good a dinner as any.

She slung her purse strap crosswise over her shoulder, grabbed her keys from the ignition so she could get back in the building, and the bag with her two bottles of wine, took a deep breath, and exited her truck into winter's fury. The icy air stole her breath. Snow pelted against her face. She marched as fast as she could with her head down to the building entrance.

Inside, she headed back up to her studio. Just inside the door, she removed her sodden coat and boots, dropped her things by the door, and went into her bathroom for a towel. She rubbed the moisture from her hair and leggings the best she could then took the towel with her to dry her stuff enough that it wouldn't wreck her floors.

Once she'd wiped down her things, she studied the studio. It might not be her hybrid gel mattress at home, but she could make a pallet out of a bunch of yoga mats and blankets. She'd be warm and relatively comfortable. Plus, at least her wine bottles had twist-off tops and not corks. Because then she would have cried.

She texted Tessa: *Stuck at the studio. Truck battery is dead. I'm fine. I have food and wine. See you tomorrow.*

Tessa replied: Yikes. Stay safe and warm. I made a batch of white chicken chili from a recipe Abby gave me. So we'll have that all weekend. Let me know if I have to call out the National Guard to rescue you.

Cybil: I'll be fine. See you tomorrow.

Cybil organized herself for the night, constructing a bed of yoga mats and blankets which, after testing it, didn't seem so bad. But she straightened as a thought occurred to her just as she was about to break into her wine. She could sneak into Miles's office and sleep on one of the couches in there. It would be infinitely more comfortable than sleeping on the floor in her studio, even with the yoga mats and blankets.

While Miles locked up every night, he hadn't installed an alarm system yet. That was slated for some time next week, if she recalled correctly. And she knew how to pick a lock. It was a skill she had picked up years ago from a guy she'd briefly dated who had been a locksmith.

She stuffed a few of the protein bars into her purse, grabbed a flathead screwdriver and paperclip, and shoved them into the front pocket of her purse as well. She hefted the bag with her wine and slung one of the folded blankets over her shoulder.

She left the door to her studio unlocked. The building was locked up after hours and could only be accessed if you had a key, so she wasn't worried that someone would enter, not in this storm. This way, she could leave her coat and boots up here to dry and retrieve them in the morning.

Cybil descended the stairs with her haul. At Miles's door, she knelt, retrieved the tools she needed, and got to work on the lock. She listened and felt her way through, found the catch mechanism, and finally heard the tiny, satisfactory click. A grin split her face. Not bad, even if she did say so herself.

She picked up her belongings and hurried through the door before anyone saw her. She closed the door, damn proud of her ingenuity. If there was a crisis, she could fix it. Usually. Being snowed in wouldn't be so bad.

"Cybil? What the hell are you doing in here?" Miles asked, standing in the doorway between his office and the main room with his arms crossed, stretching the material of his pale yellow linen dress shirt.

She winced. Dammit. She hadn't counted on Miles actually being in the office.

"Sorry. My truck won't start." She held up a hand when he opened his mouth. "I know I need to get it into the garage, I've just been busy. With the blizzard hitting full force, I didn't want to chance walking home in the stuff, and figured I'd camp out here on one of your couches."

"Okay, that's fine by me. But how exactly did you get into my office? The door was locked. And I don't remember giving you a key."

She bit her bottom lip and gave him a sheepish glance. "Yeah, about that. I sort of picked the lock."

"Breaking and entering. Tsk, tsk, that's a new one," Miles said with a sardonic grin.

"I just wanted to use you," she explained, and almost dropped the wine when she realized what she had just said.

A golden eyebrow rose and a grin tugged at his lips—his sexy-as-sin lips she had thought about non-stop since their last encounter.

She sputtered over her gaffe. "I meant one of your couches. To sleep on. Instead of on the floor with a bunch of yoga mats."

"You sure about that? Anyway, I might be persuaded to share my couches with you, but that depends."

"On what?"

"On what you have in there." He nodded toward her wine bag.

She sighed and held up the bag. "This, my good man, is some of the finest wine of the twist-off variety one can find at Fitzgerald's Market. Plus, I have a rather decent selection of protein bars that I would be happy to let you share for dinner, in return for one of your couches."

"Ha ha. I can do you one better. The casserole brigade hasn't taken the hint since I shut down the dating app. Follow me." Miles gestured and walked into the breakroom. With her stomach grumbling, she followed him. Cybil gasped as he held the refrigerator door open.

"What in the world?" The shelves were stuffed with dishes. And she noted the coffee creamer in the door, as well as some sodas, and bottled water. This night was getting better and better.

"Courtesy of Jacob and Nate. I had three casseroles delivered this morning alone. Apparently, on the dating profile those two knuckleheads I call friends cooked up for me, it says one of the things I love most is a good casserole. I admit, some of them haven't been half bad. My assistant and I have been eating our way through them at lunch over the last week, and judging them."

"I propose a trade. I'll give you some of my wine in exchange for what's in the fridge and one of the couches," Cybil offered, setting the blanket and her purse on one of the chairs before placing the wine on the table.

"Sounds like the best proposal I've had all day."

They pulled out dishes and piled fixings onto plates, then nuked them in the microwave. They sat at the small break table, eating taco casserole, some cheesy potato casserole that Cybil already wanted seconds of, and a chicken and dumpling casserole.

Cybil handed Miles one of the wine bottles, and she took its twin. Twisting the top off, she drank wine directly from the bottle.

"So, long day, huh?" Miles said around a bite. His eyes crinkled in merriment.

"Yeah. At least Burke closed Smitty's so I don't have to worry about a shift tonight. Why didn't you head home already?"

"Nate called an hour ago; told me the streets to his and Abby's places were being shut down because the weather's so bad. He's sleeping at the station tonight. Told me it would be best to stay here since I hadn't left yet."

"What about Abby? She's all alone at the house."

Miles shrugged. "She'll be fine. She has Rufus and a backup generator. Why hadn't you left yet?"

Cybil sighed. It was her own fault she was stuck. "I was trying to get some paperwork squared away. There always seems to be so much paperwork involved in owning a business. And I thought I had more time before the brunt of the storm moved in, but this squall blew in faster than expected."

"That's what Nate was saying. Apparently, the highway is a mess. Highway patrol shut it down right before he called me," Miles explained.

"Boy, did you hit the jackpot with these casseroles. They're definitely coming in handy tonight."

"That they are, and the wine definitely complements them. Plus, there's dessert too."

"There's dessert? Really? You do know the way to a woman's heart, I'll give you that."

"Yep, peach cobbler, which I can say—after taste testing a piece at lunch—is spectacular," Miles admitted. His plate was already empty as he went over to the fridge.

"I can make room for peach cobbler." She only had a few bites left of dumpling and then it was on.

"I figured you might. You always did like dessert." He returned with the dish. He peeled back the aluminum foil and set the pan between them. They eschewed the plates and ate directly from the dish.

Cybil realized Abby and Tessa were right, and she was a scared ninny, letting fear drive her. She was tired of being afraid. "Miles, I'm sorry for everything that happened earlier this week. And for keeping the grave a secret."

"Cybil, you don't owe me any explanations. If I had been there for you when you needed me most, things would have been different. And I'm sorry that I let you down." He covered her hand with his. Warmth shot through her at the innocuous touch.

"The thing is, for a long time, I've blamed myself for what

happened to my parents. That if I'd not gotten pregnant and miscarried then…" She swallowed the lump in her throat.

Miles quietly finished the sentence for her. "Then they wouldn't have died. Jesus, Cyb. That was not your fault."

It was still hard to accept. She figured it would get better, that *she* would get better, with time. "Realistically, deep down, I know that. And I'm working on believing that. Can you forgive me for keeping her grave a secret? She was both of ours, and I had no right to keep it from you."

Miles surprised her. He scooped her up and settled her on his lap so that she was curled against him. With his thumb, he wiped the stray tear from her cheek and pressed his lips against her forehead. "Babe, there's nothing to forgive. It was a hard time for both of us. I was still in a bad mental state over losing my dad the previous spring. I think it was just an awful situation all around and we did the best we could. I'm glad you did tell me, though, no matter how long it took."

"Miles." She shifted her face into his shoulder. It felt like the most natural thing in the world to slide her arms around his neck. The exposed skin still bore traces of his woodsy male cologne. He stroked a hand over her back, soothing her, offering comfort. But the caresses also stirred her, making tendrils of heat coil in her belly.

Cybil stayed curled in his arms. Her body melted with each stroke. She was a moron for pushing him away, for making that promise in the first place—the one she had regretted ever since. Her sister was right; a promise like that, made under duress, wasn't something anyone could still hold her to today. They weren't a couple of kids anymore. And the answer to what she wanted became startlingly clear.

Lifting her head, she cupped his face between her hands. "Be with me, Miles. Put your hands on me."

His eyes blazed with lust. "You sure? Be certain, because once I start—"

She put her finger over his lips. "I want you, Miles. I never stopped."

Cybil slid her finger from his mouth, keeping her gaze open and on his as she leaned in until his lips were a breath away. With a groan, Miles eliminated the remaining distance and took her mouth in a hot, hungry exchange. One kiss bled into two until she wasn't breathing unless it came from him.

Her hands worked at the buttons on his dress shirt, tugging and pulling on the linen material until his flesh was bared to her seeking hands. She moaned in the back of her throat. His chest hair tickled the tips of her fingers. Good God, he was even more ripped than he had been back then.

The man tore his mouth from hers long enough to tug off her top and sports bra. His eyes roved over her chest. Hunger darkened his gaze. His large, strong hands cupped her flesh as his mouth claimed hers once more. He grazed his thumbs over her nipples, and bolts of pleasure shot straight to her center.

Cybil threaded her fingers through his hair, imprisoning his mouth against hers. She was lost in him, in the heady tangle of heat and passion, in the way he nipped her bottom lip and ravaged her mouth while he kneaded her flesh.

Miles shifted an arm beneath her knees and rose, carrying her over to the plaid couch, his lips never leaving hers. With a tenderness that made her sigh, he laid her back and lifted his mouth. Her breathing heavy, she watched him remove his shirt the rest of the way and toss it over one of the chairs as he toed off his shoes.

The man was simply gorgeous in that big, alpha man refined way, brimming with electricity. And for the life of her, she couldn't fathom why it had taken her so long to say yes to this, to him. He withdrew a condom from his wallet before he removed his slacks and boxers in one single, smooth move.

Miles still looked like an avenging archangel with his hard, rangy build full of rippling muscles and sinew. His golden skin stretched taut over broad shoulders and washboard abs, with a happy trail that led to one of the finest cocks ever on a man. She licked her lips at the sight of his long, thick erection. "I forgot how much I enjoyed seeing you naked."

"Yeah? Back at you. What do you say we get those pants off you?" Miles's simmering gaze made her breath catch.

Cybil nodded as he returned, toeing her socks off. He laid the foil packet on the arm of the couch above her head before lowering himself down. Leaning over her, he took her mouth in a torrid tangle of tongues and teeth. He ran his fingers along the sides of her body, past the curve of her breasts, to the waistband of her yoga pants. Then his mouth left hers on a meandering erotic journey down her neck and over the slope of her breast.

He took his time, placing open-mouthed hungry kisses on each spot as he relearned her form with his mouth, teeth, and tongue. She threaded her hands back in his hair, her gaze lowered as he seduced her. Liquid pulls of need drew tauter with every caress, each touch and nip of flesh until he moved to his knees beside the couch and was lowering her pants, drawing them down her legs. Once he'd removed them, tossing them over his broad shoulder, he gazed at her with devastating hunger.

"You're so fucking gorgeous. I need to taste you. I've dreamt of this, of you," he said huskily, parting her thighs, and tearing off the strip of lace covering her.

"Miles." She moaned as he angled her body, letting her calves rest over his shoulders.

"I'll buy you a hundred just like it." And then his mouth was on her most intimate flesh.

Her back arched as he drove her body up into the heavens, sucking her skin, torturing her in the most pleasurable way imaginable. Miles was relentless, using his tongue and teeth. He held her steady as he plundered, drawing out the ecstasy. Cybil moaned and writhed. She panted, her body enflamed at his wicked assault on her senses. He took her higher, and pleasure boiled over as he sent her body hurtling over the edge.

"Oh god," she cried at the waves crashing.

She reached for him when he rose over her and rolled the condom over his shaft. Only when he'd protected them both, did he join her on the couch and position himself between her splayed thighs. He held himself aloft with one hand as he settled the head of his cock at her entrance.

"Look at me," he demanded in a low growl.

Cybil lifted her eyes and met his carnal gaze, and only then did he plunge inside. One moment she was empty, and the next, he filled her to the point where she was overflowing. She moaned at the intensity of sensations that swamped her. "Miles."

He lowered his forehead to hers. Breathing heavily, he held still, giving her body a moment to adjust. "I know. I feel it too. It's like coming home."

Miles claimed her mouth in a torrid, hungry mating and began to rock his hips. She joined him, undulating, and writhing beneath him. The tempest between them was as wild and raging as the one Mother Nature was raining down upon the outside world.

Cybil met him stroke for stroke, lifting her hips. Her nails dug into the rock hard muscles of his back. This was what had been missing from her life. *He* was what had been missing; this connection that went deeper than merely physical. It was a passion that eclipsed all else until he was sole focus of her universe.

She knew his body, remembered the way he moved. Their hips met, shifting seamlessly. It was like coming home after being lost in the wilderness. It was lovemaking that re-forged her into something more because he touched her, vanquishing the sorrows of yesterday, and restoring her faith in the promise of tomorrow.

This, right here with him, was everything. It always had been, and deep down, Cybil understood the reason why she had never moved on, had never been able to. It was because the moment he had rocketed into her world, there was no one else who would ever come close to him.

Miles's mouth left hers and he watched her through his hooded eyes. Need gathered and built. Their bodies writhed with the storm as it increased in intensity and fervor. She lost herself in his eyes. He plunged as her hips rose to meet him. Their gazes locked as the tide swept up inside, and hurtled her body over the precipice.

"Miles!" She keened as her body imploded. Cybil quaked around him as he thrust, and his body strained as he followed her over the ledge with a rough groan, and buried his face against her neck.

Her hands lay limp against his lower back, but she was too languorous to move them. Their limbs and bodies were entangled, her legs wrapped around his waist, and she felt the rapid thumping of his heartbeat against her breast. His breath tickled the delicate skin of her neck. Cybil didn't want to move from this spot.

She still loved him. Had always loved him. But she wasn't quite ready to admit it. The words stuck in her throat. Holding him tight, she kept the words to herself.

It was Miles who finally shifted, lifting his head slightly, and gazing down at her, his eyes warm and heavy lidded.

"Well. I see we haven't lost our touch," he murmured, stroking his knuckles over her cheek.

Cybil felt the delicate, tender caress down to her toes. "No, we haven't. Why did we wait so long to do that again?"

The grin that spread over Miles's lips caused her heart to tremble. "I have no idea. But I want to do it again and again."

She sighed. "Well, Counselor, I would have to agree with you. But there's something else."

"What?"

"I've missed you." It was as much of an admission of her feelings as she could make right now.

"God, I've missed you too, babe. And I'm not going anywhere. Now or later." His mouth descended again, and it was quite some time before they surfaced for air.

Chapter 22

13 years ago

"So where are you taking me?" Cybil asked. Miles navigated his truck around a sharp curve with a sheer two-hundred-foot drop-off that made her belly flipflop around like a fish tossed onto dry land.

"You'll have to be patient. I promise you'll love it." He shot her a seductive, lop-sided smirk.

How had she ever thought moving to Echo Springs was a bad idea? It had turned into the best thing ever. If her dad hadn't gotten the job with the police department here, she never would have met Miles. And that was unimaginable to her.

This was the best Fourth of July so far in her short life. The day had dawned with a crystal-clear Colorado blue sky, with temperatures rocketing up into the nineties. They'd spent the better part of the day at the local town fair. Every year, Main Street was closed to car traffic to allow for pedestrians. There was a parade along the main drag in the morning that ended at the high school, and was where the bulk of the holiday celebration occurred. Carnival rides were erected on the high school football field. Vendors sold everything, from tee shirts to handmade jewelry and artwork from their booths. And then there was the food, hotdogs and funnel cake. The scent of barbecue, cotton candy, and beer filled the air.

Her dad was working crowd control today, which wasn't unusual. Most holidays, he was either on call or on duty. Her mom and sister were working the Echo Springs Police Department booth, where they were selling hot dogs, burgers, and funnel cakes to help raise money for the department. She'd worked the early morning shift for her dad. Cybil had to admit that this town, the community of people here, had grown on her—most of all, Miles.

She sighed and watched him drive. An easy smile hovered over his handsome face. Every time he looked at her, her breath hitched in her throat. Since their first bowling date, they'd been inseparable. It was hard for Cybil to think about her life before Miles's advent into it.

They talked for hours about nothing and about everything, from theories about life on other planets, to dreams of what they wanted to be, to topics as innocuous as who should play the villain in the next superhero flick.

Last weekend, she'd introduced Miles to her parents. It had been his idea, not hers, and it had gone over better than she expected. Her dad didn't even break out his gun. Cybil had a feeling her mom had played a large part in that. It was nice because she no longer had to hide her relationship from them, even though a part of her wanted to hoard Miles all to herself. Not because she was ashamed of their relationship, far from it. It was just that she had never felt like this before—like she was standing on top of a bridge with a bungee cord, ready to jump over the side for the thrill of the ride. Her feelings for Miles staggered her and were a little terrifying, too, because of how quickly she'd fallen for him.

She loved him. As in the big L love. This wasn't a girl's love either.

Her untried heart trembled with the force and depth of her love for him. She'd not told him yet. She worried that it was too much too soon to bring it up because guys were not as in touch with their feelings as girls. And the last thing she wanted to do was scare him off.

"I can see the wheels turning in that big brain of yours. Talk to me," Miles said, turning off the paved road onto what was little more than a dirt path surrounded by evergreens.

"Well, it just seems like we're going to a place where I'm going to have to worry about running into an escaped convict with a fishhook for a hand."

"Worried about my safety?" Miles grinned as he teased her.

"Nope. About mine. Everyone knows the boyfriend gets it first," she replied, holding her breath. It was the first time she'd called him that out loud to his face. In her mind, it was what he was, even though they had never defined their relationship.

"Not all the time. Sometimes the boyfriend saves the day and rescues his girlfriend," he shot back, his features alight with mischief and warmth.

Her breath caught in her throat. "And is that what I am?"

He slanted her the side-eye and said, "Of course you are. Why would you think otherwise?"

"Because you've never said it before now."

"Ah, so you were fishing, huh?"

"Little bit."

Miles brought the hand threaded with his up and brushed his lips over the back. "I wouldn't have risked your father's wrath—or his gun collection—if we weren't. You're mine, babe."

She felt the blush spread over her cheeks as her heart rolled over and exposed its soft underbelly. "And that means you're mine too, and no one else's."

"Yeah, it does."

She had a retort chock full of sarcasm on her lips when the

line of evergreens shrouding their view parted, like a curtain being drawn back, to reveal an achingly beautiful mountain meadow full of tall grass and wildflowers waving in the breeze, with a tiny mountain stream glistening silver on its path. The sun neared its descent on the western horizon, casting the field in a golden-orange glow. At the far end of the park, rising in sharp, jagged edges, was the slate megalith of the mountain peak, its towering crest dotted with patches of white glacier that refused to melt.

The air up here was markedly cooler at the higher elevation, similar to what it was at Echo Lake. "It's gorgeous, Miles. Where are we exactly? Is it okay that we're up here?"

"It's another one of my favorite spots. The locals call this spit of land Prospect Point. Used to come camping up here with my dad. It was his land, and now it's mine."

"This is yours?" Cybil said, shocked at his admission. To own something this grand at nineteen made him even more austere and adult in her mind.

"Yep. I thought we'd camp out under the stars. From up here we can watch the town's fireworks display with almost a front row seat."

He pulled the truck up next to the creek bed, then got out and arranged the provisions he'd brought with them in the bed of his truck. Cybil glanced at the spread. He had sleeping bags, two of them that he zipped together, extra blankets, and a cooler with soda and snacks. He hauled her up into the back with him.

"What do you think?" he said, nodding at the spread. He'd packed a picnic with deli sandwiches, cheese, apples, and chips.

"Miles, it's wonderful. Can we eat?" she asked him.

"Absolutely." He tugged her down, and handed her a plate. They gorged on the feast, with their backs propped against the cab of the truck as night descended around them.

Miles built a small campfire near the truck.

"You sure no one is going to come out with a hook?" She had

one of the blankets wrapped around her shoulders to ward off the chill.

"Yeah, you don't have to worry about that. We need to be more concerned with cougars, wolves or bears. The fire should keep them away, but that's why I'm going to lock all the food and trash up in the truck cab. So they don't smell the food."

"Cougars, bears? I'm not so sure about this. Are you sure it's safe?" Cybil glanced around the firelit clearing and Miles laughed.

"Haven't you ever been camping?"

"No." She harrumphed as he clambered back into the truck with her.

"You know I'll protect you. You have nothing to fear. I have a shotgun in the truck cab in the event we get any unwanted visitors," Miles said, and drew her into his arms. Her heart fluttered in her chest, and her pulse sped up. She shivered against him. "And you're freezing. Come on, let's get you in the sleeping bags. The fireworks are about to begin." He helped her climb in and joined her. This way, they could cuddle.

She snuggled up against him just as the first explosion of light lit up the sky. The fireworks were so close, she could practically reach out and touch them. In fiery reds and golden flare, in blues and vibrant greens, the brilliant display flashed.

"It's amazing," she whispered, awe-struck by the display.

"Yeah, it's not half bad." He brushed his lips against her forehead, his arm around her as they watched the fireworks.

After the spectacular grand finale had ended, they lay under the inky velvet sky dotted with stars, surrounded by the sounds of nature settling down for the night, and the scent of wood burning in their little campfire. And Cybil couldn't help but think it was the most perfect night of her life.

She pointed out her favorite constellations, from Pegasus to Cassiopeia to Perseus.

"You've got such an intriguing mind," Miles said.

"I like learning. And putting that knowledge to practical use. I'm not necessarily a scholar."

"Pretty close."

"I just like knowing, is all. Thank you for today, by the way. In case I forget to tell you later, I've had the best time."

Miles shifted his large frame so that he was looking down at her, and the look in his eyes caused shivers to erupt inside her. He was beautiful with the firelight shading his face.

"You're welcome. But you know, it's not all one-sided. It means I get to spend time with you," he said. Dipping his head down, he brushed his lips over hers.

The light caress speared her clear down to her toes. When she sighed, Miles deepened the kiss. Cybil's hands slid up his chest as need hummed and flowed over her body. She knew in that moment, he was it for her. That she would never love anyone the way she loved Miles. And she wanted him, wanted to show him what he meant to her even despite her smattering of fear of the unknown, over whether her untried, virgin form would know what to do.

Her budding passion and love guided her movements. Miles settled himself between her thighs. He was still fully clothed, but the hard masculine lines of him, the solid feel of his body pressed against hers, and the swollen bulge of his member intimately fitted against her groin, heightened the sensations washing over her. A fever stole into her, a need that was pure and feminine. She desired him like no other, and wanted him to show her what their bodies could do together. Their breaths merged into one as the kiss turned hungry and deep.

Cybil could kiss him this way forever. When they were like this, when he kissed her, the rest of the world fell away.

Miles lifted his head, panting. He moved to shift away, his face strained with need.

Before he could retreat, she placed her palm tenderly against his cheek, her gaze unwavering. Then, with her heart in her throat, she whispered, "Make love with me, Miles. I want you to be my first."

Tension entered his face, and he said, "Cybil, are you sure? I don't want to rush you."

"I love you. Make love to me, make me your woman."

He tenderly cupped her face, his eyes searching hers with an intensity that stole the air from her lungs. "Christ, I love you, Cybil. I promise I'll be gentle."

"I trust you." She smiled up at him, feeling like she was floating in this euphoria of love for him that was so fierce, she was surprised she didn't burst with happiness. He loved her. It was amazing. It awed her that this man could love her so much.

Miles lowered his mouth back down to hers and claimed her lips. There was a new urgency, a new sensation behind it, and she dove into the deep end of the pool, ready to experience the adventure of what their bodies could do together.

Cybil returned his passionate kisses as they bled from one to another. Miles was rock hard above her, and she gyrated her hips against his. The air thickened. She panted and sighed at every tingle and new sensation full of pleasure. Need swamped her movements. They shoved at each other's clothing. Miles drew her top off and unhooked her bra. He gazed at her naked breasts, the first man to ever do so.

"You're so fucking beautiful," he whispered huskily.

Then he skimmed his hands over the tender globes, cupping and kneading them. Her lips parted on a small gasp. Miles dipped his golden head and sucked one of her nipples.

Oh my! So this was what she had been missing. Cybil arched her back at the exquisite sensations. Each tug of his mouth on her spiraled pleasure like lightning through her body to coalesce in her belly.

Miles paid homage to her breasts until they felt swollen, the nipples taut. She tugged at his tee shirt, impatient to see him, to feel his chest. He helped her draw his shirt off. In the firelight, she stared at the hard, muscled planes of his chest. His muscles rippled, drawing her fingers to his flesh. Entranced by him, she trailed her fingers over his impressive shoulders, down over his hard pectorals, scraping them through the dusting of short chest hair to the flat discs of his nipples, marveling at the way they hardened beneath her touch, and the way Miles's chest rumbled with a deep groan as his lips crashed over hers. An urgency settled over them, a furor of mouths and tongues, tasting one another. After they'd shoved their shoes off, Miles drew her shorts down her legs and whisked them off until she was before him in nothing but her panties.

The hunger on his face sent her heart tripping over in her chest. She'd never had anyone look at her the way Miles did.

He shoved his jeans off, but not before retrieving a small foil packet from his wallet and placing it beside her.

"Planned ahead, I see," she panted.

He glanced at her. "I didn't expect this tonight. If you don't want this, it's okay, I won't rush you. I would just rather we be safe."

Looking at the protrusion of flesh tenting his boxers, Cybil for the first time in her life, felt her power as a woman. Of course Miles would be prepared. That's who he was to the depths of his soul. He prepared for every scenario.

She rose so that they were both kneeling in the bed of the truck, face to face. A hum of anticipation, of expectation, flowed in the space between them.

Cybil trailed her fingers down over the firm ridges of his abdomen, while Miles didn't move. His hands clenched at his sides as he let her explore his body. At the waistband of his boxers, she teased the edges and then slid her hands beneath and cradled his length.

"Cybil," he hissed as she explored his shaft, running her fingers over the velvety smooth crown, down the firm length to the soft sac at the base of his member.

She looked up at him then. "I want you, Miles. I want this."

With a groan, he cupped her jaw, and his mouth ravished her. Kissing her, he maneuvered her onto her back. Her body was on fire. He trailed his lips down her skin, over her breasts and belly. He hooked his thumbs around the slip of her lace panties and drew them down her legs, his mouth following them down.

And then his mouth was on her most intimate flesh, his tongue sliding over nerve endings she hadn't even known she had. Cybil's legs fell open wider as he tasted her, driving her body up to an exquisite peak of pleasure so profound, she could do little but ride the waves of it.

When her body crested and broke, tautening in on itself as her swift, sudden climax stole over her, she gasped, "Miles," like a benediction.

Then he shoved his boxers down and rolled a condom over his member. He settled back between her thighs. With gentle care, he guided himself inside her, pressing forward slowly until he encountered a flimsy barrier.

"Cybil. A moment of pain only," he said. His voice shook with the effort it took him to hold himself back.

"I know it will hurt at first. I trust you. Don't stop. Please don't stop. I love you."

With a ragged groan, Miles rolled his hips and pushed past the small barrier until he was fully seated inside. A piercing lance of pain shot through her system. Tears glistened at the corners of her eyes. He stayed still, allowing her body to adjust to the fullness of him inside her. He gazed down at her with such concern, such love. Then he kissed her, holding her until she was ready. Her arms clasped around his back, she let him guide her.

They stayed that way, connected in every way possible, until Cybil felt the urge to move, to undulate her hips. And when she did, pleasure unlike anything she'd ever experienced descended over her.

Miles needed no urging. He rocked his hips, gliding through

her over sensitized tissues, slowly at first, allowing Cybil to find the rhythm of the dance. Instinctually, she wrapped her legs around his waist, and he slid inevitably deeper.

They held each other tight, moving together in a sinuous melding that wasn't purely physical. She poured her heart into her movements, caught up in him. And he did the same with her, trapped under the same hypnotic spell. They moved as one, reveling in the feel of one another, muscles and sinews bunching and contracting. His mouth moved over hers, his tongue delving inside just as his hips canted and rocked, plunging his shaft.

Her body crested and broke over the summit of ecstasy.

Miles strained within the shelter of her arms. His body shuddered and jerked as the same madness swept over him. They moved until the final thrumming of pleasure diminished and every ounce of ecstasy had been expended. Their bodies were slick with perspiration, their arms wrapped around each other. Miles had buried his face in the crook of her neck.

At her shiver, he shifted, pulling the covers back over them both but not letting her go as he rolled them so that she was nestled at his side. He tipped her face up, his hand caressing her cheek.

"I love you, Cyb."

"I love you too. Oh, Miles, is it always like that?" she murmured, unable to keep the awe or the love from her voice.

"No, it's not," he said earnestly, his gaze warm.

She stayed in the circle of his arms, certain that no other woman had ever lost her virginity so wonderfully. And she knew it had to do with the arms that held her close, the man who sighed with contentment, his lips pressed to her forehead.

Cybil loved him. She knew he was leaving for college in the fall, but in her mind, as long as he loved her, they could overcome anything. Even distance.

Chapter 23

From Old Man Turner's Journal:
Make every day with the woman you love count. Don't let a day pass without telling and showing her how you feel.

There was a small boulder pressing down on his bare chest. Miles lifted an eyelid to discover what it was, and found the large tomcat staring at him. Gus glared like he wasn't quite sure of what to make of him in Cybil's bed, especially when the woman was no longer in it.

"Good morning," he mumbled to the feline.

Miles didn't want to startle the cat and end up with claws in his chest. With care, he lifted his hand up for Gus to sniff with the hope that he could move the butterball off his chest and go in search of Cybil.

After the blizzard had dumped twenty-two inches of snow on Friday night, he was able to dig his Escalade out of the snow the next afternoon. The roads up to Abby's house were still impassable, but he was able to at least get them to Cybil's place.

To say that they had binged on one another was putting it mildly.

Gus snuffled at his fingertips for a minute before rubbing his cheek against Miles's hand and purring loudly.

"You're not so bad, for a cat."

Gus stared blandly.

"Don't take it personally, I just happen to be more of a dog person." Miles stroked his hand over Gus and winced when the furball began to knead his paws, claws and all, into his chest.

"Oh, I see someone is making friends," Cybil said with a smile, entering the room in nothing but a towel. Her wet hair was slicked back from her face and fell over her delicate shoulders. Miles couldn't help it—one look at her, and a very male part of him was up.

That he could want her again after they had done little more than indulge in pleasure for the better part of thirty-six hours still amazed him.

"Yeah, he seems to like me. Although he wasn't whom I was hoping for… Why don't you come back to bed, and I'll show you?"

She cast him a sly grin. "I wish I could. I have to get to the studio. I have classes to teach today. And a shift at Smitty's tonight."

Miles gently shifted the cat off his chest, much to the cat's dismay. "When does your first class start?" He slipped out of bed, unmindful of his nudity, or the fact that he was very up. He nipped her around the waist and tugged her in, imprisoning her in his arms.

"Forty-five minutes, so no monkey business."

"I only need ten minutes," he murmured, scoring his teeth along her neck. His hands worked the towel from her fingers and backed her up against the wall beside the nightstand.

"Miles," she protested feebly.

"Say yes, and I'll buy you breakfast on the way." He nibbled on the pulse in her throat as his hand dipped between her thighs to tease her flesh and found her wet.

"God. Yes, but hurry," she moaned.

Miles grabbed a condom from the box on the nightstand and rolled it on. Then he was lifting her up, pressing her back against the wall. Cybil wrapped her legs around him, panting in his ear.

With a rough groan, he penetrated her sheath until he was surrounded by her. He palmed her ass, using the wall for leverage, and lost himself in her. It was this way every damn time. She blotted out the rest of the world until the only thing he could see, the only thing he wanted, was her. Need and love drove him as he plundered and took.

Her cries echoed in the room. Miles claimed her mouth, wanting—nay, needing—to impart that this wasn't over. He wanted to imprint himself on her body so that he was all she craved. Because he knew she was it for him.

Cybil met his passion with her own; her lithe legs wrapped about his waist, she undulated, taking him deep. He felt the first shudders of her climax as she moaned his name.

And he followed her over, straining, plunging, thrusting deep as he came so hard, his knees almost buckled from the force. Miles looked at her, still embedded inside her, and said, "I love you, Cyb. And I know you're not ready to say it back to me yet. I will give you time, the time you need to believe in us again. But I'm not playing around here, I'm in this for the long haul."

Her expression changed; she withdrew slightly. He tried not to let it affect him.

"Miles. I care about you. I'm not there yet. I want to be, I just..."

"We've got time. No rush, and no pressure. I'll drive you to the studio." He helped her disentangle their limbs and placed her on her feet.

He took care of the condom and started to dress, giving her his back. Only then did he grimace. She was holding back. As open and giving as she had been with her body, she still wasn't letting him back in.

"Miles, I'm sorry. I just need time."

Sliding his wrinkled dress shirt on, he turned her way, buttoning the shirt up while she pulled on yoga pants. "I realize that. And I'm not mad. I know it's going to take time for you to trust me, trust that I'm not going anywhere."

"It's not that, I just," she blew out a breath, "need to hurry or I'm going to be late. We need to pick this up another time," she said, shoving her feet into her boots.

"Count on it." Was there something else she was hiding from him?

They finished getting ready and were out her door in five minutes after waving goodbye to a smirking Tessa in the kitchen. On the way to his building and the studio, they picked up coffee and breakfast sandwiches, with minutes to spare by the time they arrived.

Miles escorted her into the building and up to the studio. Once it was open, he said, "Give me the keys to your truck. I'll contact the garage and get it towed so Mike can look it over. I have to shovel my mom's drive. What time do you need to be at Smitty's? I'll make sure I come back by and will drive you."

"Five, but you don't have to, I can get Tessa—"

"Cybil, I've got it. You're not alone anymore. Now, truck keys." He held out his hand, patiently waiting until she complied.

"It's sweet that you want to help. I appreciate it. Just tell Mike to call me when it's fixed and I'll take care of it."

"Sure thing," he said, like he was going to go along with that. The least he could do was get her truck fixed. He'd been in her place and seen the furniture that had been her parents'. He was so damn proud of her, but he also knew life had been harder on her than it had been on him. He also had a need to assuage his guilt over leaving her high and dry.

"Miles. I know that look. Don't even think about it, mister." She huffed.

"I don't know what you're talking about." He kissed her quickly. "See you in a couple hours."

And he strode out, hearing her exaggerated sigh. But he didn't waste any time. From his office, he contacted Mike O'Toole, who had a slate of tows to do today because of the weather but promised to get to Cybil's truck at some point if Miles dropped off the keys with him. On the way to his place, he stopped at the garage and gave Mike his credit card, instructing him to bill him.

Cybil wasn't materialistic in any way; Miles just wanted to ease things for her. Make life better than it had been, and yeah, in some ways, show her how good it could be.

After the garage, Miles headed to Abby's place for a shower and change of clothes. He'd likely need a shower again after he shoveled his mom's driveway as well, but it couldn't be helped. The roadways were slick up Echo Lake Drive.

That gave him an idea for the unused space on the second floor of his building. Instead of leasing it out, he could have Aiden turn it into another living space. Make it into a place he and Cybil could stay in if they were caught out by the weather again.

Until that time, while he was still at Abby's house, he packed a bag with a dress shirt and shoes. If he was picking Cybil up from Smitty's at midnight, the roads to get back up here would be more treacherous than he wanted to risk with her. And he planned to convince her to let him stay the night again.

In fact, from here on out, he didn't plan on spending a night without her.

Chapter 24

From Old Man Turner's Journal:
Falling in love is easy. Being in love, learning to value the other and working toward a lasting relationship takes time, trust, and honesty.

The following Friday, Cybil finished her morning classes, failing yet again to approach Ella. Every day that passed, Miles nudged her about her feelings. But until she could speak with his mom about that promise, and ask her to tell Miles, they were in a stalemate. As much as she wanted to have their conversation face to face, Cybil panicked each time she saw Ella. And that was why she was sitting in her office, staring at her phone with Ella's contact information on the screen, debating whether she should click the green button to call her or not, when Cybil heard male voices across the hall. With an hour before her next class began, she headed out to investigate.

In the hall, she recognized Miles's deep baritone, and couldn't help the thrill that shot through her.

This past week had been nothing short of spectacular. Since

their little snowed-in couch session, they had spent every spare second together, with sleepovers taking place mainly at her house. This morning they were in the shower when Tessa walked in to use the facilities. There was nothing quite like mortifying your sister at six in the morning.

At least Tessa hadn't seen anything, only heard their laughter when she realized Cybil wasn't in the shower alone.

The door to the suite across the hall was open. Being nosy, Cybil poked her head in and found Miles with Aiden O'Toole. Aiden's rangy frame was in jeans, a tool belt, and boots. His rugged jaw was covered with a short black beard. He spied her first.

"Hey Cybil," Aiden said in acknowledgement with a friendly smile.

"Cybil," Miles murmured in a low voice, his eyes traveling over her form down to her bare toes until he met her stare with a seductive grin.

She cleared her throat, ignoring the blush Miles's heated stare caused to flare in her cheeks. Damn him. "Hey, is there going to be a new tenant?"

"Yep. Me. Give me just a minute with Aiden and I'll explain," Miles said, and shifted his attention back to Aiden. "How soon can you get started on this space?"

"Well, with it being winter, in the next week or so. I have one interior remodel across town that I'm finishing up on now. Once that job is in the books, I can get started here. If the specs we discussed are what you want to go with, I will start ordering materials so they get here in time for me to begin."

"I say let's do it. If last week's storm was any indication, I will be spending a lot of nights here. Better to be safe than sorry," Miles replied.

Aiden nodded and tucked his metal clipboard beneath his arm. "Right you are. I'll get an order of drywall put in and get you sample books for all your fixtures, flooring, knobs, and such by Monday. That way, if anything needs to be special ordered, we can get it in. Might be some delays because of the holidays, but we'll work around it best we can."

"Great, Aiden, thanks for stopping by." Miles shook his hand.

"Not a problem. I'll see you later. Cybil, good to see you," Aiden said with a nod, and headed out the door.

"What's going on? I thought you were building a house at Prospect Point," she said, confused.

"I am, but I forgot how treacherous the roads can be the further away from town one lives. I've been driving in the stuff since I was sixteen but I figured it would be a good idea to have a place here in town. That way, if I'm caught in a storm again, I'll at least have a bed, shower, and the sports channel."

"So this is going to be an apartment for you? In addition to the house up at Prospect Point?" she said, liking the idea. Then she could spend the night with him here and not have to worry about her sister walking in on them.

"Yep. And, I figured it could be an apartment not just for me, but for us." He tugged her close, sliding his arms around her waist. "I'm not trying to get ahead of ourselves, but I want a future with you. One where we aren't living out of overnight bags. I think it would be a start for us."

"And here I was going to offer you a drawer and some closet space—then you go and offer me a whole apartment." She slid her arms around his neck and clasped her hands.

"Is that right? I like the idea. It will suit until this place is reworked into what we need, but Aiden figures it won't take more than a month. Let me show you what I plan to have done with the place. I realize it's all fitted for a business, but Aiden assures me it can be retooled into a perfect apartment space." With an arm still around her waist, Miles drew her over to what currently was a small breakroom for employees, and a bathroom. He was always doing that, touching her, making sure he had a hand on her, as if he couldn't stand not to be. It was something she had missed—for all her bluster and independence, the way he would hold her hand when he drove, or had an arm around her waist when they walked, was a comfort and intimacy she loved.

"This area here will be a bathroom with both a tub and shower stall. There will be two doors to get into the bathroom; one that walks out right about here, into what will be the kitchen area." He showed her. "Basically, he's going to knock out all the walls, pull up the current office grade carpet. Sand and seal the hardwood floors beneath. This area here will be a full kitchen with an island with an overhang countertop. We can get a few barstools, make it a nice eat-in kitchen. He's also going to install a closet between the bath and kitchen for a washer and dryer in the unit.

"The second door for the bathroom will take you through a walk-in closet and into the bedroom. And then the rest of the place will be for a decent sized living room. If we want to work out, then your studio is across the hall."

She could envision it just as he described, and how it could be between them. After a long day, when the weather took a nosedive, instead of battling the elements, she could walk across the hall and be with Miles. Or any time they wanted it to be just the two of them. "I like it." A little too much, and it reminded her of the apartment they had talked about getting all those years ago. They seemed to be coming full circle, and it rattled her. "I think it will be fantastic. Are you sure you want to give up a space you could be renting out and making money from?"

"Babe, I have money. That's not an issue. And truth be told, I'm already paying for this space, so I figured this would be the best use of it. Besides, Nate's sister is moving back, so it might behoove me to free up Abby's place for her to stay in. Don't you think?"

"Well, in that case, I think it's a fabulous idea. And in the meantime, if you want to store some things at my place, I've cleared out a drawer and some closet space for your suits."

She leaned up on her tiptoes and grazed her lips over his in a light caress.

What began as a *hello, happy to see you* kiss quickly transformed into a scorching, ravenous fusing of lips. One kiss blurred into two and then three, each hotter, deeper, darker than the last. When Miles tore his mouth away, they were both panting, gulping for air. Cybil craved him. With a mere kiss, her body electrified.

"I only have thirty minutes before I have clients coming into my office," he said, nipping her bottom lip.

Cybil figured that should be just enough time for what she needed. Because she would never make it through her day otherwise.

"Come with me," she demanded, then gripped his hand and towed him across the hall to her studio. Not that he put up a fight. Quite the opposite; he nibbled on her neck while she locked the studio door behind them. They weren't going to do it against the front door. Someone could see, and it would be a public relations nightmare for them both.

She hissed at his fingers cupping her cleavage through her workout gear and kneading her flesh. She needed him. Now. She dragged him into the tiny bathroom in her office. The moment the door was shut, her hands went to his pants as his lips crashed over hers. She unbuckled and unzipped, slid her hand beneath the waistband of his boxers, and closed her hand around his shaft.

Miles groaned against her mouth. He tugged up her shirt and sports bra, exposed her chest, and cupped her bare breasts, teasing the sensitive flesh.

With her free hand, she fumbled in the vanity drawer for a condom. *Eureka. Found it.* Cybil wrenched her mouth from his and proceeded to sheath his shaft in latex, shoving his pants and boxers further down.

"I need those pants off you, babe, pronto," he said. "Christ, this bathroom is tiny. I don't know if there's room for you to—"

"Here." She swiveled, shoved her pants down to her knees and bent forward, bracing herself against the countertop and vanity with her thighs spread. Staring at his visage, which was shrouded in dark desire, in the reflection of the mirror, she demanded, "Take me. Hard. Fast."

"Jesus," he growled, gripping her hips and positioning himself. One minute Cybil was empty and the next, her body overflowed with him, stretching to accept him, to surrender to his invasion.

With their gazes locked in the mirror, Miles dug his fingers into her hips and took her. This wasn't making love, but a mating. Elemental, carnal, greedy for the pleasure only the other could provide. Miles had always been a consummate lover. He always took her needs into consideration. He palmed her breasts and gripped them tight while he plundered, pounding in hard, deep strokes. The slap of flesh echoed off the walls. Her mouth hung open, moaning and keening. Her breathing was ragged, heaving in and out. She watched his face, infused with desire, lust and, what was more, love.

And it was the love that made her tremble, made her weak, made her feel as if she could do anything as long as he kept loving her. She gripped the edges of the vanity, sobbing as he obliterated the last of her defenses.

Love for him swelled inside her until it was a tangible, living, breathing entity.

His hand snaked down her belly, rubbed against her sensitive nub, and sent her flying. Cybil keened, her gaze going blurry. At the next deep, melding thrust, Miles followed her over with a loud, hoarse growl. He lowered his forehead to her shoulder, their breathing rough as their heart rates returned to normal. Her knees trembled.

God, she wanted to tell him. She wanted to shout her love, her joy in it, to the world.

But she couldn't. Not yet. The past still stood in the way. Until the promise was no longer a secret and his mom admitted the part she'd played, Cybil had to keep those feelings to herself. And there was a part of her that wished with everything she was that she had never let Miles go. In truth, she had caved and conceded defeat first.

Miles lifted his head and cast her a cocky grin that she felt to the depths of her heart. "I must admit, I never had lunch hours like this in Denver."

She laughed. "Well, I would hope not."

He cupped her chin, turned her face, and kissed her, cuddling her for a moment as she sighed into him.

"We make quite the sight," he teased, since their pants were still down at their knees. "It will be nice to have a bed available across the hall."

"We'll never leave, or at least, we won't want to—like, ever."

He chuckled darkly. "That's the idea, babe. That way you'll never want to leave me."

Miles's manner was teasing and loving. But she could see the hint of frustration, and hurt, he tried to hide. Cybil drew up her pants. "I'll give you a minute to put yourself back together." She kissed him quickly and left the bathroom, needing a moment to gather herself.

Sex in her bathroom at work. Only Miles could push her to those extremes. And she wasn't sorry at all. When he joined her out in the studio, he looked for all the world like a professional, giving no hint of their exploits… until you looked into his eyes.

"Well, Counselor, thanks for stopping by."

"Anytime, babe. I'll be ready to get you to Smitty's by quarter to five."

"I need to check with Mike and see how soon my truck will

be ready." It would be nice to have her truck back in working order. Then she wouldn't have to depend on Miles all the time.

"Should be finished today. If you bunk with me tonight, I can drive you to the garage in the morning."

"Great. I just need to know the cost. I'll give him a call here in a bit." Even though she hated dipping into savings, if the work Mike did on the truck meant she could keep it going a few more years, it would be well worth the cost.

"Cybil, it's taken care of already. You don't have to worry about a thing," Miles told her.

"Wait, what? Why would you do that? Miles, I can take care of my own bills. I don't need you paying for my truck repairs."

He shrugged. "It's not a big deal. You had a problem. I fixed it. I can afford it."

"And you don't have to go around buying me things to win my affection. It's the principle of it. It was my bill, my responsibility."

"Don't be mad. I did it because I wanted to do something nice for you. And I need you to understand, I have a lot of guilt over leaving you alone. It's my way of easing your burden a bit."

"But they're mine."

"Well, for us to make this work—you and me—I'd like to think of it as ours, yours and mine; that we help each other out where and when we can, and we don't question the whys of it. We say thanks and move on. Unless you don't want the same thing. If all this is to you is a couple of screws and you plan on leaving me in the dust, tell me now."

Miles wanted to know why she'd ended things all those years ago, or at least a part of him did. He didn't trust that she would want to stay this time. "It's not like that, and you know it."

"You sure about that?"

"Yes," she promised. It left her feeling small and petty when he'd done something nice. Guilt and regret were tricky bastards. She hugged him, planting a big smacking kiss on his lips. "Thank you. You didn't have to take care of my truck for me, but thank you just the same. What am I going to do with you?"

"Loving me forever ought to do it." He kissed her brow when the words stuck in her throat. There was a flash of disappointment he tried to hide. "See you in a few hours."

"Okay, bye." Cybil watched him stride out of the studio.

The words he longed to hear were ones she couldn't express out loud. Not until he knew about the promise she'd made, and to whom. And the problem was, the admission couldn't come from just her. She prayed that when the time came, he would listen with an open heart and wouldn't wind up hating her every bit as much as he loved her.

Would he walk away again—and this time for good—when he knew the truth?

Chapter 25

From Old Man Turner's Journal:
We all make mistakes in dating. Be sure to forgive at every turn, and have a short-term memory.

With the Christmas holiday bearing down on them, Cybil decided to use her day off to shop for gifts. This year, not only did she have presents to buy for Tessa, she also now had Abby, Miles, Nate, Jacob, and even Gus. She figured that for Nate and Jacob she needed token, gag gifts. She already had a few things for her sister, like the dress she'd picked up for her.

It was also an excuse to get out of the house for a few hours, to put Miles off from meeting for lunch, and to run an errand she dreaded—one she couldn't avoid any longer—talking to Ella Keaton about the promise. To convince her that the need for secrecy was doing more harm now than good, and that Cybil was ending her moratorium.

Her stomach churned at the coming confrontation.

"Where are you going today? I thought you had the day off?" Tessa asked, sizing Cybil up in her jeans.

"I do, but I was thinking of doing some Christmas shopping. Getting that stuff out of the way."

"Oh, where are you going? Can I come with? I've got a few more presents I want to pick up," Tessa asked with excitement.

"I'm sticking to town, since there are all those new shops that have been opening on Main Street."

"Oh, that sounds like fun. Let me come with you! We could grab some hot chocolate from the new coffee shop, and maybe have some lunch in town."

Cybil held up a hand. "I have an errand to run first, one that you can't come with me on."

Tessa cocked her head. "What's the errand? Maybe I could help."

"No, you can't. I need to run by Ella Keaton's house. That promise is like an axe over my head. I can't move forward with Miles, or even consider telling him how I feel, until we come clean."

"Are you sure that's a good idea?"

"Miles keeps dropping these hints, like he's fishing for the reason I broke it off with him."

Tessa sympathized. "Yeah, that does throw a wrench in the good times, doesn't it? And how do you feel about him?"

Cybil sighed in surrender. There was no point in hiding it from her sister. "I love him. I've always loved him, Tessa. I feel like my entire future hangs in the balance and this one stupid promise I made, the secret I've kept all these years, might tip the scales—and not in my favor. I have no idea how he will react when he learns the truth. And I can't say that I love him until he knows. It wouldn't be right of me."

Tessa winced. "I don't agree that holding your feelings back is the right call. It might be better to reassure him that you love him first before dropping that bit of news in his lap. But it's your life."

"Do you really think so?" Cybil asked, worrying her bottom lip.

"Well, if it were me, and someone I loved didn't tell me they loved me, and then I heard a rather big secret exposed that they had been intentionally keeping from me, I'm not sure I would listen to their side of things. I don't know. Think about it. You know him better than I do. Why don't I just come with you? I'll be there for moral support, and can wait in the truck while you and Ella talk. That way, you have backup if you need it."

Cybil mulled it over. "Okay. Can you be dressed and ready to leave in fifteen minutes?"

Tessa grinned and did a victory dance. "Be back in a flash." Then she raced upstairs like her feet had wings.

Tessa was as good as her word. They were on the road in less than fifteen minutes. Cybil's nerves were frayed as she drove into the Echo Heights subdivision. Snow still covered the lawns but the roads and sidewalks were clear, for the most part. There were a few patches of ice here and there.

The rich, mocha wood of Ella's house blended in with the surrounding forest. Cybil inhaled a deep breath before opening the door. Cold air filled the truck cab.

"You've got this. I'll be right here if you need me." Tessa laid a hand over hers, still on the steering wheel, and squeezed.

"I do. Be back in a minute." Cybil pasted a smile on her face, hiding the tumbling riot of worry. She focused on the house. The wooden set of stairs leading up to the front porch. The holiday wreath was bright red and green on the tan, oak door that thudded when she knocked.

Cybil heard footsteps approach and dug her nails into her palms. When Ella answered the door, her throat closed, and she feared she would hyperventilate.

Ella smiled in surprise. "Cybil, I wasn't expecting you. Come on in out of the cold. Is that your sister in the truck? She doesn't need to sit out in the cold." She waved Tessa inside.

"I can't stay long. We have some errands to run. But I needed to talk to you," Cybil explained, and wished she sounded more confident.

"Okay. It sounds serious. Come on into the living room."

Cybil stepped inside. She loved Ella's house, she always had, especially the open airiness of the living room and dining room with their high ceilings. She trailed after Ella.

The living room was the focal point of the house. A large, tan sectional sofa with deep seats and leather chairs decorated the room, in front of a stone fireplace. There were warm touches all around. The vase on the center of the coffee table was spilling over with holiday poinsettias. There was a Christmas tree resplendent with ornaments and tinsel by the fireplace.

"Have a seat. Can I get you anything to drink?" Ella asked, playing hostess.

Cybil shook her head, too wound up for pleasantries. "No, thank you. Please, I just need to get this said and then I will get out of your hair."

"All right, what's this about?" Ella sat in one of the chairs across from the sofa where Cybil had opted to sit.

"Thirteen years ago, you made me promise that I would let Miles go, let him live his life and go after his bright future. I did as you asked. My parents agreed with you, and I swore I would uphold the promise I made you that day."

"Oh honey, if you think I don't want you to see him now, you would be wrong. You were just kids. It was different back then. I think it's wonderful that you two are seeing each other again." Ella smiled.

"Be that as it may. The thing is, I love Miles. I never stopped loving him. But before I can tell him that, I need to be completely honest with him. There can't be secrets between us."

"Miles doesn't need to know. It would only hurt him." Ella shook her head and leaned back in her seat, dead set against it judging by her clipped tone.

Cybil leaned forward, pleading. "Yes, he does. Because if I don't tell him, I'm not being honest, and it's not fair to him. Aren't you tired of keeping this secret? I know I am, and I won't do it any longer."

"He'll hate me. He'll hate us both. Miles has a very clear, distinct opinion of what is right and wrong," Ella said quietly.

"I know he does. It's one of the things I love about him. But I don't think he will. He might be angry for a time. But he deserves to know the truth regarding why I broke things off so long ago. He's asked me about it in subtle ways."

Ella closed her eyes and lowered her head. "I'm sorry, but I don't think I can. I know that's not what you want to hear."

"Ella, I won't lie to him; not for you, not for my parents, not anymore. The question is there in his eyes. He wonders if I'll end the relationship with him again. And he's never going to fully trust that I'm all in if he doesn't understand why I broke it off in the first place. It's not fair to him, and you know that. I will give you until the end of this year to tell him, or I will. I'm sorry, but it's a secret and promise I can no longer keep."

"Don't do this, Cybil. He'll hate you too."

Cybil rose. "He might. It's a chance I will have to take. Because the thing is, I love your son. I've loved him from the first. I never stopped loving him. And I won't keep this from him much longer. Talk to him. Please. I'm begging you."

"I think it's best if you leave. I will think about what you said."

Cybil left Ella sitting in her living room. So Miles's mom was staunchly opposed to telling him the truth. Cybil understood where she was coming from; she was afraid her only kid would never speak with her again, would hate her. They both ran that risk.

Cybil joined her sister back in her truck.

"How'd it go?"

"Can we not talk about it? It went about as well as you might have guessed. Ella's refusing, but I gave her a deadline. We'll see. Right now, I just want to focus on presents," she said, pulling out of the driveway and heading toward the heart of town.

"Sure. I don't know about you but I'm dying for some hot chocolate."

Tessa chattered away, trying to lighten the mood, and Cybil let her.

As painful as exposing the truth might be, it had to be done, and soon. Miles was making plans for them, plans for permanence, and Cybil wanted it, wanted those more than she had ever wanted anything in her life.

And if he hated her, walked away and never spoke to her again when he discovered the truth? It would hurt, likely more than anything ever had before because it would be final. All she did know was that she couldn't continue living with this secret, and living a lie.

Chapter 26

From Old Man Turner's Journal:
Old things can be like new again. Sometimes they just need a little polish.
Don't be afraid of getting your hands dirty.

December sped by, closing in onto the holiday at sonic speeds. It seemed like just yesterday it was Thanksgiving and bam, suddenly Christmas was next week. And Cybil and Miles had been in a relationship and dating for two and a half blissful, sexy weeks. They had gone from zero to sixty in a blink. She wished she could say that it felt rushed, but it didn't. It felt right, given their history.

It might be crazy, but in many respects it was as if the last thirteen years apart had never happened. They'd always worked well together, and he'd integrated himself back into her life seamlessly to the point where she could no longer see herself without him.

And because of Miles, the season she had dreaded had taken on an unexpected joy as she fell for him all over again. In her heart of hearts, she'd never thought she would look forward to Christmas again. But she caught herself imagining the days, weeks, months, and hopefully years ahead with Miles.

It was his fault—all that talk about sharing an apartment. Aiden had started demolishing the interior on the space this week, with an estimate that it would be ready for occupancy mid-January.

Miles had taken her up on her offer of the drawer and closet space in her room. The little things like his toothbrush beside hers, and a bottle of his cologne beside her hairbrush gave her a jolt of pleasure.

And he was why she was now sitting at her computer at the kitchen table with her mouse icon hovering over the *close account* button on Matchmakers.

"Are you sure about this?" Tessa asked from her seat across the table.

Her sister was in the middle of a deadline, her hair piled in a messy bun on top of her head, her glasses perched on her nose as she looked over the rims with her endearing way of piercing Cybil with a glance.

"Yep. There's a reason no one ever made any inroads—because they weren't Miles. I've been in love with Miles for thirteen years. It never went away. It was just set aside for a while."

"But don't you think you should wait until his mom broaches the big elephant in the room, aka the reason why you broke up with him? The secret you worry he might not forgive you for. Remember that?"

"Yeah. The thing is, even if he decides he can't live with the reason it ended and the secret I've held on to, there's not going to be another man for me. He's it." Cybil clicked on the button. When asked if she was sure, she clicked *yes*.

"If you're sure, then I support you. I just don't want to see you hurt. I know you guys are having fun and it's all thrilling now. But what happens when the sheen wears off?"

"I don't think it will, and it's not just because I love him. I mean, some of the rush of being intimate will cool some, but that's true of any relationship. I know you're worried, and I love you for it. I'll be okay, no matter which way it turns out. Besides, I just confirmed that I am officially done with Matchmakers."

"Maybe I should try that site, as I'm having zero luck these days."

"I can give you some of the guys to avoid from the get go if you do. I'm staying at Miles's place tonight, unless you need me for something here." Cybil closed her laptop.

Tessa sighed dramatically. "Nope. I'm good. I've got final projects to grade and a comic due in the next two weeks. You kids have fun. You're staying over there a lot more lately."

"We figured we would give you a break; that way, you don't have to worry every morning if you'll walk in on us in the shower again."

Tessa agreed with a nod. "We really need to get that door latch fixed. That's a horror that will live with me for quite some time."

"You should have knocked. It would have saved us all the embarrassment."

"You were too caught up… 'Oh Miles, harder'!" Tessa imitated her with great exaggeration.

"And my man knows how to deliver." Cybil laughed.

Tessa waved her off. "Just go. I already got to hear it in full surround sound, I don't need an instant replay."

Cybil stood and blew her sister a kiss. "Good luck with the grading and comic."

"Will you be home tomorrow night?"

"Probably. Text me though, if you need anything." Cybil walked around the table and hugged Tessa from the side. "I love you, you know that."

"I do. Now go have fun playing with Miles. I have zombies

crash-landed on a deserted planet to deal with." Tessa wriggled out from her hold with an eye roll.

"Have fun with that." Cybil grabbed her purse and a bag with a change of clothes. Miles was right. It would be much easier in a space together, just the two of them. Not that she wasn't going to miss living with Tessa, because she was.

On the way to Miles's house, she mulled over the conversation with Tessa. Would Miles end things when he discovered the secret? If she told him how she felt, would that soften the blow, or heighten it?

She wasn't sure. Cybil hated that feeling. Especially since she was waiting on someone else to broach the subject. At least she had given Ella a deadline. She just hated that she was continuing to be less than honest with Miles.

At Abby's house, beyond the ridiculous gargoyles guarding the stoop, Miles opened the door dressed in jeans and a tee shirt. It was a shock to see him in something other than a suit and tie. Not that she was complaining. His sexy smile cut her to the quick. "Cybil. Glad you made it, I—"

Cybil stepped into him, yanked his head down, and kissed him. She poured her heart, her soul, her entire being into the kiss. With unrepentant greed, she kissed him until the rest of the world faded from existence and there was only him.

She wanted to climb him like a tree. Her fingers sought the flesh beneath his shirt. At his husky murmur, she tore her mouth from his. "I want you. Now. I need you," she said urgently.

Just because she couldn't tell him, give him the words she knew he longed to hear, didn't mean she couldn't show him.

"We should at least shut the front door first, don't you think?" he said sardonically. But his eyes were anything but amused. They were hot, intense flames burning bright with desire.

"Good call. Off." She tugged at his shirt.

Miles slammed the door shut. Her purse and bag dropped to the floor where they stood. He hoisted her up, sliding an arm beneath her knees, and carried her up the stairs and into his bedroom. He kicked the door shut.

Cybil rode the wave of need that had taken hold the moment he opened the door. When he laid her on the bed, she rose, shrugged out of her coat and demanded, "I need you naked."

Miles scorched her from the inside out with a look, and reached over his head to remove his shirt. There was a drumbeat on repeat in her mind, screaming that she should hurry.

Hurry, hurry, hurry.

Her fingers tugged, unzipped, and shoved at her clothes until she stood before him naked. They tumbled onto his bed; Miles's mouth claimed hers as they fought for dominance until she settled on top. The wealth of her hair shrouded their faces in a black curtain, blotting out the light so that it was just them.

And something shifted, Miles's touch gentled as he caressed her back. Lifting her mouth, Cybil nipped his bottom lip. Instead of the heated race to the finish line that normally comprised their lovemaking, she seduced him. A shiver of a caress over his delicate flesh. A press of her lips against the strong column of his neck. A slight flick of her tongue against the ridges of his abdomen.

Cybil went on a carnal exploration of his body, infusing each touch with love. She ran her fingers through the hair on his chest, nibbled along his victory lines, and was thrilled when his stomach muscles clenched under her caress.

Miles watched her through heavy-lidded eyes. Cybil grasped his shaft and he hissed. His skin was silky smooth, but strong. Lowering her head, she enveloped his wide length in her mouth, flicking her tongue against the crown before drawing him deep inside.

Now Miles was the one to buck and tremble as she loved him. His hands threaded through her hair until she couldn't wait any longer. Cybil needed him; her body thrummed in sweet expectation. Releasing him, lifting her head, she grabbed a condom from the nightstand and put it on him.

She straddled his hips, their heated gazes clashed and then, in a single thrust, she took him inside. Her back arched at the deep penetration, at the wealth of pleasure overriding her system. Miles gripped her hips, rocking his pelvis, urging her into action. She rode him, planting her hands on his chest as she undulated. She watched his eyes go dark as she writhed and rocked over him, taking his shaft deep inside, over and over. His hands dug into her hips and he thrust up, spearing her flesh.

In a move that stole her breath, he tugged her down and rolled them over. His hands threaded through hers as his pace increased in intensity. Cybil sobbed his name. Her breaths shuddered out, her moans turning into low howling.

Sweat slicked their forms and still they raced toward a blinding pinnacle, holding on to each other as if the other might disappear—until the ecstasy struck her blind, left her keening his name, and sent her hurtling into oblivion. Miles followed her over not a second behind with a loud, fierce groan.

"I'll move in a moment," he mumbled next to her ear.

"Take all the time you need. I don't mind." She didn't mind his weight pressing her down into the mattress, she happened to love the feel of him on top of her, or beside her, or behind her. She just loved being with him. He was smart and funny, loyal and honorable, and without a doubt, the best lover she had ever had. He drove her crazy with his sometimes overbearing attitude. And he made her heart melt and tremble at the force of his love. She trailed her hands over his back in whisper-light caresses.

Miles shifted until he was staring down at her, then the corners of his lips quirked. "Not that I'm complaining because I'm not, at all, but what brought this on?"

"I canceled my Matchmakers account today."

"Ah, so you're wanting what, exclusivity, longevity?" he teased her, playing with a strand of her hair.

"Yes. Isn't that what we're moving toward?" she probed.

"It's about freaking time. I told you from the start that I'm all in, that I love you and want you. In fact," he nibbled along her jaw and she moaned low when she felt him harden once more, "I want you now."

"Again?" she gasped as he began to move.

"Always. I always want you," Miles replied and pulled her back under, into the torrid heat that burned bright as the sun.

Later that night, Miles came to with Cybil snuggled up against him. She was awake and tracing patterns on his chest with her fingertips in light, whisper-soft caresses. He was pleased with the progress they had made. Cybil was his again. When her hand dipped to his favorite body part, he caught it and brought it up to his lips.

"Later." He brushed a kiss over her knuckles. "I need to eat first before I ravish you again."

Cybil lifted her head from his shoulder to smile at him. "I could eat. But it's going to take a while to make something, and I'm hungry now."

"Not to worry, I made a lasagna and stored it in the fridge."

"That was thinking ahead."

"No, I just know you. Know the way you work." A shadow passed over her eyes. "What is it?"

She shook her head and changed the subject. "Nothing. I'm just tired."

Miles wouldn't dig. He didn't want to ruin the night by bringing up things that made her sad or wary. Anytime he tried to push, to get her to open up and talk about her feelings, she shut down. And when did he become the woman in the relationship?

For now, he dropped it and kept the mood light. "Too tired to eat and let me have my way with you again?"

"No. I'm starving. I need to eat." Cybil rolled out of his bed and searched the floor for her clothes.

"Come on." He tossed her his shirt and slipped on his boxers. He'd made progress breaking down her walls. She loved him. He could tell she did. But it weighed heavily on his heart that she refused to say it, to admit that she loved him. And he didn't understand why.

Hand in hand, they headed downstairs. He couldn't help but shake his head at the sight of her bag and purse dumped on the floor by the front door. Cybil padded over and picked them up, hanging them up on a hook by the door.

"I was in a little hurry earlier."

"So I noticed." In the kitchen, he removed the lasagna out of the fridge and dished up portions onto a plate before popping it in the microwave. While dinner was heating, he grabbed a beer for himself and the bottle of wine Cybil favored.

He handed her a glass of wine before removing the meal from the microwave and splitting it between their plates. Ravenous, they ate at the table in silence for a few minutes.

"It's good. Like, really good. Where'd you learn how to cook?" she said.

"I picked up some skills over the years; a man can't live on take-out alone."

"I'll say," she flirted.

"Right back at ya. You're more flexible than I remember," he teased. Miles loved seeing Cybil like this, in his shirt and nothing else but a satisfied smile, relaxed and open, without her defenses being sky high. Her hair was mussed and tumbled over her shoulders. She was so beautiful, she took his breath away.

"Now you're just fishing for a compliment. You've got skills, and know that you do. Changing the subject… Aiden was saying something about your house earlier when I saw him in the apartment today?" Cybil asked him before taking a sip of her wine.

"Here, I'll show you." He put their empty plates in the sink. "Stay here, I'll be right back." He went and retrieved the plans from the coffee table in the living room. Perhaps seeing these would melt the last of her walls.

Back in the kitchen, he unrolled the design over the table to show Cybil.

"Aiden finished the schematics. They may change a little, but those will just be minor adjustments as we go along. But this is what I'm planning. It's a decent sized two-story at four thousand square feet. Four bedrooms on the second floor, with a private master bath, and an attic space for storage—and that could be converted later on to another bedroom if need be. On the main floor will be a den, living room, dining room and kitchen. The living room and kitchen are open, one flowing into the other. The basement will be fully furnished with a home office, gym, and movie theater room with a large flat screen and comfy couches, as well as a nice storage area to install a deep freeze."

"And what's this one here?" Cybil pointed to a room off the kitchen in the back of the house.

"Ah, that will be the sunroom. It will be a nice place to soak up some sun without worrying about freezing in the dead of winter," Miles explained, studying her reaction to the blueprints.

"Miles, it's amazing, but it's also a lot of room for a single guy. Who's going to use those bedrooms?" she asked.

"Well, I'm building it for the future. Maybe for a kid or two. We'll have to wait and see."

"Kids. You're planning for kids?" she asked him.

"When I told you I love you and want a future with you, what did you think I meant? That I want to just keep casually dating and would be fine with that? I want it all with you, Cybil, the whole enchilada. I know you've got commitment issues."

"I do not," she denied with a huff.

"Babe, you're the only one dragging her feet. You know how I feel about you. Ball's in your court. And I'll wait until you're ready to tell me. Just don't make me wait too long, yeah? I mean, I moved back here to be with you."

"You did what? I thought you moved here to be close to your mom and open your own practice."

He'd put his foot in it, now he might as well fess up. "Yep, those are two of the reasons. And the third is you. A few months back when I was with Nate and the guys at Smitty's, when he and Abby were in their preliminary rounds, and I saw you again… It had been a couple years, and it was like someone had plugged me into a wall outlet being repeatedly struck by lightning. I hadn't felt that alive in years.

"It took me a little bit to come to terms with what that meant for me. Initially, it pissed me off, mainly because you initiated the breakup, not me. But then I kept seeing you, felt like I was coming out of my skin each time, and started asking myself why it happened every time I saw you. It didn't take me long to figure out that I was still in love with you. That I've always been in love with you. And that this time, I was going to move heaven and earth until you were mine."

Tears slipped silently down her cheeks. "Miles. I…" She shook her head.

He pulled her in and said, "I know, babe. And I'll wait because you're worth waiting for. I think we had to go through what we did for me to figure that out."

"I'm sorry that I'm letting you down. I just… need you to be patient with me."

He pressed his lips against her forehead. "Take all the time you need. I'll wear you down eventually. Let's get you up to bed. We've got an early start."

"Miles, make love to me."

He flashed her a grin. "Oh, that goes without saying. Just put your arms around me, babe, and I'll get you there."

At the sharp hitch in her breath, he grinned as he lowered his mouth to hers and swept her up in his arms. It might take the patience and resolve of a saint, but Miles would keep showing her, continue proving that they were better together than they ever were apart, and that he loved her still until she said the words.

Until then, he would love her enough for the both of them. And if there was a part of him that wondered if he was wrong and that maybe she didn't love him, he muffled that worry as best he could.

For now, he'd worry later about her refusal to admit her feelings. Much later, he thought as he carried her up to his bed and showed her how much he cared. Twice.

Chapter 27

From Old Man Turner's Journal:
Sometimes it takes healing a wound you didn't realize was there, to mend the bridge between you and the love of your life.

Two days later, Cybil cuddled against Miles in his bed. They were boneless, naked, and Miles couldn't think of anywhere he would rather be than nestled against Cybil on a cold winter night. Her killer backside was spooned up against him. His lips pressed against the delicate skin beneath her ear. Their legs were tangled together, and he wondered if he could entice her into another round.

"What's that?" Cybil pointed at the leather-bound journal on the nightstand.

"Old Man Turner's journal. I've been reading through it."

"Really? Abby and Nate gave it to you?" Cybil asked, glancing at him over her shoulder. Her storm-cloud eyes were becalmed and suffused with a languorous glow.

"Not to keep, no. But to read."

"Well, where did you leave off?"

"You want me to read it? Right now?" Miles quirked a brow in question. That was not the plan he had been pondering.

"Yeah, well, why not?"

"Well, I was thinking we could—"

Cybil rolled her eyes and chuckled. "You're always thinking that. Later. I promise. Journal now."

He clutched a hand against his chest in mock astonishment. "I'm wounded."

She eyed him. "No, you're not. You're just horny. Besides, if you read some of it, I would be ever so grateful."

"It's only you, Cybil, who seems to make me rather insatiable. And how grateful are we talking?" he asked, his hand roaming over her abdomen. He loved watching her skin flush with desire, the way her mouth parted on a breathless sigh.

But then it was his turn to hiss when she wriggled her rear against his pelvis. "Use your imagination."

He sucked in a breath. The woman would be the death of him. But he would gladly follow her to meet his maker. He reached across her supple form and grabbed the journal. "You asked for it," he replied.

They rearranged themselves against the headboard, pillows behind their backs. Cybil turned into his side and drew the covers up around them. With her head resting on his shoulder, Miles flipped to the bookmark holding his place and began to read.

Those first few times Evie and I visited, we sat in white wicker chairs on her porch and talked. We discussed the weather. We discussed politics. We discussed what our lives had been like in the days, weeks, months, and years since we had parted.

I told her about my marriage. That we'd loved one another. How I still loved my wife and felt the pain at losing her so suddenly. Evie held my hand when I told her about losing Charles, my only son, after his mother had already passed in the same car accident that would take him from me as well.

And in the soft, quiet gloom one evening, as we sat together on her porch, staring up at the stars, the ease of friendship made the years fall away between us.

Evie said, "I'm sorry, Bill. Sorry that I wasn't stronger back then."

"You have nothing to be sorry for. We both made mistakes. I should have married you before I left. But then, when I look back, it would mean regretting my life with Lilah. Regretting my son and my daughters, and I find I can't do that."

"I'm sorry just the same. When I miscarried our baby, something clicked off in me. I wish I could explain it so it doesn't sound selfish. I wanted our child so much, Bill. I loved it with everything I was back then. I rejoiced when I felt the first flutters of movement inside me. And then, when I lost the baby, and the doctor told me I'd never be able to bear a child of my own, more than just the baby died that day. A part of me also died, and grief at my own misfortune settled over me that I was unable to shake for many years.

"And it took a long time before I started to feel like me again. I didn't want to deprive you of your chance to have children. Knowing what I do now, about the love you had with your wife, I no longer regret the choices I made. I regret hurting you. I regret ever letting you doubt for one second that I loved you with everything I was. But I knew I would have been cheating you."

It took me about two seconds after Evie's tear-stained confession to gather her close. "I'm sorry too, Evie. For the way life treated you. I know I left you alone to deal with the loss. And I do regret not contacting you, not trying to fight for us. But I am so glad that life, when you give it enough time, brings what is meant to be back to you. I feel very strongly, whether it's fate, a higher power, or just pure happenstance, that we were meant to find our way back to each other."

"Bill, you always know the right thing to say," she said with a slight laugh through her tears.

"No, hardly. It's just when it comes to you, I say what's in my heart. I love you, Evie. Always have, and I think—I mean, I know—that I always will."

Her eyes glimmered like pools, and for the first time in more than twenty years, I kissed the love of my life. It humbled me, the depth of love I had for this woman. The trials and tribulations we'd both experienced had brought us back to this point. I made a vow with myself then and there that I was not going to let her get away from me ever again.

I lifted my head and smiled down at her. "We should get married, Evie. I love you. I've never stopped."

"Bill, I can't." Her eyes grew serious, and she started to withdraw from my arms. But I wouldn't allow her to put up walls between us. Not after everything we had been through to find one another again.

"Can't or won't?" I replied, unable to hide the rawness in my voice.

"Bill, what about your girls? They just lost their mother. The last thing they need is for their father to marry again so soon."

"But you love me. I know you do."

"Of course I love you, Bill. Loving you has never been the problem. Can't we just be together and enjoy each other? Why do we have to put a label on it if we're both committed to one other?"

I shook my head. "Evie, I will ask you every day until you say yes."

"I won't mind that at all," she admitted with a twinkle in her gaze.

I realized then that, no matter what, whether we were married or not, I would be with her until the end of my days. My love for her was boundless. It had grown and changed over the years, just as I had, for I was looking at her with the eyes and heart of a man who had seen war and experienced the ravages of grief and time.

And so every day, I asked her to marry me. And every day, she told me she loved me, but no. It wasn't long before Evie and I were once again inseparable. My girls loved her too. I think they were both relieved in the end that their old man had found someone.

Miles shut the book when he spied the twin trails of moisture running down Cybil's beautiful face. He gently grazed his knuckles over her cheek, wiping the wetness away.

"Cybil," he murmured, his heart bleeding for her because he could see the parallels.

"I didn't realize they had such a history. Abby told me little bits. But I didn't know they lost a baby together," she said in a solemn, ragged whisper as she fought against grief of her own.

He stroked a hand over her hair, offering comfort and support. "They did. But the important thing is that they found each other again. Don't you think?"

Her eyes met his and searched his face. "I know you said that you were relieved, but I need to know, were you upset I miscarried at all? You've never said, and I—"

He cupped her face. "Have there been times that I wondered or thought about what it would've been like had she lived, and we'd had her? Of course I have, many times over the years. And I did mourn the loss of her—and then you. I know you doubt my feelings because I walked away instead of fighting for us. And for that, I only ask for your forgiveness. There's nothing I can do to erase the way things happened, I can only swear to you that I'm all in now and not going anywhere," he promised.

"I didn't give you much of a choice. There's nothing to forgive. It makes me happy to know that I wasn't the only one who mourned her," she replied.

"Cybil, let me show you something," he said, then shifted and scooted off the bed. He padded naked to the dresser and rifled through the bottom drawer until he found what he was looking for. He withdrew the gray slip of material not much larger than his hands. Miles didn't know why he'd kept this thing for thirteen years, but he had. Every time he had told himself to throw it out, something stopped him. He'd like to think perhaps he'd kept it for just this moment.

When he turned around with the item in his hands, Cybil was sitting amidst the covers, her hair in a mussed spill around her shoulders, her lips still a mite swollen from their last tumble. She was the loveliest thing he had ever seen, and he thought maybe they needed this clearing of the air to begin to move forward.

He approached and sat beside her, then placed the material in her hands. She looked down at what he'd given her, her curiosity evident. He watched the moment she realized what she was holding. Emotions, like billowing, fast-moving rainclouds, blew through her eyes as she met his gaze.

"When did you get this?" she whispered raggedly.

"I found it at the campus bookstore of all places, right after I found out about the baby. Who knew college campuses carried onesies, huh?" he joked, trying to lighten the mood.

"And you kept it all this time?"

"Yeah. I lost her too, and you in the bargain. I don't regret the life I've lived since then. But don't for one second think it wasn't hard for me too. I loved you, Cybil, and I would have loved our daughter if she had lived. But that wasn't the cards we were dealt. I felt the loss just the same. Not in the way you did, but you weren't the only one in pain," Miles explained.

Cybil moved, wrapping her arms around his shoulders and hugging him tight. His eyes slid shut as he cherished the feel of her there.

"I'm so sorry I didn't see your pain. Forgive me, Miles. I didn't see it," she said, her voice raw and full of unshed tears.

"Hey, it's all right. You were dealing with way more than any teenager, hell, any *adult* should ever have to deal with. You were blindsided and hurting, and you didn't know what else to do. I don't blame you for that. I think in a way we were meant to come back together so we could share the grief and finally lay her to rest. She's been a ghost between us for long enough, don't you think?" He wiped the tears from her cheeks.

"Miles, I love you."

He lowered his forehead to hers as elation filled him. "Tell me again."

"I love you. I never stopped."

"Then why did you end things? You've never said, and since we're clearing the air…"

"I can't tell you."

"Why not?" he asked, trying not to be hurt at her refusal. He wished it didn't matter. She had never told him why, just that it was over and it had been fun, but that she no longer had time for him.

"Because I made a promise, and it's not just my secret to tell. Do we need to rehash the why? I love you. Isn't that enough?"

It wasn't. He wanted it to be, more than anything, but the need to know the truth ate at him. And it likely would until she confided the truth. But he didn't want to press her. It would only cause a fight. They were in a really good spot. They'd made progress—just not as much as he would have liked. It was going to take a bit more patience on his part.

"For now, I will let it slide. It's something that I hope one day you will feel comfortable enough—confident enough in the fact that I love you—to tell me. It's late; we should get some sleep."

"You want to sleep? I thought we would… you know."

"Have wild monkey sex?"

"Something like that."

"I did promise to ravish you after reading some of the journal, didn't I? Well, a promise is a promise." And he kissed her then, pouring himself, his love, and some of his frustration into his kiss. Deep down, he knew he shouldn't be angry.

They had made headway.

But he couldn't seem to get past the fact that she was keeping a secret from him. She'd admitted so herself.

Miles laid her back on the bed and let himself slide into her hot need. Kissing her did that; blotted out the rest until all he could see was her. He didn't waste time with preliminaries when he stroked her form and discovered her wet and ready. With desire hammering in his veins, he thrust inside her.

Cybil writhed and undulated, meeting his thrusts, as lost in her need as he. Her touch gentled him as she caressed his back, cooling the raging beast inside so that he slowed and savored the way she clung to him. Propped up on his elbows, he watched her eyes go cloudy. She bucked, dug her nails into his flesh, and still he tempered his strokes. She moved with him, his beautiful, passionate Cybil. Her movements were sinuous, her hips rocking as she met him thrust for thrust, rising to meet him, her body clasping his and drawing him deeper.

He thrilled at the way she surrendered, let him set the pace, and allowed herself to get swept up in the tide until she was crying out, quaking in his arms. Only then did he let go and willingly follow her overboard.

Chapter 28

From Old Man Turner's Journal:
Some days, you're the bug. Other days, you're the windshield.

Oh, thank heavens!

Class was done. Cybil breathed a hearty sigh of relief when her power yoga class finally came to a close. Most days, she had no problem focusing on the task at hand, losing herself and all her worries and cares in her yoga practice. As the instructor, she had to remain present to guide her students through the movements and poses, to foster a calm, cool collectedness, regardless of whether she felt that way or not.

But today, yoga and her students were the furthest thing from her mind. Her thoughts were scattered, like toddlers who had just been given cake and left unattended at playtime.

"Namaste. Great class, everyone." *Except for yours truly.*

And why, one might ask? Because there was one student who hadn't shown up, one whom she needed to talk to, one who had been avoiding her studio. Cybil had to beg Ella to reconsider her stance of refusal before she exposed the truth. It was the last hurdle between her and Miles. And it was causing him pain, making him doubt that she loved him.

"I will see you all next week," she murmured, moving around the room, and helping students get their mats and blocks put away. She complimented each one and sent them on their way.

Miles had silently for the last two days been waiting for an explanation from Cybil. Each time she told him that she loved him, it was there: this shadow of doubt. And it was killing her. She couldn't wait until after Christmas or she would go mad.

Miles had errands to run at lunch today. It was the perfect opportunity. With not a moment to lose, she locked up the studio and drove to Ella Keaton's house. This situation, the stalemate it was creating between her and Miles, couldn't go on any longer. Cybil wouldn't let it.

If Ella refused, Cybil would tell Miles tonight. And then they would see.

At the door to Ella's house, she pressed the bell and waited, tapping her foot in impatience. They needed to get this show on the road before her anxiety got the better of her and she chickened out.

"Miles, did you forget your key?" Ella asked, opening the door. "Cybil?"

"I just need a moment of your time," Cybil explained.

Ella stared, obviously not happy to see Cybil, but then she caved with a loud, reluctant sigh. "Come in. I should warn you, I don't have a lot of time. And if this is what I think it's about, you're wasting your time."

Cybil followed her into the living room, building up her courage along the way. "When we talked the other day, it was because I wanted to give you time to tell him, but you haven't. This is putting me in a bind, keeping this secret for you."

"Cybil, I'm sorry but I'm not going to get into this with you again. My answer is no. I don't plan on ever telling Miles. I never figured you would get back together, I assumed it was just a teenage infatuation."

"It was always more than that. It broke my heart to do what you asked of me, but I did it. And now, when I'm here, clearly in love with your son, you want me to shortchange him and what we could be by making me continue the lie. How is that right?"

"I'm sorry but I just can't do it. That's not the answer you want and I'm sorry, but I won't do it."

Frustrated, Cybil snapped, "Ella, dammit. I can't go on like this. It's time. It's past time; Miles deserves to know what happened back then. He needs to know what you asked of me, the promise I made you. It's not right. I can't tell him I love him and then not be honest with him. If you don't tell him today, I will."

"Tell me what?" Miles said.

Cybil's heart dropped into her toes when she spied him in the doorway between the foyer and the living room. His face had turned into a block of granite. All the warmth, the joy, the love of the last few weeks had vanished without a trace.

"Mom? What's Cybil talking about?"

His mom began to softly cry. This was not the way this was supposed to go at all.

"Cybil?" He glanced her way with a pointed question in his eyes.

"The other night when you asked me why I broke it off back then, and I told you I couldn't answer you because it wasn't all my secret to tell… Well, shortly after I lost the baby, when I was in the hospital, my parents called your mom," Cybil explained, her heart twisting into knots.

"And?" Miles pressed.

"And when I visited her in the hospital, I asked Cybil to promise me that she would let you go. I told her that it was the right thing to do for you and your future. I'm so sorry, Miles, I did what I thought was best at the time. I love you so much, please don't hate me," Ella explained with a sob.

"You asked Cybil to break up with me?"

Ella nodded through her tears. "Yes, honey, I did. And I'm sorry if that hurts you or if you think it was wrong on my part. We'd just lost your father and I was trying to navigate being a single parent. At the time, you getting Cybil pregnant was devastating, and I worried that you would end up back here without getting the life you deserved. I did it because I love you, and I was just thinking of your future."

Miles whipped his head around and glared daggers at Cybil. "And you? That's it? Because my mom asked you to you broke up with me? And if she asked you to leave me now, break things off now, you would just do it without a by-your-leave?"

Cybil sucked in a ragged breath at his fury. "No. That's not all of it. Miles, my parents agreed with your mom. When they left the hospital later that night, they made me promise the same thing your mom had earlier."

"And you didn't think I had a right to know this until now?" Miles snarled, his fists clenched in fury.

Cybil pleaded with him. "That promise was the last thing my parents ever asked of me. It was the last time I saw them alive. What was I supposed to do?"

"And the fact that I loved you meant so little?" Miles shook his head. "I can't do this, with either of you. I can't even look at you." He turned away from her and stalked out of his mother's house. The door rattled on its hinges as it slammed shut behind his retreating form.

Cybil stood, frozen, unsure how it had all gone so wrong so quickly. He'd not cared about her explanations, had just angrily accused her and walked away.

"I think you'd better leave, Cybil. I told you it would end badly for both of us. Now please leave." Ella nodded toward the door.

"It's better that he's knows the truth. He's furious now, but when he calms down, he will understand and be reasonable." At least, Cybil prayed that was what he would do. It felt like a thousand knives were stabbing her in the heart.

He would come around, eventually.

With tears streaming down her face, she left Ella Keaton's house without another word. She drove home on autopilot. Through her tears, she arrived home in an agonized daze, replaying the conversation and wondering how it had all barreled out of control so fast. At least she'd had the foresight to send out an email blast saying the studio was closed for the remainder of the day, and had called off work at Smitty's that night. She was not in the mood for peopling.

Cybil stumbled up the stairs. Pain lanced through her chest. Her breaths came in short, shallow pants. She made it into the bathroom before she lost the contents of her stomach. Tears still streamed down her face.

Tessa was visiting a friend in Vale tonight, so she had the place to herself to mourn. Her deepest fear had been realized. Miles knew the truth and no longer wanted her. Cybil never liked admitting defeat. But in her bedroom, she curled underneath the blankets, the little butterball Gus cuddled against her as if sensing her decimated heart. It was her own fault. She never should have made that promise in the first place. And then she did something she hadn't done since the night her parents died: she cried herself to sleep.

Chapter 29

13 years ago

At the sharp, hammering knock on her front door, accompanied by the deep murmuring voice intoning her name, Cybil moved like she was eighty years old instead of on the burgeoning cusp of eighteen.

With every step, her battered body protested. She gritted her teeth at the agony. The deep, throbbing ache in her belly radiated outward in lacerating sonic waves that would have felled a man twice her size. But she persisted, through sheer, stubborn determination, using the pain to help keep her focused on the task at hand. She had made them a promise and she would keep her word; it was the last thing they had asked of her.

Everything had happened so suddenly but the vicious, heart-rending fallout continued. The game table of life had been upended, then scattered in pieces across the interstate. And Cybil was reeling in a spinning vortex of darkness, a turbulent sea of emotions so deep and dark as to be an absolute antithesis of everything she'd lost.

The potential for life—gone.

All but one member of her family—gone.

And she was hollowed out and furious. At the world. At her own rotten life.

Cybil wanted to rage her soul's fury to the world; screech like a mythic banshee until everyone heard her pain. She wanted to stand on the mountain top beside Echo Lake and shriek at the top of her lungs, letting the world know her wrath and the wrenching agony that had obliterated her soul with a single swipe.

But throwing a tantrum would not resurrect the dead. Because those who mattered most were corpses and nothing, no amount of weeping, no bargain she could make, would change the awful truth.

Cybil had to send the person at the door away—let him go live his life, away from the sucking mass of despair her own had become overnight. There was nothing but love tying them together, and it was because of that love that she would do what she must to make sure she didn't drag him down with her.

Now. Today. This moment, she must say goodbye. But the very thought of it gutted her, and she physically staggered under the heavy burden of the forthcoming separation.

All that remained were jagged pieces for Cybil to use to attempt to rebuild her life. Her baby sister was counting on her to make sure she was safe, that she grew up, that she was cared for and loved. Cybil was the only adult left in her family. The time for fun and games, for being a child herself, was over. Due to the most brutal circumstances, Cybil was now her sister's guardian—or she would be once she turned eighteen next week.

With a deep, shuddering breath for courage, Cybil opened the front door of the little two-story house her parents had rented. She prayed the trembling and the fear, the anguish nearly suffocating her, were hidden beneath a mask of indifference. And the errant, erratic thought occurred to her that it was now up to her to figure out some way to afford this house and support her sister.

Cybil was surprised she didn't collapse under the weight of responsibility residing solely on her shoulders.

Her breath hitched in her throat at the sight of him: all big, lanky college sophomore dressed in blue jeans and a brown leather jacket, projecting a touch of badassery in his swagger.

He took her breath away. Always had, from the first moment they'd met.

Her avenging archangel's turquoise gaze was strained, his sunglasses pushed up so they looked like a crown on his golden head. He had come to the hospital but she had pretended she was asleep, too wrecked over the news about her parents to be able to fight another battle. It had been one of the fellow officers who'd helped get her home the next day, not Miles, because there had been things she had to do for her parents.

"Cybil," he murmured, his voice awash with kindness, with sympathy and tenderness that were nearly her undoing. They battered against the wall she'd erected, tearing at the barrier as if it were nothing more than tissue paper. Straightening her spine, clasping on to the pain as a tether, she knew what she had to do. She couldn't hold on to him. Not now. Not with everything that had happened. She had to set him free to follow his dreams, to make the life they'd talked about, dreamed about, that she could no longer be party to. Just because her dreams had ended, didn't mean she could kill his as well. There had been enough destruction. She couldn't be the reason he chose to destroy his dreams. And he would—for her—if she asked him to.

Miles stepped forward, reaching for her to offer comfort and support. He would give her his strength. She knew that. It was who he was, as solid and steady as the nearby mountains. But it would be inexcusable for Cybil to hold him back, selfish of her when he had such a bright future ahead of him—one she'd once believed she would be a part of.

Her heart clutched in her chest with the pain of a thousand daggers, and she almost staggered under the weight of them.

"What do you want, Miles?" she asked, her words short and clipped. She was proud of herself that her voice was flat, with no hint of the writhing mass of sorrow churning through her system.

"Cyb, god, are you okay? I'm here, whatever you need." Miles placed his hand on her waist to pull her close, his big palm firm against her lower back. It was a move he'd done a hundred times. It should have been comforting. It should have felt wonderful. But the familiar touch was agony piercing her chest. The pain slashed at her composure and nearly made her buckle; nearly made her abort the plan she must carry out.

He was her weakness, at a time when there was no room for it.

"Just go, Miles. I don't want you here."

He flinched back like she'd struck him, and then he tried to pull her up against all the hard planes and muscular angles of his body which she loved with a fierceness that still rocked her. Yet she pushed back, her palms on his chest. She was being rent in two as she shoved him back, because heaven help her, all she wanted to do was collapse into his warm embrace and let him shield her.

As she struggled, Miles attempted to soothe her. "Cybil. Don't do this. I know you're hurting. I will be here and I'll help you."

In a flash, Cybil could see it—them—if she allowed him to stay. He'd give up the promise of his future for her. Fast-forwarding ten or twenty years, she knew he'd resent her, come to hate her for the chances he'd not taken because of her. The way she could love him best in this situation was to let him go. "I don't want your help. Go back to your dorm and your classes. Date one of the many co-eds."

"I love you. Don't do this. We can figure it out together." He scowled, a mingling of panic, and pain on his features.

Cybil looked at him then—a last look, because after this, she couldn't see him again. As much as she would hate herself for the words she had to say, she understood now that the only way he would leave was if she pretended she didn't love him. It would be cruel, the cruelest thing she had ever done, but he would leave after that. She murmured, with as much conviction as she could muster, "This thing between us was just fun for me, nothing more. I don't have time for it, for you, now. Go live your life. Goodbye, Miles."

At the barbed words she launched, Miles's face hardened to granite and his eyes went cold. A tick worked its way into his jaw. The warmth and sympathy in his expression were replaced by anguish and something more—defeat. She'd not expected him to cave so swiftly. He had always been stalwart, so willing to enter the fray, that seeing the defeat in his eyes was almost too much to bear.

She should be glad that he wasn't going to fight her decision.

Miles's sharp gaze searched her face. She did her best to present a strong front, hiding that she loved him, pretending as if he was just an annoyance to be dealt with. But she'd believed that she'd already lost everything that mattered to her, and she'd been so wrong. She'd had so much more to lose.

Whatever he saw in her face, she knew the moment he closed himself off from her. She knew him far too well.

"Cybil. Take care of yourself," he chewed out. His voice grated with bitterness, as if the action of speaking exasperated the fabric of his being and was a herculean effort. Then he slid his sunglasses back over his eyes, shielding his tempestuous emotions from her, and walked away.

Clutching the door handle for support, Cybil stood, frozen like a statue, until he climbed into the driver's seat of his truck. Only then did she close the front door. It took every ounce of strength within her being not to go tearing after him and apologize. To tell him that she had made a mistake, the biggest error of her life, and couldn't do this on her own. The torment nearly brought her to her knees. The closed oak door blocked the temptation to run after him and beg him to come back.

"Who was that?" Tessa asked, her voice thick with tears and desolation.

Cybil steeled herself, swallowing her own misery. Like closing a garage door, she barricaded her bleeding heart under lock and key. With a pasted smile on her face, she turned toward Tessa. "Just another well-wisher. Nothing for you to be worried about."

"I thought they were coming to take you away from me too," Tessa said. Tears lined her eyes.

Cybil gingerly walked over to her baby sister—who was not yet fourteen, with her big haunted eyes, dark hair so like her own, her smaller frame still at the crossroads between girl and woman—and pulled her in for a tight hug. "No one's going to take you away from me. I'll make damn sure of it."

When Tessa's arms shook as she hugged Cybil back, Cybil understood she'd made the right decision by following through on the promise she made to Ella and her parents. Her sister needed her. She couldn't be divided.

Miles would move on. He would find other girls to date in college. He would have a life full of adventure… while she would be here, raising her sister, watching the world pass her by.

As much as she loved Miles, she resented the hell out of him too. His life would go on, while hers would just stand still.

Chapter 30

From Old Man Turner's Journal:
Sometimes the lemons in life cannot be turned into lemonade. But that's a truth about love, sometimes you must take the bitter along with the sweet. It all balances out in the end, because love is the only thing that matters.

Miles left his mother's house in a red haze. Anger vibrated through every fiber of his being. They had lied to him. For thirteen years, his life had been a lie.

He could see it: the scene they'd described. Cybil lying in a hospital bed and his mom asking her to stop seeing him. Making her promise to do so. How could they have done this? What the hell had his mom been thinking?

Using his cell, he called the office. "Eva."

"Hey, so your two o'clock—"

"Actually, I'm sorry to do this, but I need you to cancel the rest of my appointments for the day. I know next week is a holiday. Try and reschedule the ones that are urgent for Monday. If that doesn't work, try to get them in after Christmas."

"Sure, I can do that."

"Thanks. I'm also going to need you to field calls and lock up at the end of the day. I won't be back in the office until Monday."

"Is everything okay? Do you need help with something?" Eva asked him.

He snorted a laugh. *Only to rewind my life over the last thirteen years; no mean feat.* "No. I'm fine. Thanks. Have a good weekend and I will see you Monday."

"Sure thing, boss."

He ended the call before it became more personal. Miles drove to Abby's place. The best thing for him to do right now was take some time to think over his decision to move back to Echo Springs—hell, all his decisions regarding the move to Echo Springs.

What the fuck had he been thinking, getting involved with Cybil again? Thinking they might actually have a shot this time around?

Jesus, he loved her though. But that didn't mean he wasn't pissed as hell and questioning everything.

He pulled into the driveway and spotted Abby and Rufus out in the yard between the two houses. Pinching the bridge of his nose at the headache setting up camp there, he attempted to stuff his fury down to manageable levels before he finally climbed out of his Escalade.

Spying him, Rufus bounded through the snowy yard with an excited grin.

"Rufus, stop." Miles held out a hand, in no mood for wet dog, no matter how goofy and lovable the mutt could be at times. Today he was in no mood for the shenanigans.

Abby came up behind Rufus in a hurry. "Rufus, Miles said no." She caught the dog around the collar and held him back from jumping on Miles. "Sorry about him. I know he can get over excited. Are you okay?" she asked him with a tilt of her head, sending the brunette waves of her hair tumbling over her shoulder.

"Why wouldn't I be okay?" he snapped, then winced at her wounded look. "Hey, I'm sorry."

"Bad day?"

"The worst." His mom had lied to him for thirteen years. And, as an added bonus, the woman he loved more than anything had kept that lie a secret, in cahoots with his mother.

"Want to talk about it?"

"No. Thanks, though." He started to head toward the house, but then stopped and said, "Abby?"

"Yeah, Miles?"

"What would you do if someone had lied to you for a long time? How would you react?"

She slid her hands into her coat pockets and considered the question for a minute. "Well, that depends on the lie. For instance, was it done out of malice, to cover up a sordid deed? Or was it done out of love to try and protect the person from harm?"

Miles could see the direction she was going with this and staunchly refused to back down from his stance. "It's still lying, though."

She nodded in agreement. "Yes, but if it was the right thing to do at the time… Say like when I was five, and caught a bunch of fireflies in a jar. I was so excited by their lights. But I didn't know you had to punch holes in the lid."

"Killed them, didn't you?" A grin tugged at the corners of his mouth.

"Every single one. And I was heartbroken, calling myself a killer. I remember my mom sitting me down and saying that they had to move on to the next realm so that they could be fairies, and that when a firefly died, they were transformed into a fairy. And you couldn't catch fairies."

"So she lied to make you feel better. Did it work?"

"At the time, yes, it did. May I ask who lied, and why? Maybe I can help give you another perspective."

What the hell. He didn't have any idea how to move past today's revelations. "Basically, my mom asked Cybil to break up with me thirteen years ago. Cybil did what she asked, and kept the promise a secret. My mom and Cybil, in the same lie together. Doesn't that beat all?"

"Cybil told you about that?" Abby asked him.

"You knew?" he snapped accusingly. His head spun. Jesus, had they taken out an advertisement in the local paper? Did the whole town know why Cybil had dumped him all those years ago? For fuck's sake!

Abby held up her hands up defensively. "Whoa! I just discovered it a short time ago. And it wasn't my place to tell you. I was sworn by the bonds of friendship to keep it to myself. I didn't even tell Nate."

"Everybody's fucking lying. Dammit."

"Miles, let me ask you something. Did you let Cybil get to the part where it was her parents' last request of her—that she end things with you—the day before they died? Or did you only hear that you were lied to without fully listening to the reason why?"

"There was no reason for it. I could have helped Cybil. I would have been there for her. I could have left school."

"And do you think she didn't know you would do that if she asked? That your mom didn't know that? They were both trying to protect you. It might not have been the right thing, but we will never know that. What I do know is that it was done from a place of love. Cybil loves you, Miles. So does your mom. Otherwise they wouldn't have fought and sacrificed the way they did to ensure you had every opportunity."

"I wasn't given a choice. They took that from me," he replied, pride warring with his anger even as her logic began to spear through the furious haze.

"But you don't think that life took away Cybil's choices

without asking? Are you kidding me? I will tell you what I think, because we're friends, and I'm about to be brutally honest with you. I think you're scared. I think your relationship with Cybil escalated and moved so quickly that, even though you love her—which I can see you do, otherwise her lying to you thirteen years ago and keeping the secret for thirteen years wouldn't be affecting you the way it is—you got scared, and have been looking for a reason… maybe not to end things, but to toss on the brakes a bit, or some other stupid male decision."

"We've been clearing the air, moving on from the past. She lied and kept this from me," Miles defended his fury.

"Honey, look me in the eyes and tell me you would have been okay never knowing why Cybil dumped you in the first place."

Chagrined, he chewed it over. No. He wouldn't have been. It had been scraping his scars raw and making him bleed a little bit more each time she refused to tell him. Conceding slightly, he said, "Maybe. Thank you for your brutal honesty. I'm going to go inside your aunt's house and have a beer or two."

"You're welcome," Abby replied. "Rufus, come on, sweetie, let's go inside. I've got a nice treat for you being such a good boy."

Rufus woofed and pranced in delight, and followed his mistress into the house next door. Miles headed into the old Victorian. Abby had given him plenty to consider. He checked his phone. There were a half dozen missed calls from his mom.

But none from Cybil, the woman who said she loved him. Could he trust her words of love? Or were those just another lie?

Miles woke the next morning with no clearer idea as to what he intended to do about Cybil—or his mom, for that matter. He loved Cybil, and he always had, but now he wondered if he could trust what she felt—or said she felt—for him.

When he looked at the events surrounding their breakup thirteen years ago, deep down, he knew that if he had stayed and fought for them, their relationship likely would have not survived. Cybil had been too shattered by the events. He had been way too freaked out over the whole situation. Eventually, he would have become frustrated and resentful toward her.

Perhaps Abby had been right yesterday, and that lie had been told out of love, to protect him. It was still a hard pill to swallow, regardless of the reason behind it.

Abby was half right about his fear, but it was more not knowing the full story behind the breakup that had made him hesitate. Well, now he did know it. Now he understood why Cybil had held herself back for so long before finally caving—and that had only been because of the onesie.

He tried to imagine if his dad had made him promise to do something, perhaps something he didn't really want to do, and then died the next day. Would he have done it? Especially if it had been the last thing he said to Miles?

Son of a bitch. He could see it: Cybil in that horrid hospital gown, pale, heartbroken over the miscarriage, only to have two of the people she trusted most ask her to make them a promise not to see him. To agree with his mother and exact a promise from her at a time like that.

And he was a fucking idiot.

Grabbing his keys and coat, he headed out. He'd stop at his mom's first so that they could clear the air. He understood why she had done it, for the most part. Things wouldn't bounce back to normal between them right away, but he wouldn't shut her out. She was his mother.

After that, he and Cybil were going to talk. If it took the rest of the day and into the night, they were going to hash everything out. He strode out to his Escalade and noticed that Jacob's vehicle was parked next door. He must have gotten in late last night, long after Miles had poured himself into bed.

While Miles drove, he recalled the last passage he had read in Old Man Turner's journal last night when he couldn't fall asleep.

I realize I'm coming to the end of this tale. My story is almost over as the cancer eats away at me more each day. Looking back on my life now, I understand the choices we all face, daily. The choice to love someone versus being alone. Taking chances and losing everything to the point where you don't know if you can go on.

Even with the heartache I've faced, I regret only that the time is coming when I will have to move on without my Evie by my side. I'm not upset that my life is over, only that my time with the love of my life is coming to a close. The rest of the world could fall into perdition and none of it would matter but my Evie. She's been my everything, my love, my rock, and a gift this crusty old bastard has been lucky enough to call his these past forty years.

And in the end, when I finally stopped asking her, knowing what my fate would be, Evie said yes, and told me it was about time she made an honest man out of me. It was a simple ceremony in the yard between our two homes, presided over by the justice of the peace, with my two girls and their families as witnesses.

That woman can make me smile like no other.

In the end, love was always the answer. The words, the vows we spoke that day, were just the icing on the cake of the sweet life we've had together. And I finally understood why it took her so long to say yes—because, in Evie's heart and in mine, we were already more connected and committed than anyone can be. In our hearts, we were husband and wife, and no piece of paper could say otherwise.

Evie did it for me. Knowing I was going to wither away before her eyes in the days that followed, knowing that our time together was drawing to a close, she's held nothing back from me. She's been only a comfort and joy as the days pass and the sun sets on my life.

If soul mates do exist, and I believe they do, then Evie is mine. And in my heart, I know we will be together again. Whether across time and space, life and death, my soul will always find hers.

In the end, it's the love we've forsaken, and the chances not taken that we regret. Never the love we've shared. So my advice is that when you do find yourself standing in front of the one person you know you were meant for, don't be stingy with your heart or let pride and ego get in the way of the magnificent love to be had. Don't be afraid to get lost in love, because when it's the right person, they will always be your port in a storm.

Love, as I have said before, is always the answer.

Miles was driving around a turn, focusing on what he would say, when the deer appeared in the middle of the road. He slammed on his brakes. The wheels of his Escalade skidded over slick pavement. He tried to avoid the deer and correct his course but he was seconds too late, wrapped up in his mind and not paying attention to the road.

The force of the impact jarred him. The sharp jab of pain as his head smacked against the side window shocked him. Agony stole his breath along with the screech of tires on pavement. And then nothingness. The world came to a shuddering halt.

Chapter 31

From Old Man Turner's Journal:
Fate will try your soul, but don't make that close your heart to the one you love.

It was a bustling early Saturday night at Smitty's. Everyone seemed to be getting their holiday spirit on. And she was back to hating the holidays once again. In abject misery, Cybil wondered if Miles would forgive her as she waited tables. The world kept turning even though her heart was bleeding out.

She really wasn't in the mood to be here, but considering she'd canceled classes yesterday and then again this morning, she needed the money.

"Hey, Cybil. Looking fine tonight." Alex Dotson's comment was a bit slurred. His buddy Martin Long sat beside him on a bar stool and snickered, leering at her through narrowed eyes.

"What the hell do you want, Alex?" she snapped, in no mood to deal with the likes of him.

"Now, is that any way to treat a customer? I'm sure Burke

would get mighty pissed to know this is how you treat them." Alex sneered.

As if the last twenty-four hours hadn't been bad enough, now she had to deal with this moron. "I'm sure because it's you, Alex, he would applaud me."

"Bitch," he muttered with a nasty glare.

She rolled her eyes at his juvenile antics, thankful she wasn't waiting on him. She turned to leave to pick up empties from her tables, when he smacked her on the rear, hard enough that the sound of the smack reverberated. "That's it. I've had it with your crap."

She slapped her empty tray on the bar top, turned to Alex, and without thinking about what she was doing, balled her fist and sucker punched him dead in the face. The force of it snapped his head back.

With his hands on his nose, he howled. "You bitch! I'll make you pay for that."

"No, you won't. I saw what you did, Alex. You're banned from Smitty's. I don't take kindly to patrons manhandling my staff that way. Now, get your sorry ass off the bar stool and get out. Or do I need to call the sheriff and have Cybil report you for sexual assault?" Burke threatened, leaning against the bar, looking for all the world like he was just waiting for Alex to do something stupid so he could have a crack at him.

"Come on, Martin. This place is overpriced and the service sucks." Alex said, wiping at the blood leaking from his nose. The two stalked out of the bar.

Her hand was throbbing like a bitch, but Cybil shook it off. "Thanks, Burke. Sorry. I just can't stand that he thought he could put his hands on me."

"It's not an issue. I was about to step in when you clocked him good. You'll want to put some ice on that hand. But that wasn't why I was on my way over in the first place. Nate just called," Burke said, his eyes on her.

Her heart dropped through the floor at his solemn tone. "What's wrong?" Was it her sister? Had something happened to Tessa?

"It's Miles. He's been in a car accident."

Terror jolted through her. Miles, in an accident? The room spun. "Is he okay? Is he…" *Dead?*

Miles couldn't be dead. Not now, not like this, when there was so much left to say. When she needed to beg his forgiveness for the stupid promise she had kept all these years.

"Nate didn't have an update on that. Only that Miles was transported to the hospital and is in surgery now. He has Abby and Ella with him. Jacob's on his way here to pick you up. Don't worry about your tables and cashing out. I'll take care of it. You go check on Miles. We'll be thinking about him here," Burke said.

"Thanks, Burke. How soon will Jacob get here? I need to go. I need—"

Jacob strode through the front doors of Smitty's, his face grim. "Cybil, I figured you could use a lift."

"Thank you for coming to get me." She handed Burke her booklet with all her receipts and orders, and he handed over her coat and purse. Fear pumped through her as Jacob escorted her out to his vehicle.

"Do you know anything? His prognosis, injuries?" she asked when he opened the passenger door for her.

"No. Just that he was alive and heading into surgery."

"That's good. Alive is good." She nodded. It was a sliver of hope that she could hold on to.

Tessa's car screeched into the parking lot and pulled up beside Jacob's. She hopped out of her car and clambered into the back of his SUV. Tessa put a hand of support on Cybil's shoulder as Jacob drove them to the hospital.

Thank god he was driving; Cybil was too scared for Miles to be able to concentrate on the road.

At Echo Springs Hospital, she rushed into the waiting room ahead of Jacob and Tessa. She had to know how he was. She found Nate, Abby, and Ella in the waiting room.

"Anything," she asked breathlessly, glancing from one person to the next.

"No. He's in surgery but that's all we know," Ella said, and her bottom lip quivered. She wiped at a stray tear and lowered her head. Cybil wanted to go to her, to comfort her, but didn't know how it would be received after everything.

"Nate, surely as you're the sheriff, they can give you more information," Cybil pleaded with him. It was unfathomable that there was a possibility she could still lose Miles. They had no idea how bad his injuries were—or, hell, he could die in surgery.

"Doctor Townsend is with him. He's the best in the area. I was at the scene with my deputies. Miles was pretty banged up. Hit a deer up on Echo Lake Drive and then skidded into a tree. The best thing to do now is have a seat. We'll know more soon," Nate explained.

Cybil lowered herself into one of the chairs, pulling her knees up to her chest. Miles had been pretty banged up in the accident. What did that even mean? Banged up like oops, slipped and now have a few bruises, or ruptured organs, bleeding out into the snow banged up? Why couldn't her life be easy for a change?

Miles had been so angry with her yesterday. Had he been reckless and drinking because of her and what she had done? Was someone else she loved going to die because of her?

She studied their small group. Jacob sat with a small tablet, doing some tech thing. Abby was next to Ella, keeping her mind off Miles being in surgery by talking to her about a show she and Nate had been watching. Nate sat on the opposite side of Ella, flanking her. A wall of solidarity and support.

If she lost Miles, she would never forgive herself for the

damn promise. It had wrecked everything. The small bits of good, the joy, the love. It had torn it all away from her.

Cybil sat in misery, replaying the last few weeks with Miles. Praying to whomever would listen that he would survive, that he would live, that she could apologize and beg for his forgiveness. Pride didn't matter, it never had. All that mattered was that he live, and know she loved him, that she had always loved him.

Interminable hours passed as they waited. Tessa brought Cybil a soda that she sipped at, more to have something to do with her hands than because she wanted to drink it. She shifted in her seat just as Doctor Jonah Townsend entered the waiting room, pulling down his surgical mask.

Ella stood. They all did.

Doctor Townsend went to Ella and said, "Miles is a trooper. He made it through surgery just fine. His appendix, not so much. It ruptured in the accident. He has three broken ribs and a mild concussion along with that. The surgery was a success. Now it's up to Miles's body to recoup and heal. He's going to be fine, and I expect him to make a full recovery. Once he's out of recovery, and in a room, you can all get in and see him."

"Thank you, Doctor Townsend," Ella said, before promptly bursting into tears. Abby held her.

Miles was alive. Oh, thank god! The fear and grief that had put a chokehold on her evaporated. Cybil sank down onto her seat and sobbed with relief.

Chapter 32

From Old Man Turner's Journal:
When it comes to the woman you love, be willing to forgive. Everyone makes mistakes in relationships, don't compound it by making another.

"Mom," Miles murmured, and his mouth felt thick, like it was full of cotton balls. The soft whir of machines, the scent of stale coffee and antiseptic suffused the air. He was flat on his back, the bed he lay upon was raised slightly at his head, giving him a view of the hospital room he was in. And beside the bed where he was hooked up to all manner of machines was his mom.

He wanted to be angry, but seeing the lines of worry on her face, he knew he was just sorry—about the whole situation.

"Well, you look a little worse for wear. And you definitely took ten years off my life," his mom said with a light smile on her lips, despite the strain in her eyes.

"What happened?" Miles asked. He recalled flashes of being in his car, and then nothing.

"Your truck hit a deer, and then slammed into a tree on the side of Echo Lake Drive. You were unconscious at the scene, transported to the hospital. They had to do surgery, I'm afraid."

"My injuries?" He felt like he had all his limbs intact. But there was a low hum of pain, mixed with some pretty spectacular painkillers.

"Your appendix ruptured. Doctor Townsend had to do an emergency appendectomy. You have three broken ribs, and a concussion, with some minor cuts. But you'll live. And now that you will, I need to ask you to forgive me. I never should have interfered the way I did. It was wrong. I know at the time, I thought I was doing the right thing, when really I was just fumbling and doing my best after your dad died." She gripped his hand and there were tears in her eyes. Dammit, he'd made his mom cry. "I love you, and I hope you can forgive me."

"I get why you did it. I love you, Mom. Sorry to scare you like that. But I'm going to ask you: from here on out, I need your complete honesty about things. I don't have a long-lost sibling somewhere, do I?" Miles asked.

His mom laughed. "No, that I can promise you."

He glanced around the room, and his gaze landed on Cybil curled up in a chair in the corner, sleeping.

"She's been here since you were brought in. I couldn't convince her to go home and get some sleep. I know I'm the reason things ended between you back then. Don't hold my mistake against her. She loves you, honey. Anyone with eyes can see it."

Cybil had always been stubborn. Once her mind was made up about something, nothing could stop her. It was one of the qualities about her that he'd always admired—and which had always frustrated him no end.

"Let's let her sleep," Miles said and turned his head back to gaze at his mom. "Sorry for giving you a scare," he said, noting the film of moisture in her eyes that she was trying hard to hide.

"Thankfully, you've always had a hard head. I'll be fine as long as you are."

Miles let go of the anger and said, "I love you, Mom. And I forgive you. We'll figure it all out."

"I love you, too. Now get some sleep. We'll be here when you wake up."

As the morphine pulled him back under, the image of Cybil curled up in the chair stayed with him.

When he woke a few hours later, Cybil was gone, vanished as if she had never been there. He had other visitors: Nate and Abby stopped by. Jacob was there with his mom, making sure she was getting a break. The casserole patrol visited, one by one. Even Tessa stopped by to check on him.

But no Cybil.

Chapter 33

From Old Man Turner's Journal:
Celebrate and cherish the love you have, and don't be afraid to fight for the one you want.

On Christmas morning, Cybil rose early, just like she did every year, and went to the cemetery. Every year, she took Christmas wreaths for her parents and her daughter's graves. Tessa didn't like to go, and Cybil had stopped asking her to join her years before. Once she knew Miles was going to make it and was out of the woods, she had left the hospital and buried herself in work for the last few days.

Yes, she was avoiding him—avoiding the whole rotten mess they had made of things, that *she* had made of things. It was fear, mostly; fear that he would never forgive her. She didn't want another reason to hate this holiday. Her sister was still sleeping when Cybil had left the house with a hastily scrawled note, telling her where she'd gone and that when she returned, they would open presents.

At the cemetery, she noticed other headstones where friends and family had left Christmas flowers and wreaths. It was a cold, blustery day with dark, billowing, foreboding clouds. The weather seemed to match her mood these days. She made the trek with her head bent against the cold, carting the wreaths in her hands. When she reached the familiar plots of land and looked up, she slowed to a halt.

Her heart leapt into her throat.

Miles was standing at their daughter's grave. A full bouquet of white roses had been laid over it. Cybil's gaze soaked him in, from the cut on his forehead to the bruising around his eyes, and the way he held his side as if it ached. Even battered and bruised, he looked better than any man she had ever known.

She loved him so much. All she wanted to do was wrap her arms around him and reassure herself that he was really there, alive and well.

Instead of staring like a lovesick fool, she laid the wreaths on her mom and dad's graves first, fitting them against the headstones. "Miles. I didn't expect to see you here. Did someone drive you? How are you feeling? I'm sorry I haven't been by to check on you, but—"

"You've been avoiding me," Miles said, his face an unreadable mask.

So, apparently he wasn't going to waste time on any pleasantries. She admitted it with a nod and laid the wreath on Amber's grave. "Yes. I have been. The way we left things, once I knew you were out of the woods, I wanted to give you time and space."

"Well, I was coming to your house next after this stop, so you saved me a trip. There are things that I need to say that I need you to listen to."

"Okay, let's get this over with," she said. *Might as well rip the bandage off fully.*

Miles tilted his head. "Over? Babe, this is just the beginning.

And now, I owe you an apology. I've had a lot of time to think. Lying flat on my back for days on end has given me that time. I can't be mad at you for the choices you made thirteen years ago. It was the only sensible thing you could have done. I'm sorry for getting as angry as I did."

"You have nothing to apologize for, Miles. I need you to know that I did love you so much that it almost killed me to let you go. I didn't want to, I did it because they asked me to." She nodded at her parents' graves.

"You did love me, or you do?"

"I never stopped loving you. I just had to set it aside for a while."

"Are you done setting it—setting me—aside?" he asked.

"Yes. You should know, I have been in love with you since the first time you asked to sit with me on the bench up at Echo Lake. I loved you then, I love you now, and I know I will love you for the rest of my life."

"That'll do." He approached her, a little unsteady on his feet. He cupped her face with one hand. "Cybil, I love you. I've never stopped loving you. And I want the chance to love you for the rest of our lives."

"What are you saying?" Cybil whispered, her heart thumping wildly in her chest.

The look he gave her made the breath hitch in her throat. "I'm in too much pain to kneel, so you'll have to forgive me for that. Marry me, Cybil. Make a family with me. Be with me forever. I didn't just come back to Echo Springs because I needed a change. I came back because I need you. I've always needed you. What do you say?"

She blinked through the tears filling her eyes. With the headstones of her parents and their daughter standing as witness, she said, "Yes, I'll marry you."

She hugged him and he hissed. "Easy. The ribs are a bitch. And you'll be needing this now." He drew a ring from his pocket.

It was a simple white gold band with a solitary diamond in the center. "I love you, Cybil. And this is only the beginning," he said, slipping the ring over her finger.

"God, I love you," she said, staring into his turquoise eyes, which glowed with love for her, with the promise of their future.

His lips descended, claiming her mouth in a kiss that left her breathless. When Miles finally lifted his head, the joy, the love, was written all over his handsome face. "Talk about a Christmas to remember."

"It's one for the record books, I'll give you that. Miles, look. It's snowing." She glanced up. Big, fat, white flakes were spilling out from the clouds like a sign that her parents approved. She laughed at the joy filling her up. "Merry Christmas."

"Merry Christmas, babe. You're the only present I wanted. Come on, Mom's cooking up a feast today for everyone at Abby's house. Jacob's waiting in the lot," he said, trying to steer her.

"Wait a sec." She tugged on his hand in hers, keeping him there.

"You're not reneging. You said yes, and I'm not letting you go. If it needs to be a shotgun wedding, so be it. No takebacks."

"No, not on that, silly man. I'm never letting you go ever again. I think they're all finally at peace," she said, looking at the three headstones. With the snow falling around them, everything had finally clicked into place.

Miles kissed her temple. "They are. And we'll always carry them with us. Let's go home."

Home.

With her hand in his, she finally understood that home wasn't a place, but a feeling. And with Miles, she was home. Hand in hand, with the snow falling all around, they walked toward their future—one full of hope and, bursting with love, one that they would face together.

Epilogue

18 months later

Cybil awoke to the soft whirring of machines and dim lights. She glanced at the chair beside her bed and love swamped her. Miles sat, his head bent forward, his eyes closed, but protectively holding the tiny, swaddled bundle in his arms.

She reached out a hand and ran her fingers over his face. His eyelids lifted, and the force of love in his gaze humbled her.

"Hi," she whispered, not wanting to wake their daughter.

"Hey there, yourself. She was fussing a little."

"She seems to like having you hold her."

"I have a way with the ladies." He cast her a sexy, smoldering grin that drew a chuckle out of her.

He certainly had her number, that was for sure. Miles rose and handed her the sleeping bundle, then joined her in the small hospital bed. He slipped his arm around her shoulders and held her close. His lips brushed her forehead.

"Have I thanked you properly for our daughter?" he murmured.

"She's perfect, isn't she, our Willa?" And she was, Cybil thought, with her head of dark hair, tiny fingers and toes, and blue eyes that she had a feeling might end up the same color as her father's.

"Both of my girls are perfect."

"I'm surprised the hordes haven't descended once again," Cybil commented.

"Oh, I asked them not to. I wanted to give you some time to rest, but I won't be able to keep them at bay for long. Mom's already chomping at the bit, and talking about sleepovers so that her granddaughter can stay with her."

"And Willa will have Abby and Nate's little boy, Michael, to play with too." Cybil could see the playdates already.

"I'll have to keep an eye on that one. I know who his father is, and I don't trust any boy with my daughter."

Cybil laughed. "He's two months old, Miles. I don't think you have to worry about protecting her from him for quite some time."

"Doesn't matter."

Cybil smiled. Life with Miles was everything she had ever wanted, and loving him, opening her heart back up to him, was the best decision she'd ever made. "I love you, Miles."

"Cyb, I love you so much," he murmured and leaned down, kissing her with all the sweet passion, all the love he felt for her.

Then she snuggled against him, feeling his solid warmth surrounding her and Willa, knowing that, against all odds, they had made it. She leaned her head against his shoulder, their daughter safe and secure between them. Cybil knew that life didn't get much sweeter than this. She might have taken the long road to get there, but she didn't regret a minute of it.

In the end, taking a second chance on Miles had given her everything she'd once dreamed they could have: a family.

~ The End ~

Maggie Mae Gallagher

Born in St. Louis, Missouri, Maggie grew up listening to Cardinals baseball and reading anything she could get her hands on. She remembers her mother saying if only she would read the right type of books instead of binging her way through the romance aisles at the bookstore, she'd have been a doctor. While Maggie never did get that doctorate, she graduated cum laude from the University of Missouri-St. Louis with an M.A. in History.

Maggie is a bestselling and award-winning author published in multiple fiction genres. She also writes erotic romance under the name Anya Summers. A total geek at her core, when she is not writing, she adores attending the latest comic con or spending time with her family. She currently lives in the Midwest with her two furry felines.

Visit her website here:
www.maggiemaegallagher.com

Visit her on social media here:
Facebook: FB.me/MagMaeGallagher
https://www.facebook.com/MagMaeGallagher/
https://www.instagram.com/magmaegallagher/
https://www.goodreads.com/author/show/7846308.Maggie_Mae_Gallagher
https://twitter.com/magmaegallagher?lang=en
https://www.amazon.com/author/maggiegallagher
https://www.bookbub.com/authors/maggie-mae-gallagher

Don't miss these exciting titles by Maggie Mae Gallagher!

Echo Springs
THE FIXER UPPER
THE PROMISE KEPT

The Mystic Series
REMEMBER ME
CASKET GIRL

The Cantati Chronicles
RUPTURED
ANOINTED
ASCENDED

And if you like your romance with a bit of spice and kink, be sure to check out Maggie Mae Gallagher writing as Anya Summers!

Blushing Books

Blushing Books is one of the oldest eBook publishers on the web. We've been running websites that publish spanking and BDSM related romance and erotica since 1999, and we have been selling eBooks since 2003. We hope you'll check out our hundreds of offerings at http://www.blushingbooks.com.

Blushing Books Newsletter

Please join the Blushing Books newsletter
to receive updates & special promotional offers.
You can also join by using your mobile phone:
Just text BLUSHING to 22828.

CPSIA information can be obtained
at www.ICGtesting.com
Printed in the USA
LVHW041918230820
663958LV00002B/168

9 781645 634294